"*Seven Wonders* is everything that's great about superhero novels – a fast pace, a complicated plot, iconic characters, and an unlimited effects budget. Absolutely wonderful."
   *Seanan McGuire, New York Times bestselling author of* Discount Armageddon *and* Ashes of Horror

"A blast of pure pleasure. This is *Watchmen* meets *NYPD Blue*, while *The Incredibles* stroll by; fast-moving action infused with Christopher's infectious love of pulp fiction and the superhero genre."
   *Philip Palmer, author of* Version 43, *and* Artemis

"Adam Christopher maintains a punchy, bestseller prose style that keeps the action rocketing along, and protagonists that seem right both in their own setting, and appropriate to what we already recognise as super heroes. *Empire State* is an excellent, involving read, and it fully deserves to be the start of a new universe."
   *Paul Cornell, author of* London Falling

"With *Seven Wonders* Adam Christopher has proved himself the master of a new type of noir for the modern age. A noir where Chandler meets the Avengers on pages of delightfully crisp prose. A noir flavoured with echoes of *Sin City* and *Watchmen*. A noir that's simply marvel-ous and entirely his own."
   *Sarah Pinborough, author of* The Chosen Seed

"Witty and cinematic, packed full of spectacular set-pieces, labyrinthine plot twists and devious double-crosses, and populated by an imaginative array of superheroes as flawed and fallible as the citizens they're sworn to protect, Adam Christopher's *Seven Wonders* is the literary equivalent of a lazy Saturday morning with a stack of your favorite comic books: pure, unadulterated fun!"
   *Owen Laukkanen, bestselling author of* The Professionals

"An awesome heroic adventure that cannot slow down. This book was so much fun!"
*Mur Lafferty, John W. Campbell Award winner, and author of* The Shambling Guide to New York

"Adam Christopher is a bold new voice in the prose world, merging the literary with genre into a explosive new vision for modern fiction."
*Joshua Hale Fialkov, Harvey, Eisner and Emmy-nominated writer of I,* Vampire, Echoes *and* Tumor

"*Seven Wonders* is a modern day superhero novel done right. Never too dark and never too campy, this book's just the right amount of fun."
*Stephen Blackmoore, author of* City of the Lost

"Adam Christopher grabbed everyone's attention with his debut novel *Empire State,* and his follow up *Seven Wonders* will surely please all of his readers who have been waiting breathlessly for more. A smart, entertaining, energetic take on the superhero genre."
*Victor Gischler, writer of* X-Men *and* Deadpool

"A daring, dreamlike, almost hallucinatory thriller, one that plays with the conventions of pulp fiction and superheroes like a cat with a ball of yarn."
*Kurt Busiek, Eisner Award-winning writer of* Astro City

"The sequel to last year's *Empire State* sees Christopher's pocket universe alt-Manhattan under threat from earth tremors, endless winter, and an army of killer robots. The nuclear terror of the Red Menace era is filtered through a fusion of SF and gumshoe novel to superb effect."
*Financial Times*

## BY THE SAME AUTHOR

*Empire State*
*The Age Atomic*
*Seven Wonders*

ADAM CHRISTOPHER

# HANG WIRE

**ANGRY ROBOT**
A member of the Osprey Group

| | |
|---|---|
| Lace Market House, | Angry Robot / Osprey Publishing |
| 54-56 High Pavement, | PO Box 3985 |
| Nottingham | New York |
| NG1 1HW | NY 10185-3985 |
| UK | USA |

www.angryrobotbooks.com
The greatest show on earth

An Angry Robot paperback original 2014

Cover art by Will Staehle
Set in Meridien and Titling Gothic by EpubServices

Distributed in the United States by Random House, Inc., New York

ISBN: 978 0 85766 317 7
Ebook ISBN: 978 0 85766 318 4

Printed in the United States of America

9 8 7 6 5 4 3 2 1

*For Sandra.*
*La la love you.*

# A SINGULAR AND EXTRAORDINARY BODY

"Another of those singular and extraordinary bodies has made its appearance within view of our globe... Those who may have the necessary apparatus, and the ability to use them, are respectfully advised of this opportunity for adding to the stock of astronomical knowledge, by ascertaining the elements of the orbit of this aerial visitor, and making such other observations and calculations as its appearance and short stay within our view will admit of."

*The Chillicothe Gazette*, June 5th, 1811

"It was midnight on the first of October, 1811, that the *New Orleans* dropped anchor opposite the town... The roar of the escaping steam, then heard for the first time at the place where, now, its echoes are unceasing, roused the population, and, late as it was, crowds came rushing to the bank of the river to learn the cause of the unwonted uproar. A letter now before me, written by one of those on board, at the time, records the fact that there were those who insisted that the comet of 1811 had fallen into the Ohio and had produced the hubbub!"

JHB Latrobe, *The First Steamboat Voyage on the Western Waters*, Maryland Historical Society, Baltimore, 1871

"We have been very much alarmed by a repetition of earthquakes since the morning of the 16th of Dec.... Various conjectures have arisen in the minds of our readers philosophers as to the causes that may have produced them. Some suppose they are occasioned by a volcanic eruption, others seem to think they were produced by the comet's near approach to the earth. There are, however, a few who are of a differing opinion and ascribe it to electricity alone. The latter opinion I have adopted."

Letter from Robert Morrison, Esq, of Kaskaskia, Illinois, *Western Spy*, February 22nd, 1812

"The great scale upon which Nature is operating should be a solemn admonition... at such momentous periods when Nature appears, in spasmodic fury, [to] no longer tolerate the moral turpitude of man."

*Pittsburgh Gazette*, December 27th, 1811

# THE YEAR OF THE FIRE HORSE

# SAN FRANCISCO
## APRIL 18, 1906

"Not in history has a modern imperial city been so completely destroyed.

San Francisco is gone."

*The Story of an Eyewitness*, by Jack London
*Collier's*, May 5th, 1906

Fire, and smoke, and the end of the world.

Buildings shook and buildings fell as the city convulsed, the very earth beneath it caught in a terrible spasm. Solid rock, permanent, forever, moved like water as one tectonic plate shifted, just so, for precisely thirty seconds, one side sheering against the other, as something moved far, far, far below.

And death, and pain; punishment from the gods perhaps for the greed of the city, for what the people had dared wrench from the ground, the hills, the rivers. The gold rush had been a boon, the *foundation* of a whole region, transforming nature to industry and birthing the city of San Francisco.

And perhaps, as the miners and the prospectors had delved deeper and deeper, blasting and digging and blasting again, perhaps they had disturbed something. Something dormant. Something... asleep.

Perhaps it wasn't an earthquake at all.

••••

Robert ran, his feet bare and bleeding as he trod on broken glass and shattered stone and splintered wood. He ran, ignoring the pain he knew was only temporary, knowing that once he had a chance to slow down and to focus his injuries would no longer be a problem. But for now, he had to run, into the city, into the devastation, to where people needed him. And they needed him, all of them, the whole city. The earthquake had been just the start. The worst came after, Robert knew, and he knew that it had started already.

The earth had moved, cracking San Francisco into a million pieces. If that was all there was then perhaps the city could recover, given time. If that was all there was.

It wasn't.

Robert reached the crest of California Street. On his right, houses and shops were missing their frontages, reduced to a collection of stacked, open boxes, brick and stone spilling out across the street in great triangular piles that looked somehow organized, arranged. He glanced up and saw a bathtub in the upper grid of the building nearest, and in the next cubicle a heavy sideboard of dark wood hung over the edge, one door swinging open. The story below, a table and a gramophone, the machine's horn lying funnel-down on the floor, the edge of a rug flapping in the morning breeze.

On his left, the buildings were intact, or appeared to be, until Robert noticed there was nothing left that was perpendicular, every upright now an angle, all pointing down the hill, toward the city proper.

"Sweet mother of God."

Robert turned at the voice, thinking perhaps someone was talking about him – bloody, barefoot, shirtless, his blue jeans now dry but his long blond hair still salty and crisp from the ocean. On any other day he imagined he might be arrested on a vagrancy charge, locked away for a spell with others on whom hard times had also fallen ever since the gold had become harder and harder to steal from the ground.

But not today. Today, Robert was one of many battered and bruised. All down the street, people stood and stared, or sat on the piles of rubble and talked and sobbed. People in suits and hats, some immaculate, having come to this vantage point to bear witness the wrath of God. Others were monochromatic, shadows of gray and black, covered head to foot in dust. So much dust. On some, the thick gray coating was splashed with blood, dark and thick. Some of the bleeding were standing, some sitting. A lot more were lying in the street and not moving, some only half-visible underneath the piles of rubble.

Below, down the steep slope of the street, lay the city: broken and ruptured, equal parts buildings standing proud and tall and a jagged, low landscape of destruction. In the center smoke rose – black, almost a solid curling mass, like the earthquake had opened a shaft straight down, through the crust, to hell itself.

Robert rolled his neck and lifted first one foot, then another, taking the moment's pause to focus, to reach out to the world and feel it.

And then, a new arrival.

The man waved his hat in one hand as he heaved himself up the street, shouting, calling out to anyone who would listen. The people around Robert stirred at his approach, their voices growing in a steady murmur as they turned to their companions. The man had come from the city center and was bringing news, clearly. Although not any that made much sense. Robert watched as word spread from farther down the street as the shouting man passed. Some of the onlookers were confused, some frightened, some even amused. Robert had a bad, bad feeling about the information the man brought.

"Dynamite!" the man shouted as he reached the crest of the hill. Then he turned and stretched his arms out, like a preacher conducting a sermon. The crowd moved toward him, and Robert stepped back, down the street, letting people past. They all ignored him, even shirtless and bloody, but it was well not to draw too much attention, not yet.

"Dynamite!" the man shouted again, and this time the crowd was more vocal in their response. –They're using dynamite! They're going to blow up parts of the city, whole streets!"

Robert gasped in surprise, along with the rest. Then he turned and ran down the hill, his ruined feet healed, as he headed deeper into the city.

It was the gas mains. The earthquake had ruptured thirty or more, releasing gas from a hundred thousand pipeline fractures to collect, unimpeded, in the ruined buildings. The first fire had started almost immediately, then another, then another, eventually all coming together into one great blaze. San Francisco had been ruined by the earthquake, and now those ruins were being razed by fire.

Robert ran on, the devastation more awful the closer he got to the wall of fire that bisected San Francisco, moving with devilish speed from one side of the city to the other. Up on the hills, people had stopped to watch, feeling safe perhaps but unwilling to venture any closer.

But here, down in the city proper, it was chaos – people running, shouting, crying. People bleeding and screaming and dying. Even as Robert ran on, the city shook again, a sharp jolt that felt as if the world were trying to flick San Francisco from its surface like dust from a rug. The aftershock lasted only a second, but threw Robert off his feet. He fell forward onto his hands, skinning the palm of one, a shard of glass embedding itself an inch into the fleshy pad above his thumb on the other. Robert cried out and rolled into his back, more glass and rubble cutting into him in a geometry of pain.

"Help me, please. Somebody, help me!"

Robert sat up and glanced around, wincing. The voice was weak, coming from a towering collection of brick and stone that had once been a building – offices, he thought, or maybe a bank; if only he could work out where exactly he was.

"Help me... somebody."

The voice spoke the words almost without emotion, or hope. It was a woman, a victim trapped but alive. She would be dead soon, Robert could sense it. The city was filled with death on a scale that he hadn't sensed for a long, long time.

Death on a scale he hadn't *tasted* in a long, long time. And despite himself, he let the flavor infuse him for just a moment. It gave him strength. Power.

Robert raised his injured hand and pulled out the shard of glass. The two sides of the wound slicked together, the sensation oily and nauseating. Robert gasped. It hurt. It all hurt, his hand, his back, his feet. That was part of the arrangement. Injure him enough and he would suffer beyond all reckoning, but he didn't think he could die, not really. Even if his body was destroyed utterly, he knew he could come back. He didn't remember what that felt like, although he knew he must have experienced it at least once. That was why he was here, after all.

"Help me, please. Help me."

Wrist healed, back healed, Robert scrambled to his feet. Brushing his hair from his face, he edged forward toward the rubble, toward the voice.

There. In a gap, an angle of black formed by fallen masonry, he could see something moving and something shining wetly in the morning sun. A pair of eyes.

"Help me. I'm over here!"

Robert glanced around. This street was quiet, although there was plenty of traffic at the intersections ahead and behind. Most people were too preoccupied helping others to notice the tall man with long hair wearing nothing but a pair of blue jeans, his torso naked and shining in the morning sun. Too preoccupied to notice.

He had to help. Had to.

Robert turned to the pile of rubble and slid his fingers beneath the largest single piece, a slab the size of a mail carriage, at the very least. Then he lifted. It was heavy – more than a ton, maybe even two or three, he wasn't sure. Robert lifted it with the tips of his fingers and then when it was high enough shifted his hands underneath it so he could push with his palms. He stretched up, until the slab was balanced along its furthest edge, and, with a small push, Robert flipped it back. The slab hit the ground with a dull thud and split into two, shaking the street.

"You there!"

Robert froze, then looked over his shoulder. Two men were running fast toward him, one with a bowler hat jammed on tight, the other man bareheaded and one sleeve of his jacket nearly torn off, his trousers ragged at the knees.

Had They seen? Robert wasn't sure. And what if They had? Today was a day like no other. Surely it would be permitted. Even *They* wouldn't be able to stand by and let the city die.

Would They?

"Here!" said the man in the hat as he arrived with his companion. He immediately bent over and grabbed another, smaller slab, his friend in the torn suit giving a hand. Neither of them said anything further to Robert, the man in the hat, his face red, his cheeks two balloons as he heaved at the block, just nodding at Robert to indicate they were ready.

Robert reached down and began to lift.

Robert had been swimming, out at Ocean Beach, when the earthquake struck just after five in the morning. Robert swam every day, had done so for as long as he'd been in San Francisco. Ocean Beach was nice and quiet – slightly too far out from the city itself for there to be anyone around so early. As the sun rose, he had the place to himself. The beach – the *ocean* – was his.

Swimming was important, something he *had* to do. The ocean was a part of him, something he was now and always would be connected with. When he swam, it felt like he was leaving the world, as his feet lifted off the sand, as his ears were filled with the dull and epic sound of the sea. He wasn't out there in the open ocean, of course, but he knew that all the oceans of the world were connected, one great continuous body of water. Here in San Francisco, as he swam the cold waters of Ocean Beach, he felt connected with his home, so many, many miles out in the Pacific. Out here, swimming, he could open his eyes and look at the green and blue and imagine himself elsewhere.

Then the water churned and bubbled. At first he thought it was a big wave, and that maybe as he floated beneath the surface and dreamed of home he'd drifted, turning himself around without realizing, perhaps going out farther, much farther than he usually did, out to where the seas were rougher, untamed by the city shoreline. Not that it mattered. Robert knew he could swim from here to forever if he wanted, but he had to be careful in case *They* noticed.

When the second surge threw him up to the surface, and the third pulled him down, he knew something was wrong. When he surfaced again he could hear it, a moaning, like a deep wind howling through a canyon a million miles away. It was primal, animalistic, like something wild in pain. As he trod water he turned and turned. The sound was everywhere, everything. It came down from the sky; it rushed in across the surface of the water like a cold wind. Robert felt for a moment that he was the center of the world, and then he looked back at the beach. He was, in fact, much closer than he'd thought. But the beach looked different, rough, as if someone had come and turned the sand over, exposing the darker, wetter material beneath. Beyond, the trees were swaying, left to right, left to right, as though a great godly hand were reaching down and flicking them like springs.

And beyond that rose a pall: pale, too light for smoke, more like a dust storm from Arizona had suddenly arrived, impossibly, over the Golden State.

The deep howling stopped, and for a moment all Robert could hear was the sharp slap of water as the sea began to calm. He trod water a moment longer; then he started to head ashore.

Thunder rolled, the bass so deep Robert could feel it in his chest. He looked up, but the lightening sky was clear. Then came another roll, softer, farther away. Robert paddled around until he was facing the dust cloud again, now stretching nearly across the whole horizon. Dotted along it, lower down, were smaller clouds, these ones black and ominous.

He reached the shore, sinking to his ankles in the disturbed sand, his mind racing as he searched for his clothes. His pants – blue jeans, dotted with rivets like the gold miners favored – were floating in the surf farther along the shoreline. Of his shirt and boots, there was no sign. He jogged over to his jeans and picked them up, squeezing the seawater from the heavy denim, just as the earth moved again, sliding from side to side like a prospector panning for gold. Robert went with the movement, riding it like he used to ride the waves so many years ago, back home.

Then it stopped moving, and the air was still, and Robert realized what had just happened.

It was an earthquake. San Francisco had been struck by an earthquake.

Robert pulled on his jeans, the wet fabric sticky and difficult as he tried to button the fly, and then ran up the beach, toward the street, toward the city.

Robert helped all morning. At first he checked his strength, matching it to those around him (perhaps a little more). But it soon became a problem, requiring far too much concentration when time was so short for the people he was trying to aid. That was more important than rules, than agreements, and perhaps today – just for one day – *They* would turn a blind eye. He wasn't even sure *They* were still watching, truth be told. They had lost interest, all of them – even his brother, his friends – centuries ago, abandoning those they had once tended, aided, watched from afar. They'd let Robert remain, and that was the last he had heard.

And as he helped shift the debris, nobody noticed. People were too busy trying to cope with their world being destroyed, with their friends, families, business, lives crushed under the collapsing city. One man with long hair, shirtless in jeans, lifting rock and iron and wood like it was paper, he was a hero, but then everyone was a hero today. Robert lifted the rubble like it was nothing, but he was just doing the best he could, like everyone else. And hell, maybe gold mining had been good for him (he was a gold miner, in those jeans, with that hair, wasn't he?) and had made him big and strong.

It felt good to stretch his power, even just a little. It felt like waking up from a long sleep. Perhaps that wasn't far from the truth.

Today, San Francisco needed heroes. As he worked, Robert felt a connection, one stronger than he ever had with the people who lived and worked and breathed and loved and ate and slept in the city. He remembered, just for a moment, what it had been like, before the Agreement, before the Retreat. Before *They* had left the world to its own devices.

Today Robert was a hero but today was also dangerous. Not physically, although he had to make sure his own efforts weren't injuring others as he dug through the remains of the city. But there was another problem.

Robert was surrounded by the dead and the dying. It was everywhere, the air thick with dust and the smell of gas and the smell of something else, something only he could sense. It was death – the smell of life ebbing away, of the energy that animated living things dissipating, evaporating. Energy that filled the earth, that danced over Robert's skin like lightning. And it felt good. So very, *very* good.

He had to stop, now and again. After freeing children from behind a stuck door, after lifting half a house off an elderly couple (one dead, one alive), he would excuse himself, back off as others moved forward, some slapping him on the back for a job well done and thanks, mister, we can take it from here. Robert would walk backward and close his eyes and breath it in.

Death. So much death. And it was *delicious*. It sated a hunger deep inside, one that Robert thought he had expunged years and years ago. He felt like an addict taking a hit of opium long after the habit had been kicked. It was all still in there, somewhere. He was just waiting for it, had been waiting for it forever. And all he had to do was reach out and embrace the dying city, and he could have his fill of death and decay and terror and horror. Oh, what a wonderful, beautiful day it could be, if only he gave in, if only he let the hunger take over.

Robert blinked as the clouds parted and sun bathed his face. He looked around him, watched the people of the city digging and running, saving lives.

The moment passed. Robert's hunger was replaced with disgust, self-loathing, and sadness. He had to focus. The city needed him.

The fire. He had spent too much time clearing rubble when the greater danger lay ahead. The fire was growing, and to stop it the army was going to dynamite whole streets, creating a network of firebreaks.

There, the need was greatest.

Robert dusted his hands on his jeans and continued his journey deeper into the city.

It was quiet on Van Ness, the broad avenue that circled the western edge of San Francisco's downtown. The army had cordoned it off, their trucks arranged at one end. Soldiers were busy running cables, while officers in caps studied plans stretched out over a stack of wooden crates. As Robert watched from the shadowed eaves of a still-intact house, he saw the officers point first at the map and then down the street, and then back again. They were agitated, and Robert could sense their fear. And he could sense... something else.

Something that didn't belong. Something... *moving*.

He peeled out from the shade, keeping close to the buildings as he looked down the avenue. Ahead a few hundred yards, the road was riven in two, a great canyon opened horizontally from one side of the street to the other. The edges of the ravine were curled and blackened, and from within rose smoke, lazy and brown, thick and tangy with something that made Robert's nostrils twitch. It was chemical, but nothing quite like anything he had ever smelled before.

And then he saw it. Along the street, radiating out from either side of the canyon, the road *undulated*. Robert stepped out from the building behind him and braced himself, ready to act quick if the aftershock sent more debris crashing down to the street.

No aftershock came. The ground was – for the moment – solid, stable, unmoving. But ahead, the street continued to ripple. Robert could see now the movement was in thin, discrete lines, like there was something alive under the paving, its tentacles stretching out and moving the roadway as they stretched and flexed.

The dynamite trucks started to make more sense. The fire was steadily eating the city, but it didn't seem to be sweeping in this direction. The dynamite was for something else.

Robert moved in for a closer look.

The soldiers, so busy laying fuses for the explosives, were easy to avoid. Robert skirted clusters of them, and soon found himself at the edge of the smoking fissure that bisected the avenue.

"Help me, please, help me."

Robert stopped, and ducked down, trying to locate the voice whilst staying out of sight of the soldiers. This side of the street was rubble, nothing but a few isolated walls showing the outlines of where tall buildings had stood. There could be any number of people trapped here, and with the area cordoned off, it seemed the army was prepared to let them die for the greater good.

Robert moved away from the canyon and crept along the side of the street, searching for any movement, any sign of life, within the shattered buildings. There was nothing, so he took a chance and tasted for death, that familiar, *divine* tang on his tongue.

Nothing. The row was empty, the only dead things near a dog and a horse. Robert stopped, and heard movement behind him. He turned, pinpointing the sound from the split in the middle of the road. Retracing his steps, he moved back to the edge and, keeping low to avoid the soldiers at the far end of the street, looked down into the fissure.

There was someone in there. Someone had fallen into the crack and couldn't get out. It was shallow, only six feet deep, but it wasn't a clean wound in the city's fabric. Inside the fissure were jagged shelves and black openings, the bottom buried under crumbling, burned earth.

There was an arm, bare and waving, covered in black ash, reaching out from underneath one of the rocky shelves, the hand scrambling against the crumbling dirt.

Robert jumped into the trench. It wouldn't take a moment to pull the rock and dirt away and free the person. He'd bring them back to the soldiers, and then they could search for more survivors. He reached down and grabbed the hand.

At his touch, the other person wrapped their fingers around Robert's hand with enough strength to crack bones. Robert pulled back instinctively, hot, sharp pain coursing up his forearm. He stumbled backward. His bare feet slipped in the dirt, and his back collided with the jagged shelf behind. Robert cried out and slid farther, clawing a fistful of carbonized earth with his free hand as he tried to pull himself back up onto the road. He realized the hand that held his own was cold, freezing.

Another hand grabbed his ankle so hard it felt like his leg was caught in a vice. Robert kicked out blindly with his other foot, and was rewarded when it connected with something soft. The icy grip released his ankle, and Robert tore his broken hand free from the other. Ignoring the pain, he pulled himself over the lip of the fissure. He lay on his chest on the road; ahead, he saw soldiers point in his direction. One of them shouted.

The voice from the trench came again. It was calm, emotionless.

"Help me, please, help me."

Robert rolled on the road. There, in the trench, a blackened form reached up toward him; the hands grabbed at the air, fingertips straining.

It was a person, wasn't it? Someone caught in the earthquake, caught in the fire that clearly scorched the earth here. They were injured – dying. All Robert could see were two wet eyes in a face caked entirely in thick black ash.

Some of the dirt below crumbled away, and another hand broke the surface, close to the first figure. This hand too was blackened, grasping, the quiet, calm plea for help coming from under the rubble.

Booted feet pounded the road, getting closer. Robert glanced over his shoulder and saw a group of soldiers running toward him. He looked back along the trench, trying to work out what had happened to these victims of the earthquake. The road had split, parts of the surface collapsing into the trench. There must have been traffic, pedestrians, people out early. They'd been swallowed whole, and then trapped as the road caved in. That may have saved them from the fire, but Robert knew they'd die if he didn't get them out, and soon.

Then Robert saw it. A small packet, like meat from a butcher's shop wrapped in brown paper, wedged into the rock just underneath the opposite lip of the trench. The packet was wrapped in string, which trailed off, horizontal to the street. About half a dozen yards farther along was another brown packet, stuck at the same angle in a crack in the earth. More string, and then farther on, another.

Robert looked to his left. The pattern continued, all long the trench, from one side of the road to the other.

Dynamite.

"Help me, please, help me."

The army wasn't going to blow up the street; they were going to blow up the trench.

"Help me, please, help me."

The road moved beneath Robert, undulating waves out from the crack in the Earth. The wave pushed him up, and then continued down the street, the cracked paving clicking as it was lifted and lowered.

Something *moving*. Something under the street. The army knew, had seen it, and were going to try to kill it.

Robert pushed himself to his feet and took one step into the trench, careful of his footing, aware the charred earth could crumble beneath him at any moment. Black hands reached up toward him. He bent over, reached down, and then a black hand was in his. It burned like fire, although it was cold, so very, very cold. The hand pulled him forward with surprising force; then another burst through the black dirt and grabbed his forearm, then another his elbow. Robert toppled head-first into the trench as the black figures – two, three, four – emerged from the ground.

The gunshots were loud, each leaving Robert's head ringing like a bell. He felt the heat on his face and was showered with dirt and dust thrown up from the ground as the soldiers fired into the trench. Big hands – *hot* hands – grabbed both his legs and yanked him backward. Robert hit the road with his chest, the air driven out of his lungs. He rolled onto his back, and squinted into the sun, blinking away the ash and dust and blood from his eyes.

The soldiers formed a row – five men, rifles raised. They continued to fire into the trench. From where he lay, Robert couldn't see the carnage within.

"Stop!" he yelled. "For god's sake, stop!" But his voice was weak and choked with dust and dirt. The soldiers kept firing. Robert clutched his aching chest and arched his neck, looking back at the trench and the soldiers upside-down.

A black figure leapt out of the trench – lithe, naked, caked in black ash, long matted hair swinging. A woman, the first victim Robert had tried to pull out of the ground. Either the soldiers had somehow missed their targets at point-blank range, or the bullets were having no effect. The woman leapt onto the front of a solider, and then pulled him backward. The pair toppled into the trench.

"Retreat!"

The firing stopped. Robert felt himself lifted by four soldiers, one on each limb. As he was carried back to dynamite trucks, he looked back at the receding trench. More black hands appeared over the lip as the creatures began to pull themselves up.

The soldiers had seen. As he got nearer to the trucks there was a flurry of movement, orders shouted. Someone cried out that they couldn't be stopped, that they'd be out soon, all of them, that they would be all over the city by nightfall, that the street had to be blown right now.

There was a crump, like a gunshot underwater, and the street and the trench disappeared in a cloud of brown dust and red and orange flame.

Then the shockwave from the explosion hit the trucks, and Robert's world vanished into darkness.

# WHAT HORROR SLEEPS BEYOND THE KNOWLEDGE OF MEN

# INDIAN TERRITORY, OKLAHOMA-TO-BE
## APRIL 22, 1889

Now, this is the story of a young man by the name of Joel, a young man with nothing to lose and everything to gain by traveling west into Indian Territory, where the Unassigned Lands were ready and waiting for those seeking their fortune, for those wanting to start something special, something new.

Young men like Joel, who had arrayed himself with the multitude assembled in one great line that stretched north to south. A train of wagons and horses, men and women and children, the young and the old, the fit and the infirm alike. The way ahead was free, and at high noon the land run would begin, each settler able to stake a claim on one hundred sixty acres of the finest soil that had once belonged to the native people, but no longer did.

Those on horses would be first off the mark and they'd get the best of the best, of course. Those in wagons would be slower, but the Unassigned Lands were big and even if there were fifty thousand people standing in the line like the whispers rippling back and forth through the crowd said there were, then there would be plenty to go around. And if you were in a wagon, well, then maybe things were looking better for you already, if you were smart and had that there wagon loaded with the tools and means to improve the land you staked.

If you were desperate, you could go on foot. You'd be slow, you'd get the scraps, but maybe, just maybe, you'd find your lot and live happily ever after.

Joel was on foot, and he was desperate, and that was yesterday. Today he watched the sun rise in the east from his camp, nothing more than a makeshift bivouac of blankets over a fallen log. The sun rose into a clear blue sky, the color so deep, so real that if he lay on his back and looked straight up into the apex of the dome above him, the sky was almost black. It filled his vision, and made him feel like he was swimming in an ocean of nothing but color. Joel lay there in the dirt for a spell, staring at the sky until a shining diamond of light struck the edge of his vision as the sun crawled higher, toward the west.

Toward the future. Joel's future. This he knew, somehow, like it had been foretold, like it was written in his blood and the blood of his father and in the blood of *his* father before him.

Joel hadn't known his father, not really. His daddy had left to fight in the war back in, oh, must have been '63 or '64, marching to Atlanta and never marching home again. But before he'd gone, he'd given Joel something. A coin, a double-eagle. He said it was gold and it sure did shine like it was gold, and his daddy said he wanted Joel to look after it and he'd come back for it.

He didn't come back for it, but that was OK. The coin was in Joel's pocket and when he carried it he knew his daddy was with him, marching by his side. Heading west, toward the future, toward the light.

Joel packed up his bivouac and rolled his blankets and turned his back to the sun, and marched onwards across the Unassigned Lands.

By the end of the first day of the Oklahoma Land Run of 1889, the dusty Unassigned Lands had become two cities,

Oklahoma City and Guthrie. After the sun had set, two newspapers and one bank had already been established, serving those who had carved a future not just for themselves, but for their children, and grandchildren, and so on down the line.

Joel knew nothing of this. After the first day, as the horses and wagons had raced past him, as men had run past him, he walked onward, due west. He was desperate, he had nothing to lose, but he was patient, and he knew that a patient man was a man whose reward would come, in time.

The morning of the second day was still, and quiet. Joel felt like the only man in the whole world and maybe that was so, because the only thing he'd heard in the night was someone calling, far away, the voice carried on a dull wind even before Joel was fully awake. He thought of the voice now, and as he walked west, across a dusty plain of dry grass, with not a soul from horizon to horizon, he wondered if maybe his daddy really was there with him, calling out for his son to keep on marching and keep on fighting because a patient man would find his true reward.

The coin in his waistcoat pocket felt heavy. Joel kept marching and dipped a finger and a thumb into the pocket. He stopped, pulling his hand away, hissing like he'd just been bit.

Because the day was getting hot already and the blue sky above was an unbroken dome, and the coin in his pocket was cold, cold like the bottom of a blue ocean, the ocean Joel often dreamed of.

He stopped and kicked the dirt and looked around, but he was alone in the world. He looked down at his waistcoat, his eyes following the line of buttons running down to his belt. His suit was old and black, dusty, a relic from another time, something his daddy left behind when he marched to war. Like the silver gun with the creamy pearl handle that hung from Joel's waist. Why his daddy hadn't taken the gun to war with him, Joel didn't know. He'd found it in the closet, along with the suit and a box of ammunition. He hadn't fired the gun yet, not even to test it, perhaps afraid that the weapon was too old and would explode in his hand. Maybe that was why it had been left behind. But with the gun on his waist and the coin in his pocket, Joel felt as though his daddy was watching over him.

Joel gritted his teeth and slid his fingers into the pocket where the fob watch should have been, had he not hocked it somewhere back in Tennessee the previous week, getting just enough money to reach Indian Territory by high noon. The watch was nothing and was worth virtually the same, but it had been just enough. The coin was worth a lot, Joel knew that, even if it wasn't gold like his daddy told him (but it was, it was). But the coin was his father and his father marched with him, to the west, to the future.

Joel took the coin between two fingers and pulled it out. It was cold, although not burning cold like it had been moments before. Joel held it up and turned each side in the sun, the embossed bird on each catching the sunlight and shining, shining like the eagle itself was alive.

And then Joel heard the voice again.

The cave was deep – less a cave, more a long trench in the otherwise smooth and rolling dusty plain. It started as nothing more than a crack to catch the foolhardy traveler (although, Joel knew, if they were walking in his footsteps across this particular part of the godforsaken Unclaimed Lands that he found himself in somehow, then they were fools already) but widened and deepened until it was big enough for a covered wagon to fall into, breaking the axle and probably the horse in the process.

Joel had neither. He stepped into the trench and walked down toward the opening in the earth. The ground was dry and brittle, covered with a darker kind of dust than the surrounding plains, something more like ash. It was like the hole in the ground had been burned through the crust of the plain. But there was only scraggly brush nearby, dry enough but still alive, simply baked under the summer sun. If there had been a fire here then it had died long, long ago.

A riverbed then, or a creek – perhaps an underground spring run dry. The cave entrance was a black abyss. Joel slipped and slid forward, dirt and rock cascading from under his old boots, the skin on the heels of his hands soon red and raw.

He stopped when he realized the angle of the gully was steeper than it looked, but he kept sliding a foot or more toward the cave entrance before he came to halt. Nothing but dry dirt and loose rock, of course... except for the fact that Joel was sure there was something drawing him in. Not like being pushed, like some fellow settler desperate for a valid claim in the land run had hidden in the cracks and crevasses of the gully and had come out to shove Joel to his death, hoping his neck would break, and if that failed that he would be on the ground long enough for his attacker to smash his brains out with one of the heavy stones that lay scattered in some abundance around the cave.

No, this was more like being *pulled*, like there was a lasso around Joel's middle, drawing him gently, slowly in.

Joel's fingers found the coin again. This time it was cold but there was something else too, a sensation he couldn't quite describe, like when you sometimes touched the metal rim of a wagon wheel just as you got off after a long journey. A spark, a pinprick, like being licked by the trailing edge of a whip. The sensation was gone in a second and Joel took the coin out, now used to the cold.

But not used to the force that seemed to emanate from it. The coin was moving, or wanted to move, toward the cave. It wriggled in his fingers, back and forth, back and forth. Joel took a step forward, watching the coin, watching the cave.

Then he let go of the coin, and it dropped to the sandy soil like any coin would, and it did not move. With his other hand he brushed the handle of the gun on his belt, ready to draw.

Then a cold wind came from the cave, carrying with it the smell of metal and the voice, calling out, far away. The sun dropped in the sky and caught the face of the coin in the dirt, throwing up a shining, glittering flare into Joel's eyes.

The cave called again, and hand on his daddy's gun, Joel stepped forward.

# MURDER IN THE CITY

...and in developing news this hour, the San Francisco Police Department has released the name of the woman whose body was found in a back street close to City Hall last week.

The woman has been identified as Lucy Winters, 23. Relatives have been informed.

Police are appealing to any witnesses who were in the vicinity of Olive and Polk in the city center in the early hours of July ninth, and have conducted a door-to-door of nearby businesses and residences. While no further statement has been made by the SFPD, a source close to the investigation told this news organization that the death of Lucy Winters followed the same pattern as that of an elderly resident of Chinatown the previous week. The unnamed Chinese male was found hanged in an apparent ritual murder inside a food import warehouse, but our sources could not speculate on the connection between the two deaths.

We'll have more news as it comes to hand.

# I
# SAN FRANCISCO
## TODAY

Ted gave up fighting after a while. No matter how much he insisted he was OK, no matter how gently he protested at being led to the back of the ambulance by two paramedics, resistance was most definitely useless. The whole damn street was caught in the red and blue strobe of the vehicle's lights, bleaching the faces of the Chinatown onlookers in alternating flashes of color.

Reluctantly, Ted now sat in the back of the ambulance and let the paramedics fuss as much as they wanted. It was their job, after all, and a mighty fine and important one at that. Pissing off the San Francisco Fire Department was rather low on his list of priorities. Figuring out what had caused the explosion at the Jade Emperor was currently at the top.

One of the paramedics pressed a button and the blood pressure sleeve inflated for a second time; Ted felt fine, really, no problem, no pain except for his upper arm being crushed by the damn cuff wrapped around his biceps.

"Hey," Ted said. The paramedic didn't move his eyes from the digital readout, but his eyebrows went up half an inch.

Ted sighed and closed his eyes and focused instead on being the model patient. He felt fine, honestly, no problem, and just hoped they wouldn't decide to take him to the hospital. Now *that* would be embarrassing.

"Stop fidgeting."

Ted opened his eyes and saw Alison leaning against the open door of the ambulance, arms folded, the crowd behind her still eager for a quick glimpse at whatever tragedy was unfolding. Well, thought Ted, sorry to disappoint, but there is no gore, no blood, no wailing and gnashing. Rubberneckers.

The cuff hissed and deflated, and Ted felt an almost nauseating relief as the blood surged back into his arm. The paramedic moved farther back in to the ambulance. Taking his cue, Ted rolled his shirtsleeve down.

"Where's Benny?" he asked. He had no idea where anybody was. The only thing he did know was that his thirty-seventh birthday had ended with a bang a little bigger than intended, but as he was the only one sitting in the back of an ambulance, he assumed everyone else was OK. Alison seemed to be in one piece, anyway.

She jerked her head back up the street. "She's talking to the owners. Material for the blog."

Ted nodded. Made sense. A journalist had to be ready, eyes and ears open, forever searching for the story, the scoop. Ted included. That the little explosion had disrupted the dinner arrangements of a table full of San Francisco's finest online reporters was perhaps a happy coincidence. The story had landed, almost literally, in their lap.

"What did the police say?" he asked.

"Why don't you ask them yourself?" Alison backed away from the door and a uniformed officer appeared from around the side of the vehicle. He took one look at Ted, and, as though he'd forgotten a common courtesy, knocked on the inside of the door with his knuckles. The paramedic reappeared from the recesses of the ambulance with some paperwork, and the two nodded a greeting.

"He's all yours," said the paramedic, his attention now shifted from his patient to his clipboard.

Ted sighed. Great. First paramedics, now the police. This was not quite his idea of a fun night out.

"Mr Kane?"

Ted nodded. "That's me."

"How are you feeling?" asked the officer, in a tone that suggested he lacked any interest in Ted's wellbeing at all.

Ted glanced at the paramedic, and nodded at the officer. "Just fine," he said, but as he stood from the gurney and moved to hop out of the back of the ambulance he rocked on his feet, dizziness threatening to overcome him. He sat back down. Alison gave him a look, and Ted frowned. "Well, little woozy, maybe."

The officer took a small notepad from inside his jacket and flipped it to a blank page. Alison crept forward a little and stood on her toes to watch over the officer's shoulder as he began to jot his notes.

"Tell me what happened tonight, sir." The officer had his pen at the ready. The pen was short. Ted didn't think it looked that comfortable to write with.

He thought for a moment, and nodded slowly.

This was going to take some explaining.

"It was a fortune cookie."

The officer licked his lips, and his pen remained resolutely motionless. The cop's eyes remained fixed on Ted's.

"A fortune cookie?" asked the officer.

"Yep, a fortune cookie. An *exploding* fortune cookie."

"So a fortune cookie exploded, blowing out half the windows down the street and landing you in the back of an ambulance?"

"In a word, yes."

The officer licked his lips again and turned to Alison, who just shrugged.

"Look," said Ted. "We were out for my birthday…"

••••

Alison organized it, of course, although Ted thought he might have given a hint here and there. He didn't think it was quite right to organize your own birthday dinner. Not that it was a milestone age, but he was turning an odd number – not just odd, but *prime*. Ted wasn't good at math, but he had a thing for numbers. Alison knew this, although she thought his little numerical obsession was pretty dumb. But she organized dinner and drinks and friends, and kept the prime nature of Ted's age to herself. Ted was just *dying* to tell everyone. Because, he rationalized, they were all friends and colleagues, right? Some from the blog, some not. And they wouldn't mind if he waxed lyrical about the beauty of the number thirty-seven, would they?

OK, maybe they would. Well, some of them. Not Benny. Ted wondered, through the haze of a little too much wine, whether he was stereotyping by assuming the young Asian woman would be good at math. He immediately felt stupid and decided not to bring it up.

There were other guests from the Bay Blog: Alison, of course, the two Kevins, Daisy and Zane. Ted didn't really care much for Zane's company, but it was one of those situations where if you invited so-and-so and so-and-so, you really had to invite Zane as well.

Then there was Andy and Lisa. Andy was an iPhone developer and he had an office that was far too plush and had way too much of a nice view of the Golden Gate Bridge. Lisa was his wife, and Ted didn't think she worked, although he'd never quite figured it out.

Rounding it off had been Victor, Kate, Klaire-with-a-K, and Barry and Amos. Ted was always vaguely jealous of Amos, having a name like that. It sure beat Ted.

Ted was just thinking about someone else he knew with the frankly *outstanding* name of St. John when the table went quiet. He blinked and smiled sweetly at Alison, finally noticing that particular look she was giving him, the look that indicated sharp and stabby death was imminent if he didn't start paying attention.

Zane licked his lips and for a moment Ted thought he was being too harsh on him. So he was a bore. Ted had known worse.

"Sorry," said Ted, "what was that, Zane?"

Zane's smile grew two inches, and he pushed his glasses up the bridge of his nose a little. They were nice glasses. Thick black frames, gold arms, the design perfect for his face. He had taste. Maybe, thought Ted, he needed to be friends with Zane, proper friends. They could go fishing, or catch a game of whatever-it-was that they both liked, and then shoot the shit in a bar and eat peanuts. Zane had cool glasses. If Ted needed glasses – and he didn't, but if he did – then he thought he might go for a pair like Zane's.

"I was saying," said Ted's new best friend, "don't you think the new paper recycling policy at the office is just ridiculous?"

He snickered. It was unpleasant, a sort of snort through the nostrils and hiss through the teeth, in rapid alternation. Ted watched Zane's hipster glasses slide down his nose as Zane looked around the table, catching the eye of each diner to ensure that he had their full attention. Most of them smiled and then glanced back at their food. Benny's grin was the widest, but then Benny seemed to get on with everyone at the blog. Even Zane.

Ted decided he didn't like Zane after all. He probably didn't like football. Ted didn't like football either, but that was beside the point.

Ted laughed a little too loud and quickly stuck his nose in his wine glass. Under the table, Alison nudged his calf with the side of her foot, but as Ted emerged from his sweet Californian rosé she was looking the other way.

"You're right," said Benny through a mouthful of noodles. As she spoke the tail ends rotated through her lips, wet with sauce. It was fascinating and revolting. Ted wondered if she was doing it on purpose.

Benny swallowed. "I don't know what gets into Mazzy's head, but the last thing we need is another two sides of company policy to hang from the noticeboard. Am I right?"

Now she was looking at Ted. She was doing it deliberately. Ted was sure Benny had even winked. Ted opened his mouth to say something but before he could figure out quite what he wanted to say there was an intake of air from the other end of the table and Zane started up again.

Please God, thought Ted. Save me, or kill me. Whatever you choose, do it soon.

"I officially declare I have eaten all the prawns in the Bay area."

Alison laughed at Ted and leaned forward for a kiss. As their lips touched, the table erupted in applause.

"Sir, madam, sir."

Ted stretched back in his chair as the waiter set down a tiny white plate for each guest, a single golden fortune cookie in a crisp, sealed plastic bag sitting on each. It really had been a mighty fine meal. The wine had been mighty fine too. Mighty fine. Ted closed his eyes and listened to the crackle of plastic being torn and the dull snap of cookies breaking. For a second it sounded like someone was whispering over his shoulder. Ted jolted in his chair and opened his eyes quickly, feeling slightly foolish. But nobody had noticed.

"'A rising tide lifts all boats,'" said Andy. This was met with *hrmms* of appreciation from all.

"'You are a leaf on the wind, a leaf on the wind,'" said one of the Kevins. Benny laughed, and proceeded to explain at length how this was from the TV series *Firefly*. Ted wanted to tell her it was probably a coincidence but as Benny got into it Ted decided not to shatter the illusion.

"'As the sun rises in the east and sets in the West, seize the day!'" Klaire sat back and admired her tiny strip of paper with a nod and a downturned mouth. Someone suggested her fortune would have sounded better in Latin.

Benny played her cookie around on its little plate, and as soon as Klaire had dropped her fortune back on the table, she picked her little plastic bag up, like she'd been holding back and the excitement had finally gotten to be too much for her.

"My turn!" she said. She loved this stuff, really she did.

She examined the cookie at first, still inside its plastic envelope, turning it around in her fingers like a rare and wonderful thing. Then she carefully grasped the bag on either side of the main seam, and tugged. Kate hooted and slapped the table, begging her to get on with it. At this interruption, something dark passed over Benny's face, but it was replaced quickly with a smile and as Ted looked around the table he wasn't sure anyone else had seen it – except maybe Kate, who dragged her hand off the table and onto her lap quickly, her own smile suddenly gone.

Benny extracted the cookie from its bag. She turned the cookie around, grabbed it by the horns, and pulled. The cookie split neatly in two, nary a splinter out of place. With almost surgical stillness, Benny reached inside for the curl of white paper.

"'Perhaps you've been focusing too much on yourself,'" she read. The table was silent for a moment.

Then Kate hooted and slapped the table again, and everyone burst into laughter. Ted smiled and drained the last oily dregs of wine from his glass, but when he put it down he could see that Benny wasn't happy. She was staring at his little piece of magic advice, pulling the strip of paper tape so tight it began to twist at the center. True enough, it was a strange fortune. But sometimes the makers liked to spice things up a little and get funky with their words of wisdom, didn't they? If anything, Benny was lucky, having received by random chance a keeper, a fortune odd enough, good enough, to slip into your wallet as an amusing reminder.

Ted watched in silence as the conversation was re-ignited around the table, everyone discussing the best fortunes they had received in the past. Benny was as still as Ted, and Ted realized that his friend really *did* love this stuff. She was disappointed, that much was obvious, but perhaps she was taking it a little too seriously.

"Great advice," Ted said, reaching past Klaire to knock Benny's shoulder with his fist. It was just a light touch, but Benny rocked on her chair a little too much. Ted frowned and Benny placed her strip of paper back down on the plate, between the two neat halves of her cookie.

"Hey," said Alison. Her wine glass had miraculously refilled itself, and she used the base of it to point at the untouched cookie on Ted's plate.

"Aha!" said Ted. He glanced at Benny and gave a wink, although his friend didn't react. Ignoring her, Ted carefully rolled the cuffs of his shirt up, stuck his elbows out, and flexed his fingers like a concert pianist about to play Chopin. Andy laughed and someone nudged Benny, who smiled weakly now but still rocked on her chair. Ted saw it out of the corner of his eye, but quickly returned his attention to the cookie. The party may have come to a halt for his friend for some reason, but not for him.

"OK, OK..." said Ted, clapping his hands. Then he picked the cookie up and yanked the bag open. The cookie clattered onto his plate.

"Sounds like you gotta good one there!" said Amos.

Ted laughed and picked the cookie up, feeling over its surface with his thumbs, picking the optimal line of weakness to shatter the puny confection in one mighty push.

"Here we go," he said. He pushed.

Ted felt the rough surface of the thing give under the pressure. It didn't occur to him that anything should be different, that one of these things was not like the others. As the cookie collapsed in on itself and he was lit by a bright red and white light from within, Ted had this absurd vision of the *Sesame Street* four-square, three monsters holding up fortune cookies and, in the top-left, Benny holding hers delicately with a smile. *One of these things is not like the other.* He shook his head and blinked the vision away. Too much wine, too much salt, too much MSG. Didn't MSG make you crazy?

Then the world exploded in red and blue and yellow like a Chinese firecracker, and Ted cried out as the restaurant disappeared into a black void filled with falling stars.

Ted blinked, and blinked again. He was flat on his back on a thick carpet. He raised himself up, enough to see an overturned table, the floor covered with broken crockery and glasses, the sticky remains of a large meal scattered about. There was movement all around, as diners scrambled to flee. The waiters, in their white jacks and black bow ties, were shouting and running, helping people out.

Ted looked up, and saw it was snowing.

He blinked again and watched tiny strips of paper fluttering down from the ceiling.

Ted held his hands out, amazed at the tickling sensation on his palms and fingers as the tiny paper strips drifted from the ceiling. He craned his neck up, but it was dark above, like there was a stormy cloud deck above the swinging green lanterns. The paper strips were falling from somewhere higher, and they weren't stopping.

Ted blinked.

"Ted? Are you OK?" Alison was beside him.

"Ah, yeah, yeah." He looked down at his legs. He moved his arms. He had a sore head but seemed otherwise intact. He drew one leg up experimentally; Benny and Alison stepped back, each of them holding their arms out. Ted offered his in return; they pulled, and Ted was on his feet.

The paper – the *fortunes* – continued to fall. They were all over the table and covered the floor. Klaire looked around, her mouth open wide in shock, wider still when Ted smiled at her. She had fortunes in her hair and some stuck with static to her front. Ted turned, and found himself facing a rank of waiters in their white jackets and then another gentlemen in the middle wearing a black one. The manager. He reached out and grabbed Ted's hands with his own, his face tense with concern. He asked Ted something, but Ted wasn't listening.

The paper storm finally came to an end. Ted reached down and picked a fortune from where it clung to his shirt.

*You are the master of every situation.*

Ted frowned. His head was beginning to ache more than a little. He dropped it, rubbed his eyes, and tried another.

*You are the master of every situation.*

And another.

*You are the master of every situation.*

And another.

*You are the master of every situation.*

All of them said it. A single fortune, repeated a thousand times on a thousand strips of paper that couldn't possibly have fitted inside a fortune cookie. Ted gazed up again, looking for whatever the Chinese equivalent of a piñata was. But he saw only the green paper lanterns spaced at regular intervals, still swaying gently from the impossible paper shower.

"Four hours."

Alison shook her head. "You should still be there. You know that, right?"

Ted walked into his apartment, rolling his shoulders. Truth be told he did feel a little... woozy. But he hated hospitals.

"The doctor said I could go. You were there, remember? I'm fine, really," said Ted, putting a little effort into the act. The apartment had an open-plan living area and kitchen, the counter in a direct line from the front door. He went to it, resting his palms on the cool surface; then he turned around and gave a smile, trying not to let on that he needed the support of the counter against his back just to stay up.

Alison frowned. "You don't look well."

Ted laughed. "I've just spent three and a quarter hours sitting in the emergency room doing nothing, and it's now – " he checked over his shoulder, at the large faux-vintage railway clock that was on the wall in the kitchen, " – three in the morning. Of course I don't look well. It's been a hell of a long night."

Ted blinked and suddenly Alison's arms were around his waist. He rocked a little, leaned back against the counter, and then drew into her hug.

"I'll stay," she said, her cheek hard against his chest.

"You have an early meeting tomorrow."

"I'll cancel."

Ted breathed in the scent of her hair. He'd like her to stay, he'd like that a lot, but what he really needed now was sleep, and lots of it. Glorious oblivion, to go swimming in black nothing. It was more than an urge of his body, it was a demand, like there was something pressing down on the back of his mind, someone standing over his shoulder, whispering in his ear.

He pushed her away and felt bad doing it, but she didn't seem to notice. She looked up at him and he looked down at her and they stood like that a while, then she nodded.

"You're sure?"

"I'm sure," said Ted, and he chuckled. "You heard what the doctor said. There's nothing wrong. No head injury. No concussion. Not a scratch. I'm fine, really."

"You don't look fine."

His smile turned into something else, frustration perhaps, the itch to sleep so great he wanted to pick her up and toss her out the door. And then he felt bad again. Damn, what a night he was having.

"I just need to sleep."

"Make sure you do."

"I will," he said, "and I'll see you tomorrow."

"Come in late if you have to. I'll cover it with Mazzy."

"Great, perfect," said Ted, and he pushed himself off the kitchen counter. "Now get, otherwise you'll be useless at your meeting tomorrow."

Alison selected her car key, nodded, walked to the door. Ted kept by the kitchen counter, his hands braced against it behind his back. Just in case.

"OK," said Alison. She smiled and Ted knew that he loved her and knew that he wanted her to stay, but she couldn't. The blackness was calling, loud and clear enough that it frightened him a little.

Then she was gone, the apartment door clicking shut behind her. Ted stood at the kitchen counter, enjoying the first moment of quiet, of solitude, of the whole evening. He smiled, and pushed away from the counter.

He staggered a little, and stopped on the way to the bedroom. He rubbed his head, turned on his heel. He felt like he'd just heard the mysterious nothing talking over his shoulder again. Then his knees gave way of their own accord and he hit the deck.

# II
# SAN FRANCISCO
## TODAY

The city stretches beneath him like a canvas drawn on by another artist. The work is not his, but is familiar somehow, and if he looks at it, studies it long enough, he can *learn* it. If he works for long enough he will be able to see the artist's true intent, his achievement, maybe even his message. If he works for long enough he might even be able to get inside the artist's head, figure out what makes him tick, how he does what he does. And when that happens then he'll understand, finally, and then the canvas will be wiped clean, ready for something new. Ready to start again.

He hasn't been to this place before, but that doesn't matter. Cities are the same the world over, only the language and the food and the smell is different. This city is famous, too, which is almost like cheating. From the Golden Gate Bridge to the Coit Tower, from the Painted Ladies to Haight-Ashbury, it feels like he's been staring at this canvas his whole life. The sea lions on Pier 39. The science fiction bookstore over on Valencia Street. The way the city tour buses depart from Union Square and how Big Alma, immortalized in stone on top of the Dewey Monument in the middle of that same square, had called her husband Adolph her sugar daddy.

The man crouching on the rooftop has never been in this city before, yet he feels like he's lived his whole life here. San Francisco feels like home. He knows it isn't, it can't be, but the city wraps around him like a warm hug from a favorite relative.

He shrugs in the cold night air, like he's trying to disconnect himself, stop himself getting too close. All cities are the same. Seen one, seen them all. He felt the same way in the last place, he's sure he did. If he could remember what the last place was.

He doesn't know how long he's been here, and he doesn't know how long he's going to stay. Keep moving, that's the ticket. He has a job to do, not that he has a choice in the matter, and then when its done, he's done, and it's on to the next one. At least, that's how he feels it works. He can't remember before this night. He only knows that he's here with a purpose. He has skills to be used. He knows that when his task is complete and he moves to the next place, he won't remember San Francisco. The cycle will begin again. That's how it works, or at least, that's how he feels it works. He doesn't know, because he doesn't remember.

So maybe he has been here before. Maybe he does know San Francisco like the back of his hand. Maybe it's the same wherever he goes; his canvas cleaned, his task begun anew, wherever it is needed, and maybe that means he's sent again and again and again. And perhaps he goes through this every single time, when he arrives, and...

He stops and breathes the night air. No, that way lies madness. The only thing he can do is perform the task, do the job for as long as it takes until it is done. He is a tool to be used. And an effective one at that.

There is someone else in the city. Someone else new, someone else who doesn't belong.

Someone who needs to be stopped.

He doesn't know how he knows this, but he does. It's all part of it, of how it works. All part of the job.

And then he jumps.

The next building is a floor lower, separated by a narrow alley. He pushes off on the balls of his feet and pulls himself into a curl. The city's horizon spins like the silver band of a gyroscope at full tilt as he rolls in the air. At the top of the curve, above the alley, he stretches out, transforming the roll into a dive. He hits the roof of the other building and rolls along it. The aerobatics are silent, fluid. He is more than just an expert. He has power.

On the other roof he stands and shakes his hands and rolls his neck, his costume stretching as he flexes. Then he walks to the edge of the building and looks down.

Chinatown glows in red and green below. His quarry is near.

Highwire takes a few steps back, holds his arms out straight as he calculates his next jump, and then runs forward, toward the edge.

# III
# SHARON MEADOW, SAN FRANCISCO
## TODAY

"What the fuck is this shit?"

Jack Newhaven's voice was high and his accent the broad, flat strokes of New England. To anyone who didn't know him, or who wasn't familiar with the dialect peculiar to his tiny native corner of Vermont, his exclamation might have been difficult to decipher, but everyone in earshot on this particular occasion was well used to the accent and his colorful vocabulary. As the Magical Zanaar, ringmaster of The Magical Zanaar's Traveling Caravan of the Arts and Sciences, he was a showman *par excellence*, wooing the crowds that gathered each night, welcoming them to his traveling roadshow, and proclaiming the amazing feats of agility they were about to see under the Big Top.

But when he was regular old Jack Newhaven, he was somewhat less charming company.

Jack – the Magical Zanaar – stood in his metallic blue top hat, his red tailed jacket shimmering like water as its hundreds of sequins caught the morning sun, his handlebar moustache, long and curled with wax at each end, quivering sympathetically with his rage. Beside him stood a clown in an old-fashioned checkerboard costume, his face hidden behind a black half-mask, and two young women – late teens, early twenties, both blonde – dressed in matching gymnastic leotards, silver with black swirling patterns the mirror image of each other. One of them, Kara, jumped at Jack's shout. Her partner, Sara, clutched her arms across her chest.

"Hey!" said Jack, taking the unlit cigar from his mouth. He took a step forward and pointed it at the circus performers and workers gathered in front of him. "Hey!"

He was ignored for a second time. The fight continued.

They'd been in the middle of a business meeting, Jack the ringmaster and Nadine, the circus business manager. He in his blue hat and red coat and moustache, and she in a plain gray suit. The circus office was a Winnebago, and through the louvered windows Jack could see Kara and Sara practicing a new part of their ribbon routine in the open air outside their own smaller motorhome.

Nadine was explaining a spreadsheet. Jack was trying to understand it. Then came the first scream, and financial concerns went out the louvered window.

Jack looked from the laptop screen, saw Kara and Sara standing stock still, staring in the same direction. Behind them, a clown – David, one of the troupe of six who dressed in full harlequin – appeared in the doorway of another motorhome, mask in situ. Jack saw him look toward the girls. Then Kara looked over her shoulder, into the Winnebago. Jack knew that with the sun bright outside, the interior of the vehicle would be nothing but darkness, but somehow Kara managed to meet his eye.

There was a second scream, louder than the first, and female this time. Someone shouted "Hey!" and someone shouted something else, but it was muffled.

Jack swore and moved to the door, throwing it wide. Sara and Kara jumped, and the silence stretched for a few long seconds before the breeze changed and the sounds came drifting from Jack's left. Scuffles, dirt being kicked, bodies sliding around on the ground.

It was a fight, on the other side of the Big Top. *Another* fight. The third in just this week after arriving in San Francisco.

"Ah, Jesus," Jack said, taking the cigar from his mouth and licking his lips. He knew who was fighting. He also knew it was a risk, putting himself in the middle of that. It wasn't that he didn't have control over his employees, his performers – of course he did. It was just that the disagreement between the two parties under his watch was getting worse and worse, and...

He clamped his teeth around the end of cigar.

"Jack?"

Sara, her arms folded as tightly as Kara's. The morning was warm but it looked like she was freezing in her silver and black leotard. "You gonna do something about it this time?"

Jack rolled the cigar between his lips. Over his shoulder, Nadine appeared, breathing hotly on his neck. He turned, and she shook her head.

"She's right. This has gone on too long."

Another shout, the breeze bringing it so close it sounded like the fight was taking part right outside Jack's Winnebago. David took off at a sprint, not bothering to remove his Harlequin mask.

"Right," said Jack. "Fuck. Whatever." He jumped off the steps and jogged toward the sounds of the scuffle.

Jack's jog was slower than it could have been. They were right, of course, all of them. But maybe he didn't have quite the control they imagined he had. Perhaps he could assert himself over one side in the conflict. But over the other, he knew he had no chance.

Jack Newhaven was *owned* by the man.

He stopped at the curve of the circus tent and removed the cigar to suck in some air. He was getting old and fat. One day he was going to put his portly, sixty-year old frame in between the two groups and take a blow, accidental or not, that might put him down in a somewhat permanent fashion. Worse, if word got out that all was not well in the Magical Caravan, then not only would they kiss goodbye their fancy permit to set up in Sharon Meadow, in the heart of the city's famous Golden Gate State Park, they might not make another tour.

Perhaps, he thought, that was not a bad thing. If *he* let him, of course. Which would never happen.

Around the rear of the Big Top was a corridor, a smaller tent itself, which was the performer's entrance to the main ring. Behind this, acting as an effective barrier for the public, was a blue semi truck, its trailer tall and shiny. Beyond this was the part of the circus not accessible to the public – more trucks and trailers, an assortment of cars and wagons, portable toilets, and small marquees. One truck was an old model, practically vintage; it sat, incongruous, the elaborate hand-painted signage on the side proclaiming the vehicle to be from JIM'S AUTO AND GAS.

This was home to the troupe as they toured, a big family camp, housing the performers and some of their families who like to travel with them, and the ancillary staff who, on the present tour, came to two lighting techs and one AV guy.

The trailers, trucks, and tents were arranged in a circle around a large patch of empty ground, the dirt grassless, bare and brown save for a blackened, charred center where the nightly bonfire was set. On this burned disk, one big man in a leather waistcoat, bare arms bulging, punched a smaller man, thin, in a black suit already covered in dirt. Nearby a battered top hat sat on the ashen ground.

The big man held the other by the lapels of his jacket. He punched him again, with force Jack was sure was lethal, and then let go. The man in the black suit hit the ground, and immediately scrambled blindly, his hands and feet kicking up a cloud of gray and black ash, enough for the crowd of people gathered around to turn away for a moment.

Just like before. Just like all the times before.

"What the *fuck* is this shit?" Jack took the cigar from his mouth and threw it, not onto the ground but straight at his two sparring employees. It bounced off the back of the big man and fell to the ground. That got his attention. The big man straightened up, flexing the muscles of his back before turning around to face the ringmaster.

"Not your business, Jack," said the man. He was a pillar of muscle, built like a heavyweight boxer, the skin of his chest shaved smooth and glistening with sweat over the top of an intricate tattoo in a deep green ink. The design was of concentric circles, bisected apparently at random by crosses and curved tangent lines, and continued under his waistcoat and down his arms. The pattern was Celtic, matching the swirls of the silver studs on leather bands that circled the man's wrists and waist. Bearded, bald, he was surrounded by companions similarly attired, similarly tattooed. Men and women alike, leather-bound and sweating in the Californian sun. Most were smiling, some even cruelly, as the man in the black suit sat himself up on the burnt ground.

"Not my problem, Malcolm?" Jack's mouth hung open as though the cigar rolling away on the ground would be magically sucked back into place, like a film in reverse. "Jack *shit* it isn't my problem!"

Jack took a step forward, peering up at Malcolm from a foot and a half closer to the ground. Malcolm folded his arms and the two stared at each other. Jack held his ground, wondering if today was the day he was going to get thumped. Then Malcolm bared his teeth and hissed, spit onto the ashy ground, and walked away. As he did so, he caught the ash on the ground with one toe and kicked a cloud over his opponent. The man sitting on the ground flinched and coughed, and as the circle of Malcolm's companions broke up, some laughed.

"Hey!" Nadine walked toward the retreating group, waved an arm. "Hey! Dipshit, I'm talking to you!"

Kara and Sara moved to help the man on the ground.

Malcolm stopped and turned around. "This doesn't concern any of you."

"The fuck it doesn't," said Nadine. "This concerns all of us. Keep this up and there's not going to be a circus anymore. You got that?"

"Leave them," said Jack.

Nadine spun around, and Jack saw her face was red and angry. "What? Jesus, Jack, really?"

Jack had one eye on the man in the black suit. He was covered in ash, and a thick tentacle of blood and spit trailed from his mouth. Jack grimaced.

"Earth to the Magical Zanaar, come in please?"

He turned to Nadine. "Leave it to me."

Nadine sighed. "I don't know who's the biggest idiot," she said. "You, or me for staying here." She swore and marched away.

Jack rolled his shoulders. She was right, of course. He took off his top hat and rubbed his forehead.

Malcolm's Celtic dance group, Stonefire, were a relatively new addition to the troupe, having joined only this year for the circus's West Coast tour. Jack hadn't been sure at first; dancing didn't seem quite the traditional circus act, and he wasn't sure how authentic Stonefire was, their choreographed dancing and acrobatics more a modern pastiche, a romantic ideal of the noble Iron Age tribes of Europe. But they'd been a wow with the crowds, something foreign, *exotic*, dancing to drums and pipes, the main ring alive with braziers and torches. Crowds loved fire, and there was fire-juggling and fire-eating. Some of the dancing was pretty acrobatic, and some of the dancers were just pretty. Barefoot Celtic lasses in skimpy leather was good for business. Tickets sales were up; the ringside was packed on every night of the tour.

Jack sighed and picked his cigar from the ground. He only had two left, and didn't want to waste them. He turned to the man in black, flanked by Sara and Kara. The girls looked pale. Jack wondered if that was because of the fight or because of the man they were helping keep upright.

"You OK?" Jack asked, brushing dirt from the cigar.

The man in black's face was gray, the same shade as the ash that covered the ground – the ash that covered the front of his suit too, and his hair, thick and curly. The only color on him was the splatter of bright, arterial blood across the bottom half of his face that dripped thickly from his jaw. The blood on the ground was darker where it had mixed with the ash and dirt.

The man pulled his arms away from the gymnasts, and straightened his jacket. He looked at Jack, and Jack flinched. One of the man's eyes was a dark brown; the other was light gray, almost white. Jack was used to it but that didn't stop him being a little repulsed now and again.

The man in black smiled, showing his teeth red and pink. "Mr Newhaven, I'm perfectly fine."

Sara and Kara had shuffled away, and Sara was playing with the cuff of her leotard, like she wanted to be somewhere else, anywhere else, away from the man in black.

Jack waved his cigar at the pair. "You girls go get cleaned up and back to practice. Another show tonight, remember."

The girls exchanged a look.

Jack coughed. "And maybe talk to Nadine. Make sure she hasn't called the cops or anything, OK?"

The girls nodded in union, and left. Jack watched them leave, then reached forward, brushing the dirt and ash from the man in black's suit.

"Jesus, Joel, this is too much…"

As his fingers brushed against the man's chest, the man in black grabbed Jack's wrist and pulled it up. The fingers of his other hand found the fob pocket on the front of his waistcoat and disappeared inside, like he thought Jack was going to pickpocket him there and then. The two men stared at each other as the seconds grew long, then Joel released Jack's wrist. The ringmaster staggered backward, rubbing his forearm. Joel's grip had been as cold as ice.

"I'm sorry," Jack said, quietly. "I'm sorry."

Joel walked across the burned ground, and picked up his hat. It was tall, narrow – not a top hat like Jack's, its sides gracefully curved, the brim curled, but something far more old fashioned. A stovepipe hat, Lincoln-style. It was partially collapsed and covered in ash, but Joel popped it back into shape and began brushing it with his sleeve.

"Are you OK to operate the carnival tonight?" asked Jack.

Joel stopped brushing and held the hat out in his hands, turning it this way and the other, like the battered antique was in prize shape.

"I don't need to operate the carnival. You know that, Jack."

"I know, but –"

"You know, so why ask?" Joel fixed Jack with those eyes, one so brown it was almost black, one as light as the sky before a snowfall.

"I'm sorry. I…" Jack rubbed his forehead. It was the stress, making his world wobble, making his ears fill with the sound of the ocean.

Joel landed his hand on Jack's shoulder, and Jack jumped. He ground his teeth together, tight, tight.

"How much longer?" he asked.

Joel smiled. "Soon, Jack. Soon."

Jack nodded toward the marquee of Malcolm's dance troupe. "And them?"

"They're part of it, even if they don't know it. They're tools to be used," said Joel.

"And the fights? Will they stop?"

Joel chuckled. "They can't help it. It's not them, remember."

Jack looked at the ground. "Does... does *it* know? About us? Is that why it makes them fight?"

"Maybe," said Joel with a smile. "It doesn't matter. *We* control *it*. Not the other way around."

"It's going to get worse, isn't it?"

Joel clicked his tongue and walked away, saying nothing but "Soon, Jack, soon" over his shoulder. But Jack didn't know if he was talking to him, or to the power sleeping beneath their feet.

# IV
# SAN FRANCISCO
## TODAY

Morning. The best time of day – of that Ted had no doubt whatsoever – and the most perfect moment is when you wake and it's dark and you glance at the clock and it's 5.58 and the alarm is going to go off in two minutes and you lie back and close your eyes and prepare for the day ahead and you're had exactly the right amount of sleep and your body's own internal alarm clock has gently lifted you back to consciousness and you're not tired and you're ready and with a second to spare you reach over and turn the alarm off even before it has sounded and you're ready to go ready to go ready to–

The phone's ring was like warfare, like a construction worker opening a seam in the side of Ted's head with a pneumatic jackhammer. Ted had got what he'd wanted – out and under, a deep, deep sleep, the kind of sleep that isn't to be disturbed. And when you are disturbed, when you are brought up from the abyssal depth like a diver rising too fast, too fast, your day is not going to go well.

Ted reached out and his fingers knocked against wood. He opened an eye, wondering how the bedside table had managed to move itself during the night, and saw unfamiliar shapes. No, not unfamiliar. He knew what they were, but half asleep he couldn't reconcile them. There was a TV, and the table next to him was low and long, red maple, scattered with magazines and remote controls.

He lifted himself up on the couch on one elbow. How had he gotten there? His phone continued to ring, its vibrate setting making it dance on the coffee table. He grabbed it, didn't check who was calling, and collapsed back onto the couch, his eyes firmly shut.

"Mm?"

"This is some sleeping in." It was Alison. The line was clear and lacking in the usual muffled quality of her cell. There was noise on the other end, too. Someone else talking.

Ted thought about Alison's statement, pondering it for a few seconds. She could have spoken in Chinese for all he knew.

"Ted?"

Eyes open, heart pounding.

"Shit," he said. He was awake now, lying on the couch. His head wasn't sore but his body was, like he'd just finished a workout. Sleeping on the couch would do that.

Alison laughed in his ear. "Don't worry. I told Mazzy about last night."

"What did she say?"

"She asked me to ask you how you were. So?"

Ted frowned, rubbed his forehead. "Mm?"

Alison sighed. "How are you? You sleep OK?"

"Um," said Ted. Then he paused. He concentrated, hard. "Yeah, I guess. I think I overslept though." He scrambled for the TV remote and waved it at the set. The screen flickered and Ted's eyes searched the screen, looking for the ever-present clock displayed against the breakfast news.

"I think you needed it," said Alison.

On the TV, someone in blue spandex was trying to sell Ted an exercise bike in fifty-two easy payments. There was no clock on display. He was lost, deep in infomercial territory.

"Oh, shit," he said.

Alison laughed again. After a moment, Ted joined her.

"Damn, do I need coffee."

"Forget coffee. It's nearly lunch. I'll come get you."

Ted looked around like he was expecting Alison to be standing behind him, behind the couch in his apartment. The feeling that he wasn't alone was still there from last night. In the dead air that followed Alison's voice, it sounded like there was someone else on the line, whispering into his ear.

"Ted?"

"Where are you?"

"Still at the Asian Art Museum. Meeting went fine."

"Oh," said Ted. "Sorry. Great, I'm glad."

"So, lunch?"

"If lunch comes with coffee, then count me in."

"See you in twenty."

"See you," said Ted. Alison disconnected. Ted kept the phone to his ear, listening, his other hand massaging his forehead. But there was no one there. Then he put the phone down and watched a whole troupe of spandex-clad aerobics junkies do synchronized cycling on their machines as the camera panned and zoomed like it was the finale of a Hollywood blockbuster.

Ted heaved himself off the couch. A shower. Coffee. These were, right now, his two most favorite things in the world. Throw in some sunshine for good old vitamin D and some fresh air to blow the cobwebs away, and he'd be back in business. And, really, starting his thirty-eighth year with a hangover – of sorts, anyway – seemed entirely appropriate.

He tossed the phone onto the couch and headed for the bedroom, unable to shake the feeling that his head felt like it was made of lead. Heavy, slow, like his neck couldn't support it properly and if he moved it too quickly it would wobble. Maybe it would fall off.

Between the living area and the bedroom was a dining area, another red maple table, the bigger brother of the coffee table, square in the center. There were some papers, and Ted's laptop. As Ted passed it, he saw the laptop was on. It showed an empty white window, a new document opened in his word processor.

Not empty. There were lines of text in a column. A short sentence, the font italic. Repeated again and again. Ted stopped, leaned on the back of the nearest dining chair, and stared at the screen.

*You are the master of every situation.*
*You are the master of every situation.*
*You are the master of every situation.*

Ted reached forward, swiped his fingers on the trackpad, scrolling down the page. The text went on. And on.

Ted withdrew his hand and the scrolling stopped around page sixty-four.

He rolled his lips, unsure. He didn't remember falling asleep on the couch, and he certainly didn't remember sitting down and typing the fortune out on his laptop beforehand. But he remembered the restaurant, the bang and the flash, and the paper strips raining from the ceiling. Alison hadn't mentioned the fortunes. In fact, nobody did, not in the immediate aftermath. Ted wondered if, lying where he had, he was the only one who had seen. Seen how there was nothing up on the ceiling of the Jade Emperor except rolling black clouds, how the paper was falling, falling like autumn leaves. How when he looked up again, once he was upright, there were no black clouds, nothing but a black ceiling and green lanterns swinging on their short chains.

*You are the master of every situation.*

Ted closed the laptop's lid and went to take a shower.

••••

It was a bright morning and it was going to be a hot day, Ted could tell. San Francisco had a peculiar little microclimate, the way it was surrounded by water on three sides. A day could blow hot and cold and hot again, sunshine in one part of the city and chilly fog somewhere else. And then things could swap over.

But not today. Today it felt different, at least to Ted. He wondered why he was so sure, but he was, so that was that.

"What's up?"

He looked at Alison as they walked down Howard Street, coming up to the Moscone Convention Center. The flags were flying, and a fleet of taxis was in steady rotation outside the front of the complex. Something big was in town, but nothing that Ted could remember. Which meant the blog wasn't covering it, which meant it was something boring like a medical conference. You know, important stuff.

"What's up?"

Alison laughed. "You're *smiling*. You're not supposed to smile. At least not in public. You must be feeling better."

"Oh," said Ted, and he realized that yes, he was smiling. The sun was warm on his face and for a moment he felt like he could leap a tall building in a single bound. "I told you I was OK."

"You did," she said, and she looped her arm through his. They slowed their pace as they came to the big intersection at Howard and Fourth. Three police cars, lights and sirens blazing, hurtled through the intersection. Ted and Alison watched as the cars pulled up a block to their left. There were more police down there, several cars and a van. Cops were walking around, along with some men in black bomber jackets and blue baseball caps.

Ted felt Alison's grip on his arm tighten. He looked down at the top of her blonde head, and she said, "It's happened again."

••••

Clementina Street, left of Fourth Street, was cordoned off, and Fourth itself was down to one lane, the police directing a growing crawl of traffic. Yellow police tape snapped and flickered in the breeze. There were people there already, just a small group of pedestrians, some in suits, perhaps convention center attendees from just across the street. There were some in orange vests and hardhats, construction workers from a nearby apartment building right on the corner of Clementina.

Ted and Alison joined the edge of the group. Ted could see another two police cars down the closed-off street, and an ambulance, its red and white paintjob instantly recognizable from just the night before.

Ted felt his heart kick, like he needed to get away, a moment of *déjà vu* so strong it made him feel sick. Perhaps it was just seeing the ambulance there. For all he knew, it *was* the one he'd sat in just hours ago.

Alison pulled on his arm. "You OK?"

Ted frowned, confused, and then nodded. "Yeah. It's just... you know." He looked down the street where people in uniforms were milling around. They couldn't see anything. Nobody could. But everybody knew what was going on.

"I know," said Alison. "You don't think anything like this would happen in your town. Right in your home, where you live. It's like –"

"Like it doesn't feel like your home anymore," said Ted. "I know."

"That's four now."

"*Jesus*," whispered Ted. His head pounded.

Of course it had happened before. Several times. San Francisco, like an unfortunate number of other cities across the United States, knew what it was like to have a serial killer in their midst. There was David Carpenter, the so-called Trailside Killer, back in the late Seventies, although he hadn't committed his crimes in the city itself. The San Francisco Witch Killers, early Eighties. And of course the Zodiac Killer, responsible for five deaths and a series of cryptic letters sent to the local press. Unsolved to this very day.

And now a new name to add to the list: the Hang Wire Killer. Unsolved, ongoing, three deaths – *four*, now – each the same: the victims were founded hanged in quiet streets or back alleys in the city, dangling from fire escapes or lampposts, strung up with a thin steel cable. And the press sure did love a nickname. The Hang Wire Killer had arrived.

"Doesn't make any sense," said Ted.

Alison squeezed his arm. "Never does."

"I mean," he said, turning to Alison, "why the wire? Why not rope? Wire is heavy, resistant. It would be awkward, difficult to do it with wire. Doesn't make any sense."

"They'll catch him."

Ted snorted, and Alison gave him a sharp look that made Ted frown and shake his head. "Don't get me wrong, I hope they will," he said. "But remember the Zodiac Killer. That guy is still out there."

Alison returned her attention to the crime scene. Clementina Street was narrow and quiet, but they were right next to the convention center. Someone must have seen or heard something, surely? This part of town would have been busy, even late.

"Come on," said Ted, gently pulling at Alison's arm. "There's nothing to see and nothing to do. We just have to let the police do their job."

"You're right," she said as they walked away. "We're lucky, in a way."

"Lucky?"

"The blog," said Alison. "Lucky that we only cover community events and local news."

"Roller-skating dogs."

"Exactly. Roller-skating dogs. I'm not sure I could handle reporting on something like this."

"Real news," said Ted. He glanced at the flags fluttering outside the convention center as they walked back along Fourth, to the intersection. The offices of the blog were just a few minutes away. "Important stuff."

"Hmm?"

Ted smiled as the crossing light went green. "Nothing," he said.

# INTERLUDE
# PHILADELPHIA, PENNSYLVANIA
## 1903

"For the last time, Mr Duvall, we're leaving. It's over, finished. The circus is breaking up. Each of us is going his separate way, never to see nor speak to the others again. We have to do this. It's over, Mr Duvall. *Over*."

There was no arguing with Mr R S Barnett. He was the boss, the ringmaster, the manager, the accountant. He was everything. The Great Barnett Show was more than just his creation, his livelihood. It was his life.

Mr R S Barnett was shutting the circus down. It was hasty, thought Joel. A bad decision, the wrong decision. The circus was a wonderful thing, full of lights and music, life, laughter.

"Mr Barnett, please," said Joel. He held his hands out, pleading, to Barnett's retreating back. To his credit, Barnett stopped, sighed, and turned around.

"For God's sake, Joel," he said. "There's been a murder. We can't go on. We can't."

The Great Barnett Show. Full of life, and laughter.

Full of death and screaming.

The night was cold and the sky was clear. Joel lay on the grass in the middle of the dark carnival, stared at the stars, wondered what he was supposed to do now. In his waistcoat pocket, the Double Eagle his daddy had given him felt heavy and cold. His imagination, of course. But it was his lucky coin, and when he carried it his daddy walked with him.

Maybe the lucky coin was trying to tell him something.

A star fell, high above the circus, a cat scratch of white against the heavens that faded almost as quickly as it appeared. And then another, larger, brighter, flaring for a second. And then it too was gone.

Falling stars. They were either good luck or bad, depending whose folklore you followed. Joel hadn't grown up with much in the way of folklore, or religion. When his daddy marched to war and never came back, it didn't seem much like there was a god smiling down on His creation.

Or maybe there was, and maybe it was a cruel and capricious master and the world and the people in it were merely toys, a distraction.

Joel wasn't sure he believed that. He didn't believe in much.

Not since the voice had started whispering in his ear.

Well, no, it wasn't a voice, he thought as he stared at the starry sky. It was a feeling, like there was someone over your shoulder, leaning in to mutter secrets. A breath in the ear and a tickle of hair. But there was nobody there. Joel was alone – always had been, ever since his daddy had left – and there wasn't a voice, not really. It was the *memory* of a voice, like he'd been told something long, long ago in a conversation that had never happened, and then it swam back into his mind, making him dizzy like a dose of the *déjà vus*.

It had started in Oklahoma. The thing he found, buried in the ground. The thing that had come from far, far away – from the stars, perhaps. Although he wasn't really sure how he knew that for a fact, not really.

Maybe there was something in the stories about falling stars bringing luck. Good or bad, maybe both. Comets too. Comets were omens, portents, inscrutable somethings that arced across the sky, seeding cold evil from stars wherever they traveled.

It had told Joel how to build the machines. There was no instruction, no command; Joel just knew what he had to do, and he had an urge to do it like he had an urge to eat or drink or breathe or sleep. It was part of him. It had told Joel to cut the stones from the cave until he had two shining jewels, the red gems which were now the eyes of the carved wooden monkey which sat as the centerpiece of the carnival's star ride, the great carousel.

Joel turned his head on the grass, and looked toward the carousel. It was dark and still, but in the center he thought he could see the eyes of the monkey glowing softly in the night. Then he blinked and the red light was gone, and he returned his attention to the sky above.

He never staked his claim in Oklahoma. He abandoned the territory. Traveled to Philadelphia, although he didn't know why. Found Mr R S Barnett, although he didn't know why. Started building the machines, started painting them with stars and planets and moons and comets. Didn't know why, but he knew he had to. Carved the gems out of the cave rock. Carved the monkey.

The moon was rising, brightening the sky, blotting out the stars. That annoyed Joel. He wouldn't be able to see any more falling stars.

The machines were carnival rides. Barnett had paid for them, given Joel a workforce, funded a workshop. It was simple enough to Joel. He knew just what to do and how to do it. Barnett had been happy. More than happy. No one in the whole wide world would have pleasure machines like his new circus show. Barnett had thanked Joel, given him money, offered him a partnership.

But Joel didn't need money. He had no interest in the business of the place. All he had interest in was his machines and their running. His machines, and the power that lived within them. Like a hermit crab in a new shell.

The circus had opened and the crowds had been wowed, been delighted, been entertained and enthralled and sent home with happy memories and music playing in their ears. Barnett had been happy. Very happy.

Joel too. The machines ran. People were amazed. So many lights, so many colors, all planets and stars and comets.

Then there had been the first accident. A girl, aged eight, had been crushed by one of the carnival rides. She'd fallen from a spinning car, and had got stuck in the gears of the machine. The mechanism had continued to operate, obstruction or not, and there hadn't been much left of the girl when they'd managed to stop the ride. Joel remembered the great gears lubricated with blood, so much blood. Barnett was a rich man and had paid the family a fortune. The circus continued, and the news stayed quiet. Nobody would know about the first accident.

But they would learn about the second. Another woman, older this time. She'd fallen from the top of the Ferris wheel and had hit the frame at the bottom. The impact had split her nearly in two. Barnett hadn't been able to pay his way out of that one, but he had greased the wheels of the press. It was no accident – it had been suicide. The woman had been disturbed. She had planned it all. So the papers said.

Maybe she had. Or maybe the machines of the carnival wanted more.

There were more accidents. None fatal, and most – a half dozen, at least – happening to workers and carnies. This suited Barnett, because he owned his employees like he owned his circus, and it was easy to keep trouble away with a steady flow of money brought in by the customers who enjoyed the show, oblivious to the blood spilled within its perimeter.

And then the carnies wouldn't work in the carnival, sticking instead to the Big Top, to the animals, preferring even the man-eating lions and tigers to being around Joel's machines and rides. There was evil there, some said. Carnies were superstitious. Joel was not. But he knew they were right. Barnett said he didn't believe them, but Joel knew he did. He had felt it too.

The carnival was alive. More than that.

The carnival was *hungry*.

As fewer and fewer workers would go into the carnival, leaving Joel to manage the machines and rides on his own, so the accidents ceased.

The carnival was hungry. Joel knew it, like he knew how to find Barnett, like he knew that he needed to build the machines to host the empty cold nothing that had fallen from the stars. It didn't need blood. The machines didn't feed on human flesh. No, the machines fed on terror and horror – the feelings, primal instincts and emotions. That was why it had shown Joel how to build the machines, because the machines generated fear, a little at a time, controlled but genuine enough. The thing from the stars fed on fear.

Fed on death.

And it was hungry. And then had come the murder.

The victim was a clown, one of a troupe of two dozen. Some had left, reducing the group to numbers too thin for Barnett's magnificent show. So Barnett showed some of his famous money around and soon the troupe was back up to strength.

With any newcomers, there are tensions. For circus performers, perhaps it's worse, because circus life is hard and so are the carnies who live it. One of the new clowns laughed at the warnings not to go into the carnival. One of the mechanics took exception to this. They fought while others looked on, carnies baying for blood, like animals. Joel had been tending his machines at the time.

The mechanic killed the clown in front of everyone, and had fled, the crowd – suddenly dazed, as though released from some evil spell – allowing him his freedom.

That was the final straw. The circus was finished. Barnett was packing it up, and everyone, everyone knew that it was because of Joel and his carnival machines.

Everyone knew.

Footsteps approached. Joel blinked, his eyes dry. He rolled onto his stomach, and saw a shadow move, ducking between two rides, trying to keep hidden. Not someone from the circus, then. Someone else, sneaking around. A thief, perhaps.

"Hey!" yelled Joel. The night was silent, the circus performers sleeping in their tents. They wouldn't hear him. After the fight, after the way they had all fallen under some weird spell that left them spitting and snarling for blood, they'd all gone quiet, everyone keeping to themselves, perhaps ashamed of their blood lust. Perhaps afraid at what had, momentarily, seemed to take them over.

Joel walked over to the edge of the carnival. Toward the Ferris wheel, one hand inside his jacket, on the handle of his daddy's gun. The fingers of the other hand played over his daddy's coin in the pocket of his waistcoat.

The shadows didn't move. Joel stepped closer, peering into the gloom. The moon was doing a fine job of illuminating the circus and the carnival machines, but the shadows the rides cast were deep, as black as the sky above.

Joel pulled the gun, its silver shining in the moonlight. "Come out. You have no business here, my friend. None at all."

The shadows moved and resolved into a man. His clothes were rough, tattered, and he wore a kerchief around his neck, his face streaked with grease.

"Come back to the scene of the crime, then?" asked Joel. At this, the other man smirked. In one hand he held a cloth cap, which he batted impatiently against his leg.

Alexander Harrison. Mechanic. One of the workshop men Barnett had employed to help Joel with the upkeep of the carnival machines. The man who had picked a fight with a clown and won.

"There's evil here, Duvall," said Harrison, his eyes sharp and bright in the moonlight. "You know it, and I know it." He nodded toward the carousel, his eyes wide. Joel followed his gaze, saw the red eyes of the monkey glowing.

Joel smiled and turned back to Harrison. He cocked his head, kept the gun level. "Maybe you're right. But then so says every man who has stolen the life of another, I suppose."

Harrison took a step forward, not apparently inconvenienced by the weapon pointed at him. "That wasn't me, Joel! I swear it. I was like, I don't know, like–"

"Like you was possessed, I suppose you're going to tell me. Like you weren't yourself and you couldn't remember. A moment of insanity that clouded your vision."

"It wasn't like that. You know it wasn't."

"Oh," said Joel. He lifted the gun, pulled back the hammer. He wasn't afraid, wasn't worried. He had the gun, and Harrison was a man on the run.

But there was something else. The coin buzzed in his pocket like a trapped bee.

Had Harrison heard the voice? He'd spent as much time among the carnival machines as Joel had. Maybe more. Had the cold dark thing touched his mind as well?

Harrison snarled and leapt forward, grabbing Joel's gun arm and forcing it up. Joel slid his finger from the trigger for safety. Harrison was strong – he'd hammered most of the carnival into shape himself – and he growled like the lions that slept in the cages on the opposite side of the Big Top.

Joel hit the ground on his back, Harrison on top of him. There was a light in Harrison's eyes, something red and bright that might have just been a reflection of one of the lights on a carnival ride, if the lights had been on. But they weren't – the carnival was dark – the only light a flare like a falling star from the black center of the carousel, from where the monkey with the gemmed eyes sat, watching in silence. A moment later the light was gone.

They scuffled on the ground, grunting, kicking up dirt and dust. Joel brought his gun arm in, sticking the barrel into Harrison's stomach. Harrison was already grabbing Joel's wrist, twisting his body sideways, out of the way. Joel screamed with the effort; then his wrist cracked. The gun was pulled from his hand, and Harrison scrambled backward in a crawl, then stood.

Joel stood, held his hand out.

"I know the power, friend. I know what it is you feel, what it is you hear. I hear it too. I feel it in my very bones. And I know what that power wants." He took a step forward. "I know what you–"

Harrison fired. The bullet entered Joel's head through his left eye and removed most of the back of his skull. Joel toppled to the ground. In his dead hand was the gold coin, burning cold, humming like something electric.

The second gunshot brought him back. Joel coughed and opened his eyes. He took a breath that was cold, cold. The world looked different. Brighter, like there was a light shining to his left. Unsure of where he was, he turned his head, and the light moved with it. He closed one eye, opened it, closed the other. Something was wrong with his left eye. The world looked different through it.

He uncurled his outstretched hand. The Double Eagle felt as heavy as a boulder. Clenching his teeth, Joel lifted his hand, but suddenly the coin was just that, a large gold coin, heavy but ordinarily so.

He pulled himself to his feet, dusted himself down. People were coming – he could hear running, muted chatter. They were coming toward the gunshot. The *second* gunshot. Joel remembered the first, remembered spinning white light and pain, hot and exquisite. He fingered the back of his head, felt something wet and sticky. He looked at his hand. It was covered in something that looked black in the moonlight.

Joel followed the sounds. Out of the carnival, toward the Big Top. People were huddled around something. Barnett was there. As Joel approached, Barnett directed a couple of workers clad only in nightshirts to fetch the police.

Joel made his way to the front. People drew away from him, fear and confusion rippling around the crowd.

On the ground lay Alexander Harrison. He was face down, the top of his head was missing, and in one hand he held Joel's gun. It was pointed in such a way as to make the cause of death clear. Suicide by gunshot wound. He'd blown his own brains out.

Joel eyed the gun, his gun, his *daddy's* gun. He reached down to pick it up, but Barnett's hand closed around his wrist.

"I don't think you should touch it. Not until the police get here."

Joel stood back and looked at Barnett.

Barnett frowned. "What happened to your eye?" he asked.

Joel smiled and said nothing. In his fist the coin grew cold, as cold as the abyssal black of the ocean, and he saw a light, bright, like the glint of gold on a distant hilltop.

Joel walked away. He could feel the eyes of the others on him, but he didn't care. Barnett would close the circus.

It was a setback, true, but now that Joel could see the light shining, he knew what he had to do. Barnett could destroy the machines, the carnival, Joel knew that, but he also knew that Barnett wouldn't. That Barnett couldn't, because some of the power that filled Joel, that had seeped into Harrison and driven him to death to feed that power, some of that had seeped into Barnett also. Barnett couldn't destroy his machines – *it* wouldn't let him. Instead, he would separate them, splitting the carnival into component parts, some big, some small. He'd burn through his family fortune to scatter and hide pieces rather than burn the evil that lived inside the machines, inside the monkey with the glowing red eyes. And all the while Barnett would fight it, without knowing what it was that he was struggling against.

And then it would begin again. Joel would bring it all back together. It would take time, but the circus would be reborn and the carnival would go on.

In time.

# V
# AQUATIC PARK, SAN FRANCISCO
## TODAY

"One-two-three, *two-two*-three."

Bob led the tourist around in the sand of Aquatic Park in the hot morning sun. His partner was from Alabama, had a laugh and an accent to die for, and had kept her blue flannel hat on. She burned easily, she said, as he swept her into his arms, leaned her back so far she screamed in delight, blue hat firmly in place, as the others watching from the low tiered seating clapped and whistled. And then the music started, and Bob began to give a dance lesson.

Bob was a fixture, as much a part of Aquatic Park – at least in the eyes of some – as the squat, curved Maritime Museum, sitting like a cream-iced Art Deco cake farther along the beach. As much a permanent feature of the beachfront and park as the pier that stretched out in the cool water, as the twin fans of concrete tiered seating that many found a restful spot on a hot summer's day. And today it would be hot, no doubt about it.

Bob danced, slowly teaching the woman from Alabama. Her name was Julie and her friends catcalled from the tiers, the gang of late-fifties housewives transformed into a group of teenage girls by the sight of their old friend in the arms of a bare-chested, barefooted Adonis, all blond hair and bronzed skin, as he dragged her slowly, slowly around the sand, teaching her to dance. She would be the first of many that day. Bob and his free dance lessons were something to check out, for sure, if you were on vacation in the Bay Area.

"Is it true you don't sleep at all, Bob?" asked Julie, her eyes fixed on Bob's face while Bob spent most of the time watching her feet, keeping his own out of the range of her shuffling steps. He glanced up at her, his eyes as blue as the water, and she smiled. "Because that can't be right, can it? I mean, ain't nobody can go without any sleep at all, can they?"

Bob smiled. There were many stories about him, how the handsome beach bum was a retired champion surfer from Hawaii, had to be, a build like that, his hair long and salted, his stubble *just so*. He'd made it big back whenever and didn't need money anymore, and had retired to the beach to teach ballroom in the summer because that's what he liked to do.

Or that he was a retired software engineer from Silicon Valley, Cupertino maybe, and he'd hit a certain age and had cashed in his shares, swapping boardrooms and annual keynote speeches down at the Yerba Buena Center for something more important, for swimming and enjoying the summer and for dancing in the sunshine on the beach.

Or that he didn't need to sleep; that he'd already slept for twenty years and because that was all you needed over a lifetime, he didn't need to sleep again, giving him more time for the sea and the surf and the sand, more time for dancing in the sunshine. More time for enjoying life.

Bob smiled at Julie and her own grin grew. One of those stories was at least partially true. There were others as well, some true, some not. So many, in fact, and Bob had been dancing in the sunshine for so very long that maybe he himself couldn't quite remember which were real and which were not,..

"You don't want to believe those stories. Well, not *all* of them," he said with a wink, and Julie laughed. He pulled her around in a circle, swept out his right foot in a move that didn't really belong to any ballroom dance but that kicked up a fan of sand that people watching seemed to like, and then released Julie, keeping hold of one hand and bowing deeply to the crowd. Julie seemed to get the message, and curtseyed to the hollers of her friends. Her dance lesson was over.

Bob turned to his partner, and bowed, and brought his lips to her hand and kissed it gently. "M'lady," he said, and Julie rejoined her friends, and the crowd clapped.

Dancing on the sand was not ideal, as any ballroom teacher would say. Bob knew the moves – he'd had enough time to learn them, along with many other skills and talents – but it was a gimmick, nothing serious. Most of his partners couldn't dance at all, although occasionally he got some partners who liked to show off. And when he did, he let them. This was their vacation, after all. And although the lessons were free, there was a collection box near the seating, donations welcomed for the upkeep of the park.

And he needed to be near to the sea. He needed to feel the sun on his chest and the sand between his toes. It kept him connected, to the present, to the past. He looked out to the sea and rolled his shoulders. Just a couple more dances and he'd earned himself a nice swim.

"Young man? Young man, excuse me!"

Bob turned his gaze from the sea with a film-star smile, ready to greet his next pupil.

The woman was old and frail, heading toward eighty if not ninety, one of those elderly folk you saw who didn't look like they'd kept particularly fit or active. She was small, her back hunched and her skin as insubstantial as tissue. Bob saw her fingers curl as she held her hands in front of her, the knuckles red and swollen with mild arthritis. She was wearing a heavy coat, complete with scarf, ready to head out on a cold winter's morning, regardless of the fact that the morning was already pushing the mercury north.

"Madam, a pleasure," said Bob, bowing from the waist with an expansive sweep of his arm.

"I understand you teach ladies to dance?"

Bob winked. "That I do, and not just the ladies. My name is Bob. Would you like a lesson?"

"Oh, I don't need any lessons," said the woman. "But I haven't done this in a long time." She held her arms out, giving Bob his cue. He laughed and stepped into her embrace, and found himself suddenly in perfect hold. His frowned in exaggerated appreciation, although in truth he was impressed.

"Very nice, Mrs–"

The woman jerked her head to the side and closed her eyes.

"Ah!" she said. "No talking. I'll lead. I want to see what you can do. American Smooth with a quickstep." She paused, opened one eye, and regarded Bob. "I trust you know how to dance, young man?"

Bob opened his mouth to answer but the old woman had closed her eyes and suddenly her curved back was straight as a plank and he was pulled forward and swung around as the dance began. For a small old woman, the top of whose head barely reached Bob's shoulders, she had surprising strength.

From the seats came laughs and a wolf whistle. Bob smiled, shook his head, and let himself be led around the beach.

••••

By the time the dance ended, the crowd had doubled in size. Spectators were at least three deep on the tiers, with many more standing around Bob's patch of beach. Beach walkers and swimmers, children and their parents, a mix of swimsuits and casual clothing. Aquatic Park was filling up.

Bob released his grip on his partner and started to pull away, expecting the old lady to do likewise, but she pulled him even tighter like he was on a piece of elastic.

"You're doing good, young fella. Ever tangoed with a grandmother?"

Bob wondered if there was a TV crew nearby, filming the spectacle for the local news. The entire encounter felt like a set-up. It had to be. She was a former dance teacher, perhaps. Maybe a famous ballroom dancer. Bob didn't know. He lived among the people but he didn't really pay much attention to what they did.

Cheek to chest, they began a tango, promenading down the beach toward the surf, then executing a perfect turn before heading back to the crowd. Behind them, Bob hear the waves breaking.

"Did you know Lucy?" They reached the edge of the beach, turned, and promenaded to the left this time.

"Lucy?" asked Bob. Someone else he'd given a lesson to perhaps?

"She was my daughter," said the woman. "Lucy Winters. She was killed last week. Strung up with wire in a quiet street, Bob."

Bob's smile vanished. He missed his step and tried to pull away from the old woman, but her grip was firm and she tutted like he was a bad pupil. He had no choice but to keep dancing.

"I'm sorry for your loss–"

"You know anything about that, Mr Bob?"

It was a set-up. Bob broke the hold and stepped away from the woman. Then he took her hand and began walking back up the beach. He could easily direct her back into the crowd, nobody seeing anything but the smile of the charming and handsome man. Then it was time for his swim. He'd earned it now.

As they walked back, Mrs Winters laughed. Bob ignored her, his own smile fixed for the crowd, not for her.

"Oh, don't look so worried, my handsome young man."

"Lady, I have no idea what you're talking about. You need to leave the park."

Lucy's elderly mother stopped and turned. She grinned, showing tombstone teeth and gums that had receded by a thousand miles. She was much older than Ted had first thought, despite her strength and skill. Maybe a little bit not altogether there. He couldn't just pass her back to the crowd. He'd get someone to call the police, or maybe an ambulance, and they'd be able to take a look at her, maybe get her some care. If her daughter really had been murdered last week – by the Hang Wire Killer, no less; even Bob knew about that news story – then she would be in a fragile and dangerous state.

"Do you have any family we can call?" he asked, searching the park for any police or ranger who might be near.

"I'm not crazy, young man. And I'm not here to pin my daughter's murder on you, if that's what you're worried about. You might be a looker who knows how to dance, but that's about as important as you get."

"So what do you want?" The smile was gone, the warmth from Bob's voice gone. "You don't seem too cut up about your daughter, either."

Mrs Winters tutted again. "Of course I'm not upset. You didn't kill my Lucy, because she's not dead. Now, pick those feet up, I need to see what kind of Viennese waltz you've got."

Bob let her take his arms and lead him around, his feet moving on automatic as his mind reeled. "I thought you said your daughter was killed last week?"

The old woman's mechanism was gone, clearly. Maybe Lucy wasn't her daughter. Maybe she'd seen it on the news and in her dementia had formed some kind of attachment. Why she'd come down to see Bob, specifically, was a mystery, but then maybe she'd seen him in the news too. He was in and out of the back pages a fair bit, like a skateboarding dog.

"She was killed, yes. But you and I both know that's not the end."

Bob froze, mid-step. Did she know? How could she know? Was she one of *Them*? Sometimes – rarely – They did come back. And, truth be told, he had felt there was something different about the city of late. Tangun was around. Nezha too, or at least he had been, the sensation of his presence fading almost as soon as Bob had noticed it. And if they were here, maybe others were too?

They stayed in hold but they didn't move. For anyone watching, it would look like Bob was giving his pupil a few pointers.

"Who are you?"

The old lady turned to watch the spectators on the tiered seating. Bob was sure she was cooking like a pot roast under her thick coat and scarf, but her skin was as pale and translucent as it was when they'd started.

"I need your help, young man."

Bob sighed and shook his head. She did know. Somehow. But if she was one of *Them*, it was some kind of trick, trying to catch him out. Maybe *They* wanted him back.

"Help for what, exactly?" he asked, scarcely believing he was going along with it.

The old woman finally turned, glanced at Bob, and then surveyed the sand around them. "You ever built a bonfire before?"

Bob frowned. "On the beach?" He shook his head. "Not permitted in the park."

The woman laughed, high and haughty. "No, Mr Bob, not *here*. I want you to help build me a bonfire, nice and hot. Back at the house."

"A... bonfire at your house?"

She nodded. "Nice and hot. And then I want you to help me dig."

"Dig?"

The woman sighed and tutted. She stabbed a finger at his bare chest.

"We have to dig beneath it, Mr Bob," said Mrs Winters. "We have to dig beneath the fire."

"What for?"

"To get Lucy back, of course. Now, are you going to help a harmless old woman or am I going to set off the rape alarm in my handbag and scream blue murder?"

# VI
# SAN FRANCISCO
## TODAY

"Welcome back, birthday boy!"

Benny was standing by the door just as Ted and Alison walked into the office of the Bay Blog. The copier was there and she was doing a big batch of something. Her baseball cap was on backward like it always was. Ted wondered if wearing a 49ers cap with an Oakland Raiders shirt was quite the done thing, but he had the strangest feeling that Benny hadn't even noticed her clothes were mismatched. At least Benny didn't cover sports. That was Zane's area, while Benny blogged about events and local news in Chinatown, which, Ted imagined, would include the little incident down at the Jade Emperor.

Benny frowned at Ted. Perhaps she'd seen something in Ted's face that betrayed his thoughts, but as the small copier rocked on its cabinet, spitting out page after page, Benny held up a hand.

"Don't worry, I'm not going to blog it."

Alison slipped her bag off her shoulder and was walking toward her desk. "Won't someone ask about it if we don't run a post?" she called over her shoulder.

She was right. Ted knew it.

"No," said Benny, "just a fire alarm gone haywire, that's all. Nobody will ask, don't worry."

Ted frowned. "And the broken windows down half the street?"

Benny returned her attention to the copier. "Meh," she said, with a smile.

There were three other people in the office, a long, narrow room with just enough space for six identical Ikea desks. Ted could see the top of Zane's head over his monitor as he talked on the phone, and Klaire and Jake were having a meeting in the editor's office, a glass-walled partition that occupied the back corner of the space. The editor herself, Mazzy, was nowhere to be seen.

"You OK, dude?"

Ted blinked and swayed on his feet. Alison looked up at him from her desk as Benny collected her copying. She held the ream of paper under an arm and looked Ted up and down.

Ted smiled. "Fine. Just a lack of sleep."

"And the fact that we just walked past a crime scene," said Alison. Benny's eyes went wide, her head swiveling between her colleagues.

"A crime scene?" She stopped on Ted. "Seriously? *Dude.*"

Ted and Alison exchanged a look, and Ted continued his walk to his desk. "Down by the convention center, one of the streets opposite, off Fourth."

Ted swung into his chair and booted up his computer. Benny stood right where she was.

"Oh man." The Chinatown reporter shook her head and blew out her cheeks. "Was it, you know…"

Ted saw Alison's eyebrow go up, but he nodded.

"Again?" Benny shook her head. "Oh, *man.*"

Ted's computer was taking a while to boot and he had a sudden need for fresh air. In the dull shadowed reflection of his monitor he wasn't sure he recognized himself. He changed the subject. "Anyone want a coffee?"

From over his monitor, Zane waved a hand as he continued to murmur into his phone.

Benny dumped her printing on her desk. "I'll grab it. I know what everyone likes. I could use the fresh air, y'know?"

Ted sprung from his chair. "I'll come," he said. Benny nodded, and the two headed out.

Benny ordered the coffee, getting Ted a triple shot. Ted laughed, and Benny told him he looked like he needed it. As they waited at the counter, Benny pulled her baseball cap off and replaced it the right way around, threading her ponytail through the gap above the Velcro fastener at the back.

"At least Mazzy is out of town," she said.

Ted nodded. It didn't matter, the editor not being there. The Bay Blog wasn't the kind of place that required constant supervision. The writers were paid by the post, so if they slacked off it would be reflected in their paychecks.

Benny looked directly at Ted, who blinked. He felt tired. So very, very tired.

"So, look," she said. "How about we leave early today, grab a bite. You know, chillax. Shoot the shit."

Ted laughed. "Benny, my friend, please never use those phrases again."

She placed a closed fist across her heart. "I swear," she said, and then she tapped Ted's chest with the back of her hand. "But come on. Let's split at four. Grab a drink, burgers, my treat."

Ted nodded. "I'll ask Alison if she can finish early."

Benny's face dropped. "Oh, yeah, sure," she said, but Ted could tell she didn't mean it. He was going to ask when the barista called their order and Benny vanished to the other end of the counter to collect.

Ted frowned. Maybe he'd imagined it. It was just the lack of sleep and a surprising twenty-four hours. Everything would return to normal, eventually. He backed away from the counter to give the person behind him some room, only there was nobody there. Ted blinked, then followed Benny.

"Please don't tell me you're posting on Twitter about this."

Benny looked up from her phone, which she had been trying ineffectively to hide in her lap. Then she smiled and made a big show of clicking the phone off, holding it up unnecessarily high like she was about to perform a bad card trick before putting it on the table in front of her. Ted chided himself. Benny wasn't like that.

"Sorry, dude," said his friend, lifting her bottle of Bud and taking a swig. Ted watched the brown and red bottle rise and then fall, and took a sip from his mug. The coffee here was passable at best, but people didn't generally come to the Fifth Street speakeasy to drink coffee. He grimaced slightly at the too-bitter, too-cool liquid. He was feeling better, but he wondered if Benny was disappointed that her work pal wasn't joining her in some brews.

Benny took another swing from her bottle and looked around. "Quiet, huh?"

It was. They sat in a booth big enough for a family of eight, and represented exactly half of the bar's clientele. The other two customers were men sitting at the bar, both watching a re-run of a recent game on one of the bar's many large televisions. Neither spoke and they didn't seem to know each other, and Ted realized they weren't even looking at the same TV.

Benny drained the last dreg from her beer. "Early, I guess."

Ted nodded in agreement. Early was just fine for him. Early out of the office, and early dinner, and an early night. Alison had stayed behind – she was too busy on the museum story, but had insisted she had no problem with Ted and Benny getting dinner together. Benny seemed a little too pleased at this, but Ted put it down to her natural, apparently boundless enthusiasm for just about everything she did.

The clock behind the bar was slowly heading around to five. Benny and Ted sat in silence for a while. Ted listened to the ball game on the TV and let his eyes drift over the wall of bottles behind the bar. There were so many containers in so many shapes and colors, with exotic names and fancy labels. So many typefaces, illustrations of faraway places and animals: deer, birds, the kinds of things you dressed up in tweed to go shoot. The back of the bar was mirrored. Ted could just see himself in between the glittering amber liquids. He squinted a little, but there was an imperfection in the mirror and it looked like there were two Teds sitting in the booth. He took a sip of his coffee and it looked like one of the reflections moved with a weird half-second delay.

Ted nodded at the phone on the table. "So how many followers do you have now?"

Benny grinned and tapped the edge of the phone, sending it on a slow counterclockwise spin.

"Eighteen hundred and eighty-seven," she said. "Man, I'm so close to the big 2K."

Ted smiled and shook his head. "And what are you gonna do when you hit the magic number?"

Benny's grin froze for a second, and she stared at Ted, the gears working until she came up with a suitable answer.

"Aim for the next thousand, of course," she said, perhaps with not as much conviction as she would have liked, Ted thought. Benny looked down at her phone and the smile flickered off. "Anyway, it's quality over quantity. I have me a fine posse of online friends."

"Uh-huh."

Benny slid off the bench seat and tapped Ted on the shoulder. "More followers than you have, Mr Unpopular. I have to powder my nose. You want another coffee?"

Ted drained his cup. "That I do. Another beer?"

"Line 'em up, my friend, line 'em up."

They left at seven, which felt like midnight to Ted. He was fantasizing about soft pillows and darkness as they walked when he realized Benny was talking. Ted opened his eyes. They were near Union Square, heading up Stockton Street toward Chinatown, and Ted had no memory of walking that far.

"So, you think it was the firecracker, right?"

Ted stuffed his hands in his pockets and breathed in the cool evening air. It was near dark, the streetlights glowing in faint fog that was gathering between the tall city buildings.

"Firecracker?"

"Yeah," said Benny. She pointed up the street. A few blocks away, the green gateway to Chinatown was dead ahead. "Someone played a hell of a joke on you, dude. Practically blew the table up."

"Gave me a headache, for sure." Ted paused. "Is that what you think it was? A practical joke?"

"Don't you?"

Ted tongued the inside of his cheek. "I guess. But the only person I can think of who would pull something like that is walking right beside me now, and I also know that she wouldn't be able to resist admitting to it already."

Benny's eyes narrowed. "Wasn't me, chief."

"A mystery fit for Nancy Drew."

They walked in silence for half a block.

"Must have been a shock."

Ted rubbed the back of his head, trying to find the sore spot where he had hit the floor of the Jade Emperor, but he couldn't feel anything.

"Gave me a fright, sure. And everyone else."

"No," said Benny, "I mean the crime scene. You see that kind of stuff on TV, you know? Crazy, dude. Crazy. That's four now. Crazy."

Ted agreed and said he was sure the police would find who was responsible. They walked on. Ted watched the fog curl around the streetlights. "So, how's the Chinatown beat going anyway?"

Benny frowned, momentarily lost in thought. "Good," she said, "Yeah, real good. They're good people there. Nice place, has a buzz."

Ted nodded. That was good to hear. Benny had been on the blog only a few months, moving to the city from LA. She was also Korean, not Chinese, and Ted wondered if that would make it difficult for her, covering the local events in Chinatown. But clearly it didn't. Benny spoke Chinese as fluently as English and Korean.

"So just let me know if you want to talk about it," said Benny. They'd stopped by the Chinatown gateway. Benny lived in an apartment above a store. Ted's place was a short cable car ride away, toward Fisherman's Wharf.

Ted nodded. Under the peak of her 49ers cap, Benny's eyes looked sharp in the streetlight. Ted decided he didn't like it when Benny got serious.

"Sure," said Ted. Then he turned with a wave and walked down the street. "See you tomorrow."

Ted's apartment was dark and cool, just like he wanted it. He dropped his keys onto the dining table, and noticed that his laptop was on again. He closed the lid as he walked past, thinking he should check the power saving settings on it.

Tomorrow. That could wait until tomorrow. Tomorrow he would be awake and it would be a new day and life would go on as normal and–

Ted's head missed the edge of the table as he fell, hitting instead the thick pile carpet with hardly a sound at all.

# VII
# SHARON MEADOW, SAN FRANCISCO
## TODAY

Tonight he must try his hardest, because he has two crowds to please. One easy, one less so.

He makes his entrance, cartwheeling toward the ground on a blue ribbon that unfurls around him, falling with just enough speed to look dangerous. Then the ribbon's end snaps from his waist and he's still halfway to the ground. The crowd gasps, and he falls, and then catches the trapeze thrown by Jan. She times it perfectly – she always does – and he uses the momentum of his fall to push his body back up toward the roof of the Big Top. He flips, changes direction, flies toward the other side. Then he lets go, rolls in the air, and lands on the wire, an impossible feat. But this is no trick and he has no support, no hidden wires, no concealed harness swinging him from the dark above. He stands, arms outstretched, standing on nothing but a half-inch steel cable.

The crowd's not sure. They murmur. Applause starts but dies quickly. They think he is too good. They think it *is* a trick – it has to be.

But he knows this and knows how to fix it. He wobbles slightly, airplane arms swirling in the air high above the sawdust floor. He stumbles, corrects, overcorrects and leans too far in the opposite direction. The crowd gasps. He's going to fall, there he goes, it's all gone wrong, it'll be in all the papers. Then as his balance fails completely he jumps into a backward somersault, heels-over-head, and lands on the wire. He bends his knees and immediately cartwheels forward. He's working hard and now the crowd buys it. This is no trick. He's just good. The best. That's why he is known only as Highwire: a masked mystery, a man with no name, just a label for what he does.

Highwire bows on the wire as the crowd gets to its feet, clapping, whistling, shouting. It's a nice night in San Francisco but the tent is packed again, a full house. Money in, as the ringmaster would say, the goddamn bank.

Highwire belongs to the circus, is part of it. That Highwire knows nothing of his life before the circus, that he has no memory of anything *but* the circus, is inconsequential. The circus is his home, but his real work lies elsewhere, after the crowds have gone, after the carnival machines go to sleep. Out there, in the city, Highwire has a job to do.

But for now he entertains the crowd and the crowd feeds him. Jan and John, the trapeze artist couple who are part of his act, do a fine job. Mighty fine. And they're good, very good, no doubt about it. Professionals, career circus acts. Top class.

But they know the crowd is not here to see them. They're here to see *him*. Highwire isn't sure what story the Magical Zanaar gave them when the circus arrived, but he was accepted into the act. Perhaps that's how it works, new performers are hired, guest spots offered. And he's better than Jan and John. Much better. But that's not surprising. After all, they're only a couple of professional circus performers with years of training and experience under their belts.

Highwire is different. He knows this. He suspects this is why he has no memory of his life before the circus. He suspects he didn't have one, that he's part of the circus because somehow the circus birthed him, like the caravan arrived and the Big Top went up and out of the darkness walked the acrobat, ready to put on a show.

Maybe the circus birthed him because *it* knows that there is work to be done, out there, in the city.

Maybe. And maybe it doesn't matter.

Under the Big Top, Highwire flies through the air with the greatest of ease.

He doesn't expect the argument that follows their performance, but it goes like this:

"So, you think you're the world's greatest high wire artist." John. Feet on the ground, he's still in his spandex but is wearing awful square-lensed glasses like a cheap backstreet accountant. On the trapeze he wears contacts but he takes them out as soon as he can.

"Right?" John takes his glasses off, pulls at his costume near the waist and rubs one of the lenses with the purple spandex. As he does do, the costume tightens around his crotch. Highwire looks at Jan.

They're a well-matched pair. Both older than you might think, which is part of why they are so good – they've been doing it so long. She has pinched features. Sharp nose. She doesn't say anything but she squints at Highwire in the dark behind the Big Top. Highwire sees her eyes moving over his face, which is still hidden behind his mask. She probably wishes he would take it off, but that would spoil the act. Highwire is a mystery man, even to them.

John finishes polishing his glasses and puts them back on. The bottom of the lenses touch his cheeks, giving him little dimples and leaving red marks that take a while to fade when he takes them off. He frowns. He expects an answer.

"I might be," Highwire says. Honesty is the best policy. When everyone is honest, everything works out. Most people in the world could take that advice. "But I have a lot to learn, and two fine teachers."

Well, *that* part is a lie. But he has to keep his partners happy.

John nods but keeps his mouth tight. It's the nod of a disappointed father. Highwire doesn't remember his father, unless his father is the circus, in which case he is all around him. Part of him thinks this makes sense and part of him thinks the idea is hilarious. He folds his arms, his expression hidden behind his mask.

"Look," says Jan, and then she stops. She grips John's arm and Highwire can see her hold it tight. "We're not complaining about the show. Far from it. You're great. You're amazing." Jan smiles and it looks genuine, but the edge of fear is still there, lurking over her shoulder.

"But look," John picks it up. His hands are on his hips. "You're never here. We never practice." Now a stern look in the eye and the shake of the head. "I know you've got it down, no problem, but *we* need to practice, even if you don't. There's only so much we can do on our own." He jerks a thumb over his shoulder. "We made mistakes in there. We made mistakes, and you corrected for us. It's amazing, really, but c'mon, we need to work together here. It's not good for the show. You have to come to rehearsals."

Highwire folds his arms. They're right, and he's surprised. He doesn't come to rehearsals. He supposes he must have once. How else would they have worked out their trapeze act? Unless the circus did all the work for them, implanting the routine like it gave birth to its magical acrobat.

"We come to your trailer." Jan now. "Lord knows we do, but we can't raise you. It's like banging on the side of a tomb, it's so quiet in there."

"I'm sorry," says Highwire. At this Jan and John seem to relax.

Nobody says anything. Then John nods and Jan smiles. "We'll meet at eight, OK?" she says, gesturing at the Big Top. Highwire nods, and they seem happy and turn away, muttering a good night as they go.

Then comes the smell of cigars and aftershave, and the sound of hard-soled boots on the ground.

"Mister, a word, please," says the Magical Zanaar, waving his cigar in the air, the glowing red end drawing a figure eight in the semi-darkness behind the tent.

The ringmaster and the acrobat walk around the Big Top until they reach one of the trucks parked behind it. The truck is just a large black outline, tarpaulin flapping against the grass in the evening breeze.

Jack stops and removes the cigar from his mouth and smiles. He points at Highwire's chest with the cigar.

"Highwire," he says. He peers at the mask. Highwire wonders why the ringmaster doesn't ask him to take it off, doesn't know his real name, doesn't think that this is all strange and peculiar and not the way to run a circus. But perhaps he isn't running the circus. If the circus gave birth to the acrobat then perhaps *it* is running the ringmaster.

"Everything OK?" he asks. "With Jan and John. No problems?"

Highwire bows his head. "None, Mr Newhaven."

"Good, good," says the ringmaster. He puts the cigar in his mouth but then he takes it out almost immediately. "We don't see you around much. Not during the day. Sleeping, right? In your trailer. Must be a tiring act, up there on the wires."

Newhaven's forehead creases. He's concentrating. He looks distracted. Like he's trying to remember something.

"Are you OK, Mr Newhaven?"

"I'm too old for this shit," says the ringmaster, apparently to himself. He jams the cigar in the corner of his mouth. "Did you take the cable or not?"

Highwire folds his arms.

"Cable?"

"Cable. The tightrope that you dance around on. A reel is missing." He sighs and then he comes to life, his internal battle either forgotten or won. He pokes Highwire in the chest with a fat finger with a big ring on it. "That shit costs a fucking fortune, and if a cable fails now then we haven't got a replacement. Know anything about it? Short of money maybe? Thought you could make a quick buck?"

The cable. Of course. Without knowing it, Newhaven has given him a vital piece of information.

Cable. The Hang Wire killer – Highwire's quarry, out there in San Francisco – strings his victims up with wire. Not just any wire. Cable. Woven steel, thin but strong. The killings are strange, the process clearly requiring strength just to bend the cable into a working noose.

Tightrope wire. A reel of which has been stolen from the circus.

Highwire doesn't think he took it, but then he doesn't remember.

He looks at Newhaven, unsure whether the ringmaster has put the cable theft and the murders in the city together.

Highwire shakes his head. "It wasn't me. I wouldn't steal from the circus, Mr Newhaven, and I certainly wouldn't put myself and my partners at risk."

Newhaven doesn't look happy.

"Mr Newhaven, if I hear or see anything, I'll let you know. You have my word," says Highwire. "That cable is my livelihood. Is anything else missing?"

"No," Newhaven says. "Not yet." He puffs his cigar slowly. "But keep your eyes open. I am." Then he turns and walks into the night.

Highwire heads in the opposite direction, keeping close to the shadows cast by the tent and the trucks. There are a few circus folk around, doing odd jobs. Over the other side of Sharon Meadow, a light flares, big and orange, and what follows is music on the air. Drums, a pipe, a wheezing drone. Stonefire, the Celtic dancers, settling in for the night in their own way.

Highwire waits in the darkness a little longer. Then, satisfied that nobody is watching, he slips out, into the night, into the city.

# VIII
# SAN FRANCISCO
## TODAY

She'd walked this route a hundred times. Down Cleeft, onto Fourth. Along Fourth, past the titty bar, past the bums playing chess and asking for four dollars for a grande latte. Past the big streetcar stop with its long seat, slightly too low and too angled to be comfortable for sitting on – or for sleeping on, which was probably the intention. To the main intersection at First and Maple, with the Apple store on her left and the towering frontage of Macy's on her right. Ahead the road was wide and straight, and filled with streetcars and other traffic. A pause at the lights until they turned red and the cross signal shone. Then up the hill, toward Union Square and Chinatown, to her apartment.

She walked it on automatic, her mind elsewhere as her brain piloted her home. Dangerous in any big city, perhaps; maybe even more so on this particular route through downtown San Francisco when there was a killer on the loose. Her friends had told her several times – even her boss. If you want to walk, Lotta, he said, for God's sake don't go behind Grestch Street. Stick to the open. Be safe.

But the Gretsch Street shortcut knocked five minutes off the journey home, maybe more. And the narrow street was always deserted. Lotta worked nights and when it came time to head home the empty backstreet seemed preferable to running the gauntlet of leering, drinking men outside the strip clubs. They stared and said things, and sometimes they even followed her for half a block, calling out and clutching at their crotches before laughing and sloping back to their habitual loiter spot. Maybe they didn't actually ever go into the joint. They probably couldn't afford the cover.

Lotta turned into Gretsch at 2.30am. Today's shift had been nothing out of the ordinary. Like her walk home, she was so used to the routine that she switched off at work, her mind wandering in one giant daydream. Sometimes, the dream never quite went away, and sometimes she blinked and found herself pushing the key into her front door and she couldn't remember the walk home at all.

She followed the curve of Gretsch as it veered to the left, past a shuttered newsstand. A fire escape platform jutted out here as the buildings on either side crowded in, so close that, Lotta thought, you could almost step from one fire escape to the other, traveling between buildings without ever touching the ground.

Lotta sniffed. The sky was clear and there was no mist, but it was chilly. She passed under the fire escape and adjusted her coat, and as she did so the figure on the fire escape peeled out of the shadow, swung over the rail, and dropped heavily to the street.

Lotta stopped and turned around.

The bonfire had long passed its peak, when it had towered over even the Big Top like a giant pyramid of ever-changing orange and yellow. But despite the size of the blaze, it had been strangely cool. Malcolm and the members of Stonefire sat around the fire while the rest of the circus slept in their trailers.

Malcolm let his eyes un-focus as he watched the dying fire, turning it into an abstract swarm of red and black shapes, like the roiling surface of a dying sun. The heat was there all right, it was just going somewhere else.

And now it was hot enough to begin.

Malcolm stood up, ignoring the cracks of his knees and his protesting muscles as he rose from the cross-legged position. Around him, the rest of his company jerked into life, uncurling themselves from their fireside positions, brushing the dust from their leather and bare skin.

They were silent, all of them, and all of them watched Malcolm, because Malcolm was not just their leader, he was one with the spirits, chosen. Malcolm knew how it all worked because the fire spoke to him. Something else spoke, too: their true master, their creator, the thing asleep. Close, so very close.

The embers of the bonfire glowed scarlet. Malcolm moved closer, until he was standing in the ashes and charcoal that marked the edge of the fire itself. He stopped, and stared into the fire, listening to the magic in the cracks and crackles.

The glow of the embers began to brighten. Dull red became white, so bright that in Malcolm's vision there was just the fire and nothing else, his troupe – his *clan* – vanishing into abyssal darkness.

Malcolm was alone with the fire. Alone with his god.

The fire spat a shower of yellow sparks like a solar flare, cracking like electricity. Malcolm smiled, and somewhere out in the darkness someone began to clap. Soon others joined, followed by voices. The rhythm was slow, steady, primal: clapping, feet slapping the ground, moving around. Stonefire began their dance.

Malcolm stepped closer, his bare feet disappearing to the ankle in the glowing ashes. The fire cracked again and Malcolm bent down, sifting the brilliant embers with his hands. There was no heat, but a tingle, pins and needles, and his mouth was filled with the taste of rotting lemons.

Malcolm stood and turned with his back to the fire, facing the darkness. His eyes adjusted, resolving the moving figures of Stonefire as they danced and stamped and chanted. He held his arms out, and as one the dance troupe fell silent and still.

"Here," Malcolm said, and when he spoke the fire cracked again. He lowered his arms, and turned and pointed to where he had cleared a small patch in the ashes.

"We dig. Belenus commands it," he said, and he dropped to his knees. He began scratching at the blackened Earth.

The members of his clan ran forward, converging on Malcolm, almost smothering him, as twenty pairs of hands scrambled in the embers, digging below the fire.

Lotta took a step backwards and regretted everything. She regretted not taking the advice of her friends and of her boss. She regretted the shortcut; she regretted not paying attention. What she would do now for the sight of the strip club boys and their loose jeans, grinding their crotches as they tailed her down the street, calling obscenities and wolf whistles. On the other side of the street there would be people, cars, even at such a late hour.

On Gretsch Street there was just Lotta and the man in front of her. He was a black silhouette, nothing more than an oblong shadow with arms, standing under the fire escape. His shape was strange, elongated, like he was wearing a tall hat.

Lotta turned. She knew it might be a mistake, but she couldn't run backward. Fifth Avenue was just ahead. Lotta tensed herself to run and drew a breath to scream for her life.

There was a sharp sound, like someone retracting the extendable flex of a vacuum cleaner, and Lotta was pushed forward onto the pavement as something very heavy hit the back of her neck. She instinctively reached out to break her fall and exhaled heavily as the wind was knocked from her lungs, but as she tried to whoop a fresh breath in she found her airway closed tight. A second later the weight on her neck shifted and she was jerked backward a few feet. Her hands flew to her throat as something tightened around it with mechanical strength, crushing her windpipe, pushing her larynx against her spine. Exquisite agony exploded beneath her jaw, and her fingertips scrambled over and around thick, hard metal. She could feel the weave of individual cable fibers and the cold of the metal against her skin. At the back of her neck her fingers found the cable was looped through an eye, a metal ring, smooth in comparison with the wire itself, with a thick rivet or bolt fixing it in place.

The cable was tugged again, sliding tighter on the loop. The index finger of Lotta's right hand, somehow inside the noose, was caught and cut through to the bone as the metal loop was tightened and tightened. She tried to scream, but there was no air and her throat was nothing but hellish fire. She could feel her eyes bulge like water balloons, and the night disintegrated into purple spots in front of her.

Another jerk, and Lotta's last thought was that she was flying, her feet leaving the ground as she was carried into the air by her neck, her trapped right arm strung uselessly behind her head.

She swung from the fire escape on the steel cable. She was dead already but her legs kicked violently for a few seconds, throwing her left shoe off. Then the kicking stopped, and the alley was quiet and she was alone once more.

The night is cold and damp, the fog rolling in from the bay in a great opaque cloud, obscuring everything in its path and coating the city in a thin sheen of water slick with grease and oil.

Dangerous conditions for an acrobat, but even as Highwire slips for the third time as he leaps from one building to the next, he understands the problem and corrects for it, and when he lands on the next roof it is with silent, mathematical precision. He rises into a crouch and pauses, balanced forward on fingertips, and when he closes his eyes, he can sense it all: the fine fizz of the fog against this face, the sandpaper texture of the tar paper under his fingertips, the slight changes in the gentle breeze four stories from the street.

Two other things as well. Something large, nearby, breathing slowly like a sleeping dragon. It comes from all around, but seems to emanate from the ground, the streets, like there's a slow-moving river deep beneath the city. Highwire isn't sure whether he can hear it or feel it, but he can sense something is there.

The other: a vibration ahead, rhythmic, a slowly changing, slowing pattern. One object in contact with another, the two touching, separating, touching; a weight, swinging, pulling on something metal that creaks and shakes in microscopic ways. The first sound – the *sensation* – seems to be pulsing in time with the swinging too, like whatever it is beneath the city can feel it, is drawn to it.

Like Highwire. It's not just sounds and sensations that brought him here. He knows he is close. The killer is near. So very near. And perhaps, if he is quick...

Highwire skips forward on all fours, toward the edge of the building, and jumps.

The embers were heaped into two great piles on either side of the hole, like a parting of the seas frozen in blazing white and red. Now the digging had slowed, become more organized, the fire – through Malcolm – having selected the youngest, the strongest, for the last stage. As the others watched, a handful of men covered in black ash continued to dig with their bare hands as they knelt in the embers. A couple of younger dancers, a teenage girl and her older brother, spun around, kicking up ash and chanting, as a third member pounded a gentle rhythm on a leather-skinned drum.

The burned ground was dry and soft, pliable like cake. Malcolm stood over the workers, arms folded.

"Malcolm!"

The leader bent down as the diggers stopped. The one who had called his name looked out of the pit at his master, who smiled and nodded. Then two of the diggers reached down into the dirt.

The earth relinquished the body without any resistance as the diggers dragged the woman up and over the lip of the hole. She was naked and glistening, a slick, gelatinous envelope covering her whole body. Within seconds she was covered in black ash and dust.

Malcolm stood over her as she lay, face-down. As he watched, she coughed and rolled over unaided. She blinked the dirt from her eyes, and when she looked at Malcolm, she smiled.

Malcolm reached down. The woman took his hand, and he helped her up. Standing, she flexed her legs, her arms, looking down at her own body like it was new and strange.

Malcolm nodded. "Welcome, Lotta," he said. "Welcome to life."

Too late. Highwire looks down into the narrow street and there she is, hanging by the neck from the old fire escape, her body twisting on a steel cable in the gentle breeze, her legs periodically knocking against the end of the fire escape's ladder. The fog is thinner here but when the police find her she'll be wet through, which won't make their task any easier.

Highwire is too late for her, too late for all of them. But he is close to the killer. He can sense him near. He jumps to the ground, clearing three stories and hitting the street in total silence. There is blood here, lots of it. The victim has been nearly decapitated by the steel cable drawn into a noose. That in itself would require considerable strength.

Nearby a light in a building is on and there is movement. Out in the city, cars are approaching, fast. The police are coming already; someone *has* seen or heard something.

Movement in the window again. Someone pointing, down at the street. At him. Highwire ducks into the shadows and the person moves out of sight, but it is too late. He wants to go examine the body, to find clues, something that will lead him to the Hang Wire Killer who is so very, very close. But he can't. At the opposite end of the street two police cars have arrived already, their sirens silent but their lights flashing. Highwire slides along the wall in the shadows, then scales the brick and flips himself back onto the rooftop. He ducks down until he is out of sight of the street below.

And then… the killer is gone. Highwire can't sense him, not anymore. He can feel the city moving around him, people and cars and motorcycles. Dogs and cats and rats. He lays the palm of his hand on the roof and if he concentrates he can feel the Earth turn and…

Something moving. Something far away or deep below, breathing, the heartbeat of a monster.

But he can't sense the killer. Nothing. Gone. It is impossible, but it is so.

Highwire spins on the balls of his feet and runs and jumps, crossing the buildings, crossing the city, without pause or sound.

He only hopes that next time he will be faster.

# INTERLUDE
# NEW ORLEANS, LOUISIANA
## 1911

Joel kept his pearl-handled gun held high as he pressed his back into the wall. With the other hand he felt inside the fob pocket of his waistcoat, his fingers scissoring around the gold coin within.

The house was dark but the windows had no curtains, allowing a grayish glow of gaslight in from Hospital Street on the northeast side and Royal Street on the northwest. The house was empty, nothing but bare boards of a wood so dark as to be black in the dim and shaded light. The walls were empty too, just a tableau of faded squares where portraits and landscapes had once hung and been admired.

Joel stood on the stair landing, gun in the air, coin in his pocket, stovepipe hat fallen somewhere on a floor below. He looked up as the boards over his head creaked with slow footsteps. Despite the neighborhood, despite the reputation this particular quarter of New Orleans was developing, the city was quiet. And so was the house, slumbering in the night.

The creaking from the floor above stopped and Joel held his breath, imagining he was the only person in the whole city.

Even if that were the case, he knew his quarry was one of many. New Orleans was famous for shades and things that moved and bumped when they shouldn't. The

LaLaurie Mansion in which he now stood, gun raised, coin burning cold in his pocket, was perhaps the most notorious and haunted spot of all. A fire in 1834 that started in the building's not insubstantial kitchens was said by some to have been a suicide attempt by the slave cook, an old woman who feared what her mistress, Madame LaLaurie, did in the top room of the house.

The creaking began again. Joel glanced at the stairwell, an architectural splendor in carved wood. The room over his head, by his reckoning, was *the* room. The room of horrors. The room into which people were led by Madame LaLaurie and didn't come back out of again.

Joel stepped lightly across the bare floor, the boards silent beneath his carefully placed boots. The stairs were a different matter, the wood warped badly, each and every footfall sounding no matter what as Joel crept upwards.

Madame LaLaurie – slave owner, murderer, the first serial killer New Orleans would play host to – had long gone. But Joel knew that the evil that now seeped the house, the horror that lingered in the very bones of the place, drew its power from a more recent arrival, an object which had perhaps been hidden here deliberately, whoever had brought it drawn to the house like iron to a magnet. Like Joel had been, dragged by the coin, by the light that shines, by the gravity of the stars.

Joel was near. The object hidden would be his soon and then he would move on, guided to the next piece, and the next, and the next.

A bang from above, and a scraping, like furniture being moved across the floor. Furniture that wasn't there, in the empty house on French Street.

The sounds did not stop. Joel listened a moment; then he pulled the hammer of his revolver back and took the stairs two at a time.

The second landing was clear and darker than the rest of the house, the window at the end not quite at the right angle for the streetlight to shine in. There were three doors, all closed. The sliding sound came from the one nearest. Another sound too, breath, whistling, like a breeze through a cracked porch door on a fall night in the west, long, long ago.

Joel smiled and reached for the doorknob. He brought the gun to bear, his gray-white eye trained down the barrel.

In one swift movement he opened the door and took two broad strides inside, his back to the paneling and his gun panning left, right, left.

The room was devoid of life but it wasn't empty. There was a chair in the center, draped in a dusty white cloth. There was more dust on the floor, the boards caked in the stuff. Joel glanced down, and saw his boots had kicked it up as he'd stepped inside, the wood shiny beneath his feet. A series of curved streaks cut through it where the chair had been moved maybe a yard.

More footsteps. Slowly, on the landing, behind Joel, the floor creaking like a cut tree about to fall. Joel spun around, both hands now around the grip of his gun.

A shadow moved on the landing, as though someone were hurrying past the doorway. Joel tracked the motion with his gun and fired once, twice, the bullets finding nothing but air before punching holes the size of dinner plates in the wall by the stairs, the dry wood and plaster exploding in great clouds. The shadow moved again, rounding the top of the stairs and gliding down, now silent, the footsteps gone. Joel fired again and the pommel at the top of the bannister exploded, the fresh pale wood beneath the dark veneer like raw flesh in the night.

Joel wasted no time. He raced down the stairs, the shadow just ahead. On the first landing he thought he'd gained on it – enough to send a fourth bullet through the Hospital Street window. The sound of the shattering glass was appalling, a greater shock than even the report of the gun. Joel continued his chase, his boots sliding on the shattered fragments that salted the bare boards of the landing.

First floor. The entrance hall of the mansion was grand and cold, and empty like the rest of the house. On the floor near the front door sat his stovepipe hat.

Joel came to a stop at the base of the stairs and waited. The hall was silent and after a few seconds Joel shook his head. He was running out of time now. Someone would have heard the shots, and he wouldn't be alone in the house for long.

There was no time for this. He was here for a reason.

Joel took the coin from his pocket. He closed his fist around it so tight he could feel the edges bite into his palm, and he closed his eyes.

He was close, he knew he was. The coin was cold, as cold as the ocean was deep.

Then the coin moved in his grip. The prize was somewhere near…

The silence was broken by a tiny creak from Joel's left. He turned his head toward the sound, his eyes still closed. Footsteps sounded far above him. A moment later the sliding sound of the chair being moved. The haunting, a recording of a terrible act from long ago, looping for another performance.

Joel opened his eyes. He turned on his heel. There, in the paneling on the side of the stairwell, a thin vertical black space, a crack, a gap. Joel brushed the edge of his jacket to one side and holstered his gun. In his other hand the coin felt like a burning coal. He stepped back, scooped his hat from the floor, and pulled it onto his head. Then he stepped back to the paneled side of the stairwell, and he pushed.

The crack widened: a door, the paneling hinged to conceal the entrance. Beyond, caught in the gray light from the windows, was a narrow set of stone stairs leading down.

Joel smiled and pocketed the coin. The cellar. Of course. The piece was hidden in the cellar and the cellar itself had been hidden, years before, by Madame LaLaurie.

Joel rattled down the stairs and the paneled door swung shut behind him.

# IX
# SAN FRANCISCO
## TODAY

Sun streamed in through the windows, bright and hot where it hit the bed. Ted raised himself up on an elbow and with one eye firmly closed against the glare squinted at the bedside clock.

Two. PM, given the brightness of the day outside. Ted felt like he could sleep forever. Maybe he had, and when he looked out the window he'd see the ruins of San Francisco deep in a swampy jungle ruled by super-intelligent tigers.

The possibility seemed less likely as he dragged himself up and to the kitchen.

Making the coffee was a struggle and seemed to take a thousand years, but Ted made it, and then made for the couch. He considered going back to bed; it was an option, certainly, but despite the protests of his body he thought he should stay up, try to shake off whatever it was he'd come down with. Couldn't be the explosion at the restaurant. He fingered the back of his head, then the rest of his scalp. No sore points, or bumps. He felt fine. Just… as energetic as the dead. The bang had done something to his ears too, maybe damaged a drum. It sounded like someone was whispering behind him, and not for the first time Ted found himself checking over his shoulder.

Ridiculous.

Ted fumbled for the TV remote. As he did, he noticed his laptop was open on the dining table, the screen glowing.

That damn laptop. It had been nothing but trouble since he'd gotten it. Ted stood, walked over, cursing himself for being so cheap when it came to electronics. The laptop was his livelihood, after all. He really should invest in a—

*You are the master of every situation.*

Ted frowned. The word processor was open, again, and while the message was the same as it had been before, instead of being repeated in a single column running down the page, it was rendered in a large block font, a single statement, centered on the page.

Ted rubbed his eyes, then pulled his hand away from his face. His fingers felt sticky. He peered at them, unable to focus, his other hand automatically raising the coffee mug to his lips.

His hand froze. The coffee mug was plain white, but was now covered in streaks and splotches, something sticky, something that had once been liquid but had dried overnight into a tacky dark something.

Blood.

Ted gasped and put the mug down quickly on the table like it was dangerous. He raised his hands. Both were covered in drying blood. The laptop too – over the keys, and as he closed the lid, he saw more smears on the back of it.

Blood.

Ted turned his hands over and over, then felt his wrists, his arms. He looked down at his feet, his hands running over his stomach. He had no injury he could see or feel, no cuts or scrapes. And certainly nothing that would account for the amount of blood on his hands, on the computer. Tracked into the carpet from the front door to the bedroom.

Jesus. What the fuck? He paced the apartment, all the while running his hands over his body. But there was nothing he could feel; he was fine.

Had somebody broken in and bled all over the place? Had some fucking tweaker got hurt and broken in to hide?

*Jesus.*

Ted searched the apartment, then searched it again. Nothing. No dying drug addict in the closet. No meth head locked in the bathroom. He checked the hallway outside and traced the outline of bloody footprints down the stairs to the main lobby. He stood at the bottom of the stairs for a while, then realized he was wearing nothing but boxer shorts. The building's front door clicked as another resident arrived home and Ted turned tail and jogged back up the stairs, two at a time.

He re-entered his apartment cautiously, poking at the still-open door like there was someone hiding behind it. Just to make sure, he then swung in quickly and checked, but there was nobody there against the wall.

Ted turned the apartment over again, found nothing, then took a shower that was very long and very hot.

He felt better after that, but only a little. Dressed, his hair still damp, he did another circuit of the apartment, but once again nothing seemed out of place or disturbed. He was alone. He wiped the blood from his laptop and deposited the coffee mug in the dishwasher. He did these things slowly, in a daze, as he wracked his mind for possibilities. He'd obviously got covered in the sticky red stuff – it wasn't blood, couldn't be blood – and hadn't noticed. That could happen. Sometimes you stepped in something, or sat in gum and didn't know until it was too late.

He checked the clock. It was nearly three in the afternoon. There was no point going to the office. He should call in, claim sickness.

Claim sickness? No, he really was sick. Something was going on and he had to figure it out.

He grabbed the phone, sat on the couch. Turned the TV on. Local news.

"Hey, Zane. Yeah. Ted. I know. Is Alison in?"

Commercials on the TV now. It was heading up to the hour, time for the headlines. The volume was low and Ted stared at the screen, his attention on the phone. Zane was giving him a rundown of who was in the office. Finally he passed the call to Alison.

"Please tell me you're calling from bed?"

"Is the couch OK?"

"Well…"

"Good afternoon," said a woman on the television, her eyes meeting Ted's as she stared down the camera. "Our top story this hour: police are conducting a door-to-door search after the fifth victim of the so-called Hang Wire killer was found this morning in a deserted back street…"

"Ted?"

Ted blinked. His ear was hot from the phone, his eyes fixed to the TV. It showed a narrow street, cordoned off with yellow police tape that twisted in the wind. Uniformed cops and plainclothes walked around the street. Then the camera cut to a long zoom, to a big screen that had been erected down the street. There was nothing to see, except a forensic technician in white paper overalls looking at some paperwork. But above the screen was a fire escape, leading up and out of the picture.

The scene was familiar. Very familiar.

"Shit," said Ted into the phone.

"What?"

"Another killing, down on Gretsch Street."

"Yeah, I saw. How many more is he going to kill? Do you think we should run something on the blog, like a PSA or something?"

"Yeah," said Ted. That made sense. Their blog didn't cover news, only events and entertainment. But this was a special case.

Alison said something else, but Ted wasn't listening. He could hear his own heartbeat, almost feel it through the couch, the floor, like it was coming from somewhere else, from somewhere down below. He gulped a mouthful of saliva and kept his eyes on the TV. A detective was giving an interview, but Ted couldn't hear it, only his heart: *thump-thump, thump-thump.*

"Ted?"

"Ah," he said. "Look, I'm calling in sick. Maybe tomorrow too. I gotta shake this off, get back to bed."

"I'll come over later."

"Ah, yeah, sure, OK."

"Ted? Maybe we should get you back to the emergency room, get them to check you again."

"Yeah, maybe. I'll see you."

Ted clicked the phone off. A moment later he realized he hadn't given Alison time to say goodbye. He felt bad about that, but the sound filled his apartment. He winced, not sure if he was imagining it or not. His hand clutched his chest. What, a heart attack now?

Then the feeling passed, the sound abated, and he was left with nothing but the sports reporter talking about baseball on the TV.

Ted thought again about the fire escape. Gretsch Street.

He needed to take a look for himself.

Gretsch Street was a no-go. The police had the whole area cordoned off. They were desperate to catch the killer, and Ted could understand that. He loitered around with a few onlookers, but it was late afternoon now and most people had lost interest. The forensic team was still there, and a few cops on guard, but it seemed pretty quiet.

Ted nodded to one of the cops at the cordon. The officer looked Ted up and down, and for a second Ted thought the cop was looking at the blood on his hands. He quickly raised them both up. But they were clean. The cop raised an eyebrow, and Ted smiled sheepishly.

"How long you guys going to be here?" he asked.

The cop frowned. "Street is closed until further notice. Do you need access to an address?"

"Um."

"We're doing a door-to-door search of the whole street. If any of the addresses are yours, we need to take a statement." The cop turned and waved at one of his colleagues farther down the street.

Ted backed away. "Oh, no, I've never been here before. I'm just being nosy."

The cop frowned again, and looked Ted up and down. "Yeah, well, move along then, buddy. Nothing to see here."

Ted nodded and backed away. The cop didn't take his eyes off him, and then he grabbed the radio clipped to his shoulder and muttered something into it that Ted couldn't hear. Ted waved, smiled, then stuffed his hands in his pockets and walked away.

He'd lied to the cops. He'd been to Gretsch Street before, and recently too. He remembered the fire escape, all rusted and creaking, dark green paint flaking off in large slivers as the steel cable squeaked, the body of the girl swinging on the end of it. He remembered the blood, the way the girl's hand had got caught in the loop of the cable.

Ted sniffed, spotted a coffee shop, crossed the road. He needed coffee. As he crossed the street he felt OK, because all of that detail – the fire escape, the body – had been on the TV that afternoon, right? They'd shown it, hadn't they? Kind of gruesome for the main network, but that was how Ted knew.

Had to be.

••••

It was dark now and the coffee in Ted's hand was cold. He was standing at Chinatown's famous gatehouse on Union Street. A fine mist had drawn in, chilling him in his thin jacket. He hadn't meant to be out this long, wandering the city. Looking for something, but he had no idea what. And now, lost in thought, he'd somehow ended up here, in Chinatown, back where it all started. Like he was following the voice in his head.

He blinked, rocking on his heels. The voice in his head? Good lord above. Now even *he* thought he was crazy.

Ted walked up the hill. There, on his right, just near the crest of the gentle slope, was the Jade Emperor. One of the best Chinese restaurants in the city – one not on the tourist maps, one the locals felt was their own little secret.

It was closed and wouldn't open until seven. Ted realized that he didn't actually know what day of the week it was, his sleeping patterns were so monumentally fucked up.

And now he felt tired. Really, *really* tired. He'd walked for miles, trying to work out a mystery that was beyond him.

Ted crossed the street and looked up at the building. The Jade Emperor was on the third floor, and had a terrific view out over San Francisco. It didn't look any worse for wear, the windows now repaired, although Ted wondered quite what he was expecting. So a fortune cookie explodes. So what? It hadn't *really* exploded, had it? There hadn't been a fire. Paper had rained from the ceiling but that was some kind of joke, some set-up for another party that had gone off too early, scaring the diners, knocking Ted flat on his back.

Ted frowned and crossed back over the street. He needed to go home, get some sleep. That was it. Sleep deprivation. He'd hallucinated the blood. There was none on his hands now because he'd washed it off, but had there ever been any at the apartment? Hell, he'd been half asleep. Maybe it was a waking dream.

As he walked back down the hill, he passed a small alley next to the building that housed the Jade Emperor. There was a dumpster against the wall. Ted paused, looked around. There was no trash can anywhere and the cup of cold coffee was annoying him.

Ted walked into the alley, gingerly flipped the edge of the dumpster's black plastic lid up, and tossed his coffee inside. It hit a big green plastic bag, which tipped onto its side and disgorged its contents.

Ted froze, the dumpster lid held up just enough so he could see. The plastic bag was filled with shredded paper. Ted lifted the lid further, and saw there were more bags. Each green, each tied at the top, each with confetti spilling out.

Fortunes. Bags and bags of fortunes. Ted reached in, his arm just long enough for two fingers to grab at the nearest paper.

*You are the master of every situation.*

Ted dropped the paper and let the dumpster lid fall with a clatter. The heartbeat was there again, rumbling in his ears. He felt the pulse on his neck, expecting to find an artery there ready to burst, covering his hands in hot blood, filling the alley, like the blood that had filled Gretsch Street.

Sleep. He needed sleep.

Ted staggered from the alley.

The computer was open on the dining table. Ted ignored it, dropping his keys onto the red maple beside it. The pounding in his head, *thump-thump, thump-thump*, had only got worse. He felt zombified, the walking dead, so tired he wanted to throw up.

The whispering voice laughed. Ted turned around, ready to argue with his imaginary companion, but as he spun on his heel he passed out and fell over. He hit his head on the corner of the coffee table as he did so, but even that was not enough to wake him.

# X
## SAN FRANCISCO
### TODAY

In the street outside the apartment building, Benny watched Ted's window. The light had come on, so Ted had made it in, and then there had been a thud, like a door closing.

She'd trailed Ted all day. Down to Gretsch Street, the scene of the most recent killing. And then across town, to Clementine, to Taylor, to Spencer. The previous murder scenes, although the police and the cordons were long gone from each and life went on as best it could in neighborhoods traumatized by death, murder.

And then finally to Chinatown, to the Jade Emperor. There, as Benny watched, Ted seemed to wake up, like he'd been sleepwalking the last two hours. He'd jerked on his feet, shaken his head, and Benny had ducked around the lip of the nearest building to keep out of sight.

Ted had climbed into a cab. Benny followed in one behind. Ted's ride stopped at his apartment, and as Benny's cab passed she turned in the back seat, watching as Ted had paid his driver and headed into his building. Benny's cab stopped a few yards further up.

And now to wait. It wouldn't be long, by her calculation. Benny leaned against the building, still warm from the afternoon's sun, adjusted her baseball cap, and waited.

# XI
# SHARON MEADOW, SAN FRANCISCO
## TODAY

When Highwire emerges from his trailer it's 6pm. Behind the fluttering flags of the blue and yellow striped Big Top he can see the tip of the Ferris wheel and some of the other carnival machines: the big dipper, the rocket ride, their lights shining, flashing weakly in the last gray dregs of daylight. Of Stonefire's nightly bonfire there is no sign; walking between the trailers, past the Harlequin standing in the doorway of his motorhome, a silent wave and nod exchanged, Highwire comes to the circle of blackened earth where the Celtic dancers build their pyre. The space is flat, clean, but mottled and irregular like it has been dug up and filled in again, stamped flat by the dance troupe.

Highwire hears a shout, and then somebody starts counting. There is creaking, metallic, rhythmic. Inside the Big Top, Jan and John are hard at work on the trapeze. Highwire is late for rehearsal, but at least he is going this time. He said he would. He rolls his neck, feeling the spandex costume stretch over his head and face, rolls his arms, stares up at the sky, focusing on what he is about to do, high in the air above the sawdust of the ring.

"Hey, Superman! Come here."

Highwire turns. A man approaches, a head of big curly brown hair and a trucker's moustache. His bulk is crammed into jeans and a matching denim shirt, looking vaguely like a celebrity WWE wrestler getting ready to head out for a day with the family. Highwire doesn't move and then the man is in his face.

"You," says the man. Then he pauses, his head tilting from side to side like he's trying to pull focus with a pinhole camera. Highwire thinks it's supposed to be intimidating, but he doesn't move. Tension is high at the circus, he knows that. He knows that's why most of the performers stay in their trailers until show time, why they don't wander around, socialize, help each other out like they used to. There is something wrong with The Magical Zanaar's Traveling Caravan of Arts and Sciences. Highwire now realizes that maybe people think it's him.

"You," repeats the man, fists bunched, nostrils flaring. "You think you're pretty special, huh? Fucking superstar, huh? Well..." Another pause, and he draws an excited breath. "Well, ain't you just something."

The statement is made quietly, and to Highwire it feels anticlimactic. The man steps back, moustache twitching around a tight, angry mouth. Then Highwire recognizes him. Terry, one of the riggers, responsible for the tents, including the Big Top itself, and the various apparatus attached to it – including the trapeze and tightropes.

"Hello, Terry," Highwire says, reaching forward for a friendly pat on the shoulder. Terry sees the movement and jerks away; he stares at the outstretched arm like it's a live electric cable. Highwire lowers the arm and Terry's eyes follow the motion, his breathing short and quick. Highwire concentrates and can sense the man's heart rate increasing to match.

"You," Terry says, finally able to drag his eyes up to Highwire's mask. "You're not like us. You're not welcome here. You can't just waltz in and take over the show. The fuckers aren't here just to see you, bud. They're here to see the whole show."

Terry waves his hand around to emphasize the point. Highwire still isn't sure what has him riled.

Unless. Yes, there. Something else. Something... moving. Something reaching out from down below, something toxic, pushing people in the wrong direction, feeding off their anger, their fear. Making them do things like... fight.

"I have no quarrel with you, Terry," Highwire says. This is true. While Highwire needs the circus as his cover, using the thrill of the crowd to keep him in the air, his main concern lies elsewhere, out in the city, where he uses that power to hunt the Hang Wire killer.

Highwire can see it in Terry's eyes. He was right. He's being pushed by that thing the lies beneath them all, sleeping, stirring the fire in Terry's eyes, their pupils pinpricks.

Then Terry laughs and spits into the dusty ground.

There is movement at the side of the tent. A small flap flips up, and Sara and Kara duck out of the Big Top. They are in costume, each a reflection of the other.

Highwire is distracted by the two girls as Terry says something and then his fist flies forward. Highwire sees it, but whether by pure luck or through the help of some other agency, the fist connects. Highwire rocks back on his heels, hand to his jaw. The girls shout out but Terry ignores them and kicks off the ground, throwing himself bodily at Highwire.

Terry is no danger to Highwire, Highwire knows this, like he knows he could move out of the way. The power he wields so far beyond what a human is capable of that some would call it magic, but he also knows he needs to hide this.

Even so, Highwire is surprised at the force of Terry's attack. He allows himself to be grappled and push onto his back, but Terry is strong. Very strong. The fall pushes the air from Highwire's lungs, but Terry is standing already, one fist grabbing Highwire's costume at the throat and lifting him up, the other pulled back, ready for the knockout blow. But Highwire clears his head and his hand finds the dirt, throwing a cloud of dust and dry grass into Terry's face. Terry cries out and lets go, shaking his head. Highwire hits the ground again and shuffles back as the denim mountain in front of him growls like an animal.

"The *fuck* is this?"

Highwire rolls over and goes to stand but something long and black strikes him on the arm. He looks up and finds the Magical Zanaar's lit cigar in his face.

"The fuck, the *fuck*," mutters the ringmaster. He looks from Highwire, to Terry, and back to Highwire. "You fucking carnies are trying my patience," he says, and he kicks Highwire's hip in frustration.

The short man moves over to Terry, still wiping dirt from his face. He hits his employee on the shoulder with his black cane. "Jesus, Terry. I'm too old for this shit, OK?"

Terry blinks, and when he looks at his boss it's like he's just woken up. He looks around, glancing at Highwire, his eyes roving over Sara and Kara standing by the tent. Then his gaze locks over Newhaven's shoulder. Highwire follows his gaze; there, by one of the trailers, stands Joel, the carnival manager. He has his hands in his pockets and is smiling, his own black stovepipe hat at a jaunty angle.

"Ah, sorry, Jack," says Terry. He rubs his face. Newhaven peers at him and then turns to Highwire, his face dark.

"The fuck you do to him, jerk off?" He waves at Sara and Kara. "Hey, peaches and cream, go get Nadine. Get her to bring the first aid kit. *Jesus*."

The girls nod and walk away, but Kara turns and looks over her shoulder at Highwire. He frowns, and she glances over toward the carnival and holds her wrist out to the side, pointing at it with her other hand. Nobody is paying her any attention. Newhaven is fussing over Terry, and when Highwire looks toward the carnival, the carnival manager is gone. He glances back at Kara, nods his understanding. They want to meet, at the carnival, after the show is done.

Newhaven pats Terry on the back, and Terry nods. "Go clean up, pal," says the ringmaster before he turns on Highwire.

"One day, that's it," he says, cigar drawing a figure eight in the air. "One more day, and then you're out. I don't care how much money you bring in. We can manage without it and without you."

The Big Top flap opens again and Newhaven jumps; it's just Jan and John, coming to see the fuss.

"Yes, sir," Highwire says, and Newhaven's mouth twitches. He likes being called sir. He mumbles something and then stomps away.

"What was that about?" asks Jan. She and John exchange a look.

Highwire cracks his knuckles. "Nothing. I'm ready for rehearsal if you are."

The acrobatic couple pause like they expect Highwire to say something else, but then John nods and holds the tent flap open for his wife to duck under. He disappears into the Big Top and lets the flap close, leaving Highwire alone.

Highwire looks over toward the carnival, toward the Ferris wheel and the top of the big dipper, both still, their lights glowing perhaps a little fainter now.

There is trouble at the circus. And he is not the only one who knows it – Sara and Kara want to talk. Perhaps they have sensed the power stirring too. Perhaps they've seen, heard something more concrete.

There's a connection with the Hang Wire Killer too, the missing reel of cable. Highwire is surprised that the police haven't been to visit. Or perhaps they have, given that he can't remember the days, only the nights.

He lifts the opening of the Big Top and steps inside.

# XII
# DALY CITY, CALIFORNIA
## TODAY

Mrs Winters' house was a bungalow in a leafy suburb, just south of San Francisco proper. It was a nice area, and in the early afternoon, nearly deserted. Barefoot, bare-chested, Bob went unnoticed as he walked down the street. He'd only seen one other person, an old guy in short-sleeved shirt and brown shorts riding a mower around the grass outside a church. The church was new and looked just like the bungalows that flanked it, white weatherboards glowing the sun. The old man hadn't seen him, busy as he was negotiating his vehicle around a sign proclaiming IF YOU WALK THROUGH THE FIRE I'LL COME TO THEE. As Bob walked past he wondered how many gods that piece of advice might apply to. He thought it would probably have applied pretty well to him, actually. Back in the day.

He remembered how the villagers and tribesmen used to walk over fire for him. Fire and water, Bob was lord of them both.

*Was* being the operative word. Sometimes he missed it too. He frowned, and stuffed his hands into the pockets of his old jeans.

Fire was why he was here, in this quiet suburb. Mrs Winters had invited him. He should have ignored the invitation, but she knew. Knew who he was, what he could do. Why else would she have invited him? Why else would she think that her daughter could be resurrected? If she'd been sent by *Them* – hell, if she *was* one of *Them* – then it was a really damn strange way to get his attention, if that was indeed what *They* wanted.

The sidewalk ended as Bob approached an intersection. He looked right, he looked left, he looked right again. There was no traffic, just a few cars parked nearby, settled in for a day of sunbathing, the air already shimmering over them. Bob glanced skywards, and saw nothing but a blue dome, dark enough at the apex to remind him of the sea. He hadn't walked this far from the ocean for quite a while. Despite himself, he was nervous.

Bob stepped off the curb and crossed the street.

Truth was he wasn't even sure if *They* were still around. He was here to find out for himself. If she knew who he was, who *They* were, then he was powerless to stop *Them* doing what *They* wanted anyway.

Bob stopped in a cool spot under a tree, brushed his hair from his eyes. In the dappled light he curled his toes on the sidewalk and watched the ground.

There was something else, wasn't there? Something… moving. He'd ignored the signs, perhaps afraid of what they meant, not wanting to relive 1908 or 1989, unwilling to accept that something was about to happen again. It was an amorphous, nebulous feeling. There was something wrong in San Francisco. Mrs Winters' desire to dig beneath a fire troubled him. He knew what that meant. He'd seen it before.

Bob felt his shoulders rise as he tensed up. He blew out a breath and looked around. Looking ahead, he saw his destination was just a couple of houses down on the other side of the street. He walked to the curb, looked right and left and right again. He crossed the street.

Maybe if Mrs Winters was one of *Them*, she'd been sent to help. That would make three in the city, which was a damn sight more help than Bob had had in the past.

Feeling a little better, Bob trotted up the garden path that led to Mrs Winters' front door. The house was the same as the ones on either side of it. White board, two level. Not new but not old either. Bob wondered how long she'd lived in the house, and whether it was the same one she'd brought her daughter up in. Her daughter, one of the victims of the Hang Wire Killer.

Bob wondered if the killings that had struck the city had anything to do with what it was that he could sense. Something moving. Something moving under–

"You're right on time, young man."

Bob looked up in surprise. The front door was open and in its frame stood Mrs Winters. She must have been watching from the windows, Bob thought. She was dressed in a vintage ball gown that Bob had no doubt she'd bought new.

"Ma'am, you're putting me to shame," said Bob.

She looked him up and down and winked before hoisting the edge of her gown and turning around.

"Nonsense, you're just right," she said over her shoulder. "Now come on in and help me with the fire."


As he followed Mrs Winters through the hallway, Bob found himself smiling at the old fashioned floral wallpaper, the heavily patterned carpet. Bob remembered when that kind of interior decoration had been in fashion, and guessed it would have been half the woman's life ago, at least.

Not for the first time, Bob lamented the insignificant lives of those he walked among, those he had made his *home* with.

"Here we are. I've made space for us."

Mrs Winters disappeared through a side door in the hall, the edges of her puffy gown squeezing through in a cloud of silk and ruffles. Bob followed, and then stopped in the doorway.

Sometimes the insignificant lives of those he walked among surprised him, still, after all of this time.

It was a dining room, wide and long, stretching clear from the back of the house to the front, with large bay windows that looked out onto the front garden, and a door at the back next to a serving hatch in the wall, presumably leading through to the kitchen. Below the hatch was an alcove for an elaborate sideboard.

The sideboard in question lay on its front on the floor. The heavy piece of furniture had been toppled forward and then someone had taken a hatchet to its carcass, leaving nothing but a splintered frame twisting under its own weight.

The wood of the sideboard lay against a large pile of broken furniture – chairs, a multi-leafed table, clearly what should have sat with some elegance in the impressive room – in the middle of the floor toward the back of the room.

The dark, patterned carpet that started in the hall had continued into this room, but as Bob stood in the doorway his toes were over the roughly cut edge. The carpet, cut and lifted from the floor, now sat in a soft, folded stack against one wall like rolls of whale blubber. The exposed floorboards were dull with age and dusty, an unreflective, unpolished mass of grayish brown wood.

Bob stepped into the room. He could see more bits now: a different set of chairs and a smaller table; the headboard of a large bed, split into three pieces, the broken edges of each piece a bright pale yellow against the mahogany veneer.

Added to the furniture were clothes, great piles of them. And tablecloths, wooden picture frames with paintings and photos still in them. In the middle, facing the door, was a small wooden frame with a portrait photo of a young woman in it. Lucy, Bob supposed.

Mrs Winters moved to the bay windows, and laughed. "Oh, don't worry about that, Mr Bob," she said, waving off the pyre. "I was just getting ready for later. We've got plenty of room."

Mrs Winters looked at Bob, her arms held out in a familiar pose. She was ready to dance.

"Lady, look," said Bob. He walked over to her, his eyes on the pile of broken wood. Had she done all that herself? How long had it taken her? Then he remembered her strength at the beach. He looked at her outstretched arms and slipped his fingers into the back pockets of his jeans. "You asked me to come and help, and here I am. But I think we need to talk about some other things as well, don't we?"

Mrs Winters nodded quickly and then lifted her chin back into a perfect ballroom poise. "Oh, yes, there's lots to talk about. But first we have to dance. It won't work if we don't dance."

Bob ran his tongue around the back of his teeth. He felt nervous and unprepared, like how he'd felt when he'd woken from his deep, deep sleep, the sleep of a lifetime.

But maybe living down on the beach, becoming Bob, local tourist attraction, was the same as sleeping. He knew *They* were sleeping, all of them, and maybe he was too. And that's how it happened. That's how *it* had come back. Bob had let his guard down. He knew now what the thing stirring beneath the city was and what it was capable of.

San Francisco was in great danger. He needed to talk to the other one. Not Mrs Winters, she clearly wasn't one of *Them*, although she was affected by *it*, maybe even powered by *it*, caught in its field of influence.

Mrs Winters cleared her throat. "You've walked from the beach to my house in your bare feet, and I am waiting for my next lesson. So, if you don't mind?"

And with that she closed her eyes, her arms still up, her head still held to one side. Bob shook his head, took her hands, and stood awkwardly, wondering how exactly he could prevent what was to come. Was that even possible? It hadn't been before. But now he was not alone in the city. That had to be some comfort, right?

Mrs Winters opened one eye and peered at Bob. She squeezed his hand. "Viennese Waltz to start, if you please."

Bob smiled tightly.

"Anything you say, Mrs Winters."

After they danced, Mrs Winters lit the fire.

Bob let her do it. He had a feeling. If what he suspected was true, then he knew what was about to happen wouldn't obey the usual laws of physics. He needed to be sure, and then when he was he could go and find the other and talk to him.

Bob watched as Mrs Winters got on her knees and began fussing at the edge of the pile of dead furniture. Now she was old, frail, the strength and speed displayed during the dance and down at Aquatic Park gone. Her breathing had become heavy. Bob sat on the floor, legs pulled up to his chest, and didn't interfere. He hadn't for a long time. When he'd first come down, he'd wanted to become like them, *be* one of them. That was the whole point. But he wasn't, and he couldn't be. Bob had tried to live a normal life while everyone around him grew old and died. And then more people would come, their microscope lives infinitely short, and again, and again. Bob realized what was happening: the more he tried to be like them, the more he found himself distanced from them by time and decay and death.

So one day he stopped trying to be the same as them. He built the hut on the beach so he could live by his old home, the sea. That was years ago, and he watched the city grow around him. By the time there were authorities who might question what he was doing, he was part of the scenery. Then came the curious, a few at first, the wealthy who could get over to the park to gawp at the strange and handsome vagrant who lived in the hut. One night, a woman came alone, late, and instead of staring she knocked on the hut and they talked, and then they danced. She taught him ballroom, visiting at night for weeks, months. And then she stopped coming and later, years later, when she must have been long dead, Bob remembered her and thought of her often, and when the tourists came he decided to pass his knowledge – *her* knowledge – on. So the ballroom dancing began; a gimmick, a trick for visitors, but it made Bob happy. And, oddly enough, through the memory of his teacher and the contact with those he taught himself, he felt more connected to people than he ever had been when he was trying to fit in with their society.

Mrs Winters, apparently happy with the arrangement of kindling and rags in the room, reached for a box of kitchen matches by her side. She took one out, struck it on the third try, and lit the fire. She didn't move from the pyre, which was dry and already cracking with flame. Bob drew his legs a little tighter to his chest. Within moments the whole room would be ablaze, and soon enough the whole house. In any other circumstances, it was arson, and suicidal.

In any other circumstances. But he knew what was about to happen. And so did she. He pointed at the fire "How do you know about all this?" he asked.

She smiled, the expression flickering at the corners, like there was something on her mind. Her eyes, glazed, told Bob what he needed to know. She was being influenced by something else. Not controlled, because the sleeping monster beneath them had no mind, couldn't operate people like puppets. No, just... *influenced*. Caught in the field of power.

Mrs Winters ignored Bob's question and turned back to the fire. She put her hands out to the growing blaze, like she was warming them over a Girl Scout campfire, out in the woods.

Except this fire wasn't hot. While Bob could feel the warmth against his bare chest and face, it wasn't hot like a furnace, more like a brilliant summer's day. The smoke gathered against the ceiling, rolling into a turbulent gray cloud a foot thick and growing no larger.

The fire was growing quickly, consuming the old clothes, the splintered furniture, everything. The flames were tall and licked at the smoke above. But whatever heat – whatever *energy* – the fire possessed, it was being contained rather than radiated.

Or, Bob thought, not radiated but *directed*.

He sighed. How long had the danger grown, under the city? How long had he been on the beach, dancing on the sand, oblivious to the approaching Armageddon? He'd been asleep, like he had been before.

But now he knew. Mrs Winters was under its spell; the fire proved it. But if she was connected to *it*, and she had come to him, then did *it* know who he was? They had both lived in the same place for long enough, one deep below, one in the city above. If Mrs Winters was connected then perhaps Bob was too.

No. *It* didn't think. It had no awareness. Not of itself, not of Bob. Not of Mrs Winters.

Bob watched the flames as they ate through the broken shell of the sideboard. The fire spat a shower of sparks as a stack of three dining chairs finally lost structural integrity and slumped into the body of the fire. Out of the corner of his eye, Bob saw Mrs Winters smile as she tracked the path of the sparks as they swirled in a spiral toward the ceiling, caught on a hot thermal that by all rights should have set the house alight like the pile of dry firewood it was.

Bob knew what had to come next. "Mrs Winters?" He watched the light of the flames dance over her pale skin. Her cream ball gown was a rippling kaleidoscope of yellow, of orange, of red.

She flicked her eyes toward her houseguest and then back to the fire. "Patience, young man."

"How did you know–"

The old lady clicked her tongue. "You got sand and salt in your ears or something? I said patience."

The fire was dying now. A few black skeletal remains of the dining set and sideboard were the only items left taller than a foot. Above, the smoke had dissipated impossibly in the closed room, revealing a small circular burn directly above the fire, as if the whole thing had been a candle sitting on a table. Bob looked down, traced his eyes around the edge of the fire. Nearly perfectly circular, the blaze had charred the floorboards badly, yet hadn't spread more than a half-inch out from its periphery.

"Almost time," said Mrs Winters. She sat up from her haunches and pushing her legs back. Her eyes were fixed on the charred floorboards.

"Mrs Winters, why did you come to me? What do you need me for?"

The old woman turned to Bob and smiled, and then the smile broadened and her eyes closed and she began to laugh.

"I'm looking for my daughter, Bob. I'm looking for Lucy. I guess she led me to you. I knew you could help. I just knew you could. Will you help me?"

Bob frowned. Mrs Winters reached down and brushed aside the charcoal at the edge of the fire, revealing more of the burned floorboards beneath. She turned to Bob and pointed; her hands were black with ash.

"Here. We start scratching here."

Bob looked at the floorboard, split and black. Beneath would be the foundations of the house, and below that, the ground.

He hesitated. He knew what lay under the ground. He knew the power that fire had, how it could be used.

"Oh here, let me." Mrs Winters reached her lumpy, arthritic fingers into a gap in the board created by the warped wood. She pulled once, twice, and part of the board came away in her hand, nothing more than crumbling carbon.

If what he thought was down there, Bob wanted him to be the person who found it, not the old woman. She was drawing power from somewhere else, but Bob suspected it had limits. He had power he could control.

He grabbed the floorboard with both hands and wrenched. It came away with a bang – the wood was burned and fragile, but most of the nails were still firmly in place. Ordinarily, a crowbar would be the tool of choice here. Bob didn't need a crowbar. He grabbed the next board, then the next, pulling them back and tossing them over his shoulder, until soon enough there was a hole in the floor, a black, carbonized hollow, the remains of the fire piled around the edge in a semicircle.

There was nothing there. Dirt and ash, lots of it. Bob dug a little, his heart kicking, but after a few black handfuls he hit something more solid. Brick and cement, and brown dirt. The foundations of the house, untouched by the fire. The energy of the blaze hadn't penetrated far enough.

"Oh," said Mrs Winters. Bob sat back and glanced at her. She knelt on the floor, her ball gown streaked with ash, her hands in her lap as she peered into the hole.

"Oh," she said. "Oh, oh dear..."

"Mrs Winters, I–"

There was a crack like a gunshot. Bob ducked instinctively but Mrs Winters didn't move. Bob looked around, searching for the source of the sound. Then it happened again.

"What in the–"

The woodpile exploded into flame, like the remains of the bonfire had been doused in gasoline. Bob pushed himself backward but Mrs Winters didn't move, her ball gown ablaze. She lifted her hands to her face and screamed, but Bob couldn't hear her over the roar of the fire.

He grabbed her around the waist and pulled her back. Then he lifted her to her feet, and spun around so his body was between the fire and her. He wrapped his arms around her, pushing himself against her body. Behind, the fire roared and crackled. Looking up, Bob saw the ceiling was on fire. The fire was hot now, like it should have been before. The energy that had been contained, that should have been directed down into the earth but hadn't, was now suddenly released, like a nova.

Mrs Winters screamed again. Summoning the sea, the ocean, the power of gods, Bob put her dress out, and healed her burns, and ran through the front wall and into the garden as the house exploded.

# INTERLUDE
# BROWN MOUNTAIN, NORTH CAROLINA
## 1922

He parked the car on the high road that wound up the side of the valley. The vehicle was large enough to block the road completely, but Joel didn't think anyone would come by this way for, oh, maybe days.

In the valley cleft below, the river ran, heavy and fast. It washed down the valley and washed up its sides too, fed from the great thunderhead several miles to the north, where a prodigious amount of water was being dropped on the parched land. The ground was dry and cracked, and the water skittered off it like it was a hot pan.

There was going to be a flood. Joel knew this because *it* knew this and *it* had led him here. All he had to do now was wait, and watch. More would be revealed, a little at a time, a hint here, a push there, until he discovered the task he had to perform.

All he knew was that it would involve death and murder. Because there was power there, in death and in murder, power to feed the light. And the light fed Joel, and kept him moving, searching, for a decade at a time, sometimes more, sometimes less.

And the light had brought him here.

Joel sat on the running board of his car, and watched the hills on the other side of the valley, and waited for the light to shine for him.

When it was gone full dark, the lights did shine. Literally. Joel had watched the hillside all afternoon, listening to the roar of the river as it rose ever higher, breaching its banks, surging down the valley. As night fell and the stars came out, there was nothing but the roar of the water and the twinkling above. After a while, Joel could hardly tell where the valley was and where the hills ended and the sky began.

That was when he realized the twinkling stars were not in the sky at all. They were on the hills across the valley, and were small at first, then flared silently like the stars in the sky might on a cold winter's night, the air full of ice and mystery.

The lights didn't move, but they winked on and off, the entire ridgeway glinting like a box of treasure. Joel watched, fascinated. He followed the light, but the light was more of an idea, a suggestion, like the voices in his head that weren't voices at all, like the little push on his shoulder, the memories that weren't his. He stood from the car, took the Double Eagle coin from his pocket, and held it up at arm's length, lining it up with the lights on Brown Mountain. The gold coin glinted, the light moving around it, although Joel held it perfectly still. He squinted, looking along his arm with his left eye, and it looked like the coin was just another of the winking lights, over on the hill.

The river's roar was like an ocean. There was thunder, lightning, and the rain finally arrived. Joel stood in it a while. The coin in his hand was cold as it glinted, its chill crawling up his arm like icy death. The rain was warm: body warm, blood warm, and as it poured over his face he imagined the water lifting him up and floating him away.

Joel shook the rain off his face, pocketed the coin, and got back into the car. On Brown Mountain, the lights flared like beacon fires, and then went out.

In the driving rain, Joel drove out, down the road. Toward the river.

Toward the rail bridge.

It was dawn when Joel slowly drove the car down to the rail bridge, the vehicle rocking on its high springs as it negotiated the bumpy ground. The road had survived the flood, but was covered with stones from the river, some nearly half the size of the car itself.

The rail bridge had not been so lucky. It was single-track and had been low to the water already. On Joel's side, the rail bridge vanished after twenty yards. On the other side of the river, it was missing entirely, along with half of the bank. Then the rails continued around the side of the hill like they always had.

The river roared below, still a churning cascade, furious and angry.

A ranger approached Joel's car, waving his arms. Joel pulled up, the car lurching over a boulder enough for the ranger to duck out of the way.

"There's no access down here," said the ranger as Joel leaned out the window. "The road's gone out with the bridge, but even if it was still there you wouldn't be able to get this across. Too wide by far."

Joel nodded, his eyes scanning the way ahead, like he really was just an ordinary driver, like he really was just trying to find his way across the valley. There were more rangers gathered around the bridge. He'd passed their vehicles farther up the road. The light had shown him the way.

"Quite a storm last night, friend," said Joel. He looked up at the sky, and the ranger nodded.

"Record breaker, I reckon. Haven't seen the like in two generations, maybe three."

Joel whistled. "That a fact?"

The ranger nodded again, hands on his hips. "Maybe three," he said again. Then he looked down at the road.

Joel smiled, and looked ahead as he felt the push on his shoulder, the tug on his waistcoat, the coin vibrating in the pocket. He pushed himself up in the driver's seat to see over the hood of the car.

And there it was.

"Say," said Joel. "Do you need help here? See, I have my car, and it's not much but it sure can pull its weight, and more besides. I see you have something of a problematic situation here."

The ranger huffed and with some delicacy plucked the wide-brimmed hat from his head. He turned to face the rail bridge, and the river, and the rail carriages that had fallen into it.

There were two blue boxcars, half-submerged, the river surging around them. They both looked intact, and were still connected, but twisted around their coupling. They were wedged into the river between the far bank and an outcrop of solid rock.

There.

The boxcar. The one nearest.

*Inside* the boxcar nearest.

Joel blinked and shook his head. The ranger was looking at him, rolling his lips, thinking things over. Finally he said, "You know, I think we could use you. If you have the time. Could have been worse, of course."

Joel nodded like he knew what the ranger was talking about, confident that the ranger would continue.

"Last two cars of freight," the ranger said. "Oh, the train got over the bridge, but maybe that was the last straw. The bridge was weakened by the river surge, and just couldn't take the weight. Could have been worse."

Joel nodded. "Could have been."

The ranger pointed. "It could have pulled the locomotive down with it, into the river. It was all freight of course, but still."

"But still."

"Wait here, Mr…"

"Duvall. Joel Duvall."

The ranger tipped his hat. "Wait here, Mr Duvall. I'll just let the others know we have an extra pair of hands."

"I await your command, ranger," said Joel with a laugh. "Say, how many folk you have down here?"

The ranger shook his head. "Only five of us could get across from Virginia. There's more coming, but the telegraph line came down with the bridge too. Wait here."

The ranger trotted away, to his colleagues crouched near the river bank, peering at the immobile boxcars in the river.

Joel glanced down at the gun on the bench seat beside him. Then he picked it up, flipped the cylinder open. Five rangers. Two bullets spare.

He closed the cylinder, spun it, and, holding the gun aloft, opened the car door and stepped onto the running board.

# XIII
# SAN FRANCISCO
## TODAY

When Ted opened his eyes the day was already bright and old, again. The blinds were open, light pouring in.

Ted rolled onto his front, stuffed his face into his pillow, and screamed. Fuck this. He felt fucking terrible. His sleep was so monumentally fucked up it wasn't funny. He held his breath, smothering himself with the pillow until he could stand it no longer and had to come up for air. He was angry and confused and fucking fed up to the eyeballs. Fuck this.

He looked at the bedside clock, found it facing away from him. He spun it around.

7.22am.

He'd gotten back at, what, seven? Despite twelve hours of sleep, he felt tired. Wrecked. He slumped back into the bed and stared at the ceiling awhile, thinking. Ignoring the whisper in his ear.

There was a note under the door. It was a white rectangle of paper, folded in half. Ted hadn't heard anyone knock, but then again he didn't even remember getting into bed.

He picked up the note. The paper was cold. Somehow he expected it to be hot, like when a sheet came fresh out of a copier. He unfolded it.

154

The note was a single symbol, a complex Chinese character of interweaving lines, the strokes bold and tapered, like it had been drawn with the traditional brush. Ted turned the paper around, not sure which way was up. He had no idea what the symbol meant, although it looked vaguely familiar. He'd probably seen something similar in Chinatown. There were Asian tenants in his building, so most likely the note had been put under the wrong door.

Except the symbol was familiar, and the more Ted looked at it, the more he thought he knew what it said, but not quite. He blinked. It felt like the symbol was changing in front of his eyes, the strokes in not quite the same place as they were a moment ago.

He shook his head and folded the paper again. He needed coffee. He also needed to go in to work.

The tapping of keyboards, the drone of the air conditioner, the rhythmic drone of the copier. The office was as Ted had left it, though it felt like he'd been away for a lifetime.

"Hey, Ted," said Zane. He was walking from his desk toward the kitchenette, carrying a serving tray festooned with dirty cups, mugs, and coffee holders. He paused and held it up a little. "How you feeling? Coffee?"

Ted nodded. "Hey, ah…" He rubbed his forehead. "Coffee. Yes, thanks. And I'm better, thanks."

Zane nodded and disappeared into the kitchenette. Ted followed and stood in the doorway. Zane was the only one in, and suddenly Ted craved company, conversation.

"You know what I think?"

Ted frowned. "About what?"

Zane half-turned from the coffee machine. "Summer flu. It's going around. Really knocks you down, you know?" He pushed his glasses up his nose.

Ted nodded. Actually, that made sense.

"Benny's come down with it too," said Zane.

"Benny's sick?"

Zane made an *uh-huh* sound, his back still to Ted. "Hasn't been in since Monday. Which I guess makes you patient zero."

Zane laughed and turned around, holding out a coffee cup. Ted said thanks, and wandered to his desk.

Benny taking time off sick was unusual. Not that she'd been at the office that long, but she seemed to have a titanium constitution – full of energy and life. Ted had never seen her with even a single hangover after the not infrequent office drinks. He'd last seen her at the bar, where Benny had been fine and Ted had felt like crap. Maybe he had given her the bug after all.

"Alison in today?"

Zane appeared from behind his monitor. "She'll be in later. Another meeting down at the museum, working out some more coverage for their art show next month. Should be a big feature for us. Lots of hits."

Ted nodded. Page views meant advertising revenue meant the blog could keep going. The whole enterprise was risk, but they had a good team and a good editor. Even now, Mazzy was on a trip somewhere, gathering more advertising and sponsorship.

And back home, her employees were getting sick, and the city was cowering from a serial killer.

Ted turned his computer on and slipped off his jacket. As he did, he felt something stiff in the inside pocket. The note from this morning, folded in two. He pulled it out and unfolded it on his desk.

"What've you got there?" asked Zane. He had a habit of sticking his nose in everywhere. It was one of his many characteristics Ted found annoying.

"Oh, just something I picked up. A Chinese character. I like it." It was a bad lie, but Zane didn't notice. He stood and walked over to Ted's desk, and gestured at the paper with his coffee mug.

"That's not Chinese," he said.

Ted looked up at him. "No?"

Zane nodded. "Korean. Honestly, Ted, do you live in the same city as the rest of us? The alphabet is completely different."

Ted turned back to the paper. Zane was right. The symbol was squareish, more ordered than a Chinese logograph.

"Benny will be able to tell you what it means."

Ted looked up again. "Oh, yeah," he said. Of course.

The door to the office banged open. Ted and Zane turned at the sound.

Bob walked toward them, barefoot and bare-chested, clad only in his trademark faded blue jeans. His face cracked into a wide grin, and he did a salute that looked a little self-conscious. He coughed.

"Hey, Bob," said Ted. "How's it going? You looking for Alison? She's not in until later."

Alison had done a feature post on Bob just the previous week. She'd interviewed him down at Aquatic Park. Benny had taken some photos. Seeing Bob at the office was a surprise; he looked lost, out of place, and not just because of the way he was dressed.

"Oh, hey, yeah. Ted, right? Cool, cool," said Bob, hooking his thumbs into the beltless loops of his jeans. He was clearly as uncomfortable in the office as Ted suspected. Bob glanced around the office, running a hand through his sea-salted hair and blowing out his cheeks. "Hey, no problem. Don't worry about it, brah." Then he waved and turned to leave.

"I'll tell her you came by," said Ted. At this Bob stopped and turned around again.

"Actually, you seen Benny? Me and her need to have a little catch-up, is all."

Zane shook his head. "She's sick as a dog, *dog*," he said with a laugh. Bob grinned and cocked a finger at him like a gun.

Ted reached for his cell. "I can give you her number, if you want to call." As he began thumbing through his contacts, Bob padded over to his desk. Ted looked up at him. "Um, do you have a phone?"

Bob nodded and sat on the edge of Ted's desk. "Oh yeah, yeah, no worries." Then he turned his head sideways to look at the paper on Ted's desk. "Where'd you find that?"

Ted looked up from his phone. "Oh, that?" He glanced at Zane. "Ah... I just picked it up, you know."

"Korean," said Bob. "You read it?"

"Actually," said Zane, "Benny speaks Korean. We were going to wait for her to get back."

Bob nodded, lips pursed. "Cool, cool. Hey, look, I gotta run, man," he said, pointing to the door.         .

"Pretty ladies to give dance lessons too, huh?" said Zane.

Bob grinned. "Yeah, man, something like that."

Ted jotted Benny's cell number on a Post-it note and passed it to Bob.

"Sweet, brah, thanks." Bob lifted himself from the desk and slouched out. "Laters, gentlemen," he said, and sauntered back to the elevator lobby.

Ted watched him walk away. Zane slurped his coffee.

"Strange guy," said Zane.

"Yeah," said Ted, shaking his head but smiling all the same. "Isn't he just?"

Zane returned to his desk. Ted's computer had booted up, so he logged in and dared to check his inbox, not noticing the note with the Korean symbol on it was missing from his desk.

# XIV
# SAN FRANCISCO
## TODAY

"I made it!"

Ted laughed and closed the door behind him, softly, listening as the tumblers in the lock clicked just *so*. He had a headache coming on, in that all-too-familiar heartbeat rhythm, but that was to be expected. He'd lasted a full day at work, after all. The whisper in his ear had left him alone for the day, along with the weird sensation that there was someone standing behind him.

That, or he'd got used to it. He leaned back against the door, paused. Nope, gone.

Alison placed her bag on the dining table, and looped her arms around Ted's neck. She kissed him lightly on the lips. "Welcome back to the land of the living."

"Thank you very much. It's great to be here," said Ted in his best Elvis voice. He smiled and hugged Alison back. Over her shoulder he saw his laptop on. "I need a new computer."

Alison let go and turned to the table. "Practicing your Chinese, eh? You're back at work and already you want Benny's job covering the Chinatown beat?" She laughed.

Ted frowned. He leaned over the computer, tapping the down cursor with one finger, the page scrolled on the screen.

The repeated text was back, in a neat column down the page, but instead of the fortune from the restaurant, it was a string of Chinese characters. They really were Chinese, he could see that now, not Korean like the mysterious note.

"Hmm," said Ted, and he quickly closed the lid of the laptop.

"Are you OK?"

Ted turned around, smiled, but Alison's eyes narrowed.

"I'm fine, really."

"Look, I'll stay tonight, OK?"

"I'd like that, thanks." Ted stepped forward and put his arms around Alison's waist. He kissed her nose.

"And tomorrow we'll go back to the ER, OK? Get you checked out again."

Ted sighed. "OK, fine." She was right. He was feeling better, seemed to have got his sleep pattern back to normal, but he knew the dangers of head injuries, even ones that seemed mild and benign. *Especially* the ones that seemed mild and benign.

Ted smiled and studied his own reflection in Alison's eyes. Here was a woman who loved him, cared about him. He needed that right now.

"So," said Alison, "we going to stand here all night?"

Ted shook his head. "Standing wasn't what I had in mind." He grinned.

"You, my love, need to get some *sleep*."

"Aw," said Ted, mock hurt in his voice. Alison laughed.

"Come on," she said, leading him to the bedroom.

# XV
# AQUATIC PARK, SAN FRANCISCO
## TODAY

Aquatic Park was packed with tourists and locals alike. It was a fine morning and already people were sitting around on the concrete tiers by the beach. Waiting for Bob and his famous ocean-side dance lessons.

The crowd parted in front of him as he approached. Some even clapped. Phones and tablets were raised, photos taken. It was ridiculous, he thought, like he was some Z-list celebrity stepping out onto the red carpet.

But this was what he wanted, right? To live on Earth, to live among humanity. To do something that made people happy. There was nothing wrong with that. Nothing wrong with that at all.

Except the adulation, even minor adulation – cheesy holiday photos and tourists tittering over the bronzed surfer dude who like to walk around with his shirt off – was an echo of something else. Something Bob had experienced long, long ago, when crowds had parted for him, when they had looked upon him with adulation and lust. As they walked across hot coals to kiss his feet. As they skewered virgin sacrifices on sharpened poles to please him, sate his hunger.

Bob frowned, turned around to face the crowd, and

waved for attention. There were some memories he didn't want to dwell on.

"Ladies and gentlemen," he said. "Thanks for coming down here, you know, on such a nice day. I'll be doing lessons shortly, but just lemme slip into something more comfortable, OK?"

More laughter and applause. A woman in the crowd called out and Bob pretended not to hear it, but the crowd laughed in response. With a wave, Bob walked off down the beach, toward the maritime museum and his little hut. He unlocked the padlock on the door without a key – he figured a *little* magic wouldn't hurt, right? Nobody would notice *that* – and stepped into the dark interior. He yanked on the pull cord of the main light.

Benny was sitting on the floor, legs folded, chin in her hands. Bob hissed in surprise. Then he quickly checked over his shoulder to make sure the coast was clear, and shut the door behind him.

"You gave me a hell fright there, brah."

"Kanaloa," said Benny. "We–"

Bob leaned against the back of the door. He knocked on it with his knuckles, then took a breath and pointed at Benny.

"Don't you call me that, Benny. Kanaloa has been dead for a long time. My name is Bob."

Benny unfolded herself from the floor. "I'm sorry," she said, "but there's something going on that needs his attention."

"Yeah, no kidding," said Bob. He pushed off the door, pulled the folded paper from his back pocket, and offered it to his surprise guest. "I was looking for you, but found this instead. Know anything about it?"

Benny took it, unfolded it, looked briefly at the symbol. Then she held it out to Bob. Bob didn't move, didn't take it back.

"That was for Ted," said Benny. "The–"

"The sigil of Tangun the Founder, yes, I know. I can read it. Thing is, Ted can't."

"You sure about that?"

Bob cocked his head. "What do you mean?"

"You know Nezha is dead."

Bob shrugged. "I didn't think gods died. They just fade away."

"He died here. In San Francisco."

Bob pursed his lips. OK, that was different. Gods were born and gods died, but not in the mortal realm. Up there, in the pantheon, sure, they came and went, grew old or young, died, were reborn, changed form, did whatever the hell they liked. Some got fed up and bored, died, and didn't come back. It wasn't the same kind of death that life in the mortal realm knew. Heavenly death was just another change of form.

But that did explain the odd feeling he'd had, the sensation that Nezha had dropped by and then gone, suddenly.

"He was murdered," said Benny.

"And how do you murder a god, exactly?"

"That's what we need to find out. Tangun wants to talk to Kanaloa."

"Can't you give him a message?"

"Doesn't work like that."

"Of course not."

"Look," said Benny. "This is some serious shit. Nezha was murdered. In his last act, he hid his power in the city. In a damn fortune cookie."

Bob whistled. He looked around the inside of the small hut, at the Playboy calendar forever set to August 1959, at the homemade shelves with plastic Hulu dolls in a row, and the tiki mug carved with the image of an angry Hawaiian god. Bob frowned at that one, turned it around so the face wasn't looking at him. There was another image on the back – the same god, smiling. Better.

"Nezha was a trickster, for sure. Never saw the point of that myself," said Bob to the shelf.

"We represent power in all forms."

"And how do you know this, exactly?" Bob turned around, arms folded.

"Tangun is here. He's looking for Nezha's power. He tried to lead me to it, but this is the whole point – I found it, but it didn't go to me. It went to Ted."

"So, get it back off him."

Benny slipped the baseball cap off her head. "That's the plan. Tangun's plan, anyway."

"His plan involves leaving Ted little notes that he can't even read?" Bob held up the folded paper again.

"Ted can't read it, but whatever is left of Nezha within him can. He should recognize the summons."

"Ted had no clue when he gave it to me. Said he'd ask you to read it."

Benny replaced her cap, pulling her ponytail around and playing with the end of it. Bob sighed.

"Why can't Tangun just grab him, anyway?"

Benny shrugged. "No use asking me. He likes to do things his way, I guess."

"Anyway," said Bob. "There's something else too. Listen up." He explained his visit to Mrs Winters' house and the strange fire. As he did, Benny just shook her head in confusion.

"So, it's like before?" she asked when Bob had finished. "In, what, oh-six?"

Bob nodded. "And '89, yeah. Kinda. Feels different this time. Before, it just happened, no warning, no build up. Now we've got signs. Like visions and omens and all that jazz."

"And the old lady?"

Bob rubbed his chin. "She was just caught up in, I don't know, the field of power." He moved his hands around in the air, like he was shaping a globe. "Her daughter is murdered by the Hang Wire Killer and she thinks she'll be reborn from earth and fire." He frowned. "But it didn't work. The house went up instead."

"So she had no idea?"

Bob shook his head. "I don't think so. She was just... going with the flow. She's safe now, at least. I took her to the hospital and they found some family to look after her. She doesn't remember a thing."

"Do you think it's connected with Nezha and the power he gave to Ted?"

"Could be," said Bob. He ran a hand through his hair, then he turned back to his little shelf, looked at the tiki mug a moment. He turned it around so the face of the angry god was looking out again. "It's waking up. The Thing Beneath. Maybe Nezha's power did that too."

"So what do we do?" asked Benny.

Bob turned around. "We do what we can. Tangun needs to stop shitting around and grab Ted. Once we've got the power out of him, maybe then we can figure this mess out."

"OK. Good," said Benny. "Good."

"You sure?"

"Oh yeah, yeah. No problem. Tangun can be a real pain in the posterior, but I'm sure he'll understand."

Bob smiled. "Tell him that if he has a problem, he'll have to take it up with the god of death himself."

# XVI
# SHARON MEADOW, SAN FRANCISCO
## TODAY

The lull before the rush, the calm before the proverbial storm. Rehearsals over, work done, preparations complete; as the early evening drew in, excitement slowly, quietly began to build among the performers. There were a couple of hours to kill before the gates opened. Time to chill, or try to, before the curtain rose.

Sara ducked around the side of the truck and waved at Kara, who checked left and right and then jogged across the open yard formed by the circle of trailers, across the blackened circle that demarcated the site of Stonefire's nightly blaze, to join her partner at the truck. Kara pressed her fingers against the corrugated metal of the truck's covered rear and gasped at the unexpected coldness of it. Sara shushed her and pulled her partner into the shadows between this vehicle and the next.

"What's he doing now?"

Sara swung out from the truck to look. Ahead was a narrow corridor formed between two rows of transport vehicles parked nose-to-tail. It was a staff-only shortcut from the back of the main circus site to the carnival, where the tops of the big dipper and the Ferris wheel and the angled struts and colored lights of a dozen other rides towered above the trucks, all dull and unmoving.

Joel, the carnival manager, had just entered the passage between the trucks, making his way toward his domain, presumably to get the machines up and running, lights on, ready for the first members of the public to come and get a ride before the main show in the Big Top.

Joel was a loner, unpopular with the rest of the circus. He didn't socialize; he never spoke. In fact, when Sara thought about it, the only times she saw him outside of show time he was either lurking in the shadows of the trucks, watching people – watching *them* – or getting into a fight with another member of the company, usually one of the Stonefire dancers.

There had been a lot of fights recently, since they'd arrived in San Francisco. There was something in the air, something... evil. Something connected with Joel. Sara and Kara had talked about it a lot, the way the creepy man seemed to be in the center of it all. Even the ringmaster, Mr Newhaven, seemed to bow to his employee. The girls had both seen them walk off into the shut-down carnival late at night. What they were doing in there, neither of them knew.

And then there was the missing steel cable. Everyone knew about it, even if Mr Newhaven hadn't said anything to the company. The police hadn't been called, despite what was going on in the city.

Which had also started, by Sara's reckoning, around the time the caravan had set up in Sharon Meadow.

If the police came, if the local news got whiff of it... it would be the end of Zanaar's caravan. The end of the road for everyone.

"Come on," said Kara.

The sky was darkening. As the pair emerged from the makeshift tunnel leading to the back of the carnival site, they paused. The machines were turned off, their lights dead, and in the gloom they looked old and dangerous, like they would fall apart if you touched them. Or like someone was watching, and if you stood too close to a ride it would fall over onto you, trapping you between cold metal and wet grass.

It was probably Joel. The carnival was large and had plenty of nooks, and Joel seemed like the kind of guy who liked to sit in nooks and watch.

"There!"

Sara followed Kara's finger, and saw Joel disappear around one of the rides. The pair hung back at the edge of the passageway, and a few seconds later Joel's legs appeared behind a trailer as he took a left turn and walked around the back of a carnival machine.

Maybe the cable hadn't been stolen. Maybe someone had sold it – to fund a drug habit? Joel seemed like the type, the way he acted, the way he swayed on his feet and stared, his mouth moving like he was talking to himself. Sometimes he'd laugh, and sometimes he'd nod, like his imaginary friend was talking back. If he was strung out on some shit then his paycheck from the circus wouldn't nearly be enough. He couldn't steal cash – Newhaven and the circus manager, Nadine, were pretty good at financial security, the takings collected by van each morning to be banked.

But Joel could have taken the cable and then sold it – the wire would have had good value as scrap metal, and while a full reel would have weighed a ton at least it was reasonably transportable.

Did he have any idea that the wire had been sold-on as a murder weapon? Hell, did he even watch the news or read the paper or browse the net? Did he even know about the killings? Sara bit her lower lip. She'd never seen him with a phone, unlike the others at the circus. In fact, Joel seemed so old fashioned, like a man out of time, that she couldn't really picture Joel using any kind of technology. The carnival was old school, all painted wood and enameled metal showing stars and planets, and the recurring motif – a comet arcing through the heavens – was an archaic symbol, like the art of a silent movie.

They should go to Newhaven and Nadine, Kara and Sara both knew that, but they were afraid, because when it came to the manager of the carnival, the ringmaster seemed not to have too much control. The big draws of the circus were Highwire, Stonefire, and the old fashioned mechanical carnival. Newhaven wasn't greedy but he knew how much the circus cost to run and he knew which of his employees he had not only to protect but to allow a little more free reign than others.

Joel had been a fucking weirdo on the whole tour. Las Vegas, Sacramento. But San Francisco seemed different. Highwire was new. So was the Stonefire bonfire – a ritual that kept the girls awake but didn't seem to bother anyone else, almost like the whole circus was hypnotized in their trailers. Malcolm and his dancers were weird as well, taking their Disney version of Celtic warriors and princesses just a little too seriously, right down to the lack of personal hygiene. Then the fights had started, and Joel had started talking to himself.

Maybe it was the sea air and the San Francisco weather – baking hot with blue skies followed by freezing fog and gloom. But Kara had another theory. It was to do with *space*.

San Francisco was the first city in their tour in which the circus had really been able to spread out, the city offering them the prestigious patch of land in Golden Gate Park. For the first time, Joel had been able not only to get *all* of his fairground rides out of their trailers and unfolded from their trucks, but he'd been able to spread them out. The carnival was huge and drew people like a magnet, the wide-open spaces soon packed shoulder-to-shoulder.

It was nearly dark now, and still the carnival was dead, a collection of dull machines rusting in a field. In the gathering gloom their brightly colored designs and decorations looked washed out, faded, and very, very old. Sara wondered if the machines really were vintage. In the dying light, with their illuminations off, they were creepy as hell. Of Joel, there was no sign.

"Come on," said Kara. She began to walk away, but stopped as Sara caught her arm. "What?"

Sara indicated the way ahead with a nod. "What are we going to do exactly?"

"We're going to see what Joel is doing," said Kara. She put one hand on a hip. "Remember?"

"Yeah, and then what?"

"Fine," said Kara. "Go back to the trailer. I'll see you at show time." She turned and walked away.

Sara had a point, and she knew Kara knew it too. What were they going to do, exactly? Highwire seemed to have got the message, but there was no sign of him yet. They'd discussed it – the acrobat seemed to be different from the rest of the circus, separate. They didn't know him – nobody did really – but they felt he could be trusted. Maybe he'd know what to do.

Sara pulled back, watching her partner stalk off across the grass, then swore under her breath and went to follow.

Then Kara fell over. She lay on the ground, shaking.

"Kara?" Sara drew a sharp breath. "Kara! Oh my God, Kara!"

She ran over to her friend and dropped to her knees. Kara's eyes were rolled back into her head. Sara grabbed her shoulders, trying to hold her partner as she had some kind of seizure.

Kara twisted on the ground, foam at her lips, her eyelids fluttering.

"I... I... Belenus I... I... I... Belenus I..." she said, over and over. She bit her tongue and soon her mouth was filled with blood, but she kept talking, repeating the phrase that meant nothing to Sara.

Sara's heart thundered. She felt helpless – she couldn't do anything. She didn't know first aid. She'd never seen a seizure before, hadn't even known that Kara was epileptic. She had no clue. Sara stood, hands clenched, fingers intertwined, knuckles white as she rolled them, watching her friend.

Then the seizure stopped, the violent shaking and twitching fading until Kara was still. She rolled onto her side, her eyelids fluttering again and then closing, and she gave a sigh, but showed no sign of regaining consciousness.

Sara had to get help. Her racing heart had slowed and now she felt the rising tide of panic. Help. Get help. *Now.*

"Well, isn't this an arresting situation."

Sara screamed in surprise and spun around. Joel stood behind her in the shadows, one thumb hanging from a belt loop, the fingers of his other hand fumbling inside the fob pocket on the front of his waistcoat. His stovepipe hat made his silhouette look too tall, and despite the dark, his bad eye almost seemed to glow white.

"Kara's had a fit," Sara managed to say, her breath regained. She paused. Joel didn't move, didn't speak. "We need to get help."

Then Joel finally came to life. He walked around to Kara, circling the unconscious girl slowly, until he was standing opposite Sara. Behind him, across the carnival paddock, stood the dark carousel. He stared down at the body, apparently unconcerned and unwilling to lend assistance.

Sara stepped forward. "Fuck, Joel, I'm going to get–"

There was a cranking sound from somewhere ahead. Sara jumped, her attention drawn to the machines arrayed behind the carnival master.

The fairground attractions on either side of paddock had lit up faintly, strings of bare colored bulbs that outlined their frames buzzing softly in the evening air. The light flickered rhythmically, almost like a heartbeat. Like *her* heartbeat, Sara realized with growing fear. She held her breath, willing the lights to stop, but they didn't. Still Joel stood, silent, unmoving.

Sara stumbled backward, fear coursing through her body. The cranking sound increased in volume, increased in tempo, as all around the lights on the carnival rides glowed brighter and brighter, but not in synch. The light spread out from the stall of wooden clown heads to her left – heads that were all facing her, their mouths gaping – and grew in brightness as it swept around clockwise. Sara turned her head and watched as the rides on her right lit up, the wave of bright white, red and yellow sweeping back around, meeting in the middle with the light from the other side.

Sara felt her heart in her chest. The lights of the carnival pulsed to the same beat.

In the center of the field, the carousel lit up in a blaze of Victorian glory. The giant machine was an orgy of elaborately carved and painted wood: horses, unicorns, and winged versions of each; dragons, centaurs, and other things: things with tentacles and heads like starfish, undersea monstrosities that scared adults but that children loved. At the center, crouched above the steam-powered organ, sat the carved wooden form of a monkey, its eyes cut red crystals that shone as bright as the bulbs that ran along the edge of the carousel's revolving platform.

Sara fell onto the damp grass on her backside, jarring her elbows as she instinctively put her arms out behind her. She tried to push herself backward, away from the nightmare in front of her, but she felt like she weighed a thousand tons, each movement a titanic effort.

Joel spread his arms out wide as he stood behind Kara's unconscious form, then he turned to face the carousel. He tilted his head back and began to chant. Sara couldn't understand the language. All she felt was fear, cold and pure. Then her attention was taken away from Joel by something else.

The fairground was *moving*. Joel bobbed his arms up and down, the rise and fall of a conductor directing his orchestra. As he swayed here and there, up and down, so the machines around him responded. The big dipper behind the carousel rocked, the movements of the sailing ship that swung like a giant pendulum matching the side-to-side motion of Joel. The lights on the Ferris wheel looming over everything on the other side flickered and buzzed, and the wheel rolled in either direction, all in time to Joel.

Sara's eyes crawled around the ring of machines in horror. Each of them moved, twitching in time with one another and in time with their master. The lights were on full now, and they pulsed, almost organically, as power ebbed and flowed, ebbed and flowed. Far and near, far and near, as Joel swayed and swung his arms from side to side, side to side. In front of Joel, the carousel puffed like a steam train as the engine at its heart sprang to life, and it began to rotate, slowly at first, spinning about its axis as it should. In the machine's hub was a pipe organ, surrounded by mechanical puppets and automaton musicians, and on top sat the monkey, as large as a small child. It's red eyes were glowing, and the organ started to play, a drone, a tuneless wailing, a whistling of pipes that sank into Sara's bones, the sound of stars falling, the sound of the endless cold of space.

Joel swayed and the carousel began to accelerate, faster and faster, around and around. Sara watched the painted horses and elephants and monsters whip around, their forms and lights blurring in the misty evening air. The discordant drones of the pipe organ formed a familiar fairground melody. But it was slow, somehow, and out of tune. As Sara watched she felt her heart beat and her head thump, in time to the music, in time to the pulsing lights.

The pipe organ melody turned into a single shrill blast, and the carousel suddenly braked. Sparks flared from the undercarriage beneath the painted wooden skirt.

In the center of the merry-go-round, between the monsters that orbited the hub, the automatons on the pipe organ began to move. Maybe they were supposed to, maybe the carved wooden animals spinning around just gave the whole thing that zoetrope flicker. Sara blinked. She couldn't take her eyes off it. She pushed back, felt the air leave her lungs, felt the sweat on her brow.

The automatons had turned, and they were all looking at her. In the center of it all, the monkey sat, and now it was pointing at her, its eyes burning red.

Sara screamed and Joel turned around, his gray-white eye now glowing red.

He smiled, and Sara screamed again.

# WAKE UP

# INTERLUDE
# SPEARMAN, TEXAS
# 1935

Connie opened the door eventually, wiping her hands on her apron as she did. The damned man at the door had kept knocking and knocking and knocking, ignoring Connie as she'd called out from the kitchen that she'd just be a minute, that he should hang on a moment, that he should damn well stop banging on the goddamn door. She was in no mood for callers, not now. The early evening was hot and bothersome, and her husband Lawrence hadn't got back from town yet.

It was their last chance, too. Their farm was dead, the ground nothing but a dry powder, just like the ground all over the whole county, if not the whole state. If Lawrence hadn't managed to sweet talk the bank manager in Spearman for an extension... well, that was it. They'd have to move, head west, where maybe the land maybe wasn't a dust bowl, where maybe they could salvage something out of what their lives had become.

Some hope. The town was nearly empty. Connie knew that Lawrence didn't stand a chance, but they had to try, didn't they? They had to try. And after trying they could load up the truck and they could drive west, with everyone else. And while Connie's heart would ache, she knew that as they drove she and Lawrence would talk about the future with purpose, optimism, even if neither of them knew what that future would bring, where the road would lead them. But they had to. What was the point of it all if they didn't? So they'd load up the truck with the little that was left: clothes in bundles tied with rope, the dresser in the parlor that had been in Connie's family for two generations, as many farm tools as would fit on the truck. They wouldn't farm again, never again. But metal tools had to have value.

They'd leave their house to the dust, leave their farm to be buried by another storm.

Connie opened the door, taking a deep breath, ready to send the caller packing. There was no business to be had, not in Spearman anymore. They'd had callers before, quacks selling snake oil or encyclopedias. Connie knew they were as desperate as she, but that didn't stop her wishing them away, like the dust and heat and the drought.

The man was dressed nicely in a dusty black suit, old and rumpled but well-fitted. Connie pulled her head back in surprise as the man smiled on her porch and took off his hat, an old-fashioned stovepipe. His black hair was unruly and one eye was pale and gray, near to white. He bowed and pushed a book toward her.

Connie eyed the small tome, bound in soft scarlet leather, and then looked over the man's shoulder. In the dirt road that led away from the farmhouse sat a huge car, looking more like a beached yacht than an automobile. It was red, darker than the book in the man's hand, more like the blood that poured from the neck of a slaughtered pig. White-walled tires caught the last of the day's sun and glowed like blazing comets.

"Pardon me, ma'am," said the man with the smile and the book, "but I *know* you have been saved. I can tell these matters, and believe me when I say I am not here to preach the Lord's word at you, no ma'am, not at all."

Connie frowned, hands twisting her apron in front of her. The man didn't stop smiling.

Beyond the man's car, toward the town, the sunset sky was scarred with something large and brown, as light as the powdery ground on which the farmhouse sat. Connie frowned and looked at the book being held toward her.

"For you see," the man said, "the word of the Lord is His most precious gift, one every man, woman, and child on his good green earth must hold dear to the heart."

Connie laughed. It felt like a weight had been lifted from her shoulders. Her hands dropped the apron, and she leaned on the doorframe.

"Don't know if maybe it's you who needs your eyes opening, but take a look around. There's not much good and green about this earth here."

The man chuckled and hefted the Bible in his hand, like he was weighing it to see how far it would fly with a really good pitch.

"The Lord tests us in many ways. But he knows our will and our verisimilitude, and–"

"He knows our what now?"

The man smiled again. "Ma'am, if you'd allow me to sit awhile and tell you about this remarkable book and why–"

"We already got a Bible," said Connie with a sniff. Time was a-wasting. Lawrence would be back soon and damned if it didn't look like there was another dust storm on the way. A mighty big one too, size of the cloud speeding along the horizon. She only hoped that Lawrence was ahead of it in the truck, because that vehicle was their one means of escape from this hell on Earth.

"Oh, of course, every home is the home of the word of the Lord," said the man with surprise so fake Connie had to laugh. The man joined her, waving the red book in hand. "Now, there's no good to an honest Bible seller like myself traveling the length and breadth of the land just to pile the unsuspecting with unnecessaries!"

The man's smile froze and then dropped, and his eyes narrowed and he looked at Connie down the length of his nose and Connie was suddenly afraid and wanted Lawrence there, right now.

"But this book is a might lighter than the family tome you have in the dresser in the parlor," said the man, pointing past Connie with the book, into the house, although the inside of the house was dark and she knew it was impossible to see in, not from the porch. And the parlor was a room away. "And there's an awful lot of your worldly goods to pile into the back of the farm truck. It's a long way to California, Connie. A long way."

Connie wrapped her arms around herself and shivered despite the warmth of the evening. She took a step back into the house. Behind the man, the sky was getting darker and darker.

She ignored the way the man knew her name, knew about Lawrence and the truck and the fact they were going to be leaving soon. Ignored how he knew she kept the huge family Bible in the dresser in the parlor. Heck, anyone could guess such things, and she and her husband were known in town, their names hardly secret. The man was another seller of snake oil, and a smooth one at that.

Instead, she nodded at the man's car. "You might want to get your shiny automobile to cover. Looks like there's a storm coming."

She closed the door.

Joel sat in his car and turned the coin between his fingers. The coin was cold, and as he flipped it Joel could feel it move – not a pull, or a tug, or anything quite so strong, and he knew that if he let it go it would merely fall to the mat between his feet. But as he turned the coin he felt it had a tendency – an *inclination* – to lean away from him, toward the farmhouse. As he turned it, the coin caught the light and seemed to glow gold in the low sun.

"I follow the light," said Joel, "and the light it shines on thee."

Then the dust storm arrived and darkness descended, and just for a second the inside of the car was lit in gold and white by the coin turning in Joel's fingers.

Black Sunday, they would call it later. The dust storm crossed the southern United States like a tidal wave, lifting three hundred million tons of dirt from the Great Plains and depositing it on cities, towns, villages, farms, houses, people, animals. The town of Spearman was directly in its path, and little would be left afterward.

And perhaps the dust cloud, an apocalyptic fury two hundred feet high and two hundred miles wide, perhaps it pushed down on the farmstead with a force that wasn't quite natural, like there was something in the world that didn't want anything found afterward, especially not by the man sitting inside the red automobile, the dust and sand piling high against its closed windows.

Especially not by the man inside with the gold coin turning, turning, turning in his fingers, as cold as a thing out of space, as bright as a comet in the morning sky.

The sky was clear the next morning, blue and cold. Joel pushed at the car door once, twice; as it opened, finally, light brown dirt, the color of sand, the color of the sun at daybreak, leaked into the car, pouring in around his ankles, filling the well beneath the wheel. Joel pushed the door open to its full extent, and then lifted his boots and planted them firmly in the loose dirt piled high outside.

The landscape had changed, just like that. The road leading to the farm had been dirt itself but it was a road, with scrabbly and desiccated trees dotted along its length. There had been more trees in front of the house, which, while rundown and tired, still showed its proud workmanship across two broad floors.

The man and his car now stood in the middle of a desert, dirt in high dunes, the morning breeze scuffing dust from their summits like it was the middle of the Sahara.

Where the farmhouse had once stood was now a pile of rubble, twisted and broken, abused as though a tornado had hit it. It was half buried in the dirt. Within days, maybe hours, little of the house would remain above the surface. The Dust Bowl would claim another victim, and nobody would notice. Connie and Lawrence would not be seen again.

Joel slipped the coin into his pocket. Immediately his fingers hurt. He turned and looked to the west. His future lay in that direction, he knew, but he also knew there was much to be done and that he wouldn't be free of the light, not yet. The light was helping as best it could, but his road was long.

He walked around to the back of the car, pushed the dirt off the spare wheel attached to the rear in one sweep of his forearm, and opened the compartment. The trunk was large and empty save for a battered suitcase in brown leather and a long wooden pole.

Joel grabbed the end of the pole and pulled the shovel out from where it lay diagonally across the trunk.

"I follow the light," he said to no one at all, "and the light it shines on thee."

Shovel over one shoulder, Joel walked toward the ruins of the farmhouse, the coin cold in his pocket and pulling, pulling, pulling toward what lay buried within.

## XVII
# SHARON MEADOW, SAN FRANCISCO
## TODAY

Curtain up. Showtime. The circus was filling up. Ticket sales were brisk. Stonefire had lit their bonfire, and Sharon Meadow was filled with laughter, screams of delight, and all the sounds of the fair.

Nadine tore herself from the doorway of the Winnebago. Showtime, and Jack was still missing. He often disappeared. He never said where he went or what he did, but then again Nadine never asked. They were in a great location in Golden Gate Park (she still couldn't quite believe they'd scored the permit), and she assumed Jack just liked to take himself off for a wander, clear his head from the controlled chaos of The Magical Zanaar's Traveling Caravan of Arts and Sciences.

But this time, he was taking it to the very limit. The gates opened at seven. The show in the Big Top started at eight sharp with a crack of the ringmaster's whip. The stands would be packed. Already people were milling around, lining up at the four entrances of the main tent, waiting to be ushered inside for an evening of old fashioned circus entertainment.

"Fuck," she said. She left the Winnebago just as David the Harlequin came jogging over.

"There's a problem," he said. He pointed back over his shoulder at the Big Top.

"Tell me about it. Where the fuck is Jack?"

"Jack's gone too?"

Nadine pursed her lips. "What do you mean?"

"You'd better come with me."

David led her through the backstage area behind the Big Top. It sounded busy out front. Full house.

Inside the main arena, the lighting crew was fussing over settings, spotting the floor and walls of the tent in alternating colors as they made checks to the programmed sequence. At the back of the tent the AV guy messed with the mixing desk. In the center of the ring, Jan and John were having an argument. As Nadine approached, David at her side, the couple stopped. John pulled the spandex hood off his head and ran his hand through his hair.

"What the hell is going on? Where's Jack's wonder boy?"

Nadine felt her stomach turn. "Highwire hasn't shown up?"

"Nope. His trailer is empty. Nobody has seen him. This whole mystery man shtick is such bullshit. It's nearly show time and we can't even call him."

"Fuck," said Nadine. She stamped her foot, turned around, and scanned the arena like she was expecting Jack – and now Highwire – to be lurking in the shadows. She turned to David. "Can you take over as ringmaster tonight?"

David's eyes widened.

"You know how the show goes. Do your own thing as the Harlequin. All you have to do is introduce the acts."

"Well, OK–"

"Jack's not here either?" asked Jan. She and her husband exchanged a look.

"Ah, no," said Nadine. "Look, can you guys do your old act? The one without Highwire."

John smiled. "It'll be a fucking pleasure, believe me."

"John, please," said Jan. John sighed, hands on hips.

"But what about the opener? The ringmaster's intro piece."

The show's opening was a display by Sara and Kara. They ran through the stalls, dancing with streaming ribbons, before doing a short routine in the middle of the arena. At the climax, as the music swelled and trumpets blared, the Magical Zanaar appeared in a puff of pyrotechnics. The crowd loved it. Except...

"We can still do that with David," said Nadine. She turned to the Harlequin, and he nodded.

"Not with Sara and Kara you can't," said John. He seemed a little too satisfied to be breaking yet another piece of bad news.

"What the fuck?" Nadine said, hands in the air. "Who else is missing?"

"The show will go on, my dear."

Nadine, David, Jan and John turned as Jack walked in. He was dressed in the ringmaster's outfit, sequined red coat, sequined blue top hat glittering.

"Where the hell have you been?"

Jack smiled, and bowed with a flourish.

"OK. Fine. Whatever," she said. They could talk about it later. They were already late letting people in. "Sara and Kara are AWOL, so we'll need a new opening." She turned to David. "Clowns, fire-eaters, jumping around. Can you guys do that?"

David nodded. "I'm on it," he said, before leaving the tent at a jog.

Nadine turned back to Jack. His eyes seemed glazed, his smile fixed. What the hell had gotten into him?

"Jack, come on," she said. Jack blinked, bowed.

"The show must go on," he said, and he stalked off to the shadows, from where he would make his entrance.

Nadine shook her head. She looked at Jan and John, but they just shrugged.

It was going to be a strange night.

# XVIII
# SAN FRANCISCO
## TODAY

The bedside clock read a quarter after three. The big red digits were supposed to fade at night but in the pitch dark they bored into Alison's eyes like a searchlight.

She raised her head to get a better focus on the clock. She'd been dreaming, of animals sleeping and of San Francisco being hit by another colossal earthquake. That was something at the backs of all the city residents' minds, she supposed, but something you just dealt with as you got on with day-to-day living. But as she looked at the clock and rubbed her forehead, she couldn't help but feel like the building was going to begin shaking at any moment.

She shuffled around under the quilt, and turned over.

She was alone in the bed. Ted was gone, the quilt folded back on his side and the bottom sheet still rumpled with his impression.

Alison instinctively reached over and ran a hand over the sheets. They were cold. He hadn't just gotten up to go to the bathroom or get a glass of water. His side of the bed had been unoccupied for a while.

"Ted?"

Eyes adjusting to the dark, tinted a dull red by the bedside clock, Alison saw the door of the bedroom was ajar. Beyond, the rest of the apartment was a little brighter with the light of the city coming in from the big windows.

The apartment was silent. Alison swung her legs over the edge of the bed.

"Ted?"

Nothing. Alison's eyes were wide. In the semi-darkness it felt like her hearing was amplified a hundred times, the air itself making a rushing sound that seemed to reach a peak before she realized it was the sound of her own circulation in her ears.

She didn't want to turn the light on. She had no idea why – perhaps part of her wished Ted really had just gone to the bathroom and was going to slip quietly back into the room.

She shook her head. Ridiculous. She reached for the bedside light and turned it on.

In the main room Alison flicked on the lights – four switches, all at once – and squinted as she cast an eye around the apartment. The open plan lounge-diner-kitchen was empty.

"Ted?"

She knew he wasn't there, but gave it one more shot. He wasn't in the bathroom. Nothing looked amiss or out of place. Her bag was still on the table. The laptop was closed, as was the front door.

Where was Ted? Was his head injury – the seemingly innocuous bump at the restaurant something far more serious, a hematoma or swelling on the brain – making him, what, sleep walk? Had it caused amnesia? Or, what about those fugue states, like some forms of epilepsy could cause, where a person was walking and talking but unaware of what was going on and unable to remember it all later?

Or maybe he was fine, and had just gone for a walk around the block, get some air. She knew his sleeping patterns were a mess.

She darted back into the bedroom, gathered up her clothes. He couldn't have been gone long; she would have noticed earlier, surely. Maybe he wasn't far. Maybe she could find him.

# XIX
# SAN FRANCISCO
## TODAY

There is a wind up on the rooftop. Stiff, coming off the water and weaving through the streets of San Francisco, bringing with it the first fingers of fog, and other things as well. Highwire breathes it in, dissects the scents: the smell of the sea, of the sleeping seals down on Pier 39, of mossy rocks around the edge of Alcatraz. As the air is pushed through the city it collects more notes: an echo of a thousand restaurants serving cuisines from a hundred different countries, rotting garbage in a dumpster in an alley, the unmistakable tang of stale alcohol and stomach fluids from the doors of those bars and clubs still open at this hour. The cheaper the cover, the stronger the smell.

San Francisco is a big city, a living organism. Even at the dead hours of early morning, when its rhythms are at their lowest ebb, there is power moving, flowing. And not just in the buzz of a power line or the hum of a streetlight. Energy is all around, in the air, transforming, moving.

But there's something else too. Something sharp, alive. Electric. Highwire can taste vinegar, rotting lemons. A tingle on the back of the throat. The slightest pressure against the eardrums, like there is machinery nearby, *beneath*, something tunneling, something stirring.

Something moving. Alive, electric. Something not part of the city, older than it.

Something different. *Wrong.*

This is not the killer, Highwire doesn't think so. There are two evils in San Francisco. One stalks the night and strings his victims up with steel cable. The other sleeps below. Whether the two are connected, Highwire cannot say, but, yes, he suspects. Two evils, feeding each other.

The killer is still at work. He must be found. Highwire turns, closes his eyes, trusts his senses. He is here for one reason, and one reason only.

To stop him.

He takes a breath and stands tall, ready to run, ready to jump, and –

"Highwire!"

He drops to his knees, turns on the ground. There is a man in front of him who wasn't there a second ago. Highwire didn't hear him arrive, which is impossible as the man is huge, wearing elaborate armor, big, articulated metal plates over a puffy, quilted robe that flares out at the sides, giving him a triangular shape. The outfit looks more decorative than functional, and when the man moves the plates clack together like a sack of tin cans.

He is wearing a helmet that flares out at the back in a protective rim so wide it stretches nearly shoulder to shoulder. The helmet is gold, the flared edge embossed to make it look like woven hair. The front of the helmet is a mask molded into a laughing face, with gaps for the eyes, the mouth, breathing holes for the nose. The whole ensemble is that of an ancient Asian warrior, similar to a classical Samurai but not the same. The suit is from another culture.

The man laughs and Highwire realizes he can see a face through the gaps in the mask. It looks like the face of a young Asian woman, but the voice is deep and masculine.

"What do you want?" asks Highwire.

"I am Tangun the Founder," says the warrior, "and we must talk."

Highwire frowns, peers closer at the face behind the mask, at the mouth which doesn't seem to move when the voice speaks. He wonders whether the voice is coming from the helmet itself, somehow, rather than the occupant of the armor.

"I don't have time to talk," he says. The Hang Wire Killer is out there, on the loose, in the city. Soon he will kill again. Highwire ignores the fact that Tangun appeared from nowhere, that he knows his name. It occurs to him that perhaps he is not alone in his search for the killer, that there are others in the city and that this Tangun is one of them, but time is short.

Tangun laughs, his – her? – helmet and the metal parts of the armor catching what light there is on the roof and shining like they're made of bright plastic.

Then the wind shifts to blow from behind Tangun, strong enough to force Highwire to adjust his crouch. The wind is cold and brings more fog.

When Highwire looks at Tangun again the golden mask no longer reflects mirth. The features are twisted into an expression of anger, the heavy eyebrows angled downward, the thick lips curled back into a snarl. Tangun's wrath, Highwire thinks.

The warrior steps forward, clanking like a junkyard, and looks down at Highwire still crouched on the rooftop. Highwire looks up into the mask, the face of an angry god from mythology.

"You have the time, Highwire," he says. The voice is deep and resonates with a metallic tang. Highwire says nothing as he stands.

Tangun steps back and now the mask is a blank expression, a face without emotion, humor, anger.

"You will not find him tonight, friend," Tangun says. "But I can help you, if you help me."

"Help you?"

"You possess something I seek, friend," says Tangun. "Something that does not belong with you. Something we need. If you give it to us, I can help you in your quest."

"We?"

Tangun inclines the great helmet. "We are legion. We used to walk among you, but now we do not. There is another in the city who has chosen to live among you."

"Tell me more," says Highwire.

The warrior steps closer. Highwire can see more detail in the armor now. The gold plates are carved and embossed with geometric designs. The robe beneath, like a kind of quilted kimono, is white and embroidered with plants and animals: dragons, horses, sea creatures, snarling dogs.

"What are you looking for?" Highwire asks. "Because I don't have anything."

The mask is smiling now. Behind it, Highwire can see the real human face blink through the slots. The woman inside the suit seems barely more than a teenager. Highwire steps closer, peers into the mask. "And what are you the founder of, exactly?"

Tangun laughs, the mask changing in the blink of an eye. "It is as I expected," he says. "You do not know what you possess."

Tangun talks in riddles. Highwire has no time for this. Not with the killer out there. He shakes his head.

"If I had a clue who you are and what you want, believe me, I'd be more helpful. But I have work to do." Highwire turns on his heel, ready to run, to continue the search.

"Ah," says Tangun and his hand darts forward. Tangun moves with ease, his armor suddenly silent, as he grabs Highwire's arm.

"You do not know what you possess, fool!" The golden mask is angry again. "You do not understand it, cannot control it!"

Highwire pulls at his arm, but Tangun's gauntlet is firm.

"I'm trying to catch a killer!" he says. "I don't have time for riddles or games."

Tangun drops his hand, and the wind picks up again. It feels like the cold breeze is coming from Tangun himself, from behind the mask, the air flowing out through the gaps.

Tangun raises his arm, and points at Highwire, and gives a command.

"Sleep."

Highwire collapses at the feet of Tangun the Founder.

# XX
# SAN FRANCISCO
## TODAY

The horizon was a glowing belt of orange by the time Alison sat on the park bench. It was dawn. Her search had been fruitless.

She'd completed several orbits of Ted's immediate neighborhood, up and down the same streets, spreading out in a slow spiral. Maybe it wasn't the most efficient search pattern. Who knew.

The streets had been nearly empty, taxis and police cruisers the most frequent traffic. Now, as the sun rose, there was a smattering of cars. Some people on bikes and some other hardy, dedicated souls out jogging. Jesus, some people really did get up at this hour to jog. Alison had considered this to be some kind of urban legend.

She sank back on the bench. She was tired, exhausted, and cold, and alone. She'd been wandering the streets on her own, at night, which was neither safe nor sensible but had seemed like the only option at the time. She'd held it together as she focused on the search, but now? Shit. Ted could be lying in a gutter somewhere. She could have walked right past him.

Oh, Jesus. She should have called the police.

Benny. She'd call Benny. They could search again, and then they could go to the police. She could rely on Benny, and so could Ted.

Checking her watch, Alison headed back to Ted's apartment building, got into her car, and drove into the city center.

It was getting busy in town, the traffic building into the early morning rush. The clock on the dash said it was 6.10, but as she approached Benny's building she could see lights on in what she thought was the right apartment. She parked across the street, tried calling Benny's cell, but there was no answer. Although, as she watched the window, she thought she could see the shadow of someone moving around. She killed the car and crossed to the building.

"Oh, hey, Alison," Benny said over the intercom as she buzzed her up. When she opened the door to her apartment Alison was surprised to find her fully dressed, baseball cap and all. She looked fresh-faced and ready for the day. She held the door open for her, and Alison slipped into the apartment.

"I'm sorry to come by so early," she said. "I tried your phone, but nobody answered."

"Oh," said Benny with a shrug. "Battery must be dead again. Sorry!" She headed over toward the kitchen. Like Ted's apartment, Benny's place was open plan, but much, much smaller, more a studio than an apartment. Inner-city living was expensive, as Alison well knew.

"Coffee?" Benny called over her shoulder. "You look like you could use some."

Alison sighed and followed Benny. "That'd be great, thanks. You're up early."

Benny smiled as she filled the coffee grinder with a fresh batch of beans. "Oh, yeah, y'know. Habit, right? Hey, you OK?"

Alison's shoulders slumped, and she shook her head. She dropped onto one of the stools on the other side of the counter from Benny, ran a hand through her hair.

"I need you to help me find Ted."

Benny paused, one hand on the coffee grinder. "Ted? Where is he?"

Alison shook her head. "That's just it. He's gone. I don't know where. He left sometime during the night. Jesus, what do I do? Call the police? What?"

Benny rubbed her chin. "You think he's sleepwalking or something?"

Alison shrugged. "Maybe? Is that crazy? I don't know what to think," she said. "I'm worried. I think he hit his head pretty bad at the restaurant." She felt her face grow hot. "He might be hurt. I don't know what to do."

"Hey, hey," said Benny. She seemed to want to comfort Alison, but after a pause she quickly returned her attention to making the coffee. Alison rubbed her eyes, and was grateful for the cup when it arrived. The two drank in silence for a moment.

"So what do we do?" asked Alison.

Benny folded her arms, coffee mug hanging from one hand. "You tried his cell?"

"He didn't take it. He didn't take anything."

Benny nodded. "OK. You checked out the office? Maybe he headed there – either in his sleep, or because he wanted to get a head start on a project. He's been out a day or so. Maybe he just wanted to put in some extra hours."

"And not leave a note, or call?"

Benny shrugged. "He's pulled all-nighters before. Dude's a machine when he needs to be."

Alison drained her cup. The coffee was hot and bitter and wonderful, and she felt a lot better.

Benny's idea seemed like a stretch, but Ted was a good worker, and being sick had really thrown a spanner in the works for him. Knowing him as well as she did, she knew he'd want to catch up as soon as possible. So maybe he'd gone to the office and hadn't wanted to wake her. Maybe he'd meant to call but was deep in the work and had lost track of time.

"Come on, let's go," said Benny. She set her nearly untouched coffee down on the bench. "You got your car?"

Alison nodded. She slid off the stool and moved to the door, Benny on her heels. As they stepped into the hallway, Benny clicked her fingers. Alison turned, expectant.

Benny nodded. "Meet you downstairs. I forgot something." She ducked back into the apartment.

Alison nodded to the empty hallway and headed toward the elevator.

Benny clicked the front door shut. She moved closer to the wood, listening as Alison walked away. Satisfied, she slipped the cellphone out of her pocket and flipped it open. She walked towards her bedroom, separated from the rest of the studio by a floor-to-ceiling divider, and selected a single number from the speed dial.

Lying on top of Benny's bed, Ted was out cold, his chest rising and falling in a gentle rhythm.

Benny waited as she watched Ted's comatose form. Finally, the line clicked and a voice spoke into her ear.

"Dude," said Benny, "we need to talk."

# INTERLUDE
# POTOSI MOUNTAIN, NEVADA
## 1942

Joel wondered if he could fry an egg on the hood of the car. It was hot enough. Had to be. He'd been sitting in the car, which was on a dirt road out in the desert, for two days now. The road was straight. Six hours behind him was Phoenix. What lay ahead, Joel didn't rightly know. He didn't need or care to. The light had shone and shown him the way. Had led him here, to the road through the desert, skirting the western side of Potosí Mountain.

The mountain was bare brown, like the road, like the ground, like the desert that stretched from horizon to horizon. The mountain wasn't high enough for snow, at least not at this time of the year. Joel watched it through the shimmering air. Waiting patiently. It was hot outside – hot enough to fry an egg, maybe – but inside the car it was cold. On the dashboard sat the Double Eagle coin, the leather of the dash cracked from the cold that radiated from the disc of gold and dusted with frost.

The red hood of the car stretched out in front of the windshield. Joel tore his eyes from the mountain to the hood, and back again. Hot enough to fry an egg. He tried to remember the last time he'd eaten. The last time he'd felt hunger. The last time he'd felt anything, anything at all.

He laughed, long and hard, until his eyes were filled with tears and he could hear nothing but his own barking voice echo in the metal box in which he sat, in the middle of the desert.

Then the airplane came in, too fast, too low, its wings tilting this way and that, before it hit Potosi Mountain and vanished into a ball of fire.

It had been a bitch to get to the crash site. Joel had found a service road, maybe used by the parks service, maybe the rangers. Maybe those who just liked to get away from it all. The road headed toward the mountain, but then began to curve away, so Joel had stopped the car, surveyed the land, and turned off to plough his own course. The desert dirt was dry and hard-packed but littered with stones and boulders he had to weave around, and the occasional crack a little wider than he wanted to risk driving over.

So he made straight for the mountain as best he could. The red car bounced and bounced, the springs creaking, the panels rattling. He realized the car was old and that if his search went on any longer he'd need to replace it.

The car bounced but all the while the coin remained in place. It caught the sun that streamed in through the curved sides of the windshield, amplified like the glass was a lens. The coin glittered and sparkled and shone. Like it was excited. Like the coin *knew* it was close.

Joel could feel it too. He felt less hollow, less like a shadow dragged through time. He was a puppet, he knew that, but now it felt like his master had pulled the strings tight.

He was near, he was near.

He piloted the vehicle closer to the mountain, following the black plume of smoke that continued to roll into the featureless blue sky. It had been quite a plane – a passenger jetliner, not one of the big ones, but big enough. Joel didn't know where it had come from, or where it had been going. But he did have a fair idea of what it had been carrying.

At the mountain he had to leave the car and climb. It was hot outside. Very hot, too hot for most. But it didn't affect Joel. As he trudged up the side of the mountain, he took his black jacket off and rolled up his sleeves, but only out of habit, like he couldn't figure out how to keep himself occupied as he weaved his way up the slope. His hat he had left in the car, and now he wished he had kept it on. He might not have felt the heat at all, but the glare of the sun was annoying as all hell.

It took him two hours to reach the crash site. He came up over a rise, and there it was, nestled in the side of the mountain. The plane had done a belly flop straight into the flat side of a cliff, the wreckage sliding down into one of the mountain's many gullies. Despite the flash and smoke Joel had seen from the road, despite the force of the impact, the machine looked more or less intact. Maybe the pilot had wrested control in the final moments, pulling the nose up, trying desperately to clear the mountain, all too late. The plan's fuselage had split into five separate sections, each zigzagging over the terrain. The left wing was missing. The right was there, although in sections.

Smoke rose from the rear of the plane, where the tail had been. Joel looked around. The column of smoke he had been following from a distance was actually three columns up close. One, the lesser one, came from the tail section of plane. Two others came from over a ridge. The other wing, perhaps. A more substantial fire.

There was no movement. There was a lot of smaller debris – bits and pieces that looked important, though Joel couldn't tell what they were or from where in the plane they had come. There was some luggage, brown leather cases scattered, all securely fastened. There was clothing waving in the breeze, the case in which it had been packed either disintegrated entirely or buried under the plane.

Then he saw it. Blood. Quite a lot. Joel scanned the ground, recognizing an arm, a leg, another leg. There were bodies among the debris, a few intact but most a collection of torn limbs, white bones poking from shredded flesh.

And the blood. A lot of blood, thick, congealing in the desert heat.

There wasn't much time. Potosi Mountain was an inconvenient distance from most places, but the loss of an airplane would not have gone unnoticed. Already there would be people looking. They would have a fair idea of where it had come down, and it wouldn't be long before the precise spot was identified. The columns of smoke rising into the empty blue sky were a beacon that would be seen for miles and miles.

Joel stepped over the lip of the ridge, and slid down in the loose dirt and stones, jacket over his shoulder, sleeves rolled up, the coin infinitely heavy in his waistcoat pocket. He felt as though the coin were pulling him down the slope, but when he halted his slide, he stayed put, up to his ankles in loose soil. A little lower down, the late afternoon sun caught on the silver of the plane's side, casting a brilliant sliver of light across the crash site, bisecting with mathematical precision a long wooden crate half-buried in the ground.

Joel made his way to it. As he got closer the angle changed and the beam of light disappeared, but he knew he had found what he was looking for. Without much thought, the fingers of his hand found the coin in his pocket, and when they touched the cold metal he could hear the screaming in his head and the voice out of the oceanic depths of space calling his name.

The crate was six feet long, four feet wide, the same in height. Cargo. Heavy. The side was stamped with numbers and text that Joel didn't understand. Some kind of shipping number, destination codes perhaps.

Joel felt around the edge of the crate until he found a spot where the impact had loosened the nails. He lifted, the top of the crate creaking in protest. The nails holding the lid down nearest his fingers slid from their position easily enough.

The crate was filled with straw, but beneath the straw was something red and orange. It looked dull with age, but Joel recognized it at once. The screaming in his head was so loud he nearly screamed along with it.

Another journey complete. Another successful search. His quest was one step closer to completion.

# XXI
# SAN FRANCISCO
## TODAY

"Early bird, huh?"

Alison paused in the doorway. In front of her, Zane was walking back to his desk, coffee in hand. He stopped, waiting for a response.

Alison frowned. "Ah, hi, Zane."

Apparently satisfied, Zane returned to his desk.

The office was empty, save for Zane. It was early, not yet seven. Alison glanced at Ted's desk, but it was in its usual state of disarray, impossible to tell whether anyone had been working there or not.

She'd arrived alone. After she'd waited in her car for several minutes, Benny had called her cell, suggesting that Alison head to the office while she check out a couple of other places she'd just thought of that Ted might have wandered too. It made sense, and Alison was glad to have someone else helping her out.

Zane's head appeared from around his monitor. "You OK?"

Alison pointed to Ted's desk.

"Has Ted been in this morning?"

Zane lifted himself off his chair so he could survey the office over the top of his computer, like he hadn't realized he was the only one in. His eyes fell on Ted's desk, and he shook his head.

"No. But Benny was here earlier, when I arrived. Left to go get some photographs, I think. Sunrise over Chinatown or something."

Benny? That explained why she was up when she'd come by – perhaps she'd stopped back at her apartment on her way to grab her camera. But why hadn't she said anything? She'd had the feeling she was interrupting something when she'd visited.

Alison sighed, her shoulders dropping.

"What's up?" asked Zane. Alison walked over to Ted's desk and sat heavily in the chair, spinning it so she could talk to Zane.

"Ted's missing. He left the apartment early this morning, and I haven't been able to find him."

"Oh," said Zane, quietly, like he was trying to stay out of it, no doubt thinking she and Ted had had an argument and it was none of his business. "You try his–"

Alison shook her head. "He didn't take it."

"Oh," said Zane again.

Alison spun back around to the desk, looked at the phone a while. She willed it to ring, although she knew Ted wouldn't call his own desk. She took her cell out of her pocket, looking at the dark screen, waiting for Benny to call to say she'd found Ted.

She should call the police. She knew she should. But Ted had been gone, what, three hours? Four? The police would just tell her they had enough on their hands, what with a killer in the city.

Maybe Ted *had* been here early, and had left before Benny or Zane arrived. Maybe he was back in the apartment, wondering where *she* was.

She called the apartment, Ted's cell, but both went to voicemail.

"You know Bob was in here yesterday?"

Alison jumped at Zane's voice. "What?"

Zane's face leaned around his computer.

"That guy from the beach. He was wanting to talk to Benny, but Benny was home sick."

"Oh," said Alison, not entirely sure where this was going.

"You know he came up here without any shoes and not even wearing a shirt? I'm amazed the guy downstairs let him in."

Alison shrugged. "Well, that's his thing, isn't it? No point being one of the city's most famous tourist curios if you can't walk around with your shirt off."

Zane nodded and went back to work. His disinterest in Ted's welfare was beginning to piss Alison off.

The apartment. Back to Ted's, check it out, then call the police, then call Benny. It wasn't much, but it was a plan. And with the car she could cover more ground between the office and the apartment. Maybe Ted was walking back now and she could find him, give him a lift, give him a piece of her mind about leaving in the middle of the night.

Maybe she was overreacting. Maybe that's why Zane and Benny weren't that interested.

"Mazzy's back tomorrow, right?"

Zane nodded.

That settled it. She grabbed her bag, stood, pushed Ted's chair against the desk. "Ted comes in, get him to call me, OK?"

"Sure thing," said Zane, not looking up from his work.

Alison left the office, a game plan in mind.

She got into her car. The man watched her from across the street, where the awning of a small grocery store cast a shadow, deep and black, across the sidewalk. It was going to be another beautiful day in San Francisco.

He watched her pause by the car. She seemed to be composing herself, running her hands through her hair, taking a series of deep, deep breaths. Some people walked by, but nobody paid her any attention.

She wiped her eyes. He wasn't close enough to see, but he could guess she was crying. There was fear in her, and anger, and helplessness. He could feel it.

He could also feel the earth move under his feet. Tendrils of power, rippling like the tentacles of an octopus.

Soon. Soon.

She got into the car, found a gap in the traffic, and headed down the street.

He peeled out from the shadow, stepped into the day, watched her car disappear over the crest of the hill. He looked at the low sun, its light burning into his retinas. He focused on the pain, drank it in, *fed* on it, and then looked away.

It was unusual to be out so early. His domain was the night, the darkness. In the day, the city was different. He had to be careful.

The Hang Wire Killer didn't choose his victims; they were selected for him by the power, by the *thing that moved*. He was just shown the way, like he was following a light.

And the light, it shone for *her*.

The Hang Wire Killer walked off, down the street, planning his next act of murder.

# XXII
# SAN FRANCISCO
## TODAY

Ted opened his eyes. He rolled over, hit the floor, and was suddenly awake. He cried out in surprise and sat up, wincing as his fingers played over the back of his head. The floor was of polished wood and was as hard as stone. At least the bed was low and he hadn't fallen far.

He wasn't in his own bedroom. His own bedroom was carpeted in a neutral cream that he swore he'd tear up one day, revealing the original boards beneath. His bed was fairly high, two feet at least. He liked the height, had chosen it because it meant he could shove crap under the bed and not worry about it.

He wasn't in his apartment. Looking around, he saw the walls were bare brick, with various bits of plumbing, electrical fittings hanging onto it. Urban chic. The space was small, although the ceiling was high, with black iron girders crisscrossing the space. A studio loft.

The bedroom was a corner, and the third wall was formed by a folding Japanese screen. Ted stood up and gingerly walked around it.

He was at Benny's apartment. There were Asian prints on the walls, a couch and TV, and a kitchen. All open-plan, all very small. Perfect for single living in the heart of a hellishly expensive city. Ted wondered what kind of deal Benny was getting, because as small as the apartment was, it was fashionable. He didn't know much about her family, but Benny was barely out of her teens, and he guessed that she was perhaps getting a little much-needed financial aid from her parents back in LA.

More important, he wondered what the hell he was doing there. He looked down at himself and saw he was wearing his good brown jacket, the one he only dug out of the closet for those rare occasions when it was needed. A cream shirt and dark blue jeans finished the outfit. Ted blinked, trying to remember when he'd got changed and why, of all things, into this particular – unfamiliar – combo.

Then he spun around, hand waving at his ear. Someone was behind him, surely – had whispered in his ear, their fingers brushing away his hair.

There was nothing there but the bedroom screen. He was alone in the apartment. He called out – "Hello?" – just to be sure. There was no response. He could hear plumbing in operation somewhere else in the building. Cars outside.

He sat on the couch, carefully, like he thought it was going to explode. He'd gone to sleep in his apartment, and had woken up in Benny's.

Alison. *Shit*, what about Alison?

He glanced around, looking for a phone. Of course, Benny wouldn't have a phone. She'd dispensed with a landline long ago, had talked about it in the office. Ted had always thought that was a rash move. What if you were out of power? What if something happened to the network, to the cell towers?

No phone. No clock, either, that he could see, and he didn't wear a watch. Ted felt panic rise. What had happened? More missing time – but how much? What time was it? What *day* was it?

He fumbled around on the coffee table until he unearthed the TV remote. The TV would tell him the time. Twenty-four hour news. Clock in the corner. No problem.

The remote felt so very heavy. He brought it up to his eyes, but couldn't focus on the buttons, their labels swimming before him. He thought about how he needed to find out what the time was, so he could get back to Alison. He didn't think about where Benny was. He wondered if he should just go home, or go to the office, find Alison.

Find Alison.

Find Alison...

He dropped the remote and fell back on the couch. He looked around the apartment, trying to make his eyes work, but everything was a blur. The Asian prints on the walls, mostly just letters and decorative text, suddenly seemed to make sense. One picture wished for a happy and prosperous home. Another was a name, some king from Korean history. The same symbol as on that slip of paper from under his door.

Ted closed his eyes and the voice in his head said:

*Wake up, Ted.*

Highwire stands up from the couch. He looks at the sigil of Tangun the Founder, frowns, scans the apartment. He doesn't remember coming here, and he can see it is daylight now.

Daylight...

Highwire thinks a moment, formulating a plan. Yes, perhaps daylight is the answer. Time is short. He can sense it, can feel it.

Something moving.

Something moving... faster.

*Yes,* says the whisper in his ear. Highwire nods.

He sprints out of the apartment, back to the chase, leaving the door open behind him.

# XXIII
# SAN FRANCISCO
## TODAY

Bob walked into the Market and Geary branch of Apollo Coffee, ignored the looks that he got, walked straight to the back. He'd magicked up a shirt of white linen, which he thought went with the faded jeans. His feet were still bare. Some of the patrons in the busy cafe recognized him and whispered to their friends. Others, never having seen Bob before, were less impressed.

At the back, Benny was waiting at a corner table. The cafe's piped music was loud here, and most of the coffee drinkers and cake eaters and those tittering or tutting at Bob's unorthodox appearance were toward the front, where the plate glass windows let in the San Francisco sunshine and people bustled around the busy counter and the harassed baristas.

There were two cups of coffee on the table. Bob sat and raised an eyebrow; Benny indicated the drink was for him.

"What is it with you and coffee?" asked Bob. He reached for the cup, turned it one hundred eight degrees by the handle, then sat back and didn't touch it again.

Benny sipped her drink. "I like it. Tangun likes it too. Guess they don't have Colombian free trade roast where he comes from." She laughed.

211

Bob asked, "Where's Ted?" and Benny stopped laughing.

"For a beach bum you're not very chill," said Benny.

Bob frowned. "This beach bum is a retired death god who is getting a little agitated," he said. "Where's Ted?"

Benny put down her cup, adjusted her cap, picked her cup up again. She held it close to her chin, both hands wrapped around the hot ceramic.

"He's asleep."

"Where is he asleep?"

"Dude, relax. My place. He's safe there. Tangun put him under, and he'll stay under until we want him to wake up." Benny explained where Tangun had found him, and their rooftop conversation.

"So, he doesn't know?" asked Bob. He leaned on the table with his elbows, ran both hands through his crisp hair. "And what's with the acrobat thing? What's his connection with the circus?"

Benny shrugged. "Nezha's idea of a joke?"

"I never saw the point of tricksters. I mean, seriously."

Benny sipped her coffee. "He's absorbed at least part of Nezha's power, but it's totally fractured his mind. Physically, he seems fine. Mentally, well, I'm not sure how long he's going to last before the damage becomes permanent."

Bob sat up. "*Shit*," he said. "Ted could be lost forever."

Benny nodded. "I think so. I don't know. This has never happened before, but it can't be good. Tangun switched him into his own clothes, anyway. So he won't get a reminder when he wakes up."

"OK, good," said Bob. "We need to get it out of him, pronto and we don't have much time. Is Tangun ready?"

Benny pulled her baseball cap off and removed the tie from her ponytail. She shook her head, allowing her shoulder-length hair to fall free, then sat straight in her chair, her head titled until her face was covered by her hair.

"Tangun the Founder is always ready," she said, putting on a deep, mocking voice.

Bob raised an eyebrow. "Let's go."

"Well, shit."

Benny's apartment was empty, the front door open. Bob stood in the middle of the studio space, hands on hips, shaking his head. Benny had her cap in one hand, the other pulling at her ponytail.

"Sorry, dude," she said. "I left him for, like, ten minutes."

"Ten?"

"Maybe fifteen. But, Jesus, come on. Tangun put him to sleep. You can't wake up from that, not ever."

"Not unless you've got part of the power of a god inside you, right?"

Benny collapsed onto the couch. "Sorry, dude," she said, her eyes on the floor.

"Come on." Bob tapped Benny's shoulder. "He can't have got far."

He disappeared through the door.

Tangun the Founder was a god, an ancient warrior king. Powerful, trustworthy, one of the best – one of Kanaloa's few friends among the Heavenly Ones.

Benny, on the other hand, was young and carefree, a little green, a lot naïve, and had a hell of a lot to learn. As Bob stalked down the hallway, he wished that Tangun hadn't made the choice he had, to depart the Earth completely and require a host to return to it, a host whose entire family tree stretching back generation upon generation had been shaped just for that purpose. Bob had stayed as he was: a god, albeit one in disguise. If Tangun had done the same, it would have made the situation easier. Then again, foreseeing the future was not one of Tangun's – or Kanaloa's – particular powers.

Bob only hoped they could find Ted, and soon.

# XXIV
# SAN FRANCISCO
## TODAY

The Hang Wire Killer is just a person, just like everybody else. Highwire tells himself this, over and over. He also tells himself that the one thing that everybody has in common is *time*. There are only twenty-four hours in a day. Albert Einstein and Isaac Newton had twenty-four. William Shakespeare and Charles Dickens too. The President. The Pope. Everybody in the city, in the world.

Highwire wonders if Tangun the Founder has twenty-four hours available too, or whether it works differently for him. He mentioned there was another in the city. Highwire thought, at the time, he meant a friend, an ally.

Or... was he talking about the killer? Maybe the killer has more time too, if Tangun does.

Highwire curses himself. Such speculation is worthless. He has to take the twenty-four hours and use them. It is the only way.

The killer strikes at night. Five deaths now: the first, an old Chinese man, apparently chosen at random. But the next followed a pattern: young women, the time between each murder each growing shorter and shorter. Which probably means he is running on borrowed time, trying to maintain a normal existence during the day, just like everybody

214

else. Perhaps the killer senses his time is running out as his compulsion becomes ever more difficult to control. Or perhaps he thinks he is on a mission, that his crimes have a purpose, a reason. Perhaps he's a believer, following some divine plan invented by his own twisted mind.

Or invented by something else. Highwire thinks again about the movement, the thing he can sense curling tight below the city.

Highwire has to move out of the night, use the daylight hours as well. The circus will have to wait – it is his home and it feels strange to be away from it for so long, but he needs to do this, one final push, catch the killer, and then... well, who knows what will happen when his own mission is over. Highwire doesn't remember arriving in the city. If he was born of the circus for a purpose, and if that purpose is fulfilled...

Then that is how it will be.

He thinks about this as he watches the crowds in Union Square. He isn't wearing the costume from the circus; he is dressed like those around him, like those shopping and walking, sitting, laughing, talking. Across from where he sits is the stop for an open-topped double-decker bus tour of San Francisco. The bus is red and yellow, and Highwire can hear the tour guide drumming up business, ushering people on board.

Adjusting to daylight work will not be difficult, but he has to be careful. He knows he mustn't betray who he is, what he is capable of. He must hide not only from the public, from the police, but from *him*, the killer, because while the killer strikes at night, perhaps he's around during the day too. And if he suspects he is being followed during the day by the same god of the air who stalks him in the hours of darkness, then he'll go to ground, and Highwire's power will be exhausted.

Mid-morning. The day is glorious, the sky a deep blue, the streets a dappled collection of bright light and deep shadow cast by the closely arrayed skyscrapers.

He's out there, somewhere. The Hang Wire Killer. Maybe he's having his morning coffee in Union Square. Maybe he's on that tour bus. Maybe he's *driving* that tour bus.

Highwire doesn't know, but now he's ready to find out. The hunt will continue, and this time it will be successful.

The killer has to be stopped.

He gets up off the bench, and stops, looks around. Nobody is watching, nobody is listening, nobody cares.

He walks across the square, crosses the street, and heads down the hill. After a moment, he comes to an empty storefront near a big intersection. The windows of the store are big and black, and make good mirrors.

Highwire regards his reflection. The clothes he is in fit and are ordinary. Nothing to draw attention. Without the costume he doesn't recognize himself, but he doesn't expect to. He doesn't even know his own name. Only that at the circus, at night, he is called Highwire, the name that defines him.

Out here, he is nobody. Everybody. A man with no name, just an anonymous citizen. In the window reflection he sees brown eyes that match his jacket, and short hair just a shade lighter. The face is handsome enough, but plain. Clean shaven. Above the left eyebrow is an angled bruise, a dull red line, like he's hit his head on something blunt and narrow. He fingers the bruise, and it hurts a little. He doesn't remember the injury. He wonders if he should.

He drops his hand and looks around. If anyone has noticed him looking at his own reflection, they don't show it. People move around him like water; in the reflection he sees the occasional glance, but nothing more.

He turns and continues down to the intersection, lost in the sea of people, in the perfect cover, in the perfect disguise.

The killer is out here somewhere, and all he has to do is find him.

Highwire stands on the street, opens his senses, and lets the city pour into him.

# INTERLUDE
# GIBBSTOWN, NEW JERSEY
## 1951

Joel crashed through the undergrowth, and his feet twisted on a root. He pitched forward, pushing his arms in front of him and colliding with the hard ground with his elbows, his hat flying off his head. Something cracked; pain, white hot, shot up his arm. His instinct was to cry out, but he just managed to close his throat in time, stifling the sound and biting clean through his bottom lip in the process. More pain and the taste of pennies.

He rolled over on his back and then found he couldn't stop. The bank was at a shallow angle but he had enough momentum to keep tumbling, rolling like a carpet unfurled, into the gully. The water that trickled a crooked line at its base was sharp and cold, like needles pricking his skin, head to toe. This time he did cry out; he couldn't help it, but all he got was a mouthful of water and silt.

He turned and coughed, eyes blinking, his injured arm held across his chest, cradled by the other, the pearl-handled gun still tight in his hand. He fought to control his breathing, slowing it, ignoring the burn in his chest and the way his throat spasmed to clear itself. He'd made a racket already but he didn't want to make any more sound. Maybe the fall had been fortuitous; maybe he'd lost the monster that was chasing him.

Maybe. It was late afternoon, a Thursday, if he remembered right. The Pine Barrens were dull and drab, the world painted in hardly any colors other than the cigarette ash sky and the deep green of the trees and the dun brown of the soil. He was alone, or so he had thought, the wind his only companion, the wind that moaned and whistled through the pines. It felt like he was the only man in the whole world, which in a way he was, here in the middle of the Barrens.

But he was not alone. The area was remote and quiet, the perfect place to hide a part of the fairground, to keep it safe from the curious and unwise. With no people around, not for miles and miles, it was also the perfect place for monsters to live.

Joel gasped, his nostrils flaring as he sucked in the cold air. Above, up the bank, just over the lip, something was walking. It sounded like hooves, but not enough for a horse or a deer. They padded on the dirt, then stopped, then padded again. Something on two legs, walking on hooves like the devil himself.

Joel smiled. There was only one devil here, in the middle of the pines, and it was not the monster that stalked him.

He released his arm, then stretched it, flexed it. The break was already healed, the sprains and bruises gone. The burning deep in his chest had evaporated, and when he took his next breath it was light and easy. He was well looked after, and he smiled.

Joel rose from the creek, his black suit damp and rumpled. In one hand he held the gun, and the other felt for his fob pocket where the coin sat, impatient and angry and cold.

He was close.

Two more hoof-beats above, and then the sniffing of a large animal, then something else, a sound like the canvas of a circus tent being unpacked and unfolded. Something dark appeared over the lip of the bank, a triangular shape extended and flexed and then disappeared again. A wing, bat-like, the size of a kitchen table.

Joel stiffened. The sound of the creature's wings had reminded him of the circus. For a moment he had thought he could smell the Big Top, but now the moment was gone.

He pulled the hammer of the gun back, ready to move. He wasn't sure he could take on the monster, but he had the light on his side. The light was a cruel and mysterious master, its commands vague riddles, but he knew that the light would not let him die, not its chosen servant. The power out of space burned in his veins, kept him whole.

He took a step forward, one foot on the incline of the bank, ready to vault up it and remove this latest obstacle. Of course, he thought, the monster was part of it too. The fairground was near, a large piece or maybe many smaller ones, it felt like. Out there, hidden somewhere in the trees. That there was a monster here too, one that stayed hidden from mankind most times but had been seen in the nearby places, in Gibbstown and St. Peter, was no coincidence. The power of the carnival leaked into the very earth where the pieces sat, delving down, searching for the groundwater and beyond, searching for the plutonic thing beneath, the thing that moved.

Which meant, perhaps, that while he had the light on his side and the coin in his pocket, he was matched by the monster standing somewhere over the edge of the bank. What if the light was shining on it, too? Joel had traveled the United States for half a century, following the light and following the leaking evil. He'd seen what it could do to the places where the pieces were hidden, the power radiating slowly, creeping like a cancer, corrupting the world around it. Here it had spawned a monster to guard it. It must be a powerful piece indeed, hidden here in the trees.

The monster – the protector? – pawed the ground near the trees just a few yards away.

Joel took a breath and closed his eyes and his head was filled with the screaming of the coin. He knew what to do. He just had to trust the light.

He took two steps, powering up the side of the bank, and then he dropped to his knees, free hand outstretched to balance himself against the bank. He cocked his head, listening.

The monster was moving away. It stamped on the ground and snorted like a hog and flapped its leathery wings. Then it moved away, the hoof thumps growing fainter and fainter.

Had it lost his scent after he fell in the creek? Was it even tracking him by smell?

Or... did it know? Did it know that he served the same master? That he had come to find the carnival, to bring it back together? To make it whole again so it could devour the world?

Joel climbed the rest of the bank at a low crawl, until he could see over the edge. There was nothing but pine trees and their needles, dead and brown on the ground.

He raised himself up, gun in hand, at the ready. He looked around. But there was nothing, no monster, no devil. He was alone in the Pine Barrens.

Joel let the hammer of his silver gun slide gently back to safety. He kept the gun in his hand, though. With the other he took out the coin and closed his fist around it. Then he turned and headed west, parallel to the shallow embankment.

He was close.

# THE YEAR OF THE EARTH SNAKE

# SAN FRANCISCO
## OCTOBER 17, 1989

There was a moment, just before the main jolt, when it felt like the world was held in equipoise, like the world was holding its breath. The moment before impact. The moment before calamity.

The city shook and buildings fell.

Bob was on the beach this time. As the earthquake rumbled, the sound like artillery firing in the distance, his dance partner screamed and grabbed hold of him, tight. He held her, cradled her against his chest, as they rode the pulsating ground. He pushed a little – just a little – against the power of the world so he could keep upright and keep his dance partner safe. Around them, people collapsed like bowling pins.

Then it stopped and the earth was still, and he touched down on the ground again, his dance partner too. Without his realizing it, they'd been floating an inch off the rolling beach. The fact that he had done it without thinking was a worry.

Not because he thought *They* would notice. He'd thought that while *They* had abandoned the world, *They* would be looking down on it, watching, observing their experiment to see what greatness humanity would achieve. But he was wrong. *They* weren't looking. *They* didn't care.

So he wasn't afraid of *Them*, not any more.

He was afraid of himself. Of what he could do if he just gave in to the hunger that gnawed at his stomach like a parasite trying to burrow its way out.

"Oh, Bob, Bob," cried the woman in his arms. Bob snapped out of it and led her back to her friends, who were picking themselves up off the ground. They seemed OK, although Bob could see a few minor injuries among the tourists who had fallen over on the concrete steps.

"An earthquake," someone said. "It's an earthquake."

Bob looked to the southeast. Smoke rose over the trees of the park.

Where there was smoke, there was fire. It was happening all over again.

Bob pushed through the crowd, and ran.

The Interstate had collapsed. The higher tier of roadway had fallen onto the one below, crushing cars, killing dozens, and trapping hundreds.

Bob pushed his way through the chaos. There were police, ambulances, fire trucks there, but the response was still fresh, uncoordinated. People ran, people watched. The air was thick with dust and smoke. Bob pushed a little and floated up, just so he could see over the carnage. Nobody noticed.

There was a fire under the collapsed roadway. Maybe several, as the fuel tanks of crushed cars and trucks were ruptured, the kinetic energy of the earthquake and the overpass collapse converting to heat, enough for ignition.

Bob dropped to the ground. He had to help, like he had helped eighty-three years before, when the city had been a whole lot younger.

As he drew nearer, he felt a connection with the people he lived among. Here they were, in the middle of hell, the collapsed overpass in rubble around them. Another tremor and more could come down, killing them all. And yet here they were, scrambling out of cars, helping people up, digging through the rubble with their bare hands. As the trapped victims screamed, the rescuers – men and women in business suits, in jogging shorts, in jeans and skirts; the ordinary folk of San Francisco – shouted encouragement, shouted that they were coming, that everything would be OK.

Bob gently eased himself to the front, the air thick with smoke and dust. A couple of rescuers noticed him, noticed his chiseled torso, sweaty, dusty, and nodded. Here was a strong young man to help move rubble.

Bob pulled two triangular shards of roadway clear, then got a grip on a huge concrete slab about the size of a small aircraft's wing, and lifted, revealing a large pocket beneath, half- choked with rubble. Just like before, so many years ago, nobody paid attention to his superhuman strength. The rescuers around him surged forward, reaching in to clear debris and get to the people trapped within. Flame licked at Bob's bare feet. Nobody noticed.

One of the rescuers yelled something and was dragged into the hole. Others grabbed his feet and tugged him back, but their hands slipped on his pants. One shoe flew off, and then he vanished into the rubble.

Bob swore and lifted the slab higher. Then he saw, through the smoke.

Eyes, red, glowing.

Black hands reached out of the rubble. Greasy with soot, they waved like wheat in a field, fingers splayed, reaching, reaching. Bob yelled out for everyone to get clear, not to touch them, but nobody was listening. People reached for the black hands, and when they did, the black hands pulled them back into the rubble. People pulled, yelled for help, screamed in pain, and Bob stood, watching the red eyes in the smoke.

Something was moving. Again, like it had before. A power, down below. A thing beneath stirring in its sleep.

Bob held the huge fragment of roadway aloft with one hand, and reached down with the other, pulling the last trapped rescuer back by the waistband of his jeans. The people around him stood back, looking up at Bob, standing in the rubble in his bare feet, holding the slab up in the air with just one hand. He waved at them to get back, and this time they paid attention.

From the gap in the rubble came more grasping hands as the black things began to pull themselves out of the burned ground. They reached for the air, their red eyes burning.

Then Bob dropped the slab on top of them, sending up a billowing cloud of dust.

It was happening again.

Bob shouted for everyone to stand clear. They followed his instruction, no doubt fearful that more of the road was about to collapse. As the crowd backed away, Bob pushed down on the slab he'd dropped, and held it there, in case its massive weight was not enough to keep the golems trapped beneath.

Bob wished others were here, that there was no Agreement, no Retreat. But he was alone, and the city needed him again. Not just to rescue people from the calamity.

Once again, the city needed his protection.

Satisfied that the golems beneath the slab were crushed back into the dirt and ash from which they had been spawned, Bob called over his shoulder that the roadway was safe.

Work could begin again.

# GODS OF THE MIDWAY

# XXV
# SHARON MEADOW, SAN FRANCISCO
## TODAY

This was it. The worst had happened, and it was the end of The Magical Zanaar's Traveling Caravan of Arts and Sciences.

Nadine tapped at the laptop with little interest, scrolling through a vast spreadsheet of circus finances. They'd been doing well – very well, in fact. The San Francisco shows were their best ever, helped by the terrific location in Golden Gate Park and the addition of not one but two new acts – the Stonefire dance troupe and the mystery man himself, Highwire. Where Newhaven had found them, she didn't know, but they were box office magic.

And now? Now it was all for shit. The last show had been a disaster. Jack, the Magical Zanaar himself, had run through his lines without any performance at all, like he was reading them off a script. The rest of the show was lackluster at best. Jack missed his cues, and when Jan and John started their trapeze act and it became clear that the star of the show, Highwire, wasn't there, people started leaving. David and the clowns filled another gap left by the absence of Kara and Sara and then Stonefire came on.

Nadine watched from the sidelines as the Celtic dancers entered the arena, not dressed in their customary leather costumes but naked, covered in black dirt and ash. David appeared by her side, yelling in her ear that they should stop the show, that they were going to lose their permit. Gone was the choreographed dancing and acrobatics. Stonefire danced to a simple, repetitive beating drum, a relentless rhythm that lacked any musicality. On and on the drum sounded, as Stonefire twitched and stamped their feet.

People started leaving, taking their children with them. Some accosted circus staff at the entrance, telling the ushers that they hadn't paid to see this kind of show.

Then someone screamed, and the atmosphere in the Big Top changed. Stonefire had spread out, and one member had grabbed someone from the audience. The spectator tried to pull away, but the dancer yanked him bodily into the show. David and the clowns stepped into the arena. The dancer let go of his unwilling volunteer and tackled David, and the pair crashed to the ground. People in the crowd screamed, and then it was a stampede to the exits.

Jack watched it all from the shadows, oblivious to the chaos. He ignored Nadine when she tried to talk to him, didn't even flinch when she slapped him across the face. Nadine waved at the lighting desk. They got the message and brought the house lights up.

The drumbeat stopped. David picked himself up and scrambled to Nadine, his chin wet with blood. Stonefire gathered around Malcolm. He stared at Nadine and David.

"Get out!" Nadine yelled. "Get out before I call the fucking police. This circus is fucking *over*."

The group had stood a moment longer. Then Malcolm had snarled something in a language Nadine hadn't heard them use before – Gaelic? – and the group had shuffled out.

That was last night. Nadine had locked herself in the Winnebago since then. Someone had knocked on the door – Jack, she guessed – but she hadn't answered it.

Nadine thought about the stolen cable and felt sick. Jack had insisted they not report the theft, confident (he said) that they could handle it internally. Jack had insisted it was nothing to do with the serial killer who was now dominating the news; in a city the size of San Francisco, steel cable would be plentiful. Jack had been right, of course.

But now things had gone to shit, and Nadine wasn't so sure there wasn't a connection.

She tapped at the laptop again. The circus was closed, but... could they retool, rebrand, open next season, somewhere else? They'd need new acts – including a new ringmaster – need to get financing from somewhere to pay out the current contracts. But the show could go on. She and Jack were finished, that was for sure. But the circus was her livelihood. She ran the business side of things well. She enjoyed it. It provided jobs. It found talent. Maybe, eventually, when the sick feeling had passed, the show could go on.

Couldn't it?

A drumbeat sounded, once, twice. Nadine looked up, moved to the window as the drumming picked up. She knew that sound.

Stonefire. The circus was in crisis, had fallen apart because of them, and they were fucking starting again.

It was a hot afternoon. Nadine stood in the motorhome's doorway, squinting into the sun. The drumming was a fast beat now, and was joined by voices chanting, singing.

Smoke began to rise from over the tops of the tents. They'd damn well lit their fire.

Nadine hopped down the steps, the end of her rope most certainly reached.

They were dancing in front of the fire, and Nadine was ready to start yelling when she noticed the group looked

larger than it should. Stonefire was two dozen dancers, male
and female, plus partners and a few children along for the
ride. But the group in front of the bonfire was much, much
larger, twice that at least. Nadine realized the numbers were
made up of the rest of the circus acts – the clowns, led by
David the Harlequin, the jugglers, acrobats, and trapeze
artists. The non-performing workers too. They'd all joined
the Celtic group, even wearing the same costumes. Nadine
shook her head, frowning. Only Jack and Joel weren't
among them, as far as she could see. Sara and Kara too. The
pair of gymnasts hadn't come back.

The bonfire was just catching, the teetering stack of old
shipping pallets bought cheap from warehouses down by
the water making an effective chimney as the flames took
hold from the bottom. Maybe it was Nadine's imagination,
or the fact that the day was already quite warm, but the fire
didn't feel as hot as it should have.

The members – new and old – of Stonefire looked a mess.
She'd noticed them get worse over the last week – wearing
their leathers around the clock, even sleeping in them,
lying around their bonfire in the open. The costumes left
little to the imagination – men and women included – but
the group was now so dirty, covered in black ash, that it
was hard to tell where the costumes ended and bare flesh
began.

They were all taking it a little too seriously. Nadine felt a
little odd in her gray suit, but at least she was a professional,
unlike these losers.

"Hey!" she yelled. "What the fuck?" She stepped forward,
from the dry grass to the blackened, burned ground. As her
shoes kicked up the ash, she felt a tingle, a vibration through
the soles of her feet. She wasn't religious, not at all, but she
had the strangest feeling she was walking on sacred ground,
like there was something in the air, a physical presence,

someone... watching. She pushed the thought from her mind and folded her arms as Malcolm turned from the fire and looked at her. His face was covered in black ash – *deliberately* covered, Nadine realized – and when he smiled, his teeth formed a bright white line across his face.

She shook her head, waved at the bonfire.

"What the hell are you doing? There's no show, not any more. I don't know if you've noticed, but we're kinda out of business here."

Malcolm laughed. "We prepare our altar, woman."

Nadine paused. Woman? Good lord above. This was getting beyond ridiculous.

"An *altar*. Jesus, Malcolm, you can cut the whole tribal bullshit now. And put the fucking fire out. We need to start packing the tents up."

There was something wrong with Malcolm's smile. It was cruel and knowing. Arrogant.

"Malcolm," said Nadine, stepping closer, lowering her voice. "We're finished, OK? The circus is finished. Show's over."

Malcolm didn't move. It was like he wasn't even breathing, and Nadine wasn't quite sure he was blinking either. She looked around, at the other members of his troupe. The drumming had stopped along with the dancing. They now formed a circle around her and Malcolm. Still, unmoving. She turned around to face them.

"Look, I know. This isn't good for anyone, believe me. But Mr Newhaven and I need to talk about it, and then we'll discuss the future of the circus with you all. We want this to work out as best we can."

There was no reaction. The dancers stood in the circle, staring at her. Nadine held her hand up over her brow, shading the sun. Were they not breathing either? She shook her head and turned back to Malcolm.

"The business of your world is of no concern to Belenus."
Malcolm's lip curled into a snarl. Behind him, the bonfire
flared, flames as tall as the Big Top licking into the blue sky.
Then he turned around and walked toward the blaze.

"What the hell are you talking about?" Nadine followed
Malcolm to the fire. "Hey, I'm talking to you!"

Malcolm stopped. Nadine tapped the big man on his
back. His leather jerkin was moist, slick, and left a black
residue on her fingertips. She rubbed it between her finger
and thumb, which only spread the greasy substance more.
He stood and stared at the fire, ignoring her.

"Fine," she said. "Fuck, whatever. Enjoy your goddamn
fire. We're finished, but hey, don't let that stop you."

She spun around, but there were dancers right behind
her. She jerked back in surprise, then tried to sidestep. They
matched her movement, holding their arms wide like they
were herding a lost sheep.

"Get the fuck out of my way."

"We are not ended, woman."

Nadine turned around. Malcolm was facing the fire, his
arms outstretched, embracing it.

"We are *reborn*."

The feeling of presence was back, stronger now. A vibration,
the ground *humming* like an electricity transformer.

"Where there is death there is power," said Malcolm.
"Where there is power there is life."

The humming made Nadine's jaw hurt. The drumming
started again, then the dancing, as the members of Stonefire
and the rest of the circus began to orbit the bonfire. The
three dancers behind her stamped their feet, chanting in
what Nadine assumed was Gaelic.

Malcolm stepped up to the fire and fell to his knees.
Nadine wanted to reach forward, make him stop, pull him
back, but she couldn't move. Malcolm was in the edge of

the fire, and it cracked and spat around him, showering his shoulders in embers that glowed brighter than they should have in the afternoon sun.

He began to dig, clawing at the earth. It was dry and came away in great handfuls. Very quickly there were two piles of carbon and dirt on either side of him.

Then, as Nadine watched, he stood, and reached down with one arm. From the hole, a black arm emerged, grabbed Malcolm's, and Malcolm pulled.

It was a woman, young and small. She was naked, although covered entirely in black ash. Her eyes were brilliant against her blackened face as she blinked in the light. She smiled, her teeth white, white.

Nadine shook her head and forced herself to move, to run, away from the madness, away from something that couldn't be happening. But all she managed to do was trip backward, falling into the three dancers behind her. They grabbed her arms, held her up.

Malcolm kissed the girl's black hand, and turned to the dancers. The drumming reached a crescendo, and then fell silent. The dancers stopped moving.

The girl glanced at Nadine. It was Sara. She tilted her head as she looked at Nadine. Then she looked up at Malcolm.

"I am Belenus," she said. "We are Belenus, and Belenus rises."

The leader of Stonefire laughed, throwing his head back. Sara stepped over to Nadine, her black, smoking body a beautiful horror, her hair matted with something dark and sticky. She reached out to Nadine.

Nadine passed out.

# XXVI
## SAN FRANCISCO
### TODAY

"What will happen to him, do you think?"

Bob didn't answer. He and Benny had been walking half an hour, searching in vain for Ted. Benny had made a mistake leaving Ted in the apartment, but Bob thought maybe he shouldn't be quite so hard on her. Benny's entire family tree had carried the spirit of Tangun the Founder through it, down generation after generation, century after century, until such a time as the god was needed on Earth again. That time had come, and that responsibility had fallen on Benny's shoulders.

Then again, from what Bob had seen, Tangun himself didn't seem particularly cooperative. Bob considered him a friend now but, honestly, he hadn't really known him that well, back *then*. The gods and goddesses numbered in the thousands, and while they were all kith and kin, there were plenty Bob – *Kanaloa* – hadn't dealt with. Kali. Sousson-Pannan. Gozer the Gozerian. Olorun. And Tangun too, until recently, at least. After the rest had left. And there were still things he didn't understand about the warrior king.

Bob wondered what it was like for Benny. She was just a regular girl, with no particular choice in the matter, her family blessed – or cursed – by the burden of their ancestors.

Tangun had left the world like *They* all had. And, it seemed, like the others had fallen a little out of touch.

And if hadn't been for the power burning Ted up from the inside, then Tangun's little sleep command would have been just fine.

"Bob?"

Bob stopped. Benny too.

Bob smiled. "Sorry. What will happen to Ted? I guess the best option is if the power just kills him."

"Dude," said Benny, taking a step closer. They had stopped in the middle of the street, outside a clothing store. In the window was a display of vintage denim jeans, matching Bob's own pair. "That's the best option? What's the worst?"

"The worst would be if he loses control completely. At the moment, Ted is still there, somewhere. He has, what, fifty percent possession?"

"Maybe less."

"Right, maybe less. If the power takes him over completely, then what? He becomes a god. A *new* god. One who doesn't know what he can do."

"Oh," said Benny.

"Right, 'oh'. And it might be academic, anyway." He looked down at the sidewalk, then glanced sideways at Benny.

"Oh," said Benny again. "This... thing. You think it's waking up, for real?"

Bob sucked in his cheeks, then nodded.

"And when it does," said Benny, "there goes the city, right?"

Bob fixed Benny with a stare. "Maybe not just the city."

Benny's eyes went wide. "OK. So... why can't you just flex a bit of muscle? Find Ted, stop the whatever-it-is from waking up? You're a god too and–"

Bob stepped up to Benny and pushed her back against the store window. Benny hit it with a thud. Bob moved back a little, in case they were getting attention from passersby, or people in the shop.

"I am not Kanaloa. My name is Bob. I am not a god. I am a person just like you."

"But–"

"Don't ever ask me again," said Bob.

Benny blanched and shrank back, pushing herself against the glass behind her. "Sorry."

Bob took a deep breath, and brushed Benny's shoulder down with his hand, embarrassed at his outburst. Benny was a new kid but she had to know.

"It's all I can do to hold myself back," said Bob. He looked around, smiling, nodding to a few people on the sidewalk who seemed to recognize who he was, even in the white linen shirt. He spoke softly, trying to be inconspicuous. Not that it really mattered. Nobody who overhead would believe what he was saying. "If I just stretch out my hand, pluck Ted out of the crowd, I might decide I can do something else too. You know, I haven't eaten in a long, long time."

"Eaten?"

Bob turned to Benny, and he smiled. Benny flinched.

"Remember what Kanaloa was god of, Benny." Then he turned, and walked down the street, anger fading. But there was hunger inside him. He sighed, rolled his shoulders, and turned. "Benny?"

His friend pointed across the street. Then someone cried out.

"Is anyone a doctor?"

Bob jogged back to Benny. "What's going on?"

"Dude, that was Ted. He collapsed on the sidewalk."

Bob was halfway across the street already.


Bob pushed his way through the onlookers. He was surprised so many people had stopped to help. Maybe it was because the man lying on the street looked like one of them – smart brown jacket, sensible haircut, shoes that were not expensive but well chosen. Bob felt like telling the crowd that perhaps they should show the same care to those who lived rough on the streets of San Francisco, but decided to save it for another time.

It was Ted all right. He was lying on his side, curled in a fetal position. Bob dropped to the sidewalk, kneeling next to a woman who was loosening the top buttons of Ted's shirt. She glanced at him.

"You a doctor?"

"Ah, no, ma'am. I'm a friend of this guy."

The woman leaned back a little and looked Bob up and down. The ill-fitting linen shirt. The old, faded jeans. The bare feet. The long hair.

She pushed Bob away. Bob, surprised, fell back onto his ass. "Hey!"

"Fuck off," said the woman. "You're not taking his wallet!"

"His wallet?"

The woman stood up. One of those standing near had his cellphone to his ear. He tilted it down and waved at her. "There's an ambulance coming."

"Call the police too," said the woman. She turned and pointed at Bob, now standing. "This guy tried to steal his wallet."

"Ah, ma'am," said Bob, backing away, hands in the air. One of the men in the crowd stepped forward and shoved Bob's shoulder, his nostrils flaring. Someone else tapped him on the shoulder.

"Isn't that the guy from the beach?"

A ripple spread around the group.

"The dance guy?"

"That bum?"

"Isn't his name Bob?"

"That's not Bob."

"I took my mom down there just last week."

"Dude," said Benny, pushing her way in. The man who had shoved Bob turned on Benny, but Benny just nodded at him and grabbed Bob by the shoulders, pulling him back a little.

"What's gotten into them?" asked Benny.

"We have to get him out of here," said Bob.

"Dude, I know." Benny looked down at Ted. "At least he's sleeping again–"

They both turned at the sound of approaching sirens. An ambulance pulled up, the crowd parting to let two paramedics through.

"Oh great," said Bob. He reached forward to tap one of the paramedics on the shoulder, but the man who had pushed him blocked his path and shoved him back again.

"Cut it out!" the paramedic said.

The other man nodded at Bob. "This guy's trying to steal his wallet."

"Look, I'm a *friend* of his," said Bob. "His name is Ted – *Theodore Kane*. Check his wallet yourself. You'll see."

The paramedic joined his colleague, who had put an oxygen mask on Ted and was trying to talk to him. The first paramedic reached inside Ted's jacket, extracted a wallet, and from that a driver's license.

"Theodore Kane," he read.

"Went to school together," said Bob. "Ted's a freelance writer. Doing work for the Bay Blog."

"Fine," said the paramedic. "We're taking him to the hospital. You can ride with us."

Benny tugged Bob's arm. "Will he be safe in the hospital?"

"He won't be safe anywhere."

# XXVII
# SAN FRANCISCO
## TODAY

The apartment was – as she'd feared – exactly as Alison had left it. She'd even paused in the hallway, key in the lock, listening, before she pushed the door open slowly. Like it was the door to Narnia, to the magic kingdom, to her normal life and Ted's normal life. Where nothing had ever happened.

But it was just the same. The laptop on the table, closed. The door to the bedroom ajar. The apartment empty. Ted gone.

Alison sighed and swung the door closed behind her. She stood for a moment, breathing deeply. It was OK, she was following the plan. She hadn't seen him between the office and the apartment, and she'd taken some time, ducking down side streets, trying to remember old routes Ted used to walk. There were parks nearby and rows of pretty houses. He'd mentioned that he liked to take different routes, vary the routine, enjoy the walk.

Nothing.

It was time to call both the police and every hospital in the book. She pulled her cell from her pocket and sat at the table. She flipped the laptop open, frowned at the page of Chinese text that was still showing in the word processor, fired up a browser, and started searching for hospitals.

Her cell rang, vibrating in her hand, giving her a fright. She looked at the display but didn't recognize the number.

"Ted?"

"Hey, Alison. No, it's me," said the voice on the other end.

"Benny?"

"Ah, yeah, sorry. It's Benny. We've found Ted. He's fine."

Relief. Exquisite and simple. Alison sighed deeply and slumped over the laptop.

"Benny, thank God," she said.

"We're down at St Roch. The hospital."

Adrenaline pumped into her bloodstream, making her nauseous. Alison felt like she'd been kicked in the stomach. She brushed the bangs out of her eyes. "The hospital? Oh God, what–"

"No, no, he's fine. We found him and brought him in."

Alison rubbed her forehead. "Who's 'we'? Zane?"

There was a wet sort of click, followed by someone rubbing sandpaper against the mouthpiece at the other end. Benny had moved the phone away from her mouth and was talking to someone else. Alison heard the tail end of the laugh, and then heard Benny say something. Then she was back on the line.

"Me and Bob."

"Bob?"

"Look," said Benny. "Better come down here. We'll explain everything."

Alison's heart began to race. "OK, OK, hold on," she said, scrambling for a pen. There was nothing on the desk, so she opened the word processor on the laptop and began to type, the phone between her shoulder and ear. Benny gave her the address and a set of directions that sounded easy enough.

"I'll be right over," she said.

"See you soon."

Alison hung up, and stared at the notes she'd typed. St Roch was clear on the other side of town. What the hell was Ted doing way over there? It was nowhere near the office, or Benny's apartment for that matter.

And what was Benny doing with Bob, the beach bum from Aquatic Park?

Alison drove her car up out of the parking garage underneath Ted's apartment building. Ted didn't have a car, so his spot was always empty. The car drove up the ramp, bounced on its suspension at the top as she gave only the most cursory check for traffic, and then, tires squealing, she took a left and sped down the street.

The man pulled out of the shadows, into the sun. He watched the car disappear, and then looked up at the apartment building. He was on foot – not that this posed a problem; he could move around the city as he pleased, as *it* pleased. He just had to trust that *it* knew where to go next.

He looked up at the sun, felt the burn, the pain in his eyes. And then the earth shook, a micro-quake just under his boots, and then he knew.

St Roch. The hospital there.

And then it said: *Soon. Soon.*

The man opened his eyes, looked into the sun, and followed the light. The ground hummed, and the sidewalk was now empty.

# XXVIII
# SHARON MEADOW, SAN FRANCISCO
## TODAY

Nadine awoke in a room that was dark and stuffy. She moaned, and her voice echoed with a flatness she recognized. She sat up, rubbed her forehead.

She was back in the Winnebago, in the sleeping compartment. It was big, spacious enough for a regular double bed, a built-in dresser, and a mirror in one corner opposite the bed, the other wall filled with a compact fitted closet. As she sat up she could see herself in the mirror on the dresser; herself, and the back of the man sitting on the end of the bed.

"Jack?"

It was dark in the bedroom, only the light from the carnival coming in through the slats of the blinds on the left wall. Jack's face was in shadow, but he was wearing the ringmaster's jacket and hat. Both sparkled in the half-light.

"There's a power here," he said. Nadine pushed herself back up against the headboard. In the doorway of the bedroom was another man. Tall, thin, he was a black shape wearing a tall hat. He was leaning against the doorway, one hand apparently looped through his belt. It looked like his other hand was tucked into the pocket on the front of his waistcoat, but Nadine couldn't be sure.

246

Joel. Joel was a fucking creep who shouldn't have been brought into their bedroom.

"The fuck is he doing here?" she said.

"It's growing. It's moving. I can feel it." Jack wasn't listening to Nadine. In fact, he wasn't even looking at her. He was staring somewhere into the middle distance, like he was lost in thought.

"Jack, tell me what's going on," she said. She was surprised at the strength of her own voice. The last thing she remembered was the bonfire, the girl being pulled from the ashes beneath it.

"It's hungry. It sleeps and we feed it. Fire and blood. There's power there. Power in death. In murder. It's hungry and we feed it. It can create life of its own, too. They're part of it, extensions of it. They're made of the earth like it is made of the earth. We pull them from the fire. The dancers call it Belenus, but it doesn't have a name. We–"

Nadine leapt, but Jack moved with unnatural speed. He grabbed her wrists as she swung herself over the edge of the bed and pushed her back down. Nadine yelled out and struggled, but it was no good. Jack's grip was solid, his hands so cold her wrists hurt. Joel stepped out from the doorway and stood over the pair of them. He looked down at her, his white eye shining in the half-light.

"I follow a light," said Jack, and Nadine gasped in horror. Jack was speaking, his eyes unfocussed, but as he spoke, Joel mouthed the words.

"The light is cold," said Jack/Joel. "It comes from a dark place, a void of endless dimensions. It's hungry too, but weak. Intelligence, ancient and awful. It shows me where to go, what to do. It drew me here, to this city, this place. To the thing that sleeps beneath us all. A force of nature, of the world itself. But a thing without mind, direction."

Nadine gave another push, but Jack held her firm. She didn't understand what Joel was saying, how he was saying it through Jack. It was all a dream, a nightmare of earthquakes and a city falling into the abyss. Her eyes filled with tears as she struggled on the bed.

"But the light can control it. The light tells us to feed it, and soon it will awake," said Joel, through Jack. "Soon I'll be free." He turned and walked back to the doorway. "But not yet. There is still hunger, and pain. And I follow the light, and the light it shines for thee."

Jack suddenly released Nadine. She screamed and pushed herself off the bed. This time, Jack did nothing. Nadine shoved Joel out of the doorway and ran down the length of the motorhome. She reached the door and pulled it, but it was locked. She fiddled with the deadlock and catch, but the door refused to move. She thumped on it, screaming for help.

"You can't leave."

She turned. Jack was right behind her, and behind him, Joel leaned in the doorway of the sleeping compartment. Jack held up his hands, and between them flexed a loop of thin steel cable.

Nadine screamed again and pulled and banged on the door. Then the loop of steel dropped over her neck and was drawn tight.

# INTERLUDE
# POINT PLEASANT, NEW JERSEY
## 1967

Pay dirt. He'd hit big, the mother lode. He arrived in town, checked into the motel named, optimistically, the Pleasant View – of the parking lot and freeway, mostly – called the number from the newspaper, and then driven across the Silver Bridge into Gallipolis, New Jersey. It all went so very smoothly.

Joel waited patiently as Jim, owner and proprietor of Jim's Auto and Gas, stamped his feet and blew into his hands. The December night was cold and clear. A frost would dust the park just across the road tonight, and most folk would stay indoors. Christmas was coming, and the townsfolk had better things to do than come out at night and look at antique junk.

"You OK there, mister...?" Jim looked Joel up and down, unsure of the man standing in just his old black suit, old-fashioned hat tucked under his arm. Joel smiled and nodded at the padlock on the garage door.

"Let's just get events progressing in a more forward direction, Mr Jim, if you would be so kind." Joel put one hand in his pocket and slid the index finger and thumb of the other into the fob pocket of his waistcoat. The gold coin was screaming at him, inside his mind.

"Well, OK, now," said Jim. "And it's Mr Callaghan, but Jim'll do. Everyone calls me Jim." He pointed over Joel's shoulder. Joel half-turned and saw the man's name in six-foot-high letters, black and red on a white panel, high above the garage and gas station that was adjoined to the lockup. It was late and the sign was unlit, but the white enameled background picked up the moonlight, making Jim's name easy to read.

"In fact," said Jim, bending over to fuss at the padlock, "you might be the first person I've actually told my surname too." He laughed and got back to work. After a moment, the lock snapped open and Jim pulled it from the catch and dropped it into the pocket of his parka. Door unlocked, he released the catch and heaved. The door creaked and the metal roller front buckled a little, but it remained in place.

"Little help here," said Jim, shifting over slightly.

Joel took his left hand from his pocket, but his right hand was slower, the fingers lingering over the coin. In his head the coin screamed and screamed again. He ignored it and the scattering of gravel outside the garage crunched under his feet as he moved to help Jim with the door. The roller groaned in protest and the coin in Joel's pocket screamed his name, and then there was a click and the door was free. It rolled speedily upward, taking Jim's and Joel's hands with it until it left their grasp and clunked into the frame at the top.

"You got a truck or something?" asked Jim. He stepped across the threshold, vanishing into the dark. A second later a small light clicked on, and then another – single bulbs with white cone shades, set in rows in the high ceiling.

Joel's fingers found the coin again and this time he took it out and rolled it across his knuckles, almost without conscious thought, as he stepped into the garage.

The space was as tall as it was long and wide – a hollow cube, the floor thick with dust. Attached as it was to the auto workshop Joel suspected it had once been a workshop itself, now relegated to storage. It was full of machinery that looked like it was folded up, or disassembled and stacked in pieces. There were metal poles and plain sheeting, plenty of it, but the two small lights picked out something brighter – yellow and red and green paint, covered with dust but still shining. Joel saw shooting stars and the tail of a comet, paintings of ringed planets, of lions and tigers and creatures that were neither, animals that had never lived.

Not on Earth, anyway.

"Been here a while," said Jim. He stood next to Joel and surveyed the contents of the garage like an explorer standing atop a mountain. Then he swept the baseball cap off his head and ran a hand through his thick white hair. "Now I think about it, I'm pretty sure it's always been here."

"Always?"

"Well, I'm Jim the second. Jim the first – my old dad, rest his soul – started the auto shop, oh, thirty years ago, maybe longer. Built a double workshop but always used this half for storage. Guess the town just isn't big enough for the enterprise he had in mind. But I can remember the shed being loaded up and then locked. He took me on when I was fifteen, apprenticing, you know, and he didn't like me coming in here." Jim turned back to the stacked components. "No sir, that he did not like at all."

"Do you know where he acquired the, ah… *collection*?"

Jim laughed and looked at Joel. "Collection? Now that's one way of looking at it. It's just a load of parts, far as I'm concerned. A load of parts that I ain't got any use for. Business is good and we're redoing the shop, expanding out here. This all has to be moved. Just wasted space for me at the moment."

Joel pursed his lips. This was a mother lode, all right: the biggest collection of the carnival he'd yet found. If he could find more collections like this, it would shorten his quest by quite a margin, and then he could move west, where the light was shining, where the coin was forever pulling when it wasn't near to its kith and kin.

"Maybe you aren't hearing me right, friend," said Joel. "I asked you where your daddy acquired the pieces."

Jim raised an eyebrow and folded his arms. "No clue," he said, and then his expression softened. "It's old though, for sure – late nineteenth century. You think maybe this needs to be in the Smithsonian or something?"

Joel allowed himself a small chuckle. "Well now, Mr Callaghan," he said. "I'm not sure that mighty institution has a department devoted to the study of the humble fairground attraction."

"Well, it's honest Americana. Must be someone who–"

"There is, and that someone is me, Mr Callaghan."

"Oh, well, yes, now, I'm sorry I–"

"How much?"

Jim stopped and rubbed his chin. "Well, let's see now…"

Joel chuckled and waved his hand. He strolled as far as he could into the garage. In front of him was the edge of a bright yellow sign, curved like a crescent moon, now stacked upside down between plain metal flats. It was part of the carousel. The most important part of the carnival, the *nexus*. He smiled and reached out to pat the sign, the coin's scream so loud in his head he thought he would black out. His hand stopped, and he brought it back, hooking the thumb through a belt loop, his index finger rubbing the fob pocket of his waistcoat. There was so much packed into the garage, he wondered if perhaps the centerpiece was here too. The carved monkey with the jeweled eyes. He strained his neck to peer over a rack of metal panels, but he couldn't see much.

Patience, patience.

"I do believe this fine collection is worth something, Mr Callaghan, and I'm not for a moment here pretending to be anything other than an interested customer. So please, you can spare the pretense. The expansion of your commercial enterprise must be both difficult and financially troublesome. Even a layman like my own self can see that."

Jim's eyes widened a little. "Well," he said, "that's true. After this lot is moved out, we have to clean the workshop up, refit this place, put in a car lift–"

"Five thousand."

Jim coughed. Joel smiled. Good, good. Time was short. The offer was high. Joel knew that wouldn't be the end of their little business arrangement, but it would keep Jim satisfied enough to not get in his way, for a while at least. The coin burned and screamed and it was all Joel could do to stop himself screaming along with it.

"OK," said Jim. He held out his hand, ready to shake on the deal, fire in his eyes. Joel glanced down at the hand and smiled, but he kept his own hands in his jacket.

A scream echoed from down the street. Joel and Jim turned at the sound, which was followed by the long drone of a car horn and screeching tires.

"What the hell is all that?" Jim dropped his hand, the light from his eyes gone. He walked out of the garage, Joel close behind.

Someone ran toward them, down the middle of the deserted street, a block away. The silhouette waved his arms. "Hey, hey!" the running man shouted.

Behind him, a car had stopped across the intersection, its brake lights blazing red, its headlights casting a hazy white cone in the mist hanging low in the air.

"What's going on?" Jim called out, squinting at the running man. "Drew? Is that Drew Lewiston?"

Drew pulled up in front of them, then bent double and gasped for breath. He pointed back down the road, toward the car.

"We've seen it. It's here again. It's back."

Jim sucked in a breath and stood rigid, staring toward the car.

Joel lazily stepped forward, kicking at the gravel. "What's back, exactly?" he asked. Drew glanced up at him and frowned; then he turned back to Jim.

"The Mothman. The Mothman's back, Jim, and it's got Julie. It's taken Julie!"

Joel sat on the bed, his back against the hard headboard, above him a faded print of a velvet lady, her skin green, her eyes looking to a distant shore. Joel knew how she felt. He was a stranger here himself, not just to Point Pleasant but to the very year. His skin may as well have been as green as the velvet lady's, his eyes on his own lost horizon.

How much longer he had to go, to endure, he wasn't sure. Not that it was punishment. It was the opposite, a boon, a gift bestowed upon him by the light.

The light that shines, and it shines on thee.

On the other side of the motel room, beneath the thin red curtains faded to honey orange, was a sideboard, on which sat the TV. The sideboard was empty, the Gideon's Bible gone. When Joel booked the room he'd made sure to have the motel remove it before he arrived. He wasn't sure it mattered, but he wasn't sure it didn't either. He served another power now, another light, and until his journey was complete he had no intention of drawing the attention of something else that might be looking down upon humanity. In the thirty years since he had posed as a Bible salesman in the dustbowl of Texas, Joel had grown ever more wary – paranoid, perhaps, but as his journey stretched into years, into decades, he had decided to be more careful. No more Bibles.

The glass on the sideboard rattled again. It was upside down, next to the TV. Underneath it was the Double Eagle, the gold coin buzzing like a trapped and angry bee. It vibrated against the thin veneer of the sideboard and against the edge of the glass, slowly pushing it toward the TV.

Joel watched the glass and watched the coin. The light was impatient, but the screaming had stopped. It was as if the cheap glass was a cone of silence, confining the evil within.

It didn't, of course, but Joel wondered what would happen to him once the evil had left him alone, or if it ever would. If it could let him live until mid-December 1967 without aging a single year since that day in wild Oklahoma, would it let him live until… 2067? 3067? Until the Earth crumbled to dust? Beyond?

That was the dilemma. Life eternal was a dead-end road.

Joel had excused himself when Julie turned up. Something had landed on the car and Drew had slammed on the brakes as the thing flew off, something large and heavy that had rocked the vehicle on its springs and put a dent in the roof. Drew had fled toward town, Julie in the opposite direction. A cop called Willy had found her back by the Silver Bridge, the girl terrified but still, watching the bridge like the thing was going to collapse into the Ohio River. The police had called out the fire department to help search for the creature, but the town was quiet. Drew had been drinking – Julie too – so the Sheriff didn't file a report. They were good kids and chances were a heron or something from the river had got lost in the night and hit their car. Herons were a lot bigger than most folk realized.

Joel tore his eyes from the sideboard and the glass shaking on it, and glanced at the clock on the nightstand. It was two in the morning, December 17th. He needed to acquire a truck, he needed to collect the pieces of the carnival, and he needed to leave the town via the Silver Bridge. His red car had served him well but was, like Joel himself, a relic of another age. Only, unlike Joel, the car was showing its age. And besides, for the collection of large pieces in Jim's garage, he needed something else.

Jim Callaghan of Jim's Auto and Gas had a truck. Joel had seen it parked at the side of the gas station just a few hours before. Big enough to carry the pieces from the garage.

The glass buzzed again and glided along the top of the sideboard like it was the star attraction in a séance. It stopped by the edge, and the coin was still.

The size of the find worried Joel. It was a boon, to find so much intact and in one place, and moving it wouldn't be a problem. But each piece needed an offering, payment on collection, as he thought of it. Sometimes the creeping evil did the work for him: the flood in North Carolina, the end of the farmhouse near Spearman, Texas. Joel's own death. But sometimes it needed help. It needed Joel to do something, pay the toll, satisfy the hunger of it and of the light so they could move on.

The collection in Jim's garage was huge. Nearly all of the carousel, as far as Joel had been able to see, and more parts of something else, perhaps the Ferris wheel. The carousel was important. If the carousel was there, then maybe the monkey was too.

The collection payment was going to be large. The carnival demanded payment. The thing stalking the town was a manifestation of the carnival, or at least of the power that leaked from it and into the ground, but aside from scaring teenagers who were out when they shouldn't be, there didn't seem to be anything else to it. Red eyes glowing in the night weren't going to be enough.

Murder, on the other hand. Murder had power. Joel reached over to the nightstand and pulled the drawer open. He took the pearl-handled gun from inside and spun the chamber. Seven shots. One belonged to Jim – a down payment, perhaps. But there would be only six more bullets after that. It wouldn't be enough.

Unless... unless all he had to do was start the cycle. Seven murders, enough power to feed the carnival and then perhaps that was enough to start a chain reaction. The light would be fed and then the light would feed on the world around it, filling its hunger. Letting Joel move on, taking the pieces with him.

And then he felt the push from behind him, like a heavy hand resting on his shoulders just so. He was right. The cycle. All he had to do was start the cycle and it would do the rest.

Joel slipped off the bed, picked up his holster from the back of the chair, and wrapped it around his middle; then he picked up his stovepipe hat from the seat and carefully pulled it on. He watched the glass on the sideboard for a moment but it was still; he reached forward and the coin sprang to life, dancing on its edge, jumping so hard it hit the side of the glass and cracked it. Joel jerked his hand back. Then he knocked the cracked glass over with the back of his fingers and slapped them down on the coin, sliding it to the edge of the sideboard and then off into his hand.

He squeezed his palm on the coin, feeling the cold burn, listening to the screaming in his head, listening to the death of stars and comets blazing in the night. Then he opened the door and left.

The first step was the truck.

Point Pleasant was in the grip of something, and Joel knew the cause. He'd taken the truck as dawn broke, and then spent the day loading it. Jim's Auto and Gas remained closed; when people stopped by to ask him as he worked, he feigned ignorance, said Jim was just paying him to clear out the workshop.

Word about Drew and Julie spread during the day. There had been other sightings too. The creature was back, watching the town with its glowing red eyes, flying high overhead.

It was funny, in a way. That the town thought they were playing host to something monstrous and alien, a creature with gray wings and red eyes that appeared to do nothing at all but scare young lovers and children in the middle of the night.

Nobody in the town knew what was coming. Joel didn't himself, but his head was filled with screaming and he felt cold, so very cold, no matter how hard he worked dragging the metal and wood from the garage.

He'd been right about the parts. It was nearly all of the carousel superstructure, though no horses or soldiers and nothing of the pipe organ and engine. The monkey was missing too, the most important part, the center of it all, but while Joel was disappointed, he knew that finding that keystone would be the most difficult quest of all.

And there was something else in the town. Joel could feel it. There were still seven bullets in his gun but it was as if something knew he was here, who he was, what he was doing. He'd kick-start the cycle and he knew that, once it was started, it couldn't be stopped. He was on a deadline. He had to get out and across the Silver Bridge.

After the first flurry of disappointed visitors to Jim's garage, Joel was left alone. A cold wind blew and people stayed indoors. When the truck was loaded, Joel dusted his hands off on his coat, his fingers lingering over the fob pocket, feeling the ice brand deep into his flesh, into his soul.

The sun was setting, and Joel knew Point Pleasant would never be the same again, not after tonight. He also knew that there was more to do. He had to make the payment.

Taking the gun from its holster, Joel turned on his heel. He let himself into the gas station and walked through the empty store to the counter, and then around it. He reached down and pulled a trapdoor open, revealing stairs leading down to a small cellar Jim used for storing cartons of cigarettes and old oil cans.

Jim rolled on the floor and looked up as Joel descended the stairs, gun before him. His eyes were wide and wet and he shouted something, but it was just a muffled moaning behind his gag.

Joel glided across until he was standing over Jim. He smiled and raised the gun.

Murder had power and payment was due. And tonight, Point Pleasant had to pay a steep price indeed.

"I follow the light, friend," said Joel, pulling the hammer of the revolver back with his thumb. "And tonight the light, it shines for thee."

"Hey," said someone near. Then footsteps followed, heavy boots pounding on the road. Joel clicked the door of the truck shut and turned, key still in his hand. The fireman was young and built like one of the engines he drove, with a sharp buzz cut and ears that stuck out like jug handles.

"There a problem, friend?" asked Joel. The fireman pulled up in front of the truck and looked it over. It was white, JIM'S AUTO AND GAS, POINT PLEASANT, WEST VIRGINIA inscribed in elaborately scrolled, hand-painted black and red letters on the driver's door. Beneath that was a telephone number in a type little more functional.

"Where are you taking Jim's truck, exactly?"

Joel sighed. The man was still wearing his gear, big and bulky and unzipped to the waist, despite the cold. The man's skin was slick with sweat and the white T-shirt he wore under the heavy fire jacket was stuck to his skin.

"And what's in the back there?" the fireman asked. He walked around to the back of the truck and grabbed the edge of one of the yellow enameled metal signs. Immediately he pulled his hand back and shook it, like he'd got a shock.

"Hey!" the fireman yelled. Behind Joel came the sound of more booted feet running. Joel turned and saw two more firemen, just as large as their colleague.

The coin whispered to Joel, and pulled, pulled, pulled him toward the fireman. With one hand Joel brushed the edge of his jacket aside and unclipped the strap that held his gun in its holster.

"See, I'm wondering," said the fireman. "Things go to shit in town just as you blow in. Nobody has seen Jim all day and people have been talking about a whacko in a top hat messing with his stuff. And here you are with Jim's truck – what, he just give you the keys, did he?"

The man held his hand out, palm up. After a second Joel laughed and dropped the truck's keys into it. The fireman nodded, his fist closing as his two companions stepped forward.

"Now," said the fireman, "you want to tell me again where the hell Jim is and why you think you can just drive away in his truck?"

One of his friends cracked his knuckles. Joel smiled at him. Then he pushed the edge of his jacket to one side, revealing the gun. The firemen backed up immediately, the unpleasant smirks gone, their expressions now a mix of fear and surprise.

"Hey, cut it out, will you? All we want to know is what you're doing here and where Jim is."

"And I, friend," said Joel, "will tell you that I'm on a mission that no man can stop."

"Mission?" The second fireman sounded unsure. His companions looked at each other.

Joel smiled. "For you see, my friends, I follow the light, and tonight the light shines not just for me but for this whole glorious town. Penance must be paid, and the light seeks a price that is high and terrible."

He pulled the gun. One shot rang out. Then there was a pause, and another two shots echoed like thunder around the empty street. Lights came on in two houses on the other side of the street, and a dog started barking.

Joel stepped over the three bodies bleeding out on the road and climbed into the truck. He had to leave now. He'd only used four bullets out of seven, but he sensed that was enough.

The gears crunched and the truck creaked forward, toward the Silver Bridge out of town. And above, flying on leathery wings beneath the clouds, something large and gray, red eyes burning in the night, followed the truck, and the man in the black suit, and followed the light.

# XXIX
# SAN FRANCISCO
## TODAY

Alison hadn't been to St Roch before, but it was the same as any hospital she'd ever visited. She headed straight for the ER. Benny was sitting in the large, open waiting area, watching the door. As soon as Alison strode through it, she was on her feet and waving her over, smiling. Alison felt better seeing her. Benny lifted her baseball cap and replaced it backward, like she usually wore it in the office.

"Benny! Where's Ted? Is he OK?"

Benny nodded vigorously. "Oh yeah, yeah. They want to keep him in overnight, you know, observation and all that."

Alison shook her head. "Jesus, what the hell happened? Where was he?"

Benny placed her hand on her shoulder. Alison flinched, and she pulled it away, looking surprised. She smiled oddly, then turned and pointed down a corridor.

"He's down here," she said. "Come on."

Benny walked ahead. Alison hesitated. When Benny had touched her shoulder, it had gone numb, and was now alive with crawling pins and needles. She rolled her shoulder. Maybe she'd managed to tweak a nerve.

••••

Ted was sitting up in bed in an exam room, curtained off from the rest of the ER. Bob stood next to the bed in a white linen shirt and faded pale blue jeans, his long blond hair thick with sea salt. He winked and folded his arms. Alison nodded a greeting, but it was Ted she was here to see.

"Ted, Jesus!"

"Alison, hey," said Ted. He smiled and reached out one hand to her. She took it, but the pins and needles in her shoulder were starting to spread down her arm, making her fingers numb, rubbery and Ted's hand feel dull, unreal, and hot.

"What the hell happened? My God," she said, leaning in for a kiss. Ted drew her into a hug, pulling her at an angle across the bed. When she pulled away, Ted shrugged.

"Beats me. I remember going to bed and then I remember going to the bathroom. And then I woke up in here with these two fine people."

Alison looked up. Benny and Bob were standing next to each other, mirroring each other's pose, arms folded, grins wide and white.

"I can't thank you enough," she said. "Where did you find him?"

"Out on Fourth," said Bob. "I was out for a walk, bumped into Benny. Then there was this commotion outside. We thought someone had been run over, so we, like, ran out, see if we could help, and it's Ted, out cold on the sidewalk."

"So we called an ambulance. I tried to call you but my cell was out of power." Benny winced. "Sorry."

Bob shrugged. "And I don't carry a phone."

Alison laughed and waved their apologies away. "But you do carry a shirt around, I see?"

"You know," said Bob, looking down at himself. "For emergency purposes."

Alison turned back to Ted and looked into his eyes. He opened them wide.

"I'm fine!" he said.

"Uh-huh," said Alison. "What with the sleep walking and the amnesia, yes, you're fine. What did the doctor say?"

"Nothing yet, just that they want to keep me in. Maybe do an MRI tomorrow."

Alison squeezed Ted's hand. "Sounds like fun," she said. "So, you really can't remember a thing?"

Ted sighed. "Nope. Bed. Bathroom. Hospital. Such is my life. Although my insomnia seems to have gone."

"Yeah," said Bob. "Replaced with somnambulance."

Ted scratched his fingers again on the hospital sheets. "Maybe it's a concussion. I don't know. I've never had one."

"Well," said Alison, "let's wait and see what they say." She turned around on the bed to the other two. "Thanks again."

Benny jerked into life, almost jumping on the spot. She nudged Bob with an elbow and nodded toward the door.

"Yeah, well, we gotta be going. Don't worry about work. Only Zane is in at the moment. Mazzy isn't back until tomorrow, I think." She nodded at Bob. "I'll give you a ride."

"Thanks, brah," said Bob. He nodded at Alison. "Ma'am," he said, and then he nodded at Ted. "Take it easy."

When they'd gone, Alison kissed Ted again. "It's good to have you back," she said.

Ted smiled. "Glad to be back."


"So, he really doesn't know."

Bob and Benny walked across the hospital's parking lot, Bob shaking his head. "Nope, not a thing. Complete division."

Benny whistled, low. "Well, I guess that was possible."

"Yep," said Bob. "Trust a trickster god to make things difficult."

Benny laughed, but it died as she saw the look on Bob's face. Bob stuck his thumbs through the belt loops in his jeans and gazed out across the parking lot.

"Question is, how do we get it out of him?"

Benny interlocked her fingers on the top of her head. "Should we have called Alison so soon? I mean, before we got Nezha's power out?"

Bob shook his head. "The hospital was going to call her anyway. I thought it would be better if you did it first."

Benny nodded. "So... would Tangun know what to do?"

Bob nodded. "I hope so. He's here to help us, after all."

"And if he can't?"

"Well," said Bob. He looked up at the sky. "Then it'll kill him. If the world isn't destroyed first."

"Yeah. About that. How long, do you think?"

Bob frowned and looked down at the asphalt. His feet were still bare and he curled his toes against the ground. "It's different. Not like before. Before there was no warning, it just happened. This time it's waking slowly, like there's something poking it."

They stood in silence for a while.

"We need to get it out of Ted," said Benny. "We should tell Alison."

Bob laughed. "Yeah, and how is that going to go? Hey, Alison, your boyfriend is possessed by the power of a Chinese trickster god, only he isn't supposed to have it and the gods want it back. They've even sent someone to collect it. Oh, and by the way, my name isn't Bob and I've lived on the beach for six hundred years."

"Point. So, what then?"

Bob pointed to Benny's car. "We wait until she's gone. Then we go back in, and we take him out."

Benny looked around, to see if anyone was listening to their conversation in the middle of the parking lot. "What the hell? Alison has only just found him. He's going to disappear again?"

"Hey, chill, brah, no worries," said Bob. "We take him back to your apartment. Keep him there until Tangun comes back, and then we can get the power out of him."

"And then?"

"And then he'll be fine. We can say he discharged himself, take him back to his apartment. Call Alison. It'll all be fine. And *then* we can get to work."

"Work?"

Bob nodded. "To get to the bottom of this, we need to go back to the beginning. Before Nezha was murdered, he hid his power in a fortune cookie, right? We can find out where the Jade Emperor gets its fortune cookies from and check it out."

Benny frowned. "That's not much to go on."

"But it's something," said Bob. "And if we don't start on something, we can kiss goodbye to the city, and probably quite soon."

# XXX
# SAN FRANCISCO
## TODAY

Alison left Ted to get some sleep – much to her own relief, she was almost embarrassed to admit to herself. He seemed fine, he was in good hands, and he insisted she go; he was going to be there until tomorrow anyway, and she'd been up since three and hadn't stopped since then. And it wasn't like he could sleepwalk out of a hospital. He'd be moved out of ER into a room, and if anything were to happen, someone would see. Right?

It was hot outside, the sun already reflecting off the myriad windshields and rooftops of the cars in the front parking lot. Alison paused just outside the hospital's main doors and, hand shielding her eyes from the glare, tried to pick the direction her car was parked in; in the rush in, she hadn't paid attention to where she'd stopped. Loitering around were a number of people – patients mostly, dressed in hospital robes, but also a few uniformed staff, nurses, some visitors – idly enjoying a cigarette or two in the morning sun.

Alison glanced around, wondered why someone in a hospital, whether they worked there or were a patient, would smoke. Not that it was any of her business. A moment later she caught sight of a sign out in the parking lot, directing cars around to the back of the complex. She'd parked near that sign, or at least she thought she had. She stepped off the curb and crossed the lot.

Soon. *Soon.*

One of the people by the hospital doors pushed himself off the wall, watching as Alison walked into the parking lot. He took a drag on his cigar, blew a great blue-gray cloud up into the air. A couple of other people near him frowned, gave him one of *those* looks, but he didn't notice. He had eyes only for his next victim. Eyes only for Alison.

Things were reaching a climax. As the power built, so too *it* stirred, deep, deep below the city. The light was particularly bright on this woman. With the power from her death the Thing Beneath would stir once more, perhaps enough to shake the city.

The man dragged on his cigar again, watched Alison drive from the hospital. Her course was plotted. *It* knew, and *it* showed him.

There. She would meet her end... *there.* So would the two who protected her. The cold power within him stirred as he thought of it. Yes, yes! They were different – not like the women, but like the first he had killed. He had found him by accident in Chinatown, the old Chinese man in the long green coat. But he was different, he had sensed it – there was a shine on him that made the cold darkness in his mind writhe in pleasure. So he had killed the man and the Thing Beneath had stirred for the first time.

And now... there were more, like the old man? If only he had known! He would take them as well, and oh, how they would feast. There was such power living within them, the man with the blonde hair, the Asian girl. He had watched them walk into the hospital, their images almost shimmering with light in the man's eyes. They

were like the old man in the green coat. They were...
different.

Yes. *Yes*. With that power the Thing Beneath would wake,
and then it would feed. Murder would become massacre.
The entire city would die and then would be reborn, and
*its* minions, *its* golems, would crawl from the earth, clawing
their way to the surface. And then the Cold Dark from the
stars could feast, and as it ate it would grow, and grow,
controlling the mindless monster as it tore continents apart.

The Hang Wire Killer was about to slaughter his final
victims.

# XXXI
# SAN FRANCISCO
## TODAY

"Back so soon?" asked Ted. Bob gave him a tight smile. Benny pulled the curtain around the bed. Ted frowned.

"What's up?"

Bob looked at Benny. Benny nodded, stepped up to the side of the bed, and pointed at Ted. Benny's eyes rolled back into her head, her eyelids fluttering, and when she spoke her voice was deep, masculine. It echoed oddly, like she was speaking from behind a metal mask.

"*Sleep.*"

Ted shut his eyes, his head falling forward onto his chest.

Benny blinked, and shook her head at Bob. "This isn't going to work."

"Shut up and go find a wheelchair."

Benny sighed and slipped out between the closed curtains. Bob yanked the edges together after her.

Now what? Ted was asleep. They could get him out of the bed and into a wheelchair, but people would notice them wheeling him out.

Unless Bob made it so nobody could see them. Which would mean using his powers... Which would start the hunger, which would...

The hunger. Death. He was in a hospital. Death was all around him, it filled the building. He could taste it. Delicious and intoxicating, so very close.

If he used his powers, there was a risk he would lose control. He'd used them before, when the city faced disaster, but with that carnage had come distraction. He had been able to drink it in, use his powers, and the two had balanced. At least that's the way he liked to look at it.

Here, all he had to do was reach out, have a taste.

Benny was back, pushing a fold-up wheelchair through the gap in the curtains.

"How are we going to get him out, exactly? Someone will stop us. Bob?"

Bob turned around. The room looked brighter, felt warmer, and he saw Benny retreat against the bed.

"Don't worry," said Bob. "It's under control. Now." He turned and pulled the curtains of the exam room open. The ER was busy with patients and physicians, nurses and porters. Nobody seemed to have noticed.

"What the–"

Bob moved back to the bed. "They can't see us," he said. "Now, help me get Ted out of bed."

# XXXII
# SAN FRANCISCO
## TODAY

Bob watched as Benny shuffled around the warehouse, peering over wooden crates, looking into dark corners, all the while keeping her hands firmly in her pockets. Bob too. Having deposited Ted back at his apartment, they'd been poking around for an hour, but they had no idea what they were looking for, or what form it might take. It was best not to touch anything, not yet.

Even with the lights on, the warehouse was shadowy. The bulbs were bare incandescents, but they hung high from the ceiling above and were only just up to the job. Bob suspected they were original to the building. They knew how to make light bulbs last in those days. He thought he could remember this block going up in the 1920s, after the area had been razed by the quake of '06.

For the purposes of their mission, Bob considered the warehouse their "ground zero" – it was from this warehouse, full of foodstuffs imported from China, that the fortune cookies supplied to the Jade Emperor restaurant had come. Given that one of them had held a particular surprise for Ted, it was as good a place as any to start looking. But for what, exactly, Bob didn't know.

Benny stopped and turned around, shook her head. Bob sighed and sat on a packing case. Benny sat next to him, and swept off her baseball cap to scratch her head.

"I don't get it," said Benny. "Why would Nezha hide his power in a fortune cookie? Nobody even knew he was here. It was Tangun who sensed something was wrong and made me follow the trail of energy leaking from the cookie back to the Jade Emperor. He thought I could pick it up, only it was Ted who got the cookie, not me."

Bob frowned. "Why did you wait until Ted's birthday party? Why not just intercept the fortune cookie before anyone else got caught up in all this?"

"Tangun didn't direct me to the cookie until the night of the party," said Benny, "and then the cookies got swapped somehow."

Bob raised an eyebrow. Benny held her hands up.

"Dude, I swear, it just happened."

"Nezha the Trickster playing his final game? Great." He sighed. "I'm too old for this."

Benny laughed. "I thought gods didn't get old?"

"I didn't come back to the Earth to be a god," said Bob, shaking his head. "I chose to leave all that behind."

The pair sat in silence: the ancient god from across the oceans who had retired, the human host of an ancient god visiting from the heavens.

There was a sound from close by. Bob and Benny both stood from the crate and turned around. A second sound, the cracking of an old door being pushed open, and a triangle of light pierced the gloom of the warehouse, spotlighting the pair.

Two figures were silhouetted by the light from an open door – one large and chunky, the other smaller, thinner. As they stepped forward, the large shape resolved into that of a man, middle-aged and rotund, dressed in a shirt and open blue waistcoat. He had a handlebar moustache like a Nineteenth Century showman.

Next to him was a woman. Fair-haired, blue-eyed, she stared straight ahead, hypnotized, apparently unaware of her surroundings.

"You are here, as I knew you would be," said the man. He gestured with open arms, one with a thick loop of what looked like rope hanging from the elbow.

Bob looked the newcomer up and down, then turned his attention to Alison. "Alison? Who are you, and what have you done to her?"

"I'm sorry we haven't had a chance to meet, yet," said the man. "Allow me to introduce myself. I am the one and only Magical Zanaar. I killed one god, and I'm here to kill two more."

Bob and Benny looked at each other. The Magical Zanaar grinned and pointed at Bob and at Benny. The ground began to shake beneath them, the cement cracking and then breaking into angled shards. Bob and Benny stumbled, unable to move, as they sank into the ground and were held fast.

"Ladies and gentlemen," said the Magical Zanaar, "step right up and behold the greatest spectacle on Earth! One man against the heavens, and lo! See how the gods themselves are powerless against the Cold Dark. See how the Thing Beneath stirs from its eternal dreamless sleep!"

The Magical Zanaar advanced on Bob and Benny, the loop of steel cable slipping from his arm and into his hands, his eyes glowing red in the dim light of the warehouse.

Darkness and heat. Moisture and salty dampness.

Bob's eyes flickered open. Around him the world was a dark void filled with geometric brown shapes stacked in some kind of order. He blinked, and the shapes began to resolve themselves. Packing boxes. They were in the warehouse. It was night outside. And...

Something else now. Something confusing, frightening. There was no pain, although there was discomfort. But there was something else, something Bob had not experienced for hundreds, maybe thousands of years.

Lost time. Lost memories. He'd been unconscious. Bob didn't sleep. That story about him was actually true.

There were other things that Bob didn't need to do. He didn't need to eat, or drink, or even breathe. He didn't need to look like a human male in his late thirties. Everything was an illusion, from the toned physique and chiseled jaw to the carefully worn blue jeans. But he'd settled on his appearance many millennia ago. The blonde hair and fair skin had frightened his people, out in the Pacific. Fear was an emotion he enjoyed.

Bob also couldn't feel pain, and he couldn't be killed. It wasn't that he was indestructible, or impervious, or had steel skin or unbreakable bones. These concepts just didn't apply to him. They had no meaning.

Losing consciousness was therefore... unprecedented. To knock out someone who didn't even exist on this plane of reality was quite an achievement.

Bob blinked again but the warehouse still spun on a slow axis around him. He frowned, and moved an arm, but this only made his vision wobble. He kicked with his feet and found only air beneath them.

There was something closed tight around his throat. As he spun slowly around, another shape came into view.

A body, next to his, suspended in mid-air, slowly rotating. It was lifeless and covered with blood, which seemed to have poured unchecked from the throat. The body was hanging by the neck from a loop of woven steel cable tied with a simple slipknot. The body's head was drooped forward. The steel cable had nearly separated it from the body.

Bob squinted and gritted his teeth, trying to clear the smoky confusion from his own mind. Knocking out a god left a hell of a headache.

In the dark, the body next to him rotated again until Bob was able to recognize the insignia on the shirt it was wearing – a man wearing a football helmet and eye patch, two crossed swords behind him.

The Oakland Raiders football team.

Benny.

Bob gasped airlessly, and his hands flew to his own neck. There was the cable, tight against his skin. Tight enough to kill, certainly, and slick with blood. But Bob was a god of life as well as death, and his neck had healed while he'd been out. The cable was still tight enough to asphyxiate, but Bob didn't need to breathe anyway. The Magical Zanaar had been careless. He'd been able to kill Nezha, assisted no doubt by the evil power within him, but Bob was a different category of deity. Especially now he was starting to use his powers on the Earth, just a little. Bob was a god much harder to kill.

He reached up and tugged the cable above his head experimentally. It was solid, rock hard. Straining his neck against the noose, he looked up, tracing the course of the wire as it vanished upward into the dark ceiling.

Bob looked back at Benny and felt his stomach roll. Benny may have played host to an ancient god, but while Tangun was absent she was mortal. Her death had been violent, sickening. Here, swinging so close to Benny's body, Bob could feel the urges rise, the hunger stir inside. There was power in blood, in death. Bob knew it – it was part of him – and clearly the killer knew it too. He was using that same power to wake the Thing Beneath. The brutality, the savagery of the Hang Wire murders had a purpose.

Zanaar had power. Real power, enough to overpower both him and Benny. The Cold Dark – Bob didn't know what that was, but Zanaar seemed to be connected to both that and the amorphous evil stirring beneath the city. The Thing Beneath.

Bob cleared his head and began to swing his legs. The steel cable squeaked as it took his weight without strain. This amount of cable could hold up a bus. High above there was a very low groaning sound, virtually inaudible, as the rafters around which the cable was tied sighed with the strain.

As Bob moved in the air, he analyzed the strength of the cable, the tension, the flexibility. He pushed a little with his mind and understood the weft and the weave of the fibers bound inside the cable with the clarity and accuracy of an electron microscope.

Then he pushed a lot with his mind, and the steel cable around his neck broke down into its constituent atoms and fell to the warehouse floor in a cloud of glittering silver dust.

Bob floated in the air next to Benny. Above him the remains of the cable whipped back up into the darkness as the weight on it suddenly evaporated. The end of the cable snickered past one of the hanging light bulbs, then it whipped back and shattered the globe. Without thinking, Bob reduced the falling glass shards to individual molecules of silica. Then he looked up, realized what he'd done, and refocused his mind. Once he started exercising his long-dormant powers, they'd started to take over. The glass had been no danger to him, but part of him was starting to enjoy the freedom, the power to manipulate the world around him. He had to focus, concentrate, do only what was necessary.

Bob drifted down. He and Benny had been hanged ten feet from the floor, in the open space between the crates, opposite the main warehouse door. He looked up at Benny's lifeless, blood-soaked corpse, swinging on the cable, and blinked.

The cable holding Benny disintegrated into powder. He held Benny's body in the air, then gently lowered her to the warehouse floor and the great pool of blood that had collected underneath her body.

Bob shook his head. It was a waste, senseless and unnecessary, another example of what went wrong when the gods meddled in the lives of people. Benny was dead, as were five other innocents, killed by someone wielding a power with no control.

Bob could bring Benny back to life. It was easy enough, as easy as a simple command, a push at the fabric of the world. But it might be enough to push Bob over the edge. He was afraid of what the power he wielded might do to him if he decided to use it.

He had been both a god and a devil, and he wasn't sure which side was stronger.

Benny was dead, but Bob knew that Tangun the Founder could not be killed, at least not like this. But when Tangun visited Earth, he needed a host mind and body. Benny's family tree stretched back to the Three Kingdoms of Korea, nearly two thousand years of history, destined to be the host line. Tangun was wound within her DNA.

Another of the god's mistakes.

Bob stood over the body. No – Benny deserved better. He wouldn't let her just be another victim of the games gods play.

*"Benny, ho'olu komo la kaua."*

There was a gentle splash as two golden boots settled in the pool of blood. Tangun's golden mask smiled at Bob. Bob stepped back in surprise.

"Kanaloa, my friend," said Tangun. Behind the smiling gold mask, Bob could see Benny's eyes were bright and alive. Her chin and neck were clean, with no blood, no injury. He'd resurrected Benny, who had brought Tangun straight back to Earth.

Bob bowed. "Tangun, King and Founder. We must act quickly."

The golden mask was suddenly a scowling visage of rage and terror, the frozen, screaming face of hell. Bob flinched. There was something different about his friend now. Tangun was ready for war.

"We dally," said Tangun, his voice booming like thunder in the warehouse. He rose two feet in the air, his golden armor sparking with energy. "Come, the chase is on."

# INTERLUDE
# CONEY ISLAND, NEW YORK
# 1977

The city was burning. Not Manhattan, not down where people sat on lawn chairs on the sidewalk in the warm July night, drinking and talking and gazing in wonder at the empty, black glass towering over them on all sides. Not in Midtown, where cops were busy freeing the old and the wealthy from dead elevators. Farther up, where the decay of New York had really taken hold, where buildings were empty shells and where graffiti covered every surface and the gangs had control. Up there, in the Bronx, in the war zone, where the creeping failure of the city was at its most severe, where people were desperate.

There, the city burned.

The power went out at 7:23 p.m., and just like that, the largest city in the United States became impotent, floundering in the sudden darkness. It was inevitable, perhaps, the final embarrassment of a city so deep in debt that even the President had told it to go to hell.

Maybe that's where they were now, in a hell of darkness and chaos, of utter confusion, paralyzing fear. For some there was opportunity in the darkness. Fear and anxiety and hopelessness bred anger and hate and desperation. Bred crime, lawlessness.

The looting began, coupled with rioting and fighting and then, in the darkness, a light flared.

Ladies and gentlemen, the Bronx was burning.

Joel watched from shadows under the eaves of a closed restaurant as the emergency services worked, and worked hard. The power was out at Coney Island. On a hot summer's night the place should have been burning bright, nothing but lights and the smell of hot dogs and popcorn and the screams of the happy and the happily terrified.

With the power out, the shadow under the eaves was an almost impenetrable blackness, not even the strobe of the cop cars and ambulances across the street were able to penetrate. Joel was out of sight, invisible in the night.

The street in front of him was packed with people. Getting everybody out of the amusement park was a big task, and there were people still stuck inside, in a rocket-shaped car at the high point of its orbit or swinging at the top of the Ferris wheel, with nothing to see but the dark city from horizon to horizon.

There was fear here, Joel could feel it – the electric charge in the air, the cold burning in his waistcoat pocket. The fabric of the place was thick with it. But the firemen and the fairground operators were hand-cranking the Ferris wheel's gears, and people were being helped out of the swinging seats as each reached ground level. Out on the street, hotdog stands were doing a flying trade, their cookers operating on gas, the owners not needing electricity to count the dollar bills accumulating in their apron pockets.

Joel took the coin from his pocket and squeezed it in the middle of his fist. The cold hurt, like a knife plunged through his palm. Joel concentrated, focused on the screaming in his head.

Joel opened his eyes and looked to his left. There, in the darkness of the park, where the rides were black shapes jagged against the moonlit sky. Where there was no one, not anymore. Where, farther down the street, by a side entrance, sat two police cars, their lights off.

There was fear and there was death, and near too. In the dark fairground, something terrible.

The next piece.


"We need to see if we can get any of this stuff shifted tomorrow, after maybe taking down the – hey, excuse me!"

Joel walked past the cop, ignoring him, heading toward the body on the grass. The cop flipped his notebook shut and pulled the flashlight out from under his arm.

"Hey!"

Joel looked down at the body. It was a girl, face down, in a long dress. The grass was gray in the night, covered by irregular patches of something dark, nearly black. Joel smiled as he adjusted his footing. Blood, and lots of it.

"That's enough, buddy!"

Joel glanced up. One of the cops pulled his gun and walked toward him, his colleague quickly pocketing the notebook and reaching for his own weapon. Joel raised his hands and turned around on the spot, face to face with the gun. The other cop hesitated; the first seemed to sense this and called to him over his shoulder.

"Get on the radio, get Mackenzie over here, pronto." He turned to Joel. "On the ground, pal. Now!"

Joel glanced at the ground, and back at the cop.

"Well, friend, there's a lot of blood on this here grass. I'm sure you don't want me disturbing the scene of a crime, now do you?"

The cop did nothing for a couple of seconds. Then he gestured with his gun. Joel smiled and crabbed sideways until he felt the grass underfoot was dry.

The other cop turned on his heel.

The pearl-handled gun was in Joel's hand in the blink of an eye. Even as the first cop gasped in surprise and raised his own weapon up, Joel brought the base of his revolver's grip down on the man's face. There was a crack and cop's nose sank into his face, blood erupting in a thick spurt. The cop dropped his weapon but his cry was choked off as Joel's free hand found the man's throat. Joel pushed down; the cop didn't resist and hit the ground on his knees. Joel raised his gun hand up again and hit the cop on the crown of his head just once. The cop gurgled as Joel released him, then fell sideways onto the grass.

The cop with the notebook was a rookie, had to be. He turned back around in time to see his colleague topple to the ground, but then stood for a second, frozen, his eyes wide. Then he drew breath to shout and finally pulled his own gun from its holster.

Too late. Joel was faster, his speed preternatural, *assisted*. He grabbed the rookie's wrist and yanked upwards, breaking bone and causing the gun to fall from his grip. Holding the pearl-handled revolver in his other hand, he sideswiped the rookie's jaw. There was a crunch, like someone biting into a crisp apple, and something liquid and black in the low light flew from the cop's mouth. The rookie staggered, his head bowed. Joel took the invitation and cracked his skull as he had done with the first cop. The rookie sighed and fell to the ground, face-first.

Joel stepped over to the first cop's body, feeling the power swell around him as the two lives drained away in the blacked-out night. The first cop gurgled and one leg twitched; Joel fell onto his back on one knee, reached down, and twisted the man's head. Another crack, and the gurgling stopped.

Joel had dispatched the police as quietly as he could, but people would be coming soon. Joel glanced over and

up; there were still people on the Ferris wheel, high up in
the air with a view over Coney Island. If anyone had been
looking in his direction, they would have seen the flashlight
and dark shapes moving, surely.

No matter. He'd find the piece, collect it and go, off to
follow the light to the next part, then the next, then the next.

Joel moved over to the rookie and took the flashlight
from his cooling hand. He turned it on the body of the girl,
murdered in the dark night of July 13th, 1977.

No, not murdered, at least not by human hand. The death
was unnatural in more ways than one. This was why Joel
had been brought here, he could feel it.

Holstering the pearl-handled revolver, Joel took the coin
from his pocket, his fingers afire. He rolled it into his palm
and squeezed and held his hand out as he slowly walked in
a circle.

The girl's body – and now the bodies of the two cops – was
lying in a clearing near the north side of the amusement park,
an area behind a series of dark fairground attractions. A water
dunk, the back of two closed-up concession stands, and...

Joel walked around the front of the structure, into the
park proper.

It was a shooting range. Ornate and colorful, a huge
construction of wood and metal enameled in bright and
elaborate drawings of stars and a great comet arching over
the whole of the front. On each side, carved out of wood,
stood a pair of life-sized soldiers in red coats, tall hats, each
holding a rifle and bayonet. There were more at the back
of the range, framing the empty target area where paper
boards would spring up for the players to try to hit with
their own toy rifles.

The coin pulled, pulled, pulled. Joel raised the flashlight at
each solider, standing boldly to attention, rifle shouldered,
shiny bayonet pointed to the starless sky.

The bayonet of the solider nearest did not shine. It was dark, and when Joel shone the flashlight on it, it didn't shine but glistened.

Blood.

Joel shone the light over the soldier's face, chest. The carved figure was covered in it. In the flashlight's beam the soldier's red cheeks glowed and it grinned with a mouth of straight white teeth. The thing was immobile, interlocked wooden segments assembled into the form of a giant toy soldier.

Immobile, but not lifeless.

Joel flicked the light off, counted two, and turned it on again.

The soldier's carved wooden features were twisted now in anger, the mouth snarling, the cheeks still glowing red but the heavy black eyebrows dipped into a V over the eyes. Eyes now fixed firmly on Joel.

"I follow the light, and the light it shines for thee," said Joel, pocketing the flashlight and getting to work.

# XXXIII
# SAN FRANCISCO
## TODAY

There was something wrong with Tangun.

Kanaloa, god of death and of life, floated high about Chinatown, surveying the city below, Tangun hovering beside him. Bob had bent the light around them, so if anyone looked up they'd see nothing at all, least of all a man with long blond hair wearing only a pair of jeans and a man clad in antique Korean royal armor. Bob had to be careful. They could defy gravity, and Bob could play with photons so they wouldn't be seen. But any more, and who knew what might happen. Bob supposed, if he thought about it, that he could turn the gravity off over the entire city, or separate San Francisco into its constituent elements. That would stop the killer and the power that drove him. Stop the thing beneath. And so the city would be destroyed and everyone in it would die in the process. But was that a bad thing, really?

What was worse? That the city was destroyed as the thing below awoke? Or that the entire world be ruled over by Kanaloa, the devil-god? Power. Power was dangerous.

Bob closed his eyes and shivered, and jolted like he'd come out of a deep sleep. There was a soft, metallic moan from beside him. That's when he noticed the problem.

He turned to look at his warrior friend, but Tangun was no longer beside him. Instead, he had floated downward to land with a thud on the roof of the warehouse.

"Kanaloa..." His voice was quiet, merely an echo of the defiant roar that usually sounded from the golden mask.

Tangun fell onto his knees, the scalloped helmet dipped toward the ground as Bob landed beside him.

"Tangun?"

Tangun pressed his hands into the roof, like he was trying to keep himself from falling over completely.

Bob took a step closer. "What's wrong?"

Tangun straightened up, and looked at Bob. Bob recoiled. He couldn't stop himself. He took one involuntary step backward, too quickly, and his heel twisted under him. He fell heavily onto his backside.

Tangun's golden mask was a frozen visage of despair and pain. The expression was horrific, the face of the devil from Korean mythology. Blood ran in two thick courses from the eye holes, streaking the gold with bright red.

Bob watched, fascinated, as the blood trickled to the bottom edge of the mask, collecting on the lip before dripping in heavy splotches onto the roof.

Bob stood, and stepped up to his fellow god. He peered closely at the mask, through the gaps at the face of Benny underneath. Benny's face was clean and there was no blood, but her eyes were glassy and she didn't blink.

"Tangun?" Bob reached out to touch the mask, the blood dripping from it, but drew his hand back.

Tangun sat back on his haunches. "The line is broken," he said, gasping. "The line is broken. My time on the Earth draws to a close."

Bob dropped down so he was at the same level as Tangun. His eyes searched the mask. "I don't understand."

"The Golden Child. The host," said Tangun. "She passed from this realm. Without the Golden Child I am but a memory doomed to fade from this world."

"Hold on," said Bob. Tangun tipped forward and Bob grabbed his shoulders, steadying him. The armor was ice cold. "Benny died but I brought her back." He peered closer at the mask, through the slots. Benny's glassy eyes stared back. "She's in there, inside the armor."

Tangun shook his head. "Benny lives again, but her death and return has broken the line. Without the Golden Child, I soon will leave and return to the Heavenly Ones. My grip on the world becomes ever more delicate."

Bob shook his head. "I need you here, Tangun. How long can you hold on?"

"I know not," said the warrior king. "The longer I cling to the life of the Golden Child, so her time, too, becomes short."

Bob rubbed his chin. "So if you stay, Benny dies. Doesn't matter. I can bring her back again."

Tangun laughed weakly, his wide, ornate helmet wobbling, but the mask was still frozen in the expression of pain and terror.

"Even you know the price of that."

"I... I can control it."

"Ha!" Tangun lifted his head, and this time the mask's expression had softened, the mouth almost forming a smile. "You are a poor liar, my friend. But it is for the Golden Child that I worry. Your power corrodes her soul, Kanaloa. You dare to bestow the gift of life upon her again, so she will fade more and more to the shadow realm."

Bob sighed. Tangun was right. Human souls were thin, fragile things. Repeated death and resurrection would cause irreparable damage to Benny.

"Well. Shit," said Bob. He stood up. He wasn't sure he could do it alone. He needed Tangun to take Nezha's power back to the Heavenly Ones. It had to be him, thought Bob. He wasn't sure he would be able to resist taking the power for himself, given the chance.

The whole city was in danger. And how much farther would it spread? First San Francisco, and then California, and then the western United States before the monster underground crawled east, rolling over the land, shaking it to pieces as it did, growing stronger as it expanded. If they didn't stop it here, now, then maybe they never would, gods or not. Especially not with this other entity involved, the Cold Dark. It had power. A *lot* of power.

Bob watched as Tangun wobbled and crashed onto the warehouse roof on his back. Bob reached down, and Tangun took his arm. The warrior's armor was as cold as the abyssal depths of the ocean as his power, tethered to the Earth via his host, Benny, drained away, back to the home of the gods.

Bob pulled Tangun back to his knees. Through the mask, Bob saw Benny's eyes were still glazed, the lids now half closed. Tangun's metallic groan sounded again.

"I can help," said Bob. Tangun shook his head slowly.

"You cannot, friend."

"I *can*," said Bob. "I can hold onto Benny's soul. Keep it where it should be–"

"You cannot–"

"–and that should give you some extra time. I can keep Benny on this side of the shadows. It won't be like before, but it might be enough to hold your line together for long enough."

"Bob," said Tangun – said *Benny*, her voice a hollow whisper. "Dude, you can't do that. You don't have enough power anymore."

Bob felt fear rise in him, and something else too. Excitement.

Tangun slumped forward. Blood poured from the mask and splattered on the warehouse roof, splashing Bob's feet. Time was running out. And Bob wasn't sure he could face the fight alone.

He had to do it, just the once. Just enough.

"My name isn't Bob," he said. "My name is Kanaloa, and I am a god."

He closed his eyes, and he remembered.

Kanaloa. God of the ocean, god of life. God of death. Millennia ago his people had worshipped him, praised him for the bountiful seas. He kept them fed, he kept them safe, as god of the seas.

And as god of death, he took them away, sometimes before they were ready, with cruelty and pleasure, feeding on their pain as their life energies left their physical bodies. Kanaloa, a god to be thanked and worshipped. A god to be feared and appeased.

On the warehouse roof, Bob flinched, his eyes still closed. He didn't want to do this. He was afraid what Kanaloa would do, drunk on power, a whole world as his plaything.

But he had to trust himself. He had learned a lot. Had he learned enough?

Death and life are intertwined, the two sides of the same coin, one unable to exist without the other. Like Benny and Tangun. Like, perhaps, Kanaloa and Bob.

"Here goes nothing," said Bob.

A warmth spread around him, and for a moment he remembered the sea and the rolling waves on the surface, and the creatures below that made their home in his domain and who were his friends.

He remembered the islands, and the people on them. He remembered their smiles at the ocean bounty he granted them; he remembered their reverence and their ecstasy as they worshipped the god of the sea.

He remembered the joy of the departed as he guided their souls from this world to the next.

He remembered the fear of those left behind. He remembered how some believed their god was an angry but just and all-knowing lord and master, and devoted themselves to death-worship and sacrifice in his name.

He remembered being Kanaloa.

He searched. And then he found her.

Found Benny.

Bob felt the warmth spread, hotter now, and he smiled and watched the dancing colors behind his closed eyelids as the life force ebbed and flowed, ebbed and flowed.

And then...

*Something moving.*

Bob gasped. The rolling waves of warmth that swept out from his body and into Tangun evaporated in an instant, replaced by a deep chill. A cold Bob knew well. The cold of deep, *deep* water, the cold of the void, far below the surface, the deepest place, a narrow, black wound in the side of the planet.

And something moved within it. The colors vanished from Bob's vision, replaced with a darkness that itself, somehow, impossibly, felt cold. A darkness that moved, shapes black on black on black. Angular and geometric forms, moving mechanically, rhythmically, pulsing like a heartbeat, growling like an animal.

Something moving. Eyes in the dark. Hands reaching up through burnt earth, blackened, carbonized: golems born of the ground itself, the thing's eyes and ears and hands, its minions crawling over the Earth. Like 1906. Like 1989.

Like today.

The visions stopped, the sounds ceased, and Bob felt himself falling. He cried out in surprise and opened his eyes just as he felt his face hit the rooftop. And then Bob felt two things he had never felt before.

Pain: cold and deep, primal, angry, electric.

Fear: black and limitless, as dark as space. There was something there, in the darkness. Something else, not sleeping beneath the city but flying, arcing through space on a trail of fire. Intelligent, shining, yet still primal, animalistic. The power Zanaar had spoken of in the warehouse.

The Cold Dark.

Bob didn't know what it was. It had come from elsewhere, but was now in the city, its power growing. It was entangled with The Thing Beneath, the two feeding off each other, a symbiotic relationship.

Then it was gone and Bob was falling again.

Bob pushed himself up from the roof. He felt different, energized... but the fear was still there, clutching at his heart.

He closed his eyes, rolled his neck, focused on calming himself. Then he looked up. Standing before him was Tangun the Founder, his gold armor shining bright. The mask was creased with laughter.

"Tangun?"

"Dude, this is sick!" came the voice from behind the mask.

"Benny?"

"Tangun is here too," said Benny. Bob could see Benny's face behind the mask. She was looking around the inside of the mask, her face split into a wide grin. "Dude, seriously, this is radical. I'm like Iron Man, medieval style!"

This wasn't right. Tangun and his host weren't supposed to co-habit the same body.

"Kanaloa, I am healed. For this I give thanks."

Bob blinked. It was Tangun's voice – deeper, masculine, the voice of a commanding king.

"Ah, yeah," said Benny. "OK, that was weird."

It had worked then. Bob – Kanaloa – was holding Benny's soul in place. He just hoped it would be enough to keep Tangun in the world without doing permanent damage to Benny or her soul.

Bob dragged himself to his feet. "Tangun, I've seen it," he said. "The Cold Dark. We're in trouble."

"I too sense the danger," said Tangun. He flexed his gauntlets and then delicately placed his hands on his hips, his mask now one of determined, directed anger. "But my question is, brother – did *it* see *you*?"

Bob stared at the golden mask of the warrior-god, and nodded. "It did," he said.

"Then the fight is on," said Tangun. "Our quarry moves."

Bob looked around the rooftop, then realized Tangun wasn't talking about anything he could actually see. The warrior-god was looking out into the city with other senses.

"Where?" asked Bob.

Tangun titled his head. "He has the woman with him still."

"Alison?"

"She lives."

Bob sighed in relief.

"For now," said Tangun. "I fear she may be the killer's final victim."

"Final?"

The helmet tilted to the other side. "They move towards the circus. There the powers intersect."

Bob nodded as he put the pieces together. "The Magical Zanaar. He's from the circus – like Ted's alter ego. Nezha had been trying to show us, all along." He turned and jogged to the edge of the warehouse roof. The circus was in Golden Gate Park, due west.

"Wait," said Tangun, his voice booming. Bob turned around.

"Come on," he said.

"We must stop them before they reach the circus, to save the woman."

Bob moved back. Tangun stood infuriatingly still. Bob tapped the back of his hand against the warrior's breastplate, willing him to action. At the contact, Tangun jerked on his feet, and when he spoke again it was with Benny's voice.

"Follow me," she said, and she ran for the roof's edge.

# XXXIV
# SAN FRANCISCO
## TODAY

A voice calls his name, and Highwire opens his eyes.

It is dark. He lies, waiting, listening. The sounds are different. He tunes in, focuses his senses. Quiet streets outside, still in the city. Late. No, *early*. Very early.

In a few seconds his eyes adjust to the dark and he can see the room he is in. It is a bedroom, familiar. The blinds have been pulled down but streetlight leaks in between the horizontal slats.

Something stirs in his mind. He looks around for the person who called out to him, but the bedroom is empty and there are no sounds from beyond the door. Perhaps he imagined it.

He has been in this apartment before. This is the apartment of the man in the brown jacket, the man with brown hair and the bruise healing over his left eyebrow.

*Get up, Ted.*

The voice again. A whisper over his shoulder, although he is still lying on the bed.

Ted. This is Ted's apartment. *His* apartment. He is that man. He is Ted. He knows the voice was speaking to him, to Highwire, the acrobat.

He lies in the dark and waits and listens. Then he feels it.

Fire, in the sky. A bright light that shines, shines. Cold power.

And something... moving, beneath the city, channeling power, siphoning it downward. Mindless, crawling, being fed by death, by blood, by murder.

Canvas. The Big Top. The tight rope.

*Yes, Ted,* whispers the voice in his head. *There the nexus lies.*

He blinks and waits, but the voice has gone.

The *nexus.* It is at the circus, he can feel it now. The Thing Beneath sleeps under the entire city, its very being embedded in the tectonic plate. The circus, like the city, is right on top, but the circus is the channel. The circus is *feeding* it.

And...

*Well done, Ted. Better late than never.*

Highwire sits up, rubs his temples. Cold power and a vision of infinite dark.

"Who are you?" he asks the empty room, but there is no reply. Was the voice even real?

He moves on the bed and his head thumps, *one-two*, in time with his heart. He looks around. He doesn't remember getting to the apartment – to *his* apartment – but then he doesn't remember a lot of things.

But–

*Yes, Ted.*

–he *knows* about the nexus. And about–

*That's right, Ted.*

–the Cold Dark, and the Thing Beneath. He knows he must stop it. Them.

An odd feeling swims over him. There is dizziness, and nausea. He jerks his head around, sure there is someone there at his shoulder, but the bedroom still has a single occupant.

He turns back to the door. He needs to continue the hunt. The killer must be stopped, must be–

*Too late, Ted.*

"Too late for what?" he asks aloud. The voice is real then. It is not his voice, although he thinks now that perhaps only he can hear it. The feeling of someone by his shoulder persists.

*They have returned to the nexus, Ted.*

He has a purpose. To hunt the killer. Now... what? He is too late?

*Yes, Ted. We are too late. If we are to stop them, we must follow them to the nexus. We might be in time, if we are lucky, Ted.*

He gets up and he stands in the bedroom. The apartment is still. The presence at his shoulder seems to move from one side to the other. He turns around again, knowing there is nobody there.

"But I come from the circus."

There is no reply.

"Who are you?"

Silence. It unnerves him, so he leaves the bedroom, walks around the apartment. He remembers it now, all of it, as he sees individual items: the brown leather sofas. The coffee table. The dining table. The laptop on it.

The laptop is open, the screen bright in the dark room. There is something moving on the screen, black and spidery, flickering and flickering.

The word processor is open. There is a single line of text, in a repeated column. The page is scrolling, like the track pad is jammed. The text at the top and bottom of the page flickers as the infinite scroll zooms onward.

They are Chinese characters. Logotypes. It takes him a moment to notice this, because he can read the text without any problem.

*You are the master of every situation.*
*You are the master of every situation.*
*You are the master of every situation.*
*You are the master of every situation.*

Highwire reaches out and touches the track pad, and the scrolling stops.

*Follow the power, Ted,* says the voice in his head. Then, as he watches, text begins to type itself on the laptop's screen, adding new lines to the column, one word at a time.

*YOU*
*ARE*
*THE*
*MASTER*
*OF*
*EVERY*
*SITUATION*

He closes the lid of the laptop. The apartment is suddenly much darker. He leaves it, and follows the voice. He returns to the circus. To the nexus.

# XXXV
## SAN FRANCISCO
### TODAY

Tangun was nearly a full block ahead, in pursuit of The Magical Zanaar. He ran through the crowds of Chinatown, pedestrians and tourists parting around him, all unaware of his presence. Bob followed. They couldn't see him either. Exercising his powers, just enough.

Bob had already broken the rules, bringing Benny back to life, binding her soul, holding it in place to keep Tangun tethered to the world. And then there was the manipulation of gravity and of light. It was all very simple.

And wouldn't it be so much easier just to step through into the quantum foam of the city and pick out the evil? He could pluck Zanaar and send the Cold Dark back to the stars. He could extract Nezha's power from Ted. Destroy the thing under the city once and for all. He could stop it all, just like that. No more running, no more racing against the clock. Just one thought, and it would be done.

And then what? The possibilities were endless. Bob stopped in the middle of the street, the crowds now coursing around him like he was a boulder in a river. He grinned. He remembered what it was like, when he was Kanaloa, when the world was young, the universe a blank canvas, the very fabric of reality clay in his hands.

He could save the city, the whole world, and then... improve it. And why not? San Francisco could be rebuilt according to his design. And then he could apply the same to his home, Hawaii, and then to the rest of the world. And why stop there? Why, there was no power in the universe that could stop him. He was a god, and what was a god without worshippers? They would bow to him in fear.

Bob's head spun, and his eyes felt hot and wet. He staggered on his feet, and shook his head.

And that was why there were rules and why there was no need for gods anymore. Absolute power corrupts, but absolute power over everything, space/time itself bending to your will – that was not corruption, that was *consumption*. One step into a darkness from which he could never return. Bob had pushed far enough already. He dared not go much farther.

Bob only hoped Tangun possessed the same self-control he did. He looked up and saw a flash of gold ahead, where the street began to climb one of San Francisco's famous hills.

Bob followed.

He saw Zanaar, eventually. Alison too. They disappeared around the mouth of an alley. Tangun was behind them. Bob followed, miles behind. He'd spent too much time dreaming of power.

The alley was dark. The light from the lantern-shaped lamps of the main street and the hundred different neon signs in orange and red, blue and green, that lined it only spilled so far.

Bob stepped into the shadows, noticing for the first time that the street was wet beneath his bare feet. Something shone on the ground ahead. He moved closer, reached down and picked up Tangun's warrior helmet.

Bob rotated the golden helm in his hands until the mask was facing him. It wore an expression of abject fear. The eyes were wide, the mouth open, screaming in silence. Looking at the twisted mask, Bob felt afraid. What had happened? He hadn't been *that* far behind, surely?

"Kanaloa..."

Bob looked up. The Magical Zanaar – the Hang Wire Killer – was standing at the top of a fire escape. Next to him stood Alison, eyes glittering, unblinking in the night. There was something else, long and thin, snaking from Alison's neck and disappearing against the silhouette of her captor. Steel cable. He was about to kill her, but Bob had arrived just in time.

Where the hell was Tangun? Zanaar couldn't have killed him so quickly, so easily. The alley was empty, save for the three of them. Bob could feel his grip on Benny's soul as strong as ever.

Bob let the power surge within him. He floated up until he was level with Zanaar. The circus ringmaster raised an arm and pointed at him.

Bob couldn't move. Not up or down, left or right, back or forth. Bob tried to raise his arms, but they were immobile, frozen. He realized the intercostal muscles between his ribs were paralyzed. If he had needed to breathe, he would now be suffocating.

Zanaar stepped forward, into better light. He was smiling, but it was strange, almost mechanical, like whatever was inside him had seen a smile but didn't know quite what it was for. His eyes were glazed like Alison's, and when he looked at Bob they were unfocussed.

"Kanaloa, a long way from home..." whispered Zanaar. He tilted his head, and his mouth moved before he spoke again. "We know what you are."

The power that controlled him, the black nothing that had fallen from the sky, was more dangerous than the Thing Beneath, Bob realized that now. The Thing Beneath was alive but unaware, not a sentient creature but a crawling presence. This was different. The Cold Dark was intelligent, alien. A power from somewhere else, working to some hidden plan.

There was nothing left of Zanaar now. He showed no surprise, no reaction that Bob was still alive.

"Why... why are you here?" Bob asked.

The ringmaster mouthed the words, and then the voice spoke, each word carefully selected, carefully spoken. "You... cannot... stop... the... construction... build and spread... build and spread... the power now... we have the power now... to build and spread... build and spread..." He yanked on the cable in his hand, jerking Alison's body. Bob knew what would happen next. Zanaar would throw her off fire escape and let the cable do its work

"What... power?" It took all of Bob's focus to speak. He pushed at his invisible bonds; as he did, Zanaar gasped, and the grip around Bob tightened. Zanaar was channeling something very strong indeed.

"Power in death... power in death... there is power in death," said Zanaar. "Kanaloa knows this is true. Kanaloa takes his power from death. From murder."

Bob gritted his teeth. Zanaar smiled, and looked down, between his feet, to the street below.

"It wakes and grows hungry. We... feed it. We... give it power. We... build and spread... build and spread... together we build and spread..."

Tangun had been right. He'd said the powers intersected at the circus – the Cold Dark, intelligent and aware but small, latching itself like a parasite to the mindless hulk of the Thing Beneath. Feeding it power through murder, until it had enough to wake up.

Alison. The final victim, as Tangun had warned. And where the hell *was* Tangun? What had happened to him?

The Magical Zanaar looked up into the sky. "You... cannot... stop... the... construction... soon... we... shall... have... form... have... power... have... life..."

Bob struggled against the power that held him, but it was no use. Zanaar – or the Cold Dark, operating Zanaar like a puppet – held him fast.

"The... stars... are... right..." whispered Zanaar.

The earth shook. The sound of car alarms going off came from every direction. Bob could feel the bass vibration in the air. The fire escape shook and rattled like a car crash as the Thing Beneath stirred in anticipation of its final meal.

Bob was powerless.

"Now... we... have... life..."

Zanaar lifted his hand, the one holding the steel cable that looped around Alison's neck.

He pushed. Alison fell.

## XXXVI
## SHARON MEADOW, SAN FRANCISCO
### TODAY

Highwire stops, looks around. It is night, and he has returned to the circus. The gate is closed and there is a notice pasted across it that all performances are canceled, with a phone number provided for those customers who have pre-paid tickets to call for a refund. The management apologizes for the inconvenience. There are technical issues. The circus hopes to re-open presently. Thank you, San Francisco. See you real soon!

Highwire pauses, but there is no voice, no presence at his shoulder. From beyond the gate comes the beat of drums and the roar of a fire.

Highwire vaults the gate and heads inside. Toward the nexus.

They take him as soon as he steps from the darkness cast by the Big Top. They are dirty, caked in black, burned earth, their eyes shiny in the night. The two who take his arms are members of the Stonefire dance troupe, but soon others appear – other performers, workers at the circus. David the Harlequin, his checkerboard costume abandoned, his naked flesh painted in black dirt. Three of his clowns, although Highwire is unsure of their identities as their faces are obscured by thick black dirt.

He didn't hear them coming, didn't see them until it was too late and they were holding him. This is impossible, he knows, because his senses are heightened and he can see and hear all. But here at the circus, at the nexus, there is a power greater than his own at work. He can do nothing yet, so he obeys the unspoken instructions of his captors and allows himself to be dragged away. The hands clutching his arms hold firm and are burning cold. They take him to the bonfire. As they walk, Highwire glances at the dark shapes that loom over the circus – the carnival machines, all Victorian wood and ironmongery. He is sure they are moving, twitching against the night sky, and above the roar of the bonfire he can hear the fatigue of old metal and the creak of old wood.

The bonfire is surrounded by many people, all covered in burned earth. The drumming has stopped and they all stand still, facing the new arrival. At the center stands Malcolm, arms folded, his smile broad and wicked. And then the drums start again: a slow beat, the execution march, marking time.

Malcolm points, and Highwire is dragged forward and pushed to his knees. Behind, the creak and rattle of the carnival machines swells. Something moves, deep underground. Highwire can feel it, the vibration through his knees. An amorphous, insubstantial consciousness, a something that curls around itself and around the world, and as it moves in its sleep the city shakes. The air is thick with power, a presence as substantial as the voice in his head, the voice now silent, absent.

Highwire looks around at the gathered crowd of dirt-caked dancers. He knows Stonefire is a Celtic dance group that puts on a show based on a fictionalized vision of an Iron Age culture and the gods they worshipped. But here, over the nexus, over the Thing Beneath, that power is taken, twisted and exaggerated, and fed back to the group, plunging them back in time five thousand years. It is perhaps accidental, because Highwire is unsure the Thing Beneath really has any awareness or sentience. But there is another force here, a cold darkness that has become the sleeping giant's master. It uses the power from far below, directing Stonefire and their ceremonies, using them for something. Highwire doesn't know what. He fears he is about to find out.

The drumming reaches fever pitch, and the group gathered around the bonfire begins to dance around it, save for Malcolm and the two holding Highwire. Malcolm's smile is fixed, his eyes dull, like he is listening to something far, far away.

A moment later he nods and points back at the fire, and the dancers all rush forward, piling into a group, falling into the embers and ashes at the edge of the fire, throwing up great clouds of red and orange sparks.

They begin to dig.

Highwire watches. Is he to be offered as a sacrifice to their god? To the thing beneath? He is unsure. He could escape, he knows he could, but he also knows he would just have to come back. He needs to stop whatever this is.

Then the crowd at the fire begins to separate. Highwire can see two banks of dirt on either side of a hole, shoveled out of the ground beneath the fire by the bare hands of the troupe. The group parts and stands in two ranks, and Malcolm turns and walks to the fire.

The fire sparks and cracks like a firing range. The carnival machines creak and clank and buzz, and the drone of an old steam-powered pipe organ drifts across the circus.

Malcolm reaches down into the hole and a hand reaches up, out of the earth. Thin, lithe. Black. It grabs Malcolm's arm, and he pulls, and she is lifted from the ground. Naked and caked in thick carbonized earth, her eyes brilliant white against her black face.

Malcolm turns and leads her toward Highwire. Highwire recognizes her. The man in whose body he resides knows her, knows her well.

She reaches out a hand, and smiles. Her teeth, like her eyes, are blazing white against her ash-covered face.

Highwire knows her name: it is Alison.

Malcolm laughs and reaches out toward Highwire. Highwire's ears are filled with the sound of the fire and the sound of the ocean, and as the earth shakes gently he topples forward into the dirt.

# INTERLUDE
# HONOLULU, HAWAII
## 1986

They sat facing each other on a rug, both cross-legged, one in a black suit, a little rough, the remains of something smart and tailored from another age, another world. The other was shirtless, clad only in shorts. His chest was sunken and disappointing, his stomach rolling over the waistband, his feet hard and calloused. He was a man who spent a lot of time outdoors, the sun baking him, hardening him.

The room was small but full of junk, the den in a cheap house in the crappy part of Waipahu. The junk included newspapers and porn magazines stacked high, two guitars (one without strings), and a sea of discarded food wrappers and pizza boxes. And machinery. Old, rusted, none of it complete. Some parts were arranged in a pattern on the floor, on the Seventies Formica coffee table, like the man had been looking at them, examining them, trying to figure out what they were part of, how they fit together, how they moved.

Pity the man couldn't tell Joel where the rest of the machinery was. His eyes were glazed, and he rocked slowly, back and forth, back and forth. Around his neck was a tiki on a string that he pulled at with one hand. His lips moved and he mumbled, but the words were inaudible.

Joel's gun was on the rug in front of him. Across the knuckles of one hand he rolled the coin.

Late afternoon. The room was hot and stuffy, all the windows and doors closed, the curtains drawn. Under normal circumstances the room would have been unbearable, the tropical weather outside turning it into a kiln. Joel didn't feel hot, but then he didn't feel cold either and he knew that was part of how it all worked. The man opposite wasn't sweating, and Joel wondered if the light had enough power now that the cold he could feel in his hand was something real now, radiating out, chilling the room. He had no idea. He didn't know if that was important or not.

Joel dropped the coin into the palm of his hand and squeezed. It felt like he was squeezing a wet battery. But there was no pull and, more important, no light. He frowned. The light had led him here, to the house, to the wreck of a man who now sat in front of him. Surely he was in the right place. The pieces of the carnival arranged around the room were proof enough.

Joel tilted his head as he watched the man mumble, his eyelids fluttering. Joel wondered if he was talking to the light as well. Maybe there was silence in his head instead of the screaming of the stars because he didn't need the coin to find the next piece, not here. What he needed was the man. The man now gibbering and drooling on the rug.

Joel wondered if this was how the man had been before the other killings. Four women were dead already, the first raped and murdered – strangled – nearly a year ago. Three more followed, each bound and raped and killed in the same manner. The city was going crazy trying to find the perp. The FBI had set up a task force, but nobody had any leads.

Nobody except Joel.

Murder had power. Joel knew that all too well. Maybe there had been no connection, not at first. Perhaps the man was evil and had started already. But if there was a piece of the carnival near then maybe it sensed kindred evil nearby as its own power leaked like oil from a ruptured tank deep in the ground. Maybe it reached the diseased mind of the killer and contaminated it more, driving him further and further, demanding more death, more *power*. Joel didn't know the man's name or what he did for a living, but he knew the man's *purpose*. He knew that he was a killer, a sadist, one who couldn't resist the evil compunction to begin with and was now locked into the power, feeding it as it fed him.

Joel opened his palm and the golden head of Lady Liberty looked aloof and the year inscribed below – 1862 – felt like a slap in the face. Joel remembered 1862 like it was yesterday.

The coin was cold, and the man gibbered on. The afternoon was heading toward the perpetually early dusk of six o'clock.

The man must have brought the pieces from somewhere else, because there was nothing else nearby – Joel had searched. The house had no outbuildings, no shed, no garage. It was just a weatherboard structure with five rooms that sat in the middle of an empty, grass-covered lot.

Joel slipped the coin into the pocket of his waist coat, pulled the rim of his stovepipe down low, and steepled his fingers under his chin. "Do you know where the rest is, friend?"

The gibbering man gasped. A reaction or just an automatic reflex to swallow as more saliva dribbled out of his mouth, Joel wasn't sure.

"Friend, can you understand me?"

At this the gibbering man fell silent, his mouth snapping shut with an audible clack. He blinked.

"Well now," said Joe with a smile. "Welcome back, friend."

The man stared at Joel in silence.

Joel said, "I've come a long way in my search. I've been led here by the light, and right now the light is shining full well on you, my friend. I have a feeling there is something you need to give me, or show me."

Silence.

"Friend, I understand you are on a quest of your own–"

"Liar."

Joel stopped short and laughed. "Those are hard words, friend, when all I'm doing is asking you the easiest question of your wholesome life."

"The light doesn't shine for you here. It shines for *me*." The man poked his finger at his own chest, and he smiled. It was a cruel smile.

Joel nodded, understanding. He was right. The carnival was near and had latched onto the man like a tick. It was telling him things.

The man laughed. "Kanaloa cannot stop me."

"Kanaloa?"

"He is near. Kanaloa is near, and he is watching me. He cannot stop me, because *They* will not allow it. But he can stop *you*." The man pointed.

Joel licked his lips. "Friend, we can talk in riddles all through the night, but we both have our own quests to fulfill. I've come for a piece of the light, and I cannot leave without it."

"Not you, no, not you."

"Who, then?"

"The light, the light, it shines for *me*," said the gibbering man. He leaned forward until his nose nearly touched Joel's, saliva leaking from the corner of his mouth in a thick, cloudy trail. "One more," he said, "one more and I shall be whole."

"That a fact, friend?"

Joel picked up the gun from the floor, sliding his hand between the rug and the grip and pulling the hammer back even as he moved it up to the gibbering man's forehead. The gibbering man began to laugh, quiet at first, then louder until it was nothing but a ragged, hoarse gasping. He pulled at the string around his neck so hard it sawed into the fatty flesh, drawing blood, but the string didn't break.

And there it was. The pull. The whisper, far, far away. The gibbering man let go of the tiki but it stayed in the air, bouncing up and down a little, pulling the string tight around the man's neck. Pulling toward something. Toward the carnival.

"Friend," said Joel, "I follow the light and the light it shines on thee."

He pulled the trigger and the back of the gibbering man's head exploded, white and gray and so much red splattering across the crappy TV with its peeling fake wood veneer and across the curtains, making them twitch as they were plastered with brains.

The man's body toppled forward, but Joel stood quickly and kicked out, pushing it backward. It hit the floor with a wet crunch.

He took the coin from his pocket. It was cold, so cold it burned. And it pulled, just a little. Joel glanced down at the body and saw the tiki floating in the air, still tethered to the remains of the man's neck.

Murder was power. Not killing, not death, because the world was full of killing and full of death and it didn't mean a thing. But *murder*. Murder was different. Special. Murder was ancient, primal, a force all its own. The dead man had been a murderer, generating enough power that the light had shone for him like it shone for Joel.

Joel reached down and grabbed the tiki out of the air. He pulled it off the ruined neck, held it in his fist, and squeezed and squeezed, until he saw the light and he knew where to go.

# XXXVII
# SAN FRANCISCO
## TODAY

"Dude, *now!*"

Zanaar looked up.

Tangun – Benny – flew out of the sky, feet first. She landed on the ringmaster, the two crashing into the fire escape. Bob was suddenly released; surprised, he fell and hit the street, shattering three vertebrae. He cried out, healed the cracked bone, and rolled to his feet.

He was too late. In the melee on the fire escape, Alison had been pushed over the railing. She fell, the steel cable trailing behind her. As Bob watched, her body swung out sharply as the cable reached tension and the loop closed around her neck.

Bob screamed and pulled at the world. Kanaloa was the lord of the sea, and Bob commanded the water without conscious thought. The water on the ground. The brick walls of the alley, wet from a recent shower. The water that trickled from a broken outflow pipe farther down the alleyway. Water under the street, in pipes and drains. It gathered slowly at first, pulling itself off the walls and the street, out of drains, out of the pipe. Then it became a wave, condensing around Bob and shaping itself into a silver funnel, a tornado of water spinning with Bob in the middle.

Bob commanded the water again. The waterspout surged forward, engulfing Alison. She vanished into the roaring funnel; moments later she reappeared, held aloft at the level of the fire escape, the steel cable around her neck slack. Bob deleted the cable from existence and the waterspout collapsed, landing Alison on the street with just a gentle bump.

Bob dropped to his knees. He curled over, hands tearing at his hair, unable to see anything but light, shining, blinding light. He felt sick, excited.

Powerful. *Hungry*.

He could do anything.

He was a god, and he could rule the world.

"Dude, we gotta run, man."

Bob looked up. Benny was standing in front of him. She had Zanaar's unconscious body in her arms.

"You OK?" Benny looked afraid.

The hunger. The power. So much potential. So much he could do. He could end it all. Now.

"Bob?"

Bob blinked, and stood. *That* was why he couldn't use power like that.

"I'm sorry," he said. He rubbed his eyes, and they felt like hot coals burning in his face. "I can't do it. That was too much. I nearly lost it." He walked over to Alison and scooped her up. She was breathing softly and didn't seem to be injured. He hoped she didn't remember anything of what had happened.

"Yeah, but you didn't, did you?"

Bob looked at Benny. He frowned. "No," he said. That was true.

"Which means you can control it, right?"

"Benny," said Bob, "you don't understand. I'm a god. I'm Kanaloa – *was* Kanaloa. And Kanaloa was an angry son of a bitch."

"Dude, of course I understand. I'm Tangun, or at least he's in here with me now. And you're not Kanaloa."

"I'm not?"

"No." Benny grinned. "You're Bob."

*You're Bob.*

He thought on this. Then he smiled. He wasn't Kanaloa; he was Bob. Benny was right. He laughed.

"Is that the wisdom of Tangun?"

Benny shook her head. "Dude, some credit, please."

Bob knelt down, holding Alison, and grabbed Tangun's helmet from the ground.

Benny shook her head. "I can't see in that thing."

Then the earth shook again. A slow rumble that built and then faded. Out in the main street, a fresh set of car alarms went off.

Bob and Benny exchanged a look.

"Clock's ticking," said Bob. "Come on."

# XXXVIII
# SAN FRANCISCO
## TODAY

They took Zanaar and Alison back to Ted's apartment. It was quiet. Light from San Francisco's streetlights filtered in through the blinds, filling the space with bands of yellow light. Bob adjusted Alison's form on the couch so the light didn't strike her directly in the eyes. He watched the rise and fall of her breathing for a moment, and then turned to Zanaar in the armchair. He was out cold, snoring. Bob searched Zanaar's pockets and found a wallet. The expired driver's license inside that said his name was Jonathan Newhaven, and gave an address in St. Albans, Vermont. Bob smiled. He thought he'd guessed the accent. Inside the wallet was a card for his circus. He was the ringmaster.

Benny disappeared into the bedroom. "Shit," she called out. "Ted's gone."

Bob raced over, but there was nothing to see. He nodded, rubbed his chin. Benny looked at him, eyebrow cocked.

"The circus."

"Has to be," said Bob. "Nezha's been trying to lead us there all along. I think we threw a little spanner in the works – " he pointed at Newhaven – "but I have a feeling things are already in motion."

Benny looked down at Alison, at Newhaven.

"Will they remember anything?"

Bob shook his head, nodded at the ringmaster. "No. My guess is that he hasn't been himself for a while – not since the killings started. He was just being used – he's not the Hang Wire Killer, not really. I don't think he'll remember anything."

"And Alison?"

"Same thing," said Bob. "But a shorter timespan – from whenever she was grabbed."

Benny's armor clacked together as she folded her arms. "At least they're safe now."

"Yes, but you're going to have to stay here and look after them."

Benny gasped. "What? You're going to the circus alone? You need Tangun's help. That's why he's here, after all!"

"Brah, listen up," said Bob. "The Thing Beneath is being woken up by whatever it was that arrived with the circus. When it moved, it broke Ted's sleep spell."

"Like... feedback?"

"Right," said Bob. "Feedback. So someone needs to watch these two. They're OK, but they've shared a connection to the power. I don't know what will happen at the circus. There might be feedback, or it might be able to reach out and take them over again. If that happens, I need Tangun here. He's the only one powerful enough to look after them."

"If anything, Kanaloa is even more powerful."

"Yes. Which is why Kanaloa has to go to the circus, find Ted and the source of the power."

"Ted might be dead."

Bob frowned. "Kanaloa can fix that." That was true. He just hoped he didn't have to use his powers so fully again. It was dangerous enough, the hunger in his mind and in his heart. Power was addictive. And so close to the source, it would be worse. The temptation, the blissful satisfaction.

But there was a city to save, perhaps a world. And there was Ted, and everyone else at the circus, trapped in the middle of something that had nothing to do with them. They were caught in the web of something ancient and primal.

Benny nodded. "Go. Tangun will stay here. So will I." She laughed. Bob smiled and patted his friend on the shoulder.

"Thanks, brah."

"Good luck."

# XXXIX
# SHARON MEADOW, SAN FRANCISCO
## TODAY

The darkness is a living thing. It surrounds him and he can feel it move, feel it breathe. It envelops him like a blanket. It is not merely dark, an absence of light. It is the shadow of *something moving* and it is the blackness of space; two primal forces meeting, colliding, drowning in an abyss of nothing.

The Cold Dark. The Thing Beneath. One fell from the sky. One slept under the earth.

And now one uses the other. The Cold Dark, a sharp evil from beyond the stars, aware and with purpose, has found a new home, a wonderful world of life and of light. This world it wants. It will consume it, burn it up, and as it does it will send new seeds out into the universe, more falling stars, more pathogenic energy. Grow and spread, grow and spread, the fungus of space.

The Thing Beneath sleeps, and as it sleeps it slowly draws power, charging itself like a capacitor. And when there is enough power, it wakes, it moves, reshaping the world above it as it turns. But there is never enough power, never enough life. It moves, the earth shakes, and then the power is gone and it sleeps again.

Until now. Now the Cold Dark feeds it. The Cold Dark has sensed the Thing Beneath, understands its hunger, its needs. It feeds it, and by feeding it controls it, and by controlling, it will be able to use it to grow and spread, grow and spread, like never before.

Except something is not right. The final sacrifice, the last mote of power, is gone. Has been taken away, the death prevented. The tool, the killer, Newhaven, has been lost, is gone, is no longer one with the powers.

The Cold Dark grows angry. The Thing Beneath stirs, but is not awake, not yet.

Almost.

Then there is a voice. Faint and faraway, a whisper carried on the wind. The voice of someone old and wise, standing just over your shoulder.

*Wake up, Ted.*

Highwire opens his eyes.

The night is bright, and as Highwire blinks, the world resolves around him. The light is artificial. Red, yellow, green and blue and white. Blinking and flashing, strobing in many directions.

The carnival. He is at the heart of it all. He raises his head, looks up, sees the carousel in front of him, a Victorian cake tin of painted horses and monsters and soldiers, lit in warm orange. It rocks, back and forth, back and forth, like the gears are jammed. The steam-powered pipe organ at the center wails like mourners at a funeral, like animals in pain.

Highwire is surrounded by the wooden soldiers. Each is frozen in place, inanimate, oversized children's toys. Each with a scowl, each with rifle and bayonet pointed at him.

Highwire sits up, pushing himself off the ground and onto his elbows. In the blink of an eye, the soldiers have changed positions. Their aim is adjusted, the rifles higher. It is the same at the carousel. The animal rides are agitated, some standing back on their hind legs, eyes wide and rolling, lips drawn back in fear. At the center sits a carved monkey, its shining red eyes almost too bright to look at.

The carnival is alive. Highwire looks to the left, to the right. The machines have all moved, from the big dipper and rocket cars to the little stalls full of rotating open-mouthed clown heads. All elegant and elaborate, carved and crafted out of wood and metal, painted with the stars and planets and a falling star. The machines have moved to form a closed circle, a perimeter surrounding the patch of ground on which Highwire lies. There is no way in or out. He is trapped, and as he watches, each of the machines moves a little. The big dipper bobs and dips. The rocket cars are rotating around their angled hub, slowly, slowly, like they are drifting through space.

It is night. The darkness feels alive too, like the circus. There is no wind but it feels like the air is moving, something breathing in and out, in and out. There is pressure on his eardrums that follows the same rhythm. Like a heartbeat. The heartbeat of a sleeping monster.

There is someone standing behind him. He can sense his presence, although the person makes no sound. Highwire's augmented senses are clouded by the sounds of the carnival and the weird pressure of the atmosphere, but he can feel the man there.

Highwire stands, turns, expecting there to be no one there once again. But this time there is. The man behind him is not alone. He smiles, his white eye shining with the lights of the carnival. Standing next to him is a woman, her naked body caked in black burned dirt, ash drifting off her like smoke.

He knows who she is. Her name is Alison. She is connected to him – to the body he wears, the man with the brown jacket, the man from the apartment, the man with the bruise healing above his eye.

But this *isn't* her. It looks like her, is perfect in every detail, but it is not alive, not like the woman called Alison is alive. It is a copy, made from earth and pulled from the hot ground. A tool, a golem, nothing more.

Highwire listens for the voice in his head, but it is silent.

The carnival machines twitch and clank as Highwire steps toward the pair. Behind them stands the Ferris wheel, the largest part of the mechanical carnival. The wheel rotates this way and that, this way and that, a few degrees in each direction, no more.

The man with the shining white eye smiles. He wears a stovepipe hat. His black suit is old. The fingers of one hand he keeps in the fob pocket on the front of his waistcoat.

Highwire glances over his shoulder. The wooden soldiers have moved again, now arranged in a rank, their rifles raised and aimed. Behind, two soldiers in different uniforms – the officers – are at the carousel, frozen in conversation with the carved monkey perched atop the pipe organ.

The carnival twitches and turns, the organ wails, the lights flash, but the golem and the man in black do not move.

Highwire is fast, he knows this. Faster than the wooden soldiers, he thinks, although he doesn't know how fast they really are with his back turned. The carnival can move, the machines creaking and clanking as they do, but they are large and heavy, animated by a stellar force centered in the monkey. Highwire can sense anger and rage, but while the machines *can* move they are not *built* to move.

The Ferris wheel stands above them all, slowly turning. It is high, thirty feet at least, a collection of pipes, struts and bare framework – not as elegant as the rest of the nineteenth century machines, more functional, but still vintage, still beautiful. From the top you could see the whole city, shining in the night.

From the top, Highwire could *jump*. Behind the wheel is a wall of trucks and trailers. Beyond that, the west side of the circus, the open fields of Golden Gate Park. Beyond that, the city. Escape would be easy. If he could move fast enough.

"You can't leave, friend," says the man with the white eye. "You were brought here. Brought to me."

He takes his fingers from his pocket. Between them he holds a large coin, gold, heavy. The heartbeat sound in Highwire's head gets stronger for a moment, and it feels like the ground beneath him is vibrating. Above all of this, the coin appears to crackle like electricity, although it is merely a gold coin being held between the fingers of the man with the white eye.

"You followed the light, didn't you?" the man asks. "You followed it like I followed it."

Highwire says nothing. The golem next to the man tilts its head, looking at Highwire. It is smiling, its eyes are wide and bright against its black-caked face.

"I've followed it a long time," said the man. "It told me how to build the machines. Told me what it needed to grow and to spread. And then when others came and interfered, breaking the machine up, it showed me where the pieces were hidden. It shone a light for me, a light I followed, across the country, searching. And then when the machine was complete, it shone the light here. There's something it wants here. Something deep underground. There's something down there, friend. A power, sleeping since the planet was made by the hand of God himself."

The man stops. He looks excited. He looks like he wants Highwire to tell him that he was right.

Highwire says nothing. Then he pushes off with his right foot against the soft dirt. He leaps over the man, over the golem, hits the dirt behind them, and sprints for the Ferris wheel.

The air is thick now with metallic grinding as the carnival jerks into life, every machine, ride, and attraction reacting to the movement. There are no gunshots, but Highwire glances over his shoulder and sees one of the wooden soldiers is calling to the officers while the others aim their rifles, some having dropped to one knee as they prepare to fire.

Highwire blinks. The officers are running from the carousel. The soldiers screw their eyes along their rifle sights.

Highwire blinks. Gunshots fill the air, smoke rising thick from the old fashioned rifles. The shots go wide, pinging off the Ferris wheel, sending sparks into the night. The wheel's motor grinds, roaring like an injured beast. The carousel begins to spin, faster and faster, the moaning of the pipe organ increasing in pitch until it sounds like a siren. Underneath it all, the cacophony of the living circus, Highwire can hear a monkey laugh.

He jumps, catches a strut on one of the wheel's spokes that holds the passenger baskets around the rim. He swings, spins around on the strut to get up speed and momentum; then he swings again to the next basket above. Highwire finds his rhythm, leaping up and up, climbing the wheel. The guns fire again, but the soldiers' aim is poor. The bullets ricochet off the wheel, white-hot sparks flaring around him. Highwire is nearing the top of the wheel.

The wheel shakes, and shakes some more. Highwire squeezes his grip, his body bouncing against the framework. The carnival is angry and now the machine is trying to shake him off. The wheel turns, faster, but Highwire lets go of the passenger basket and catches a strut of the main superstructure. He begins to pull himself up. If he can stay in the center of the wheel's frame, clear of the moving parts, he can get close enough to the top to swing himself over the other side, and then jump off onto the trucks.

Just a few more seconds, a few more feet. The wheel shakes and shakes. Any more and Highwire thinks it will shake itself apart.

He adjusts his grip, he counts, he jumps.

Something meets him in the air.

Something hard, cold, lit in brilliant neon strips and incandescent bulbs. It catches him, closes tightly around his legs. It pulls him back down and then swings out, and Highwire is suddenly upside down. Then it swings back, and Highwire connects with the side of the wheel. Neon tubes and bulbs shatter as his body is dragged through them, burning him, broken glass tearing into his skin.

Highwire struggles, but he is held in something huge and vice-like. He looks down, sees his legs trapped in a mangled framework. It is metal, struts and pipes, but also enameled metal sheeting, painted with stars. A fist, an arm, fashioned out of carnival parts.

The arm swings out again. Highwire sees the ground fly across his vision, the man and the golem surrounded by the wooden soldiers, the carousel spinning so fast that the animal rides around it are alive and moving, like he's watching a zoetrope of alien creatures as they twist and turn and stamp in pain and fear.

The arm swings back. Highwire is slammed against the body of the Ferris wheel. His head hits the frame with enough force to shatter his skull, and the last thing Highwire remembers is that his name is Ted Kane.

# INTERLUDE
## MT DIABLO, CALIFORNIA
### 1998

The man walked out of the woods as slow as you like, one thumb hooked under his belt and his black jacket blowing in the evening breeze. He wasn't smiling, not quite; the expression was rather a knowing smirk, a curl of the lip of someone stumbling upon something they were expecting to find, but perhaps not quite where they were looking. His black boots kicked up the dust at the edge of the woods before sliding silently onto the grass of the clearing, and as he walked toward the campfire, John watched, fear coursing through his body almost like a physical thing, like his heart was encased in a solid block of cold, dead metal.

"Can I help you, sir?" was all John managed. He sat in his camping chair in front of his tent, on the other side of the campfire, which crackled and sparked. It wasn't really necessary, not on a warm Californian night like this, but he had felt the need to build it. And build it he had, and very well at that – the flames enveloped a pyramid of firewood, which stood nearly two feet high in a circle of stones John had picked up from around the edges of the campsite, within the boundary of the woods. The woods from which the stranger had come.

The man laughed, like he was surprised, and he held one hand up like he was about to swear an oath as he kept his slow pace forward. John gripped the arms of his camping chair, daring not to move just yet, but as the surprise of the man's arrival faded he began to watch carefully, waiting for the right moment. There was a gun in the tent. The man in black looked dangerous, some kind of hobo who lived on the mountain maybe, in a crumpled suit that looked positively Victorian, like the battered stovepipe hat on his head.

If he could just, somehow, dive backward on the chair, roll around, reach the gun and–

"Oh, now, I'm disappointed, friend," said the man. He stopped by the edge of the fire and put his hands on his hips. John shuddered as he saw the man had one gray eye, pale as newsprint. He wore a waistcoat under the black jacket but John didn't notice the color. What he did notice was the shining silver something on the man's hip, revealed as his hand brushed the edge of the jacket aside, quite deliberately. A gun, in a holster. "I come here in peace," the man said, "and you're already thinking of how you can get one-up on the situation." He shook his head and tutted.

John licked his lips, his eyes on the holster. "What are you, some kinda cowboy?"

Even as the words escaped his throat, John regretted it. Now was not the time to be a smartass, even if it was just the nerves talking.

"You might be closer to the truth than you realize, friend," said the man. He let the edge of the jacket fall back and then he sat on ground on the other side of the fire, folding his legs beneath him to sit cross-legged in a way that John – at least twenty years the man's senior – thought he could remember being able to do a good long while ago, back when his hair was longer, the hem of his trousers wider.

John released his grip on the arm of the camping chair, which creaked in response. The other man raised an eyebrow and the knowing smile came back.

"You're going to ask, friend," said the man, "what I want. And at the very least to that question I can offer you God's honest truth."

John frowned at the man's archaic speech. The man's accent was rich, treacle-dipped, from somewhere in the Deep South, each word drawn out and savored like the first bite of a fine meal.

"The ranger said there was nobody else camping up here," said John. "Said I was alone on the mountain. Not much call for camping on a Wednesday, I guess."

The other man's knowing smile returned and he tilted his head as the fire cracked, the sound as loud as a gunshot in the night. He lifted the hat from his head and placed it on the ground next to him.

"What makes you think you aren't alone, friend?"

Psycho. The man was a fucking psycho, John thought, and this was it, the end. The weirdo obviously watched the gate down the mountain road, watched the comings and goings, and when he knew he had the park to himself he could come out and gut the lone camper he'd been stalking all afternoon. John shivered, closed his eyes.

"Oh, don't be like that, friend," said the man. John opened his eyes and the other man was looking at him, that pale gray eye practically shining in the firelight that bathed him in a moving yellow light. "I said I came in peace, and on that subject not a lie would pass my lips."

They sat in silence for a minute or two. John wondered if maybe he could kick the fire over fast enough, then get to his car, a piece of shit Oldsmobile Cutlass Cruiser, faux wood paneling and everything, that waited under the trees on the other side of his tent. Maybe he could. If the keys weren't in the tent behind him.

John thought a moment. "Did you walk up here?" he asked. He'd arrived just before five, pulling into the park gate just as the ranger was driving back down the road to lock up. The ranger had let John in, pointed him in the direction of the best camping spot on this side of the mountain. Then, as John coaxed the Oldsmobile up the gravel incline, he'd closed and locked the park gates.

John hadn't heard anything man-made all afternoon, not even the jet that had flown high above, its vapor trail catching fire in the setting sun as John had started to gather rocks for the campfire. The main road was a long way down the hill. If the stranger had walked up from the gate it would have been a heck of a hike. But if he was a hobo who lived on the mountain, why hadn't the ranger said anything? The mountain was large but surely the parks service knew who should be there and who shouldn't.

"My friend," said the man, holding his hands out and closing his eyes, like a patient man instructing a slow student, "you are not asking the right questions."

"You're not from around here, are you? What is that, Kentucky? Alabama maybe?"

At this the man's eyes flicked open and the smile returned. He dropped his hands, and his white teeth glowed orange in the firelight.

"Now, isn't that the thing," he said. "I've traveled far and wide over this here continent, and sometimes beyond, but nobody has ever asked where it is I call my home. I knew I was right to find you, friend." He looked up into the cloudless sky, black and salt-scattered with the light of distant suns. "The stars are shining for me today."

"OK, fine, fine." Anger replaced John's fear. "What do you want?" The weirdo might have been armed and might have been talking like he was straight out of an amateur production of *Oklahoma!*, but if he was going to die then John wanted to go out with a fight. He was on the wrong side of middle-aged and weighed too much, as the creak of the camp chair reminded him, but dammit if he couldn't do some damage before the morning came and the ranger found his bloody body in a pile next to the smoking embers of the campfire.

The man lifted his hand and pointed at John. He held it there a while, and the fire cracked and the camp chair creaked and the gentle evening breeze dropped to nothing. The atmosphere suddenly felt close, softly pressing in around John and the campsite.

John lifted his own hand and pointed it at himself as he caught the meaning. "Me? You want... me?"

The man laughed and dropped his hand. "Yes and no," he said. "I'm actually more interested in what you have in that car of yours."

Relief swept over John. The car? The weirdo wanted to steal his car? Well, fine. It was a piece of shit and John had wanted to upgrade for a while now, especially as he'd be needing something even bigger than the station wagon once his shop was set up, a small van maybe to carry –

"To carry antiques and heirlooms and all manner of paraphernalia from one place to another," said the man, nodding his head. "The dealing of antiquities and curiosities is a fine profession, my friend, a fine profession. I am something of an expert myself in the finding of artifacts of rare interest and beauty. I've walked this land from top to toe in a quest of what you might call a personal nature. Maybe you might even say it was a calling, a journey guided not by my conscious mind but by the powers that be, shining a light which I can do nothing but follow."

John blinked, ignoring most of the man's rambling.

"How did you know I was an antiques dealer? Do I know you?"

The man shook his head. "You do not, but I think you will, in time. You see, friend, this journey of which I just spoke is coming to an end. I'm near to it, you see, near to the source, the magical spring, you might say, from which the mighty river flows."

John shifted his weight in the camping chair. He took a breath, and paused. Then he leaned forward. "What the hell are you talking about?"

The man sighed and pointed toward the silhouette of the station wagon under the tree. "You have something I need, friend."

"You're gonna steal my car?"

"I want what's inside your car, friend, and I'm not going to steal it. I come in peace, as I have laid out to you, and would do nothing that might breach this pleasant accord we've come to."

"OK..."

"Having said that," said the man, looking now into the fire, "there is something in your car that I have come to collect and I can't let you or anyone else stand in the way of that. But I have a feeling I've been led here for another reason. We're so close to it now, you and I. It's down there, in the city, sleeping under the rock. And maybe this close to the source, this close to the end, maybe it doesn't need the power. Doesn't need to feed on the murder of others." The man found a long twig by the fireside and poked at the fire with it.

Holy shit. Murder? John's heart kicked painfully in his chest, and he wanted to throw up.

"OK ..." he said. How could he get out of it now? Something in the car? He was on his way to San Francisco and was due to meet the realtor the day after tomorrow to look at the empty store on Fell Street. There was nothing in the car but a suitcase of clothes and a very small collection of things he thought he'd try and sell to another antiques store, to test the market, so to speak. Two pieces of jewelry, both pretty but both costume and pocket change only; a small table with folding leaves, oak, early twentieth century, nothing flashy but a solid piece; and something more unusual, a–

"A carved wooden monkey with red crystal eyes," said the man. The fire cracked, and John nearly jumped out of his chair. He felt sweat on his brow, and when he wiped it off he found his hand was shaking.

"How did you know?"

The man smiled. "I told you I was following a light, and the light it shines on thee, my friend."

"Fine, whatever you like." Maybe he wasn't going to get murdered. The psycho said something about not needing to, but not much of what he said was making any sense. "Take it. I'll get it for you." John lifted himself off the chair and made a half-turn around but then the other man spoke, more firmly now.

"Oh now, time and again things proceed in an untoward direction." He tossed the stick into the fire and shook his head. "Sit yourself down, friend. There's time a plenty for that."

John lowered himself back into the chair. His stomach did loops and his bladder was fit to burst.

The other man looked into the fire and slipped one hand into the pocket of his waistcoat, where maybe a fob watch would have comfortably sat a hundred years ago. He extracted a coin from the pocket and held it up between two fingers. The coin was large and bright, silver or maybe even gold, the firelight giving it a coppery hue that made it hard to tell. He slowly twisted it between his fingers, this way and that, this way and that, his eyes fixed on it, studying the detail. John couldn't see what it was, but he felt a dangerous twinge of curiosity.

The man flipped the coin and caught it, but he kept his fist closed. He looked again at John in his camper chair.

"You ever wondered about those eyes, the ones in the monkey, and how they came to be?"

John blinked, the spell cast by the shining coin broken.

"Ah, well," John paused and thought. "There's a label on the bottom. Says the gems were cut out of a meteorite that fell in, oh, eighteen hundred and something. Load of baloney, but–"

"But you've wondered now and again, when the hours are small and looking up you see a star fall. What if that were the case? What if those eyes were alive, and what if the monkey were alive and waiting."

Maybe he was dreaming. Maybe he'd fallen asleep in the camper chair, the warm and humid night pressing in, the heat of the fire unnecessary. Maybe it was the mountaintop – being alone in such a place, maybe it did things to you. John hadn't needed to build the fire yet he had felt compelled to do so. He vaguely recalled a few stories about Mount Diablo, the Devil's Mountain, about strange sounds and strange creatures that lived there. The night was warm and the fire, as impressive as it was, didn't really feel very hot. His imagination, surely.

And the stories? John snapped out of it, shaking his head. Baloney, pure and simple. And yet... there was something in the other man's eyes, something deep and old, like the man had sidestepped out of time and–

John blinked again. He was asleep, he was dreaming, and the ranger's truck would wake him up in the morning and the ranger would ask why he'd made such a big campfire.

"I can tell you things about the earth and the life within it," said the man. John rubbed his eyes, watching the other man over the haze of the campfire, sitting on the ground with one pale eye alight like he was the devil himself. "I can tell you about the light that I follow, about the power it seeks. I can tell you about what lies asleep under San Francisco, how it will wake again, with my help and with yours, John."

The man smiled, and reached into the fire. John wanted to stop him, but he found himself bound to the camper chair, hands clenched tight around the arms.

The man pushed at the fire and the fire sparked and cracked, flames licking at the sleeve of his jacket. John wanted to call out for him to be careful. His hair would catch fire, that close.

The man pulled out a stone, large and elliptical, from the edge of the fire. It glowed dully in the man's hand, but the man didn't seem to be affected at all. In fact, as John started finally to lever himself out of the chair to get a closer look, the other man began to laugh. He raised the stone above his head, and brought it down on another stone, still *in situ* in the fire surround. There was a sharp click, and the stone in the man's hand split open.

John was on his feet now. He shuffled around the fire to stand over the man sitting cross-legged on the ground. In front of him was the stone from the fire, neatly cleaved along some natural fissure into two equal halves. In the middle was a cavity, and in the cavity sat a frog, almost black in the firelight, its skin glistening as it breathed quickly, in-out, in-out, in-out.

"What in the world..."

The frog shifted in the cavity and hopped onto the other man's knee. Then it turned again and hopped off and was lost to the darkness of the campsite. John stared after it but could see nothing but black, the afterimage of the fire dancing in front of him like falling stars, like a comet streaking through the heavens.

The other man uncurled himself from the ground and stood up. He straightened his jacket and brushed his hands, miraculously untouched by the fire and the glowing rock. He held out his hand. John looked down at it for a moment, and then found himself shaking it with his own.

"My name, friend, is Joel Duvall."

"John," said John, like he was in a dream, falling toward the man in the black suit, the man with the gray eye, spiraling toward the cold black of space. "My name is–"

"Mr John Newhaven, of St Albans, Vermont, on his way west to seek his fortune like so many of his kin before him. But you prefer Jack, don't you? Or you did, back home. Out west in your new life you want to be called John, but you can't escape the past. Jack."

"Yes, I, but... but how do you know? Who are you?"

Joel squeezed John's hand so tight it cracked like the fire, and he stepped closer, his gray eye bright in the firelight, his smile the smile of the devil himself.

"I follow the light, Jack, and the light it shines on thee," said Joel. "We're close, friend, close to the source."

"Close to the source," repeated Jack, lost in Joel's gray eye.

"And we've an empire to build, you and me, Jack, you and me. We've come west, both of us, as far as west will go."

Joel released Jack's hand and then rested his arms on Jack's shoulders.

"And with the last piece, we can begin."

Joel slid his arms away and walked toward the shadow of the Oldsmobile. Jack stood and rubbed his eyes. Then he turned and followed.

# XL
# SHARON MEADOW, SAN FRANCISCO
## TODAY

The pounding in his head finally dragged Ted back to consciousness. *Thump-thump. Thump-thump.* A heartbeat. Not his heartbeat, but that of something large, something near.

Ted groaned, and when he moved his head it felt heavy and the pounding only increased, like his head was inside of a big bass drum, the kind a beefy guy in a leopard skin would carry in front of a marching band, each side of it thumped with a huge soft mallet.

He moved again, but only managed a slight wriggle. He felt bile rise in his throat and made to swallow it back but too late. The hot, bitter liquid filled his mouth. He spluttered, and sprayed it out of his mouth in an odd direction. Ted snorted in a mild panic as some of it went up his nose, the stench hot and strong. He coughed, clearing his burning throat, and realized he was hanging upside down. In front of him was a confusing array of angular shapes lit in bright colors.

"I'm impressed, my friend. Most impressed."

Ted stretched against his bonds, but it was no use. He was held fast, head-down, to the side of the Ferris wheel by a metal framework, the structure tight against his arms and legs. As he rolled his head, he felt something else too. The round, woven edge of steel cable, around his neck.

He jerked his head, ignoring the thumping in his head, trying to get a fix on who had spoken. It wasn't the voice in his head, not this time. That was still silent

Then the world flipped. The colored lights spun and resolved themselves into the illuminations of the carnival. Ted's head spun as the blood rushed from it. Dizzy and sick, he closed his eyes as the pounding in his head seemed to reach a crescendo before fading to a steady background rumble. He felt much better the right way up. Ted gasped for breath, and looked around again. So, he was in a fairground, behind the tents of a circus. Ted scrolled back, trying to piece the fragments of memory together. He remembered the apartment, the hospital, then someone else's place – Benny's.

Then... other things. He remembered flying through the air, but he knew that couldn't have been him. He remembered sitting at his laptop, his fingers flying across the keyboard as Chinese characters filled the screen. But again, that wasn't him. He remembered a trapeze, remembered walking around the city, watching himself in reflections. But it wasn't him. It was like he was watching a movie, his body being piloted by someone else. A whisper in his ear. A presence over his shoulder.

And then he remembered a fire escape, bodies hanging, twisting. Blood, murder, power, the wail of police sirens. An escape across the rooftops.

And now he was here, at a circus.

Maybe it was all just a dream. He remembered being in the hospital clear enough. Getting checked out after... what? He couldn't remember. The restaurant, the exploding fortune cookie. That was it. He was getting checked out, and they'd sedated him, and he was having a dream in which he thought he was a serial killer who strung victims up with steel cable, and that he was now being held in a circus fairground by the arms of the Ferris wheel.

Arms? Ted's head thumped.

"Oh, friend, don't fall asleep now. We have much to do, much to do."

Ted opened his eyes. He was ten feet off the ground. Below him stood a man in a black suit and tall hat. Beside him stood the slight, slim figure of a naked woman. The pair was silhouetted by the lights of the carnival behind them, especially the carousel, from the center of which shone twin red lights, almost like a pair of spotlights. There were others there, too: a circle of tall men dressed like old fashioned Redcoat soldiers stood unmoving, each with a rifle. Farther back, around the edge of the space formed by a ring of carnival rides were more people, maybe twenty or thirty. They were just shadows, swaying back and forth, back and forth, in time to the thumping in Ted's head, in time to the machines of the carnival rocking on their bases. It was like the circus was alive, one single creature split into different, smaller pieces.

Ted willed the voice in his head to come back, but there was nothing there. Perhaps that was part of the dream too.

"You don't know, do you?"

Ted looked down at the man in the hat. He stepped forward, into better light, and Ted could see that he had one eye that was gray, almost white. In one hand he rolled a large gold coin over his knuckles. The girl beside him followed.

Ted gasped.

"Alison! Alison! What's going on? What are you doing here?"

Alison swayed gently on her feet. She looked up at him, but it was like she didn't recognize him, or even understand what he was saying. She was painted in something black and rough, like dirt, or ash.

The man with the gray eye laughed and looked at Alison. Then he turned around, his arms out, indicating the circle of people in the carnival.

"The power works many wonders, my friend. Many wonders indeed. Why, from the very earth itself it shapes life, the arms and legs and ears and eyes that it doesn't have. It could build its own army." The man's accent was southern. To Ted he sounded like a used car salesman showing his latest model.

Ted looked around the circle. They were all the same as Alison – standing, swaying, glassy eyed, all covered in black dirt. The soldiers Ted could now see were carved wooden statues, just part of the fairground attractions.

"What have you done to them?" Ted strained against the machine that held him. The structure rattled, but held firm. He was helpless.

"I don't think you quite understand my meaning, friend," said the man in the hat. He turned around. "They're not people, only their shadows. Golems, you might call them. Including your lovely friend here. Brought to life with earth and fire by the Thing Beneath. A thing which I control."

The man on the ground craned his neck up as he walked closer to Ted. He pointed at him. "But you, my friend. Oh my yes, *you*. You're different."

He took a step back. The carnival machines began to move – two stalls, on each side, folded in on themselves, filling the air with the sound of creaking metal. As Ted watched, they screwed themselves up, tearing canvas and metal, breaking lights and signage, until they were each a bizarre, insectoid thing. They crawled toward their master; then together they unfolded their former flat frontages, enameled panels showing a starscape, into a small platform.

The man stepped onto it, and held his hand out. Alison – whatever it was that looked like Alison – took his hand and joined him on the platform.

The two machines changed again, reshaping themselves as they lifted the platform up, raising the pair to Ted's level.

"That's better," he said. "Now we can talk, man to man."

Ted looked at the golem. It was a perfect copy of Alison. If this was her shadow, brought to life, then–

"What happened to Alison?"

The man shook his head. "Alison, Sara, Kara, Lucy, Lotta, all of them. They don't matter. We have more important things to discuss, friend, than–"

"What happened to her?"

The man jumped forward, to the edge of the platform.

"There's more at stake here, friend!" he screamed, whipping his hat off, his eyes narrow, white spittle collected at the corner of his mouth.

Ted looked at the golem. It was still looking at him, tilting its head, like a baby discovering something new. Was Alison dead? Was this all that was left? Was there anything of the original within her?

"Alison," he said, "come on, it's me. Ted."

"Listen to me," said the man. He slapped Ted, hard, across the cheek. Ted banged his head against the metal behind him, and after the electric sting of the slap faded, he felt something warm spread inside his cheek.

"You're stuck here, because you followed the light, friend. You followed the same light as I!"

The man stretched his arms out. He was angry. Very angry.

"These are my machines. They're filled with another power, the cold power of the stars and the dark. You can't escape. You can't leave. None of us can. The Cold Dark shone its light and brought me here, showed me the thing sleeping under the city, showed me how to control it. And you, you were brought here too, to me." He leaned in to Ted so he could whisper. "Brought here for a reason, friend. A reason. Don't you get it? Don't you understand? The light has brought us together. It *knows*. But there's something else, friend. I know too."

Ted shook his head, and spat a sticky gob of blood onto the platform in front of him. The man's eyes didn't leave Ted's face.

"Know what?" asked Ted.

"I know what you have," said the man. "I know what's in *there*." He poked Ted's chest.

"And what do I have?"

The man pulled back, almost like he was surprised. Then he laughed. "I wasn't sure at first. The mysterious acrobat, appearing just like 'that'." He clicked his fingers. "Wowing the crowds and then chasing off into the night, after my puppet. But now I get it. Now I can *smell* it on you. You've got the secret. The means to freedom. You have the key."

"The key to what?"

The man held his arms out. "The key to this prison. You're my way out of this hell."

Ted slumped in his bonds. It was too much. The guy was deranged. He felt a tickle at the back of his neck. Like his imaginary friend was back.

"What, you think I want to be like this?" asked the man, angry again. "You think I want to live forever? I've followed the light. The light has shown me the way, has led me. I've followed it. I've been faithful to it. The light, it shines for me. But you think I *want* that? This thing, the light, all it needs to do is feed so it can grow, and spread. And then what? What happens for me then?"

Ted shook his head. The man nodded in furious agreement.

"Yes, my friend! Yes! Nothing. Grow and spread, grow and spread. It's kept me alive, nothing but a tool to be used, a puppet. I was a man like you once. And now I'm nothing. I don't exist. There is nothing but the light."

"I don't understand. How can I free you?"

"I want it. I want what *you* have. In there." The man tapped Ted's chest again.

"I don't know what you mean. What do I have?" The presence at his shoulder grew stronger. Ted felt the adrenaline pulse through his system.

"Give it to me!" said the man, "or I'll destroy the city."

# XLI
## SAN FRANCISCO
### TODAY

The man's white eye shone red. Ted tried to shrink back against the Ferris wheel, but there was nowhere to go. The presence at his shoulder was so strong now, it felt like it was pushing him towards the man in black.

"I can command it," said the man. He nodded. "Oh yes, friend. I might be a prisoner, but I can *command* it."

The Ferris wheel shook, the metal clattering around Ted. Then he realized it wasn't the Ferris wheel, it was the ground. The whole carnival was shaking with the earth.

"He can't help you, and you can't have it."

A new voice. Ted looked up, and the man on the platform spun around. On the grass below a new arrival walked forward, ignoring the circle of golems and the frozen wooden soldiers, wearing nothing but blue jeans, the lights of the carnival reflecting off his naked torso, slick with sweat. The carnival machines around him twitched, but didn't move as he walked.

Ted looked on in confusion. "Bob?"

Bob saluted. "Welcome back, Ted. Seems you found the source. Good work."

Ted shook his head and pushed his arms against the metal frame holding him. "I think it found me. I was just following–"

Ted stopped, his forehead creased in concentration.

Bob nodded. "Don't tell me. A voice in your head? A push on the shoulder?"

"I... yes. That's right. But–"

Bob held up his hands. "A little trick played by a magician called Nezha," he said. "I'm sorry he picked you, Ted, I really am."

The voice whispered in Ted's ear as Bob spoke, but Ted couldn't make it out. It sounded like it was speaking Chinese.

The man on the platform clapped, and put his hat back on.

"Well now, isn't this interesting?" He tilted his head, like he was listening to something far away. "Kanaloa? Oh, you're a long way from home. So that completes the picture for me and the Cold Dark. Now that you've joined this little soiree in person it can read you like a book, but it couldn't figure *him* out. But you're too late, friend. The means to freedom. It's right here, and it's mine."

"I'm not sure the thing in your machines would agree with that," said Bob. "And my name is Bob." He nodded at Ted. "Are you OK?"

"Apart from being held hostage by a living circus, fine," said Ted. "Do you know where Alison is?"

"She's safe," said Bob.

"Are you sure about that, ancient one?" The man on the platform gestured to the golem next to him. The creature slowly turned around, unsure on its feet.

Ted could see Bob frown.

"Oh, I'm sure," said Bob. "That construct doesn't look too good. It's not complete, is it? Just an empty shell. It's degraded already. Look."

The man looked at the golem rocking on its heels. Bob was right. Ted could see the creature was dying. With each passing moment, it seemed harder and harder for it to stay on its feet.

Which meant... Alison was alive? Alison was alive!

Then the golem collapsed. It didn't fall, it disintegrated, its legs crumbling first, then the body falling downward. It hit the platform and came apart softly, like it was dry, soft soil.

The man on the platform turned to Bob. He laughed. "So you stopped him in time, old one?"

Bob tilted his head. "You mean you don't know?"

"Oh," said the man. "Well, the connection was lost, so to speak. I have you to thank for that, I think. Oh, and your friend too. Now, tell me, where is *he*?"

Behind Bob, the circle of golems began to move. They closed in on Bob; all were clay and ash, but they moved fluidly, with purpose. The dead army of the circus. Bob glanced over his shoulder, then stuck his thumbs through the belt loops in his jeans and shrugged.

"Just you and me, brah."

The man in black adjusted his hat and rolled his lips, looking out into the night from his platform. Then he smiled and nodded. "Seems like I'm not the only one with connections in this town." He cocked his ear, listening to nothing, his lips moving. Communicating with the Cold Dark in the carnival machines. "I think maybe I should repay the favor." He looked down on Bob.

As Ted watched, Bob's hands dropped to his sides and he took a step backwards. He looked worried. He caught Ted's eye, but Ted didn't know what it meant.

"I don't know who are you," said Bob, his attention back on the man in black, "but you have to listen to me. The Cold Dark. It controls you, don't you see? It's given you something of its power, but it's using you. You need to help me. You need to fight it with me. Send it back to the stars."

The man in black shook his head. "You think I don't know that? That's why I want him. That's why I want what's *inside* him. It won't let me go, not ever." He pointed to the circle of golems, still closing in on Bob.

"But I *can* command the light, ancient one. And through it, I can command the Thing Beneath and its army of earth and fire."

The golems marched forward while the carnival machines twitched and hummed in the night.

*Now is our chance, Ted. I'm going to help you, but we only get one opportunity. Just one, Ted. Do you understand? Are you listening to me, Ted?*

Ted felt dizzy, sleepy, felt like there were hands on his shoulders. The voice was back and loud in his head, echoing in from all around him. Nausea spread out from his stomach, the dizziness sending the world spinning. He squinted, tried to focus, but could see nothing but the golems surrounding Bob and the man in the hat stretching his arms out to the sky, hear nothing but the voice in his head, repeating the same thing over and over and over again.

*You are the master of every situation.*

*You are the master of every situation.*

*You are the master of every situation.*

Ted closed his eyes.

Highwire opened his.

Bob scanned the circle of golems advancing slowly toward him. They were made of earth and fire, and while he was a god, these weren't his specialist elements. He was the lord of water, of life, and of death. The golems weren't alive, merely instruments of the Thing Beneath, channeling energy from it. Energy commanded by the man in black. Bob pushed a little at the world and extracted the man's identity: Joel

Duvall, carnival operator. A man out of time. Bob frowned. The Cold Dark had kept him alive as its puppet for a century and a half. That was some power.

The circle got tighter.

He could fight them. He could destroy them. But what would the cost be? Once he started, could he stop himself? And what would it achieve? It was a distraction from the real menace – from Joel, the controller, the conduit for a cosmic force that didn't belong on the Earth.

There was another problem, too. Benny. Bob reached out but there was nothing there, not anymore. The Cold Dark had been able to "see" Bob's hold on Benny's soul, and had cut it, just like that. Again, the power of the Cold Dark frightened Bob. He only hoped that Benny would survive long enough with her connection to Tangun for Bob to grab hold of the tether again. The short amount of time available just got a whole lot shorter.

Bob refocused on the problem at hand: on the circus, on the circle of golems crowding closer and closer around him.

Ted screamed. Bob spun around, but Ted was still trapped in the machinery of the Ferris wheel. His head turned from side to side, his face a mask of pain. He cried out again, and was still, his head slumped forward. Then it lifted again, slowly, and Ted opened his eyes. Something had changed, Bob could see that. The acrobat had taken over again.

Nezha, the Last Magician, Chinese trickster god, had been murdered by the circus ringmaster under Joel's control, the power of his death causing the Thing Beneath to stir. But Nezha wasn't dead, not really. Killing a god was difficult to do. He was still alive, in part, *inside* Ted. Like Tangun was inside Benny. But how much of Nezha was left was a mystery.

Bob called out. "Nezha! We're at the source. We can stop this, here, now!"

Ted – Highwire – stared out into nothing. Did he hear? Was he even listening? Had Nezha's power finally burned out Ted's body, leaving nothing but a shell, as empty as Alison's collapsed golem?

Joel laughed. The ground shook again, and this time it didn't stop.

It was starting.

*It* was waking up.

The golems closed around Bob. He crouched down, hands over his head, unwilling to fight. The golems weren't alive. They were just made of earth and ash and fire, animated by the life force of The Thing Beneath. Destroying them wasn't the problem; there would be no death to feed off. But Bob had already stretched his powers much farther than he had ever wanted to. That'd he'd been able to control himself so far meant nothing; he knew that with every flex, every push at the world, he took a step closer to becoming the monster he knew he really was. He had to get out, get away, remove himself from temptation.

Bob turned on the ground, ready to take to the sky, to fly away, out of reach, away from it all. But even as he summoned the power to leave the ground the golems piled on top of him, pushing him back against the earth. He got a final glimpse of the platform, of Joel laughing.

Of Highwire wrenching his bonds apart, of Highwire jumping forward, onto the platform. Then Bob was surrounded by darkness and the stench of hot earth and ash.

Highwire hits Joel, pulling him off the platform. The pair falls, hits the ground. Highwire sees the gold coin Joel holds go flying into the air. It shines with a light all of its own, like a falling star, like a comet.

Joel turns on the ground. He snarls, his white eye glowing red, the earth bucking, crumbling beneath him. Cracks appear in the dirt, and they open and close, open and close, like a fish gasping on land. His hands grab at Highwire, pulling him closer. Highwire gasps, and Joel pulls himself up until his face is in Highwire's.

"Give it to me! Give me my freedom!"

Highwire pulls free, pushes Joel off. He feels the power surge within him and he feels the presence at his shoulder – Nezha – working with him. He somersaults backward, out of reach. But the ground buckles, and he loses his footing as he lands. He crashes to his knees, to his hands, and when he goes to stand, he finds he can't move.

He looks down. The ground is holding him. It moves, like there's something under the surface, the ground undulating rhythmically. Highwire thinks of octopi, of squid, of monsters with many tentacles, many heads.

He looks up and sees Joel running toward him. He tries to get out of the way, but he can't move. The ground holds him and pulls him down. He is sinking, being dragged under.

Joel grabs Highwire by the collar of the brown jacket he is wearing. He pulls against the ground, but the earth bucks and Joel falls to his knees, still holding the jacket.

"Give me my freedom!"

Highwire shoves with his upper body, and Joel falls backward. He hits the ground on his back and does not rise, although he tries. Highwire watches as the earth moves around Joel, the cracks opening, the dirt eating his hands, eating his legs. He pulls and struggles and cries out, but he is held fast, flat on his back, as the earth drags him down.

Nezha says *NOW!* in his ear and Highwire yells out and tears himself from the ground, sending a shower of earth skyward. He rolls forward and grabs Joel's arms. He pulls, trying to free him from the ground. The ground fights back, pulling even harder. There is pain in his legs, feet. Highwire looks down, and sees the earth is trying to swallow him too.

Joel screams. He is almost under. Highwire pulls, afraid he will break Joel in two. Then a shaft of earth – an arm, blackened, as hard as stone – shoots out of the ground. The hand grabs Highwire's neck, as strong as steel cable, and squeezes.

And then Highwire sees…

…*Emerald robes and Chinese logographs and a man with a long beard and fireworks shooting from the tips of his fingers as he stands in the warehouse and laughs, and laughs…*

…*and a man in a top hat walking through darkness steel cable stretched in his hands then fire then darkness then…*

…*A world. The Earth, young, hot, its surface liquid rock. There is power here, energy, and that power and that energy is so great it is alive. It squirms in the magma, circling the globe, and then the world cools and it slows, and cools and curls, hidden far below, sleeping, waiting, alive in the rock, in the Earth, part of planet itself. And as it cools and falls into slumber, it turns, sometimes, and when it turns the Earth shakes and energy is released, but not enough, not enough, not until…*

Bob's black prison squeezed in, the space becoming smaller and smaller, the golems pushing together, fusing into one form, a dome of black stone and hot earth.

The earth rumbled, cracks opening beneath him. The golems wouldn't crush him; they were merely holding him in place so the Thing Beneath could come up and consume him.

Bob was a god. Gods had power. And if the Thing Beneath could get just a fraction of that, then it would awaken fully in an instant. The Cold Dark would wrestle with the unleashed monster, but it was strong, and it would win. Together they would consume the world. Build and spread. Build and spread.

Bob had no choice. He had to use his power, flex his muscles, become Kanaloa once more. He knew he wouldn't be able to resist the power. When he had been a god, millennia before, he had been content to rule over his island and over the seas. He was worshipped, and while he had the power to swallow the world, there were other gods walking the Earth, many more powerful than he. This had kept him in check, because to go out into the world would mean meeting the other gods, his brothers and sisters. They would have stopped him.

So he had been content to rule over his domain.

But now there was nobody else. The gods had gone, abandoned the Earth, abandoned humanity. He'd stayed behind, disavowing his powers and nature to live among the people he had once ruled. Some had come back, now and again – like Nezha had – but they didn't care, not anymore.

And now he was alone, and he was Kanaloa, and he would rule the world. And all he had to do was–

There was a knock on the black rock above him, like someone had struck it with a hammer. Bob looked up, and saw light. There was a hole in the canopy, jagged and fresh, the lights of the carnival shining through.

And there was light from the ground. Bob looked down and saw a large gold coin sitting on the earth. The ground smoked around it, flames flickered around its edge. The coin seemed to be glowing – not red, not like it was hot, but *white*, like it was reflecting the light of the sun on a brilliant summer's day.

Joel's coin. The totem of the thing that had controlled him for so long.

Bob had his answer.

The rock canopy shrank further and the ground roiled.

He reached forward, picked up the coin in his fingers, and he saw:

*...Darkness and light in equal measure, the black of space, the blaze of a billion stars. He was blind, swimming in nothing, swimming in space and...*

*...He saw a worm as big as a god swallow a galaxy whole... He saw things crawl in the heart of stars... things that were cold, so very cold, colder than space, colder than the empty nothing inside atoms... things that craved heat and energy... things that curled inside stars and wailed at the cold... things that shone brighter than galaxies...*

*...He saw supernovas, he saw stars explode, he saw stars fall. He saw comets, colossal balls of ice that burned in the depths of space, trailing debris, seeding the universe with life... seeding the universe with a disease, a pathogen, one that was cold and dark craved heat and energy and light, that needed to grow and spread... grow and spread... grow and spread...*

*...He saw a comet arc across the sky above a desert...*

*...He saw a star fall...*

*...He saw a star fall...*

Bob smashed through the stone canopy on a column of roaring water. It bounced under his feet, carrying him into the air. The salt water sprayed against his bare skin, soaked his jeans, saturated his hair. Bob felt alive, the power surging through him as he commanded the sea

But not his power. He raised his hand and uncurled his fingers from around Joel's coin, the totem. He used the power of the stars, of the Cold Dark. The more power Bob channeled through the coin, the colder the coin got, siphoning the power from some dark corner of the universe.

Bob smiled and the crest of water dropped. He stepped onto the ground. The earth was hot and cracked, but still. The night was quiet. The lights of the carnival were on but there was no movement. The machines were still.

"Ted?" Then Bob saw him. He rushed forward, past the platform to where Ted lay in front of the Ferris wheel, half buried in the ground. He fell to his knees, shook the wet hair from his face, spraying Ted with water.

"Come on, brah, don't make me bring you back to life." He leaned over and began breaking great chunks of burned earth off him. As he worked, seawater ran off his hair onto Ted's face. Ted spluttered, then coughed, and tried to sit up. Bob broke the last of the dirt free and helped him up. Bob peered at him.

"What?" asked Ted, rubbing his head.

"Is that Ted, or is that Highwire? Or am I talking to Nezha?"

Ted shook his head. "It's me. Ted. I think, anyway." He looked around. "What the hell happened?"

They were alone among the carnival machines. The earth dome formed by the fused golems was half-collapsed. Around it half of the wooden soldiers were standing, the rest lying on the ground, lifeless.

"I don't think the powers that be liked what Joel had in mind."

Ted crouched on the ground. He ran his fingers over the cracked earth, but there was nothing there. Joel had been swallowed up. Nearby lay his black stovepipe hat.

"He was trapped," said Ted. "Stuck between a power from the stars and a power from the earth. Wasn't there any way we could have released him?"

Bob knelt down next to Ted and stared at the ground. "I don't know, brah. Maybe. Maybe not. He'd been following the power a long time."

The pair stood, looked around. And then the earth shook.

"What was that?" asked Ted.

Bob shook his head. He squeezed the coin in his hand and floated up off the ground. He turned in the air, looking out over the circus, and then rose higher so he could see into the city proper.

"There's some fires in the city," he said. "But we stopped it. I guess we'll get aftershocks for a while yet. But look, I need to get back to Benny. I lost my grip on her soul.

"Alison!" Ted looked up at Bob expectantly. Bob nodded.

"Alison too. Gotta make sure they're safe."

Then Ted swore in Chinese. Bob floated to the ground and grabbed Ted's shoulder as he knelt down. Ted had his eyes screwed shut, like he was listening to something far, far away.

"Ted?"

Ted shook his head. "There's something coming. Nezha says... says it isn't safe. Not yet."

The ground shook, throwing the pair sideways. Bob squeezed hard on the coin. He couldn't let that fall out of his hands, not now. He rolled and pulled himself to his feet immediately. Shaking the dirt off him, he looked around.

The carnival was moving, every machine. The carousel began to spin, the whine of the pipe organ building. And the laugh of the monkey: hollow, metallic, like something trapped at the bottom of a well. Its eyes shone red.

The machines dragged themselves out of the ground. They twisted into shapes that could crawl, corner by corner, edge by edge, over the shaking ground. Machines touched, swung toward each other, crunched together, forming new shapes in twisted metal. Lights shattered, neon flickered as panels bent, were torn, were fused together.

The ground shook. Bob rode the movement. Ted reached out and Bob pulled him up, then yanked him to one side just as the ground opened and fell away where he had been lying.

The carnival was one single mass now, twisted and rattling, a frame of mashed metal and rippling canvas. The construct heaved and creaked, and then unfolded upward. It stood, teetering, on two legs. The thing was shaped like a person, thirty feet high, a mangled sculpture of scrap. The only thing missing was the head.

As Bob watched, the construct took two giant steps toward the carousel, now spinning so fast the pipe organ and carved monkey were clearly visible in the center, the animal rides just a blur. The construct reached down, unfolded two gigantic arms, and picked the carousel up.

The Victorian machine was huge, a circular structure twenty feet in diameter. As it was lifted, it continued to spin, the construct carrying it into the air like a gyroscope. With a crunch it placed the carousel on its shoulders. It stood tall, carousel spinning, the makeshift head absurdly large.

Ted and Bob looked up at the teetering machine. "This is bad," said Bob.

The voice blasted from the carousel – a cacophony of high and low notes from the pipe organ. It was mournful, wailing, like the death of a church organ.

WE ARE BELENUS, said the construct. WE DEMAND THE HEART OF THE WORLD.

# XLII
# SAN FRANCISCO
## TODAY

The smell woke her. Rich, strong, bitter as anything. Hot steam tickled her nose, and she blinked.

"Drink this." Benny held the cup of coffee in front of Alison's nose. She took the cup and took a big gulp from it. It was hot, hot enough that she had to gasp afterward, a cloud of steam puffing out of her mouth.

"Thought you'd need that," said Benny. She smiled and sat on the arm of the sofa opposite.

Alison pulled herself upright. On the other sofa was a large, middle-aged man dressed in shirtsleeves. He snored softly, his breath vibrating his waxed handlebar moustache. He looked like the ringmaster of a circus.

"Don't worry about him," said Benny. "His name is Jack, and yes, he's from the circus. He's going to sleep for a while now." Benny looked down at Jack and patted him on the head. Then she sighed, her other hand clutching her chest.

"Benny? Are you OK?" Alison sat the coffee down on the table and went to stand up, but the room spun around her. She sat down heavily, shaking her head.

"You need to sleep too," said Benny. "The coffee will help with post-resurrection synapse realignment. Trust me."

Alison blinked. "OK," she said. She closed her eyes and the sensation of being on a ship in a rough sea stopped. She frowned. "Are you telling me I'm dead and brain damaged?"

"*Were* dead," said Benny. "And any brain damage is temporary. That's what the coffee is for. Drink up, dude."

Alison opened an eye and reached for the coffee. She glanced at Benny, and she looked pained again. She also looked pale. Very pale.

"You're the one who looks like the walking dead," Alison said. She took another sip of coffee, then another. She felt better already. "And who said coffee was good for zombies?"

"That'll be Kanaloa."

Alison paused, then sipped again. "We haven't met."

"He's the Hawaiian god of the ocean, life, and death."

Another sip of the coffee. "OK."

"You know him better as Bob."

Alison nodded. Maybe there was something in the coffee, because she was in Ted's apartment with a circus ringmaster asleep on the other couch, and Benny had just told her that the homeless guy who taught tourists the foxtrot down at Aquatic Park was a god.

"He doesn't look like he's from Hawaii," she said, not quite believing what she was saying herself. "More like Oregon."

"Then you don't know your Hawaiian mythology," said Benny, with a laugh. "In legend, Kanaloa was fair, while his brother Kane was dark. Two sides of the same coin, I guess." She shrugged, then coughed and fell off the arm of the sofa.

"Benny!" Alison dumped the cup and knelt by Benny's side. She was white, her breathing long and deep. "What's wrong? Are you hurt? I'll call an ambulance." She looked around but couldn't see a phone.

Benny grabbed her arm. "It's OK. Figured this would happen. Kanaloa has a lot to worry about right now. Don't worry." Then her eyes rolled back and the air left her lungs. She slumped on the floor.

"Shit, Benny, wake up!" Alison shook her, felt for a pulse. She didn't find it. She wasn't breathing. She pulled her arms out of the way, tilted her head back, ready for CPR.

Benny's hand gripped her wrist, and Alison yelped in surprise.

"She is being looked after," she said. Her voice was deeper – masculine, hollow and echoing. Her eyes were still closed. Alison shook the hand off her wrist and felt again for her pulse. Nothing. She pulled back her eyelids, but she didn't react.

"Fear not," said Benny in the deep voice. Alison backed away until she was against the sofa. Benny remained where she was on the floor. "This mortal has served the Heavenly Ones well. But she has endured too much and I cannot prevent the passing of this life from one form to the next."

"What the hell does that mean?" Alison tore at her hair. This was all some twisted nightmare. Had to be. "Who are you?" she asked.

"I am Tangun, King and Founder. I returned to the Earth on a quest for a lost power, but my Golden Child has suffered too much. Kanaloa fights for us. I will protect the girl as we journey together beyond to the shadow realm. She has served with great honor."

Benny stood, her image flickering between the Benny Alison knew, in a sports shirt and baseball cap, and a warrior clad in ceremonial garb from the Far East, gold plated armor over richly embroidered white robes.

"Benny?" Alison's voice was tiny.

"It's OK." Benny now. She opened her eyes. "Look after Jack until Bob gets back. He'll be able to explain everything. I have to go now. I'm being taken to meet the Heavenly Ones." Then her image flickered and the warrior was standing there.

"We ride to the heavens, my friend," said Tangun. He raised his arm, there was a flash, and the armor collapsed to the floor. Alison slid forward, but the robe was empty. Sitting on top was the huge helmet. Its front was a golden mask molded into a face. The face was laughing, frozen in time.

# XLIII
# SHARON MEADOW, SAN FRANCISCO
## TODAY

The ground shook, another tremor, stronger this time. The carnival construct – Belenus – staggered on its gargantuan feet, the carousel head spinning, the pipe organ wailing. Then it took a step forward, the ground shaking.

"And it's awake," said Bob, backing away.

Ted stared up at it. "What the hell is it? Is Belenus one of you?"

Another crashing step forward. The giant machine was unsteady, its framework of twisted metal grinding and screeching as the body moved. But it seemed to be adapting. It took another step, this time faster, with more certainty.

"Belenus isn't real," said Bob. "It's a work of fiction, a fake Celtic god someone dreamed up. The Thing Beneath doesn't have an identity. It's alive, but it doesn't think."

BELENUS DEMANDS THE WORLD.

"You sure about that?"

Bob looked around at the torn-up carnival, the ground cracked from the tremors and carved up by the moving machines.

"It's the two of them together," said Bob. "The Thing Beneath, and the Cold Dark that lives in the machines. They've become one thing."

Another step, another roar of the pipe organ.

"I hope you have a plan, Bob," said Ted, "You're a god, aren't you?"

Ted was right. Bob was a god. He was Kanaloa. He could do anything. And if he did, then he may as well let Belenus destroy the city, because that was exactly what Kanaloa would do once he started.

Unless...

"Can you talk to Nezha?"

Ted looked at Bob. "Talk to him?"

"If he's in there with you, then I'm not the only god in town."

Ted blinked, and looked over his shoulder quickly. Then he turned back to Bob and nodded.

"He's here. He's... me... I think."

He held his hands out. A green glow played over his skin, increasing in brightness, crackling with gold sparks like a firework.

Bob smiled. "Then maybe Nezha the Last Magician and Kanaloa, god of the ocean, can fight this together. I need you to help control me. If I get out of hand, you need to stop me. Do you understand what I'm saying?"

Ted lifted his hands, and nodded. The green glow surrounded his whole body now. As Bob blinked, Ted's image flickered between the ordinary guy in a brown jacket and a Chinese man with a long beard and long green coat.

Bob looked up at the carnival monster. It was standing still, swaying, the spinning carousel like a gyroscope, keeping the top-heavy construct balanced. The pipe organ droned on, but the thing wasn't moving.

Yet.

Bob looked deep into the construct. It wasn't moving, because it was *changing*, rearranging its internal structure, converting the mash of carnival rides into something far more complex. Each piece was shifting slowly, interlocking like a complex puzzle. Nuts and bolts and bars forming logic gates and switches, creating mechanical algorithms for life. A spine had formed, reinforced at the neck to better support the huge carousel. What had once been a dozen separate Nineteenth Century fairground rides was becoming a single machine.

It was becoming Belenus, the Celtic god who never was, made real in a collection of fairground attractions.

Bob braced himself on the ground. Now was their chance, before the construct finished remodeling. The solution seemed simple: separate the machines.

He glanced at Ted. Ted was looking up at the construct, his hands green fire.

"Ready?" asked Bob. Ted nodded without taking his eyes from the machine.

Bob summoned the ocean and rose into the air on the crest of a tidal wave. It carried him up, allowing him to leap onto the construct's chest. The machine shook and sparked as the water flooded through it, shorting the electrical systems, making the lights over its surface flicker. Bob grabbed at metal panels and began to tear them off. He reached inside the grinding guts of the machine, the moving parts jamming against his arm. He began pulling at anything that was within his grasp.

As he did, he felt the hunger grow along with the lightness in his head. He could dissolve the entire machine with a thought. And... why not? It would be so easy. They were running out of time, and here they were, playing. Even as he ripped out one piece, another moved to compensate, the construct rebuilding itself around the damage. It was a waste of time.

And then, he thought, once he'd destroyed the machine, he could make sure that San Francisco was never in danger from earthquakes again. The tectonic plates could be realigned, fixed.

And then, he thought, he could make some alterations to the city. Make it better.

And then, he thought, he could begin again, teaching the inhabitants of the city what it was to have an angry god as their lord and master. Oh, they would walk over fire for him. They would feed him with their blood and their souls.

Kanaloa, god of the ocean, looked at the molecular structure of the machine he clung to, and started making some changes.

Ted watched Bob, clinging to the front of the swaying machine. He'd started pulling the thing to pieces, twisted metal debris falling to the ground as Bob threw bits over his shoulder. But the machine was large, and Bob was making slow progress. Ted was surrounded by green fire, but he knew that wasn't really him doing it. It was Nezha, the echo of a godly spirit that was still inside him, whispering Chinese riddles into his ear in a constant stream. He didn't understand any of it.

Then Bob stopped moving. He clung to the front of the construct as it rocked on its feet, but he'd pulled his hand out of its interior.

The whispering in Ted's ear grew loud as the green fire in his hands flared bright. Suddenly he understood the words being spoken to him.

*Listen to me, Ted. Kanaloa must be stopped, for if he is not stopped, he will surely destroy the world.*

Ted shook his head. "I–"

*I said we had one chance, Ted. Kanaloa must be stopped. He asked you to do this.*

"But–"

*Kanaloa has a powerful will, but even he will not be able to resist for long. The power will drive him insane. There is nothing left to check it. Except you, Ted. Except you.*

*You are the master of every situation, Ted. Remember that.*

Ted looked up at the carousel.

*Yes,* whispered Nezha. *There. The center. The nexus. I will help.*

Ted vanished from the ground in a puff of green smoke and reappeared on the carousel, riding one of the wooden horses. The world outside was a multicolored blur; the carousel was spinning impossibly fast, but within its bounds it was still and quiet, like he was not in the real world anymore. Ted swung himself off the horse. Behind his back, he heard it rear and neigh; when he looked over his shoulder it was still. Then its eyes rolled around to look at him. Time seemed to be moving differently within the ride. Slower.

*Excellent work, Ted. I knew I could rely on you.*

Ted turned back to the carousel's hub. To the pipe organ, to the monkey with glowing red eyes that sat atop it. The organ and the monkey flickered like a zoetrope. Ted realized the carousel was still rotating around the stationary center.

"Why am I an acrobat?" Ted asked.

*I needed a tool, Ted. I had grown tired, old, and was going to pass my power on. But before I was ready I was killed. So I hid the power for you to find it and use it, hunting my killer, stopping him before his own power grew too strong.*

Time slowed to a crawl. The wooden horse behind Ted neighed again.

"But why the circus? And why me?"

*Think, Ted. Think! I could feel the power of the circus. I knew that to be the source. But I was dead. I needed you to be my eyes and ears. I needed you to stop the killer in the city. I also needed you at the circus, to find the course. So I created the acrobat. With his abilities you could give chase to the killer while investigating the circus.*

"Except I didn't know anything about it, did I?"

*Yes, well. Forgive me. I'm a trickster at heart. The fortune cookie, the acrobat. It seemed like a good idea at the time. It's my nature.*

"You have got to be kidding me."

The striped wooden pole next to Ted's head exploded in a shower of splinters. He spun around, and saw the rides behind him now occupied by wooden soldiers. Here, in the in-between-world of the spinning carousel, they were alive and moving. Three reloaded their flintlock rifles while the other three were taking aim. Behind them, the world outside spun by in a silent kaleidoscope of color.

*I'm sorry, Ted. You didn't have all of my power. If you had, then we could have worked together, you and I. But it has taken this long for me to get a hold of your mind.*

Ted turned back to the monkey and felt the bullets hit his back. There was pain and green fire. Then the pain vanished.

"Was that you?"

*Quickly. I can protect you for only so long. We must reach the center.*

The hub of the carousel was a step higher than the platform itself. Ted pulled himself onto the back of a horse that had a writhing starfish for a head, swung his legs around to the side facing the hub, and jumped. Behind him, the creature screamed in agony as it was shredded by another volley of shots from the soldiers.

*The Cold Dark is there. It does not belong here, Ted. It lives in the jeweled eyes of the monkey – the last fragments of a great comet that fell to Earth.*

Ted pulled himself up the front of the pipe organ. Here, at the hub, the centrifugal force of the real world seemed to take effect, threatening to throw him spinning away.

Fighting against the force, his hands burning green, Ted pulled himself up, until he was within reach of the monkey.

Hands grabbed his ankles, his legs. He kicked backward, but it was like kicking a tree trunk. He glanced over his shoulder and saw the wooden soldiers clambering over the rides. One had crossed from the platform to the hub, and now hung from Ted's legs as it was pulled out and away by the centrifugal force.

The monkey. It sat unmoving on the organ, its red eyes glowing.

Ted felt his grip slip. He slid down the organ before regaining a hold, and felt the weight on his legs shift. He glanced down, and saw the soldier's rifle pointed at his head.

Ted let go of the front of the organ with one hand and grabbed the rifle. He pulled it toward him in one swift movement, pulling his head out of the way. The soldier fired the gun. At nearly point-blank range, the bullet was right on target.

It hit the monkey's right eye. The gem shattered and the pipe organ howled. Ted pushed backward on the rifle barrel, and the wooden solider lost his grip. One kick, and it slipped off Ted, colliding with the edge of the spinning platform and disintegrating into splinters.

Ted pulled himself up, and reached out a glowing green hand. He grabbed the monkey's remaining eye, and pulled.

The world exploded in red and green, and Ted fell backward. Waves crashed in, and the voice of Nezha rang in his ears.

*You are the master of every situation.*

*You are the master of every situation.*

*You are the master of every situation.*

And then:

*Well done, Ted. I knew I picked the right one!*

●●●●

Ted coughed up a thick mixture of seawater, bile and mucous, and rolled onto his side. A hand appeared in his vision.

"Thanks, brah."

Ted grabbed the hand and Bob pulled him up. Ted was soaked through, the water on his face warm and salty. Bob was dry as a bone.

"Kanaloa?"

Bob smiled, held up a hand. "It's Bob, please."

Ted pushed the wet hair from his eyes and looked around. The fairground field, already torn up from the earth's tremors and the movement of the machines, was a muddy morass, the churned ground covered in broken and bent metal. Ted recognized one of the Ferris wheel passenger buckets, and one of the rotating clown heads buried upside down to the nose in the dirt.

Ted held up his hand, uncurled his fingers. In his palm sat a large red gem. It shone in the night, like it had an internal light of its own.

"What happened?" he asked, his eyes on the gem. It looked – it *felt* – dangerous.

"Yeah, well," Bob said. "It was close. Good job, Ted."

Ted shook his head. "I don't understand. What did I do?"

"Well," said Bob. "Must admit I lost it there. That's the problem with power, especially power you haven't used in, oh, a long time. Drives a hunger, right here." He patted his bare stomach with a fist. "But that hunger was satisfied, just at the right time."

"I still don't know what I did. I was up on the carousel." He frowned, and listened. Nezha's whispering voice had stopped, the presence of the trickster god was gone. The circus was quiet.

"That," said Bob. He pointed at the gem in Ted's hand. "Whatever you did, you broke the connection the Cold

Dark had with the Thing Beneath. It was rebuilding the construct, so when you interfered you released a whole ocean of energy. Snapped me right out of it." He nodded. "Thanks, Brah. I mean it."

Ted frowned. "I'm not sure it's me you have to thank. I was just doing what Nezha told me."

Bob tilted his head. "Is he still there?"

Ted paused, and shook his head. "No. I feel... like me."

"You didn't have all his power," said Bob. "Maybe it wasn't him you heard, not really. Just an echo of his power. You probably burned it out of yourself when you entered the carousel."

"He said he was protecting me, but that he couldn't do it for long."

Bob shrugged. "And farewell to the trickster. You're back to being you."

Ted nodded. Then he looked around the circus ruins. "What about all this? The people in the circus."

"They were all consumed by it. Their energy converted to create the golems." Bob kicked at a pile of earth.

"They're all dead?"

Bob nodded.

Ted sat on the ground. "Jesus."

"But we stopped it," said Bob, joining Ted. "It would have taken the city, and then California, then the West Coast, then...well," he held his hands out.

Ted nodded. "So... can't you, I don't know, *do* something?"

Bob shook his head. "I can't. I almost lost it once. Any more and..." He clicked his fingers, then paused. He was looking at the glowing gem in Ted's hand, then he held out his own hand. "Give me the stone."

"What?"

"I can't use my own power," Bob said, lifting the gem from Ted's palm. "But I don't have to."

His fist curled around the gem and he closed his eyes. Ted took a step back.

Then Bob opened his eyes. Ted saw green and blue swirling colors, shining in the night, and the sound of the ocean far away, like he had put a shell to his ear.

Bob smiled. "Guess what?"

Ted shook his head, unable to find the right answer.

Bob rolled his neck, like he was a weightlifter about to go for gold.

"Tonight, everybody gets to live."

# POSTSCRIPT
# ASIAN ART MUSEUM, SAN FRANCISCO
## TOMORROW

It was a small ceremony at the Asian Art Museum. Ted, Alison, and Bob were special guests at the presentation.

The gift was spectacular: an antique set of Korean ceremonial armor, donated anonymously. The provenance was immaculate, the paperwork perfect. As stipulated in the gift, ownership of the artifact was to be held jointly between the Museum of Asian Arts in San Francisco and the National Museum of South Korea, with the piece swapping between the two in ten-year cycles. In the interim, scholars from both institutes could have full access to the armor, so it could be fully documented and researched. The richly embroidered robe included text that claimed it was the ceremonial armor of Tangun, the legendary first king of Korea, but Tangun was nothing more than a myth.

Like Kanaloa, the Hawaiian god of the ocean. Like Nezha, the Chinese trickster.

"You OK?" asked Ted, offering Alison a glass of champagne. She took it and smiled. The museum reception was a glamorous evening affair that allowed invited guests to browse the exhibits, Tangun's armor pride of place. Alison looked at the display, sipped her drink.

"I'll miss her," she said.

Ted put his arm around her waist. "Me too," he said.

Bob had burned the fairground to destroy the machines. It was ruled an accident, the giant – illegal – bonfire of the circus having collapsed during a minor earthquake that shook San Francisco, setting the whole carnival alight.

The circus fire had made headlines around the world. It was a miracle, everyone said. The entire fair had been razed, utterly, yet there were just two people unaccounted for – Joel Duvall, the manager of the carnival rides, and Jonathan "Jack" Newhaven, the ringmaster. Their bodies had never been recovered, and it was assumed they had perished in the inferno. That the rest of the performers and staff were accounted for, with only a handful of minor injuries, was a blessing. Likewise the earthquake, which had been small, sparing the city itself from much major damage. In the days after the quake there was no sign of the Hang Wire Killer. The police investigation continued, but leaks to the press from somewhere inside the SFPD suggested detectives were considering whether the serial killer was among the dozen citizens killed by collapsing buildings during the tremors.

Bob and Ted had found Alison still in Benny's apartment, watching the sleeping ringmaster. The armor was there, empty. And then Bob had sat her and Ted down, and told them his story, and the story of the pantheon of which he was a part. He told them about Nezha the Magician. He told them about Tangun, and the legacy that Benny carried down her family line. Alison explained what had happened, that Tangun had said he would look after Benny.

They considered Jack, the ringmaster. Bob told them he would wipe his memory, like he had the resurrected members of the circus. Just to be sure. Then he'd take him back home to Vermont. He'd set him up as an antique dealer, or something. His life with the circus would be forgotten forever.

"What about Kanaloa?" Ted had asked, as he and Alison held each other on the couch. Alison was shaking, afraid, perhaps, of the god who stood in front of them in his faded blue jeans.

"My name isn't Kanaloa," said the god. "My name is Bob, and San Francisco is my home."

"And me."

Alison turned around. Bob smiled at her and sipped from his own glass of champagne. He was back in the linen shirt, unbuttoned nearly to the waist.

"But," he said, "she's fine. Trust me."

Alison turned to Ted, and Ted nodded. She turned back to Bob.

"We need a new writer," she said. "Someone to cover Chinatown. And maybe write something about ballroom dancing." Alison drew in closer to Bob, eying the people around them to ensure nobody was listening in. "And look, this whole god thing kinda freaks me out, but if Kanaloa really is gone for good..."

Bob raised his glass. "Relax. He's not coming back. And thanks for the offer – it would be good to get out there, among everyone. I think Benny would like that."

Ted smiled, and kissed Alison on the cheek.

"Yes," he said. "I think she would."

Alison raised her glass. "To absent friends."

"To new beginnings," said Bob, touching his glass to Alison's and Ted's. He took a sip, then turned to look at Tangun's armor, proudly on display.

"New beginnings," he said, lifting his glass once more.

Ted appeared at his shoulder. "I can certainly drink to that," he said. He sipped his champagne, and as Bob turned away, cocked his head. He thought he heard a whisper, something just over his shoulder, but when he turned around there was nobody there.

# ACKNOWLEDGMENTS

My heartfelt thanks to everyone who helped get this book into your hands, in particular Stacia J N Decker, agent *extraordinare* and valued friend, who once more went above and beyond the call of duty with another set of life-changing editorial notes.

To Amanda Taylor, who not only put up with endless emails about San Francisco – including its history, geography, weather, public parks, bylaws, suburbs, the *works* – but also found the time to read large sections of the text and provide much valued suggestions and comments: oh boy, thank *you*. Your essential help is deeply appreciated. I do hope you enjoy the end result.

Thanks to my editor Lee Harris, and to Will Staehle for another amazing cover. It was a difficult brief, but man, what a result.

*Hang Wire* takes its title from track 12 of *Bossanova*, the third album from seminal art rockers the Pixies. My thanks to Black Francis, Kim Deal, Joey Santiago and Dave Lovering, for a lifetime of inspiration and ideas.

And thanks to my wife Sandra. Y'know, I've done a few novels now, and she *still* puts up with it all. I'm in awe. This book is for *you*.

# Miriam is on the road again, and this time she's expected...

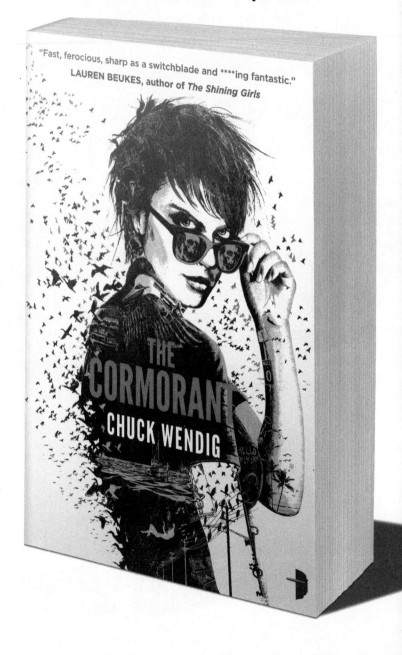

## THE CORMORANT
### CHUCK WENDIG

**David Gemmel meets *The Dirty Dozen* in this epic tale of sorcerous war and bloody survival.**

The quest for the Arbor
has begun...

HEARTWOOD

FREYA ROBERTSON

The quest for the Arbor has begun...